Algorithm

by

Arthur M. Doweyko

e·LITBOOKS

ALGORITHM

Copyright ©2014 Arthur M. Doweyko
All Rights reserved
Published in the United States by E-Lit Books
www.e-litbooks.com

Except as permitted under the U.S Copyright Act of 1976, no part of this
publication may be reproduced, distributed, or transmitted in any form or
by any means, or stored in a database or retrieval system, without prior
consent and permission of the publisher.
Cover Art and Design by Martin Blanco

For information on the subsidiary rights, please contact the publisher at
info@e-litbooks.com

This is a work of fiction. Names, characters, businesses, organizations, places, events and
incidents either are the product of the author's imagination or are used fictitiously. Any
resemblance to actual persons, living or dead, events, or locales is entirely coincidental.

ISBN: 978-0-9894011-9-7
978-0-9894011-0-4

To my wife and best friend,

Lidia

"**THE ACTION CONTINUES TO THE END** ... Hardly anything is what it seems to be. Genre readers should enjoy it; I did."

—Piers Anthony
Author of the *Xanth* fantasy series

An intriguing story from the beginning. **OLD SCHOOL HARD SCIENCE FICTION** about the modern biological sciences and nanotechnology. I loved it.

—Jerry Pournelle
Heinlein Award Winner; Denizen of Chaos Manor

"Cutting edge science delivered in mouth-watering morsels: **A COMPLETELY ORIGINAL ORIGIN STORY.**"

—Dean C. Moore,
Author of *Renaissance 2.0*

"Doweyko pulls you into his world with **TAUT, INTELLIGENT PROSE AND SUPERB STORYTELLING.** The award winning *Algorithm* is a fine mixture of literary, sci-fi, and fantasy that rewards its readers with elaborate exposition and fantastic action. Just a great book."

—J. J. White
Author of *Prodigious Savant* and *Deviant Acts*

"**HOOKS THE READER FROM THE GET GO.** Indiana Jones for the thinking reader. I was carried along by the likeable characters and the believable possibilities that the author presented."

—Martha Powers
Amazon Bestselling Thriller Author

"From the opening baseball game to the mysteries of space to the magical coin-like object that drives the story. **ALGORITHM IS SCIENCE FICTION AT ITS ENTICING BEST.**"

—Tom Palumbo
Author of *Amelia Earhart, Once Again*
Director, Advanced Institute For Motivation

Abu Abdullah Muhammad ibn Musa Al-Khwarizmi (750-850 CE) was a Persian scholar in the House of Wisdom, Baghdad. An extraordinary scientist, astronomer and mathematician, he is considered the Father of Algebra.

The European Latin translation of his name evolved into the term, "algorithm," which in modern day parlance is equivalent to a computer program—a set of instructions carried out by a machine for a definite purpose.

Prologue

Independence Park, Maplewood, NJ, August, 1979

"I'm ready when you are."

Adam's grip tightened about the partially unraveled friction tape covering the handle of his Louisville slugger. Tossing back a shock of dirty blond hair, he sucked in his breath and eased his thirteen-year old body back in eager expectation.

"Here it comes ya lil' squirt," bellowed the pitcher as he wound up.

The ball rocketed down the middle. Adam swung and the crack echoed off the dense wall of chestnut trees surrounding the ball field. The ball scaled the foliage, and for a moment looked like it would continue on into legend. However, the laws of physics, in particular those describing the unyielding effects of gravity, took over.

Elation shifted to terror as cars trundled through the landing zone. To Adam's relief, a distant 'thunk' announced the ball's contact with the street, however the respite was short-lived, for the next sound was that of glass breaking. All on the field scattered in every direction but toward the ball's unfortunate crash site.

The pitcher ran to Adam, yanked the bat out of his hands, and slowed long enough to ask, "Wattaya standin' there for?" Before taking off toward the nearest park entrance

Adam jogged after him and when he reached the sidewalk he slowed to a walk.

I just bought that ball.

He kept to the pavment skirting the ballpark, all the while casting surreptitious glances at each three-story apartment building across the street. When he reached the house next to his own, he crossed over. To the left of the wooden stairs leading to the first floor entrance something grabbed his attention. It was the basement window, or where the window should have been. A few daggers of glass remained in the opening, framing the darkness within like the gaping mouth of a sharp-toothed ogre. Adam moved past the gruesome specter, trying to remain casual. Maybe the break went unnoticed.

Like his own house, access to the basement took the form of an inside entry next to the backdoor. Seconds later, he was through the door and staring down at a wooden staircase. He descended gingerly, stepping to the side of each tread to avoid the squeal of a loose board.

At the bottom, he peered down the length of the basement toward the front of the house. The darkness felt grim and the cold air licked at the back of his neck. The light from the stairs faded as Adam crept forward, groping for a switch or a dangling chain. Bumping into musty carton boxes and storage crates, he crept farther into the gloom. He heard footsteps above, muffled conversation, and the sound of water gurgling through pipes. When his outstretched hands touched a metal post, he craned his head to the side and focused on the dim outline of the broken window. Hazy light streamed in from above and outlined a darkly smeared coal bin. He stepped up to the coal bin and needed to look no farther. The ball sat atop a mound of the dusty anthracite.

He angled over the blackened wooden planks and landed softly at the base of the coal pile. The ball was nearly within reach. He clambered up, slipping and kicking up sulfurous dust, blackening hands and knees as he scrambled to the top. He lunged for the ball, grasped it with one hand, and glided down the rocky heap in deep satisfaction. Black sparkles settled around and on him, fading in and out of the light. Adam found his other hand clutching a few nuggets. He was about to toss them back into the heap when a flash of reflected light caught his eye. He opened his fingers, releasing one lump at a time, until all that remained was a fist-sized chunk. Even in the muted light he saw the oddly-shaped golden glimmer. He rotated his upturned palm, bringing it closer. There was something metallic in the coal.

The sound of footfalls on the staircase broke his reverie. There he was, reclining in a dusty coal bin at the far end of an unlit, unfamiliar and cavernous cellar—ball in one hand and a mystery lump of coal in the other. The shadowy figure reaching the foot of the stairs was about to discover an intruder. Tucking away the coal in his dungarees pocket, he rolled off the brimstone mound, careful to avoid dislodging a 'here-I-am' mini-avalanche. He slipped over the side of the bin and felt for some potential cover. The lights came on just as he squeezed between a stack of cartons and the cellar wall. Shuffling feet with loose slippers slapped their way toward him.

I bet my ass is hanging out for all to see.

The shuffling and slapping drew to a stop.

That's it, he's got me.

"What's this?"

I'm dead.

Adam recognized the voice of his neighbor, Mr. Kurtinaitis—a gravelly, ancient and grinding timbre, which even with such a short phrase, retained its distinct Lithuanian origins. Every neighborhood had its curmudgeon, some old geezer that never got along with anyone younger than thirty, the community warlock whispered about by the children unfortunate enough to have encountered him. Mr. Kurtinaitis had the required indeterminate advanced age, the bent-over posture, gnarly limbs, the grizzled, unkempt look, an obscure foreign accent and gruff demeanor required for a fully-fledged wizard of the dark world. Adam imagined him staring at the broken window of his beloved, dreary cellar domain. A deeply furrowed brow framed the evil eye searching him out, maybe already locked in on his exposed posterior. He was about to stand and beg for mercy, when after a few more shuffling sounds, Mr. Kurtinaitis muttered, "Damned kids."

More silence.

He's seen me for sure. He's probably sneaking up on me now.

Instead of getting hoisted by the scruff of his neck, Adam heard a deep and profound sigh of disgust, a kind of snort a dragon might issue, and the shuffling headed away to the back stairs.

The Dark Lord proceeded to shut off the lights and uttered several nasty sounding phrases in the *Lord's* native tongue. Adam heard him ascend the stairs, grumbling at each step, and slam a door. A full five minutes of complete silence went by before he drew up enough courage to step out from behind the boxes. He tiptoed through the same door, all the while certain that Mr. Kurtinaitis was actually hiding just out of sight at the entrance.

He slinked outside, holding his breath lest it give away his position. After reaching the security of his own backyard next door, he parked himself on the wooden stairs and waited for his adrenaline levels to subside along with the thumping in his chest. Once he resumed normal breathing, he placed the ball in the recess of his backdoor entry, and with a satisfied exhale, reached into his pocket.

As he held the lump of coal to the waning afternoon sunlight, he beheld an odd metallic gleam, a golden slash in the side of the black rock.

Maybe it's gold!

Eager to crack it open, he struck the coal against the slate walk at the base of the stairs a few times, which only resulted in leaving black scars along the slate's surface. He was about to try and crush the lump beneath his feet when he heard his parents parking their car in front of the house. He put the coal back into his pocket and entered through the backdoor to greet his mom who was carrying groceries.

"Hey, mom. Need some help?"

"Dad'll need a hand. There's more in the car. How on Earth did you get so filthy?"

"Aw, nothin'… I just fell."

Her head bent downward, giving her the glaring look with which he was all too familiar.

"Help your dad with the bags from the car, get those clothes off, and take a bath. You do remember we have an appointment to see Dr. Wujciak this afternoon? Hurry up, you have fifteen minutes."

He had forgotten about the physical.

Damn.

Summer was nearly over and St. Harold's Preparatory School required a physical for all new students. Adam was thrilled about the prospect of starting a new phase of his life. As he thought about the doctor's office and his mystery rock, an idea emerged which got him even more excited.

***

Adam sat in Dr. Wujciak's crowded waiting room with his mother at his side. After he read and re-read the same worn out, three month old issue of Life magazine, his name was called. He leaped up to follow the nurse, giving his mom a quick wave. He was finally old enough to be on his own.

After the usual weight, height and blood pressure routine, the nurse left him in a small inner office to await the good doctor's arrival. Adam wandered over to the corner of the office and stared at a dusty old instrument that he knew from previous discussions with Dr. Wujciak was a fluoroscope.

An x-ray machine.

It looked like a washboard with some dials and switches at its base. He was staring at it when the doctor came in.

Dr. Wujciak went through his standard prodding and jabbing routine, interrupting with an occasional request to say, "aah" or to breathe deeply as he moved an icy cold stethoscope along his bare back. In the end, Adam was congratulated for being so healthy and growing so quickly. Dr. Wujciak was about to escort him out to the reception area, when Adam stopped, pointed and asked, "Is that thing back there still working?"

"You mean Old Flora? We don't use it anymore, Adam, because it generates too high a level of x-ray radiation to be safe."

"Oh, it's not for me. I was wondering if it, Old Flora, still works, 'cause I have something that I was hoping you could check out."

Adam took out a little ball of tissue paper, unrolled it, and handed him the chunk of coal. Dr. Wujciak flipped it over several times and stopped when his eyes caught the metallic gleam, a sparkling golden band.

"Aha … So you want to see what's in this coal? Why don't you just break it open?"

"I plan to do that, but maybe it's something that might get damaged. It's gotta be really old, being in coal. Do you think that Old Flora can see inside it?" he asked with a broad grin.

Dr. Wujciak looked as intrigued as Adam. "I haven't fired that machine up for years, but there should be no problem spending an extra minute or two in trying her out. Besides, it *is* a very curious piece of coal."

He rolled the stately antique out of the corner, plugged in the frayed wiring and dimmed the lights in the office. "I've been thinking about donating it to a museum."

He riffled through one of his desk drawers, and handed a pair of red-lensed spectacles to Adam, while donning a pair himself.

"We'll need the glasses to see the image."

A faint buzzing sound preceded an eerie glow from the washboard. Dr. Wujciak made a few more adjustments to the machine and asked, "So where did you find it?"

"In the park."

Dr. Wujciak pulled his red spectacles down to the tip of his nose, propped up the lump of coal on a stand behind the washboard and said, "Come over to this side, Adam, so that we both might see what's inside."

"By the way, why do you call this thing Old Flora?"

"Just a nickname. I've had this baby around for most of my professional career. They used to be very popular back in the forties and fifties." His head lolled to one side as he added, "She's kind of like an old friend."

Adam wriggled closer and Dr. Wujciak covered them both with a heavy lead-lined blanket and turned off the room lights. The spectacles gave the washboard glow an eerie look, as if they had just opened a crimson window to another world. The two were drawn in by the bright, translucent outline of the stone. The doctor twiddled with several dials and a second image appeared within the glimmering shell, denser and even darker than the rock. The encased object appeared rounded and smooth. Dr. Wujciak reached behind the board, rotated the coal and the two investigators both uttered a whispered 'wow!' almost in unison as they made out what looked like a coin or medallion having a hole in its center. Their noses were nearly touching the screen when a blinding flash of light filled the office, followed by the unmistakable stench of burned rubber. Dr. Wujciak reached up and switched on the lights. "I'm afraid that may be it for Old Flora. I think her power supply just blew."

Just when things were getting really interesting.

"That's quite a find, Adam."

Dr. Wujciak returned the enigmatic object to Adam. "What are you planning to do with it?"

"I don't know."

I'm going to crack that sucker open. That's what I'm planning to do with it.

"The object inside might be valuable. It could have historic importance. Perhaps you may consider having a scientist look at it. I know someone in the geology department at Rutgers that I could contact if you like."

"Thanks for the offer, but I think I want to wait on that. So … could we keep it a secret, sort of between you and me?"

"That's okay, Adam, just let me know when you're ready and I'll arrange for you to visit the university."

Dr. Wujciak patted Adam's back. "Now, put your shirt back on. You're in tip-top shape. Good luck this coming year at St. Harold's, and just remember to let me know if you need any help with your discovery."

As the doctor was leaving the examination room, Adam threw him the splayed finger Vulcan hand greeting. The tricky Trekker salutation was returned with a wink.

***

The next morning Adam woke alone. Both parents were at work and the opportunity for discovery had finally arrived. Still in his pajamas, he grabbed the lump of coal and flew downstairs to his father's cellar workshop. He grabbed a screwdriver from a pegboard, holding both it and the coal in one hand, and wedged it against the bench top. The other hand reached for a hammer.

He tapped the coal and cleaved off chip after chip until at last, the coal split and a golden medallion rolled out onto the bench. Adam closed his fingers around the half-dollar-sized mystery and held it up. Its golden sheen changed in intensity with every movement, however slight. There were several odd symbols running along the edge, and it had a perfectly round quarter-inch hole in its center. There would be no way he could keep the object if he made it public.

This treasure is mine and I'm going to keep it.

He never did keep his promise to get back to Dr. Wujciak, nor did he ever tell anyone else about it for the next twenty years.

***

Traveling at nearly the speed of light, a slate gray cylinder traced a path along the inside of the Milky Way's Orion Arm a dozen light-years from Earth's solar system. Its exterior, covered by numerous gashes and impact craters, spoke of a journey of an extensive length of time. Buried within its body a complex array of machines sat in silence with the exception of one. A muffled hum from its bowels was followed by the appearance of an amber light embedded in an instrument panel. Several exterior conical shapes emerged from the body of the cylinder. They glowed briefly and altered the cylinder's trajectory, after which they returned to their original, cloaked poses within the otherwise unremarkable exterior. The amber light faded into darkness.

Part I

The Medallion

Chapter 1

Dr. Adam Dove capped off his curved chalk line with an arrowhead which indicated the path a pair of electrons would take to complete a complex chemical reaction mechanism, and yet, he was still in his father's workshop twenty years ago, gripping his golden enigma. A cough from the audience shattered the flashback, and the gold in his upheld hand morphed into chalk. He turned to look at the classroom. The only sounds throughout the large auditorium were those of pens, pencils, and laptop keyboards belonging to students engaged in keeping up with second-year Organic Chemistry. A distant period bell signaled the end of class and completed Adam's return to the present day—a fall semester Monday in the year 1999 in the sprawling eastern Pennsylvania campus of the Schill University School of Medicine, just outside Scranton, where Adam taught and conducted research in Bio-organic Chemistry. His other hand had been unconsciously fiddling with the medallion hanging beneath his shirt, a habit born of many years and of which Adam had become barely aware.

A short walk along the adjacent hallway brought him to a second floor research lab and his inner sanctuary—a glass wall-enclosed, smallish office populated with piles of books, unfinished manuscripts, and uncorrected test papers stacked precariously in a random pattern of towers, each threatening to topple onto his scrimshawed oak desk. He eased into a cracked leather-lined swivel chair, balancing himself on the three working casters, and reached up to the top of the nearest and most threatening pile.

Soon I'll be wandering around the hallways, lost in my thoughts, feeling my way along the walls while students point and snicker.

He was holding a sheaf of papers when a tap on his office door drew his gaze to a young woman's smiling face framed by the rectangular door window. Her long black hair was neatly tucked into a ponytail. Her eyes were big and brown, highlighted by dimpled rosy cheeks. The collars of a white lab coat completed the portrait. Adam knew her as the molecular biology prodigy from MIT, recently hired by the biochemistry department to coordinate and analyze incoming data from the Human Genome Project. Her name was Linda Garcia, and she was outstanding, both in intellect and looks.

He nodded and she let herself in.

"Professor Dove? I was wondering if you would like to be a part of the Human Genome Project analysis team."

Her speech held the barest traces of a Hispanic lilt, made all the more exotic by her tanned complexion and beguiling smile. It was typical of Linda to speak directly, often without the usual schmooze associated with departmental politics. Most folks knew about the Genome Project, and most knew that Dr. Garcia was the hotshot coordinating efforts at Schill. To be a part of the team analyzing the human genome not only represented a great honor, but was a most desirable opportunity for many of the fledgling researchers at the university.

"It's Linda, right?"

"Dr. Linda Garcia. I just started here last month."

"And you're heading up the university's contribution to the Human Genome Project, right?"

"Why, yes. The sequence data we are generating, coupled with incoming data from around the country is huge. It's the reason for my visit. I thought that you might be interested in joining my team."

Adam's heart opted for an extra beat. The Human Genome Project began in 1990 as a massive effort coordinated by the US Department of Energy and the National Institutes of Health to identify all the genes in human DNA. Estimates suggested the project would take about fifteen years to complete. In actuality, nine years later the work was nearing a high point and was almost complete. Adam knew enough to realize that the scientists best suited to the task were molecular biologists, much like Linda. Although he was an organic chemist with some expertise in biochemistry and statistical analysis, Linda's request to join her team seemed out of place.

"Linda, don't you have enough scientists trained in DNA sequence analysis on your staff?"

Her eyes widened as she answered. "Well, yes ... however, Dr. Dove, there are aspects of the data analysis that I think someone with your background could really contribute to."

She entranced him. Adam was having difficulty paying attention to what Linda was actually saying. "Please call me Adam ... what aspects?"

Her face grew solemn as she replied in a firmer voice. "Adam, why don't you join us tomorrow morning at our review meeting? After seeing the details of our work thus far, you'll be able to answer that question yourself." She turned, perhaps too abruptly, leaving the office door to slowly swing back. Before it closed, she added, "Gotta run. I hope to see you in the morning."

When she reached the outer laboratory exit, he extended his arm to hold his office door ajar. "I'll be there. Where and when?" He noticed that his hands were sweaty.

Linda called back without turning. "Room 331B, nine sharp." With a quick backward wave of her hand she was down the hall and out of sight.

***

Room 331B was Linda's laboratory office located on the third floor almost directly above Adam's. A note on the door led him to a meeting room farther along the hallway. He approached its outer door and peered through the glass. About a dozen seated researchers surrounded an elongated conference table. All were dressed in freshly pressed white lab coats, while several fiddled with an overhead projector. A reflection in the glass revealed someone coming up behind him—Linda.

"Good morning, Adam. Glad to see you made it."

Adam feigned mild surprise and turned to see Linda's infectious smile. While she opened the door, he replied, "Me too." He followed her inside, and wedged himself into an empty desk chair in a far corner of the room.

Linda began. "As you know, we are in the midst of collating and analyzing the remaining DNA sequence data for human chromosomes four and five, which would complete our portion of the preliminary sequencing. The meeting this morning was called to brain-storm the current data, and to map out a plan of action." Looking directly at Adam, Linda continued, "Dr. Adam Dove will be joining us in a consulting capacity."

The announcement went largely without reaction, with several heads turning to look at Adam. He returned the curious glances with an innocent but studious façade as he pondered the confidence with which Linda assumed he would join the team. The meeting proceeded to detail various quirks and challenges surrounding chromatographic separation and identification procedures, sequencing options, purification issues, and other such technical bits typical of the project in general. As the presentations proceeded, Adam began reviewing what he actually knew about DNA.

The acronym was short for deoxyribonucleic acid—a polymer made up of four types of bases. The sequence of these four bases in a DNA strand represents all the instructions needed to build and maintain any biologic organism. A set of three bases, a triplet, generally encodes for a single amino acid, a building block for a protein that can be hundreds of amino acids long. The sequence of these triplets along the DNA constitutes the genetic code. Each chromosome held one DNA chain and that a chunk of DNA that codes for a specific protein is called a gene.

That's definitely all I know.

He guessed that the total amount of DNA, which describes an organism, is called a genome.

"Adam, now that you have an appreciation of the challenges we face, I would like your opinion on something."

Adam blinked, mentally filing away his DNA musings. The meeting room was empty.

It must have been a short meeting.

Linda was standing in front of him and with a smirk, turned and waved for Adam to follow. They entered her laboratory together, where she stopped just inside, letting the door close behind them.

"As you may know, the human genome project was designed to identify each and every gene, and in so doing, it would provide the world with a complete description, basically a roadmap of a human being. The idea was to determine the sequences of approximately three billion bases that make up our DNA, and then to figure out how many genes were present and what proteins they encoded for. Information obtained from this project would be invaluable to us, especially in tackling genetic disorders and developing new ways to design medicines tailored for the individual's biochemistry."

Linda furrowed her brow. Catching the look, Adam stifled a yawn. She cleared her throat and raised her hands to emphasize a point. "However, we have run into a few surprises. Originally we assumed that hundreds of thousands of genes made up the human genome. Earlier observations indicated that simpler organisms had a smaller number of genes. For example, bacteria and fungi range from about two to eight thousand genes. Fruit flies get up to about fourteen thousand, and mice are at twenty-five thousand. Although the human genome project is not quite complete yet, our data indicate the gene count for humans to be less than thirty thousand."

"Not much more than in mice. Sounds a bit disappointing. What gives?"

"No one knows for sure, but it would appear that we may be using the same basic machinery present in lower species, but in a more complex way."

"Is that the issue that you'd like me to look at?"

Linda shook her head. "Not exactly. There's something else that has emerged which may be much more of a puzzle. It turns out that our genome is largely unused. That is, not only are we limited to thirty thousand genes, but recently we have discovered that a fairly large portion of our genome appears to be nonsense."

Linda took a step closer to Adam. When he spoke, his voice cracked. "Exactly how much of the genome are we talking about?"

"Our analysis suggests that about two percent of all the sequences in our DNA codes for protein. This leaves the rest of our genome with no identifiable purpose. Some scientists have called these sequences 'junk.' I call them 'non-coding.' And, that's where you come in."

"And why would that be?"

"Experimentalists have been working on the possible function of non-coding DNA, and the most likely theories suggest that it may be responsible for the regulation of all the processes which go into creating and maintaining us, basically acting to make sure each step in the process of our growth and development takes place at the right time and in the right way. Personally, I think that's a neat explanation, however, there's no concrete proof ... and, besides, the non-coding sequences are a bit strange."

"Strange? In what way strange?"

"There are many instances where apparently random sequences repeat themselves in other parts of our genome. Actually, they seem to be both random and organized. One other thing … as I mentioned, lower, simpler organisms have fewer genes. However, they also have less non-coding DNA. The trend that we are seeing is that as an organism becomes more complex, that organism has an increased amount of non-coding DNA."

"Whew. So, how do I fit into the picture?"

"You've done a great deal of work in the area of structure-activity correlations, mathematical procedures designed to detect relationships between molecular structure and biological activity." Adam nodded as Linda continued. "I have a feeling that there may be more to the non-coding DNA issue than just a random set of sequences coupled to vague theories of cellular regulation."

"You want me to look for patterns within these sequences? Patterns that may correlate with some type of function?"

"You got it."

"Just how much non-coding sequence data do you have?"

"We are just now completing the sequencing for two chromosomes. The non-coding sections consist of about two hundred fifty million bases. We can get the sequence data from other labs which cover the rest of the human genome. Altogether the mystery sequences contain close to three billion bases."

* * *

The cylinder turned and a large engine at one end fired in a programmed series of short bursts to begin a controlled process of deceleration. The G-forces needed to be carefully regulated. Excessive forces would not damage the cocooned occupants, but could pose issues to the few awake and on duty.

Chapter 2

Adam lived in a colonial on the edge of the Schill campus in a small suburban community on the outskirts of Scranton. Settling into his favorite easy chair, he sifted through magazines and letters.

"Adam. Is that you?"

It was Helen, his mother. She was visiting for a few weeks, and although she arrived a week ago, her voice still startled Adam. After his dad passed away a few years before, the visit had become an annual ritual.

"Just me, mom."

Creaking stairs announced her arrival in the foyer outside the living room. She gave Adam a wide grin. Her silver gray hair was wrapped in a bun and wire-rimmed spectacles hung low on her nose.

"Your dinner's ready. It's so late, and you didn't call."

Adam had spent most of the day setting up the computer equipment and software necessary to handle billions of bits of information. Pattern recognition techniques were well known, but not many such approaches could handle the enormous input represented by the human genome sequence data. He had set up the processors on the university's extended network, which included the use of idle desktop computers scattered throughout the campus, as well as several sister campuses elsewhere in the state. He could monitor the process from anywhere along the network, even from his laptop at home.

He looked up at his mother and blew her a kiss. Just seeing her standing there, chiding him, gave him a warm feeling.

There was nothing like a mom.

"Sorry, mom. I'm involved in a new project and needed the time to set up a few things. Is that pot roast I smell? Be there in a minute."

Pot roast was his favorite. It reminded him of simpler times. His mother mumbled under her breath and glided off to the kitchen while Adam returned his attention to the mail. He came across an item of singular interest—a letter from his hometown, Maplewood, a small suburban community along the northeast corridor of New Jersey. It was from Dr. Ben Wujciak. He felt a pang of guilt as he recalled his childhood promise to follow-up the mystery they shared together two decades ago. He had relegated the medallion to a nightstand drawer, while prep school consumed his attention. University and graduate school provided further distraction. When he moved to Schill, he rediscovered the medallion in a shoebox and decided to adopt it as a good luck charm, something he could use in the academically competitive world of grants and tenure. His fingers walked across his shirtfront, reassuring him of the medallion's presence. He tore open the envelope. A short note was attached to a folded piece of paper. Hand-written, it had the look of a hasty scrawl, like scribbling on a prescription.

"Dear Adam. I trust you are doing well at Schill. I thought you might be interested in the enclosed article. Best wishes to you and Helen. Don't be a stranger when back in town. Please feel free to drop by."

Adam's family had moved out of the old neighborhood while he was at prep school. A letter from Wujciak after so many years was quite a surprise. Attached to the note was a photocopy of what appeared to be a newspaper clipping. On its upper edge, printed by hand, he made out 'Morrisonville Times, June 11, 1891.' The hair on the back of his neck bristled as he read the column's title, GOLD CHAIN FOUND INSIDE COAL. The article went on to describe how a Mrs. S. W. Culp was shoveling coal into her kitchen stove when a large lump broke in two and out from the center of it fell a gold chain. The chain was about ten inches long and was described as being of 'antique and quaint workmanship.' Investigators were convinced that the chain had not been accidentally dropped into the coal since one portion of the broken lump still clung to the chain while the separated part bore the impression of where the chain had been encased. The article went on to discuss the ramifications of such a find, especially as the coal was said to have been from the Pennsylvania era, which suggested that it could have been over one hundred million years old.

Adam's mind began racing. He read and re-read the article, oblivious to his mom's incessant call to come for dinner.

A gold chain in a piece of coal. Why did Wujciak send me this? Was there anything else on the chain? Where was the chain now?

His mom raised her voice. Adam refolded the clipping and tossed it on the coffee table. It was time for a pot roast dinner.

***

The next morning, after his mandatory cup of java and sugar-frosted donut, and after checking up on the progress of the DNA analysis using his laptop, he ran a few searches on the Internet to see if there was anything more on the 1891 article. To his surprise, he came across hundreds of references to Mrs. Culp and her gold chain. His elation waned as he found himself wading through a vast heap of equally curious archeological oddities—conspiracy theories of government cover-ups, ancient human civilizations, catastrophe theory, creationist dogma, and even indisputable proofs of time travel and teleportation. Aliens, mostly the gray, stringy kind, were in the mix as well—a possibility for which he felt an odd attraction.

***

The Schill University chemistry department was situated on the first floor of the science building, McArdle Hall. The newspaper article had given him a mental kick in the butt. As a child, he had always thought that the medallion was just an old coin. He had to admit that such a thing was very unlikely and that maybe he had purposefully avoided thinking too much about it.

Adam wandered along the central hallway guided only by the touch of his fingers along the wall, much as he feared he might be doing eventually as 'The Absent-Minded Professor of Schill University.' He bumped into one of the senior denizens of the analytical labs, Dr. George Freedman, a good friend.

"George, got a moment?"

"Hey, Adam. Anything for you, son."

Adam only knew George for a couple of years, however, George knew everyone in the building, and the campus for that matter. He was at least a decade past mandatory retirement age, slightly eccentric, entirely bald, and sported a prominent pair of geeky black-rimmed bifocals. A pure white triangle of a goatee punctuated his permanent red-cheeked cherubic complexion.

"What can I do ya fer?" he drawled.

"Does your lab have a way to analyze metals?"

"Why, of course. Anything in particular you have in mind?"

Adam struggled with a way to describe the item without sounding too mysterious. "Well, some time back I came across something that looked like an old coin, and I was wondering if you could figure out what it was made of. I assume you have access to non-destructive ways to do this?"

Adam's basic knowledge of analytical chemistry was spotty and relied on his recollections from sophomore days in college, at a time when everything was dissolved in acids and was subjected to a variety of tests which resulted in assorted noxious vapors and bright colors. In fact, his impressions of it all were not far removed from the age-old theme surrounding the conversion of lead into gold.

"What kind of metal do you think it's made of?"

Adam reached down his shirtfront and pulled out the medallion. Even in the indirect fluorescent hallway lighting, the object had an enticing sparkle. He pulled it over his head and handed it to George.

"Well, what do you think?"

Hefting the piece to gauge its weight, George gave it a long stare through his coke bottle lenses. "Golden in color, but based on the weight, I don't think it's pure gold. It seems just a bit light to me. Could be an alloy of some sort."

He removed the chain, handed it to Adam, and stared at him through the hole in the disk's middle. "What kind of coin is this?"

"I really don't know. In fact, it may not be a coin."

George spoke to himself. "A metal disk with a hole in the middle. Odd surface reflects light in different ways. Funny little symbols running along the edge. Where did you come across this weird little piece?"

"If I told you, you wouldn't believe me. Let's just go on the assumption that it may be quite old."

George gave Adam an odd look, one that he might reserve for clueless administrative staff and visiting dignitaries. "Adam. You're sayin' it's a coin that's not a coin. It looks like gold, but might not be gold. It's engraved with symbols that I've never seen before." George lowered his specs and gave Adam a long look.

"Oh, all right then."

Adam spent the next few minutes relating the discovery that took place twenty years ago. When he finished, George's eyes acquired a distinct squint and his head tilted to one side as he asked, "So, this coin came out of a solid piece of coal?

"That's what I'm saying."

"Do you realize how old it might be?"

"That's why I came to you. I need someone to verify something I'm afraid to say out loud."

George tilted his head back and blew out a gust of air. "Adam, as I understand it, coal takes a long time to form. All coal owes its origin to vegetation, compressed and decaying. Softer coals could be tens of thousands of years old, but if it was anthracite … hard coals like that could take anywhere from one to a couple of hundred million years to form. Are you *sure* it was *inside* the coal?"

"That's how I found it."

George gazed at the shiny little disk. A fine bead of sweat formed about Adam's brow as he soaked in the potential ramifications. George waved at him to follow and they marched down the hallway.

"I agree we should try and figure out what it's made of, and then go from there. Trace metals analysis can pinpoint the type of process used to make it, and even suggest the where and when of it … of course, assuming it was made by some conventional means."

When they reached the end of the hallway, George swung open a set of metal fire doors and they entered the main analytical laboratory. It was a modestly sized lab with four bench areas, two along the walls and two running down the middle in parallel. Equipment occupied every available square inch. Two ventilation hoods faced each other from opposite walls. Four and five foot gas cylinders stood alongside the instrumentation, connected by metal tubing to a host of liquid and gas chromatographs, mass spectrographs, and other devices Adam could only guess at. The room hummed as automated injectors and collectors processed samples and data. Cabling dangled from the drop ceiling, connecting most of the equipment to a central data collection system.

They made their way to a corner occupied by a monolithic blue-gray apparatus. To Adam it looked like one of the movie robots of the nineteen fifties—a silent sentinel overseeing its lesser metallic minions. A smattering of yellow and black radiation hazard placards surrounded the brooding metal giant, while faded Post-it notes scrawled with added warnings and illegible instructions clung to its sides. Some lay on the pitted table top beneath it, fallen years ago, judging from their faded colors and the thickness of accumulated dust.

"This is the beastie that will tell us what we want to know. It's an EDXRF unit we inherited from Penn State some years ago. The acronym stands for energy-dispersive x-ray fluorescence … basically a device that will blast your sample with x-rays and then provide a readout of the radiation that's emitted back. Each element has a characteristic emission spectrum, so we can find out what's in there and how much."

"And that won't that damage the medallion?"

"Don't worry. The x-rays barely penetrate the metal surface and the emitted radiation dies out quickly. The only problem is that I'll need some time to resuscitate my old colleague here and prepare the sample. I'll give you a call either tonight or first thing tomorrow morning."

Adam agreed, although not without pause. He was leaving behind an old friend. As he left, he saw George donning a frayed and discolored lab coat with one hand and clearing off some bench space with the other. When he reached his upstairs office, Adam sequestered himself in the rear of his lab, preparing for the next day's lectures, feeling all the while a bit naked and anxious as thoughts of his good luck charm being pummeled with huge amounts of radiation ran through his mind.

***

The phone rang. A glowing red LCD display announced that it was 2:30 a.m. Adam rolled toward the night stand and answered the phone.

"Huh?"

"Adam. Adam, I couldn't wait. You've got to come down here and see this. It's incredible."

"George? Do you know what time it is?"

"Adam, that artifact of yours is very special. I've got a fix on its composition, and I ran some other analyses. It's like nothing I've ever seen. Like nothing anyone's ever seen."

Adam rubbed his eyes open, threw his bed covers aside and practically leaped out of bed. "I'll be right there."

***

It was about three in the morning when Adam arrived at McArdle Hall. The only lights he saw came from the analytical lab on the first floor. As he ascended the granite steps, George threw open the front doors.

"Come on, Adam. I've got lots to show you," George panted, nearly out of breath.

"I can't believe you've been up all night."

Adam struggled to keep up with George who fast-walked to his lab. When they reached the x-ray apparatus, George turned to him. "Like we discussed yesterday, I ran the x-ray fluorescence analysis." George paused for a moment as if to gauge Adam's reaction. "And, the data suggest the disk is made of gold."

"I thought you said it felt too light."

"I'll explain. Aside from some debris one would naturally find on an old piece like this, the surface is definitely gold, pure gold, one hundred percent pure 24-karat gold."

"Aren't there always some impurities in gold?"

"Well, that's the thing, or more precisely, that's just one of the things. The gold on the surface has no impurities aside from normal microscopic debris."

"Is that possible?"

"Well, it's damned unusual. If it was made long ago, I'd say it was actually … impossible. But if it was made using modern technology, then that's a different matter. Besides, pure gold like that doesn't do well as a coin. Gold coins are usually minted as a mixture with other metals. Gold alone is too soft to stand up to the wear and tear of handling."

Maybe it wasn't made to be handled.

By the look of George's open mouth, Adam could tell there was more to come.

"Because the artifact seemed a little light for gold, I decided to run a few more checks—specifically, some high intensity x-ray microanalysis. This way we could see if there was any other metal present. Wait 'til you see what I found."

Adam followed George as he jogged to another corner of the lab. He grabbed a few black and white photos from the bench and handed them to Adam.

"What does this look like?"

Adam stared at what could easily have been a cross-section of the interior of a beehive's hexagonal storage chambers.

"A honeycomb of some sort?"

"You got it. But instead of wax, this honeycomb is gold. There's stuff inside each chamber. The scans I made say it is carbon. I scanned other parts of the medallion, and it's much the same. The honeycomb structure exists throughout the whole piece. I was able to make photos of the x-ray using our EM. What you're actually looking at is a section that's a couple of hundred nanometers wide."

Adam was familiar with an EM, an electron microscope, but was surprised to find out it could use x-rays to see through specimens. "How many of these chambers are there?"

"I've estimated the number to be at least several billion. It's like a solid gold sponge, but at a microscopic level."

Adam leaned back against a wall as George continued. "If you're having trouble getting your mind around this, join the club. There's no way this could be manufactured, just no way. It could not be constructed with any present technology, as well as any technology we even could conceive of." George smirked. "Or should that be 'any technology of which we could conceive'?"

After a long pause, Adam's eyes refocused and he looked up as George continued. "Hey, there's a bit more. Using the EM, I made some careful geometrical measurements of the disk. First of all, it's perfectly round. Taking into account a bit of wear, the edge transcribes a perfect circle. There's no deviation even within the limits of EM resolution. And to top it off, the hole in the middle …"

"Let me guess. It's perfectly centered as well."

To which George nodded and smiled back at Adam.

"Is that it? Is there more?"

He winked. "I know I promised to only use non-destructive analyses, but these findings got me so crazy that I just had to check one more thing."

Adam was about to say something.

"Hey, don't worry. Using a focused laser source, I managed to remove a microscopic amount of the gold from one edge of the disk, just enough to get a measurable amount of sample using a special device on the EM. Then I ran a mass spectrogram on the sample."

Adam raised his head, prompting George to continue.

"Well the mass ions from the gold are dead on. It's gold for sure." George looked down at a paper towel on which he had scribbled some numbers. "Atomic number 79. Mass 196.967 amu. The same gold we are all familiar with, that is, it looks like our gold, and the stuff we have here on Earth. But the carbon …" George paused, winked again, and went on. "Well, it's pure carbon, but with an atomic number of 13, not the carbon-12 isotope we would expect …"

"Here on Earth?" Adam finished.

He's going to start ranting about aliens any moment now.

Unflustered, George continued. "Well, as you know, carbon-13 does exist here on Earth. Basically, our carbon consists of two stable isotopes, ninety-nine percent carbon-12 and about one percent carbon-13. Although we have the technology to isolate it, how it got into that medallion in such a pure form, and why it's there, is a mystery to me."

Along with a litany of other mysteries.

Adam braced himself against a bench edge. They both stood in the corner of the lab in silence for several minutes, when Adam asked, "Can you date the piece? There's carbon in it."

George was quick to respond with Adam already nodding. "No can do, as I can see by the look on your face, you know that carbon dating relies on measuring the amount of carbon-14, and this piece has no carbon-14. Remember, the carbon is pure carbon-13. And, of course, gold is gold, only one stable isotope. Anyway, using carbon-14 dating relies on some assumptions—the primary assumption being that the object is from Earth."

Adam ran his fingers through his hair, shook his head, and asked George for the disk. Reaching into the EM sample compartment, George suggested, "You could leave it with me, you know. Just in case I think of something else we might want to check out."

"You've outdone yourself tonight, George. Get some rest. I'll be back in the morning, and with a chance to clear our heads I'm sure we'll come up with some more ideas by then."

George gave the medallion a long look and handed it over. Cradling it in his hands, Adam stared at it with a new found respect bordering on reverence.

So, what we have here is an unnatural object found in coal which means it's incredibly old, machined to perfection which means we probably didn't make it, made of a wafer of pure gold containing zillions of bits of carbon-13, which means we definitely didn't make it.

He turned to George just as he was leaving the lab and said, "Maybe the symbols running around the edge translate to something like 'In God We Trust'."

George chuckled. "Or, 'Not to be Used for Legal Tender'?" whereupon they both laughed.

The two men bade each other goodnight and agreed to keep the evening's discoveries to themselves. They would meet again sometime later in the day as it was unclear how much sleep either would get. Adam restrung the medallion around his neck and walked back to his car in the half-light of pre-dawn. He barely noticed the sheaf of photos he still held in one hand. The electric smell rising from the asphalt presaged a muffled thunder in the distance.

***

The cylinder positioned itself neatly behind Earth's moon. Final adjustments made by the conscious portion of the crew assured a secure location, well screened from direct view by Earth's inhabitants. Moments later an opening appeared on the side, through which a small, canister-like object emerged. As the opening behind it slid shut, the small object accelerated away. Several of the crew took up designated posts within a small circular room having a wide viewing screen along one side which played and re-played a receding view of that small canister as it swept beyond the moon's horizon. Before long, the opening reappeared on the outer skin of the cylinder, and a second canister flew out.

Chapter 3

Dawn brought with it rattling surges of rain against Adam's bedroom window. He couldn't sleep. His mind had been racing through the few hours of darkness that remained when he got back from the lab, looping endlessly through each analysis and each conclusion, seeking out rational explanations where none seemed possible. This went on and on until, at last, the subdued glimmer from the tempest outside heralded the arrival of a new day. Adam arose from bed and bounded down the stairs for a cup of coffee, not at all surprised that he was still dressed.

***

A gray smear of a sky hung overhead as he entered McArdle Hall. A glance along the length of the hallway leading to the analytical lab availed him of nothing but a cavernous gloom. He was about to go up the stairwell when a movement in the dark caught his attention. Thinking it might be George, he stuck his head back into the hallway for a closer look. Someone entered the single cone of light from an overhead ceiling lamp.

"Oh. Hi, Dr. Dove ... Adam."

It was Linda.

Startled, Adam took a moment. "Linda! I thought you were someone else."

Her mouth curled up slightly, pausing before answering. "Sorry to disappoint. I'm on my way to get a cup of coffee. Would you like to join me?"

God ... she's beautiful. Maybe it's the lighting. The scent of her.

The first floor boasted a small break room equipped with the requisite coffee maker, microwave and a last-resort donut vending machine. Adam had almost forgotten about the DNA pattern recognition analysis. It seemed like ancient history.

"Let me get my stuff upstairs. I'll be back down in a few minutes. Sure, coffee would be great."

At this early hour no one else had come into work, at least not into his lab. When Adam arrived at his office, he immediately fired up his laptop and downloaded a brief progress report on the analysis. With billions of base pairs making up possible patterns, he did not expect to see much. However, a cursory look suggested that even at this early stage there was some evidence of repeating patterns surfacing, and he could bring these up to Linda over coffee. He waited for the printout before going downstairs to the break room with laptop in tow.

***

Adam sipped carefully at his Styrofoam cup.

Linda said, "I'd have to check with my database, but these sequences you've identified as repeating are probably well known. They're probably what we call spacers between coding regions."

"That may be, but the results of my analysis thus far suggest a more subtle purpose. It would appear that the coding regions are more random than the non-coding regions." Adam let that comment sink in for a moment before continuing. "The coding regions, responsible for all the protein that we're made of, consist of base pairs that are statistically random, and the non-coding regions, which represent the vast majority of our DNA, are full of non-random sequences. At first I thought that this was odd, but on second thought it does make some sense. The base pair sequences coding for all kinds of protein would necessarily resemble random numbers. I guess it's weirder that the non-coding stuff is not very random."

Linda put her coffee mug down and eased back into her chair. "So, what kind of patterns are these that exist in the non-coding DNA?"

"Too early to tell. The next stage of the analysis will begin to tease them apart, and that will take at least a few days. In fact, I've got a suite of language translation programs which will automatically kick in, programs that will look for possible meaning in the patterns—basically looking for internal relationships."

Adam finished his coffee and stood up to leave. As he did, their eyes met and for a moment Adam glimpsed the promise of a deeper future connection. He was still staring when a flash of light transformed her into a dark silhouette. Hallway window panels cracked, followed by a whoosh. Glass shards blew into the room, followed by a burst of heat and a deafening roar. Insulating panels tumbled down around them. Adam instinctively fell forward covering Linda, and the two rolled onto the floor beneath the table they had shared moments before.

After a few seconds, Adam shook his head, throwing off dust and glass. A worried look on Linda's face confirmed she was all right. He stood, shaking his windbreaker of chalky debris when the wall behind him exploded with a silvery blur flying past his head. It crashed into the wall to his front. He stared at the impact site and recognized the massive silvery object as a five-foot gas cylinder. Its valve stem had broken off, turning it into a rocket. Gas shrieked out of it, enveloping the pair in a whirlwind of choking dust. The contents of such a cylinder typically exceeded several thousand pounds per square inch. Adam wasn't sure what the cylinder contained but wasn't interested in sticking around to find out, especially since it might be a flammable gas that could ignite at any moment. Linda was already on her feet. He grabbed her arm and led them out into the smoke-filled hallway. They passed by teeth-chattering alarm bells as they ran toward the building's entrance.

Adam yelled, "Is there anyone else upstairs?"

"I'm always the first one in the morning. I didn't see anyone up there."

A hissing sound provided the barest of warnings as several gushing sprinklers promptly soaked them. He was sure he had not seen any lights on the second floor. The two hurried along the darkened hallway, skirting showers and thick black smoke, and exited through the glass entrance doors. Once outside, they slowed to walk toward the parking lot. Alarms clanged within the building and were broadcast on outside speakers. Students from nearby dormitories slogged through the wet grass of the quadrangle.

Troglodytes. They look like they just crawled out of their caves.

Young men and women garbed in undershorts and nightgowns began appearing out of the twilight mist. Prodded from their dry dormitory hollows, they meandered toward McArdle Hall, transfixed by the siren call of the alarm bells. On the bright side, the rain had ceased by the time Adam and Linda reached his Pathfinder.

***

Helen finished pouring coffee. Linda nodded thanks. Her cup trembled in her hand. "Look at me. I'm shaking."

"Maybe you're drinking too much coffee," said Adam.

They both laughed. Adam placed his arm around her shoulders and their eyes met. Her straight dark hair was wet, the ends curling up. She had an ethereal glow.

Maybe that's just the wet hair.

Helen said, "Oh dear, it's a bit chilly in here this morning. I'll get a blanket for you."

"Oh, no. That's quite all-right Mrs. Dove. The coffee'll warm me up."

Adam rubbed Linda's shoulder. He could feel the tension dissolve as they huddled together.

"You can relax now. We both had a close call."

"What happened back there?"

"It looks like something in the analytical lab blew up."

"But there was no one working there this morning, was there?"

"Not that I noticed. The lights were off when I arrived. I was in that lab last night … actually, earlier this morning. We had a number of instruments running."

"We? What were you doing there so late?"

Adam wasn't sure how to answer. His natural inclination was to remain secretive, sensing that the less people knew about his medallion, the better. Although with what had just happened, he felt closer to Linda than to anyone else.

"I was down there with George. We were running analyses on … on a coin I had found a few years back."

Linda pursed her lips and asked, "Was there anything you did that could have set off such an explosion?"

"Far from it. It was just some analytical work George was doing on this." Adam pulled out the medallion and held it out to Linda.

She moved her head closer for a better look. "Wow, it's beautiful. What kind of coin is it?"

"Well, actually, I'm not so sure it's a coin. In fact, that's basically what we were trying to find out."

"And, did you?"

"Yes and no."

Adam was about to elaborate when the phone in the kitchen rang. He stood up and answered, then looked at Linda. "It's George. He's frantic. Excuse me a moment."

Adam moved away from the kitchen table, leaving Linda and his mom to chat while he positioned himself outside the kitchen door to continue his conversation with George. After a few minutes he cradled the phone and sat down.

"George is beside himself. He was calling from McArdle. It was his lab that blew up and he's afraid that everything in there was destroyed … equipment and data, even the stuff that we collected last night. He's there now with the firemen trying to sort everything out."

"What a mess. Thank goodness no one was hurt." After a moment, she added, "You could always analyze that thing again … somewhere else."

"I suppose you're right."

Actually, we found out quite a bit last night.

The photos were with his laptop, which he just recalled, he left behind in the break room.

"Linda, I've got to go back. Back to the chemistry building, to get my laptop. I left it in the break room."

"You think there's a chance it didn't get destroyed? You could call George."

It was not so much the laptop that was of concern.

"Why don't you stay here with my mom. I should be back in a half-hour."

Before Linda could respond, Adam had fetched his windbreaker and was out the door.

Linda turned to his mother. "Is your son always so headstrong?"

Adam's mother calmly topped off Linda's coffee cup and replied, "He's a very focused person. If I've learned something over these many years it is that Adam has a way of seeing things that is unique, and when his mind wraps itself around something, watch out."

***

Adam winced at the acrid stench of smoke which had reached the parking lot. There were several fire engines surrounding the chemistry building. People in red and yellow helmets were moving in and out of headlight beams. Some had gathered near their equipment while others rolled up fire hose. The fire was out.

When he arrived at the entrance, someone yelled out. "Sir. Sir, you can't go in there yet!"

Adam turned to the approaching policeman. "But I just want to get to my laptop. It was on the first floor, in the break room."

"I'm sorry, sir. You'll need the fire marshal to clear you. They've got men inspecting on the second and third floors, and I think he's up there with them. You'll have to wait until he comes down."

The policeman resumed his position near the entrance. Adam turned away and walked slowly toward the parking lot, thinking of options.

"Adam!"

It was George. He ran up and began describing the devastation in the analytical lab. It seems the explosion may have been due to a gas leak of some sort, triggered by one of the electrical contacts in the equipment. At least this was the fire marshal's preliminary finding. Then George frowned and shook his head.

"Is there more, George?"

"The only gasses we had in there were argon, nitrogen, oxygen and helium … none of which are flammable. None of those would cause such an explosion."

George was staring at the ground and muttering to no one in particular.

"Whatever it was, it scared the hell out of us. We were next door."

George's head shot up. "You were in the break room? My God, I saw that room. The explosion must have knocked over a nitrogen cylinder. It flew through the lab wall. You could have been killed ... We?"

"Linda and I were lucky."

Adam paused a second as George's mouth formed an 'o'.

"George, are you sure there was no one in the lab this morning?"

"I locked up the lab last night. Besides the janitor, I've got the only key. So, I don't think so. Why do you ask?"

"Oh, nothing. Just worried that someone could have been hurt."

Adam recalled the shadowy figure in the hallway earlier that morning.

"George, can you do me a favor?"

George peered over his glasses.

"I need to get into the break room, to get my laptop if it's still there. The firemen don't want me going in, but I really need to get to my computer. If you could talk to that cop at the door, kind of distract him? You know, get him to move away from the door?"

"While you scoot inside?"

Adam nodded. At first George grimaced, then smiled and returned the nod. In short order, the policeman at the entrance was enmeshed in an animated conversation with George who was making noises about his equipment and the fire.

Adam slipped inside and entered an alien landscape. An emergency floodlight at the far end of the hallway silhouetted snake-like tendrils of smoke hanging from the ceiling. The sprinklers had done their job, leaving everything wet and dripping. Feeling his way forward, Adam came to the glistening metal break room doors that stood ajar, as if beckoning him inside. Just then, he heard the front doors squeal open and someone say they had to wait for the fire marshal before they could go in. It had to be George and his new friend, the policeman.

Adam slipped into the break room, crunching glass underfoot and hugging the shadows along a wall for cover. The disembodied voice continued on with its cautionary monologue. Adam heard the front entry doors swing closed and the voice fade away. He looked over the overturned furniture and debris-strewn floor for signs of his black leather laptop case and spotted the upturned table that he had shared with Linda what seemed only minutes ago. Beyond that there was a gaping three foot hole in the wall through which the silver missile had flown and through which he could see into the analytical lab. His arm brushed up against the now empty and silent gas cylinder still lodged in the opposite wall. He lowered himself to the floor on all fours and crawled toward the table. A movement caught his eye. He froze. Something had shifted in the analytical lab. The only people in the building were the fire and safety inspectors on the floors above him.

So there shouldn't be anyone downstairs right now.

Adam maneuvered a little closer for a better look through the hole. He tensed when he saw a beam of light gliding along a bench top, followed by sounds of drawers opening and closing.

Who is that and what is he searching for?

After a few minutes the light disappeared and he heard only the sounds of dripping water. Craning his head forward through the hole, he confirmed that there was no one inside the lab, but he did see light coming from a window, or rather, where a window used to be.

Maybe it was a fireman and he went out that way.

The opening led to the rear of the building. His level of anxiety clicked up a notch. He looked back down and found the laptop beneath part of the wall, still inside its leather case, and only slightly wet. Since it was likely that the building entryway was guarded despite George's best efforts to distract, he slipped through the hole in the wall, baby-stepped between ruined lab equipment, and leaped out the window.

Seconds later, within the dark solitude of the lab, where the only sounds were the tick-tock dripping of water on flooded floors, the suspended ethereal wisps of smoke overhead jerked as a figure emerged from hiding in the shadows and made its way out the same broken window.

Adam met George in front of the building and the two walked back to the parking lot.

"Well, is that it … your laptop?"

"Sure is," Adam answered while lifting up the case for George to see. He opened it while they were walking, pulled out a sheaf of photos. "And, see what I've got?"

"Well, at least that's something. It's probably the only data that survived. All the stuff in the lab is gone. By the way, the cop I was talking to told me that they won't be letting anyone into the building for a few days. Looks like the explosion took out the building's electrical system. So, between that and the clean up, they'll be busy in there for at least a week. I guess that means we're on vacation."

"Did you see anyone leaving the building in the last couple of minutes?"

"Nope. I was busy distracting the guard, remember?"

"Is there any chance that someone knew about the analyses run last night?"

George adopted his contemplative, furrowed eyebrow look that Adam guessed he found most useful either to hide outright confusion or use as a prelude to pontification. "Well, I certainly didn't tell anyone. However, the instruments are networked to enable data to be archived. It's theoretically possible for someone on the network to monitor which instruments are gathering data. They could even take a look at it, but it would mean that someone had to be up late, or rather, early this morning, and have an interest in doing so. Why do you ask?"

"How would someone go about monitoring the instruments?"

"Anyone with a valid user id and password can get on the system from almost anywhere on the campus, and …"

"With the right commands, they can access the instrument files," finished Adam.

George nodded and looked perplexed.

"George, that was a great job you did last night. Do me a favor and please don't tell anyone about the medallion, especially anything about our findings. I need to see someone in New Jersey before we make any of this public."

Adam got into the car and rumbled away. He thought about George and the daunting prospect of replacing and rebuilding the lab. He had a nagging feeling that something was off, a disquieting certitude that there was something going on just out of view. As he exited the parking lot, he watched George in his rearview mirror fade off into the distance, little realizing how justified his concerns would soon prove to be.

Chapter 4

The early evening sun cast deep shadows across Walnut Street, Maplewood. Tall maple and elm trees lining the road threw shifting zebra lines across Adam's car. The drive from PA to his hometown took only two hours, but it felt like ages. His mind's eye relentlessly reran the day's events. He had dropped off Linda at her car and promised to call her later.

His medallion was an enigma. The archeological ramifications of such a find could be colossal. The analyses were carried out on a networked computer system. To a paranoiac mind, someone could have been observing the data collection. Adam didn't think of himself as paranoiac.

Did I see someone in the laboratory hallway just before the explosion? It was an explosion that should not have happened. Who was rifling through the remains of the laboratory? What were they looking for?

Adam's skin prickled as he realized just how significant the medallion could be, and that someone else may know that as well. Scientific deductions had their limits, since such reasoning required hard facts. Intuition, on the other hand, was prone to fill in the voids between, and it was intuition that drove Adam to New Jersey, to Maplewood, and to Dr. Ben Wujciak's home.

Why would Wujciak send me information about a gold necklace found in a lump of coal back in 1891? Why send it to me now?

The doctor had retired from practice several years ago. His home office was still in the same place, located on a quiet residential street. Adam parked his car on a nearby cross street, and walked over to the house.

The place looked the same as he had remembered it nearly twenty years ago. Time's passage, so relentless in modernizing the surrounding neighborhood with new office buildings, had taken a major detour to avoid the doctor's unassuming little one-family house. Faded gray wooden steps led up to a recessed porch. A rectangular patch of brighter paint over the door betrayed the former location of an office shingle. Adam pressed the doorbell, eliciting a muffled two-tone chime from within. After waiting a minute or so, he pressed the doorbell again. No one seemed to be in. Noticing a mail slot at the bottom of the front door, he stooped over, propped open the hinged flap and peered into the foyer. He spotted a small but dismaying pile of mail on the floor.

The doctor seems to be out ... maybe for quite a while. I should have called before making the trip.

He walked down the short flight of steps thinking about what he would do next. He was heading back to his car when he noticed the garage in back—a one-car affair separated from the house. The folding door was down. He walked back along the gravel driveway and peeked in through one of its square windows. There was a car in the garage, a VW Beetle, and someone was seated on the driver's side.

Adam pulled up the garage door with a screech. In moments, he was at the car, and what he saw through the rolled down window broke his heart. Dr. Wujciak sat at the wheel, looking straight ahead, dressed in T-shirt and shorts, as if ready to start out on a routine trip to the local supermarket.

His face and arms were a subtle shade of gray. The head lay back against the headrest, as if he was taking a moment to relax.

The one person I could trust. I've got to call the police.

As Adam recovered from the shock, he once again began thinking about the curious collection of events of the past twenty-four hours and decided to take a look around before making any calls. The key was in the ignition. He reached in, careful not to disturb anything. A slight but unsettling odor of decay wafted through his nostrils. Nausea and a headache began to queue up. Fighting to keep his stomach under control, he turned the key but found that it was already in the ON position, meaning that Dr. Wujciak had started the car before dying. Turning it produced a frail click. The gas tank needle was on empty and the impotent starter confirmed the battery was dead. These observations were not alarming in themselves, however, looking up at the garage door assembly, Adam noted there was no automatic door opener. The doctor had to be running the car with the garage doors closed. The facts could be consistent with a sudden death, as from a cardiac event, but it would mean that Wujciak rolled the door down, started the car and died before he could pull the door back up.

That made no sense at all.

He looked at Wujciak's face again. There was something doll-like about the pose, just sitting there with his eyes closed, head back. Adam moved in for a closer look. The lips were red. The face was gray. Adam's limited knowledge of poisons was sufficient enough to suspect carbon monoxide that might leave its victims with blood red lips. Wujciak's ruby fingertips confirmed the diagnosis. The image of this old man sitting alone in his car leaped up at Adam as he played back the events.

The garage door was closed. The engine was running. Wujciak breathed in the monoxide fumes until he was gently swept away from this reality. He breathed in the fumes. This was not a sudden, unexpected death.

Adam pulled out his cell phone. Dead. It was almost always dead, especially since he had the irritating habit of forgetting to recharge it. He walked to the back of the house. Surprisingly, the back door opened with a gentle push.

"Anyone home?"

After waiting a moment to be sure that he was alone, he entered the breakfast nook adjacent to the kitchen. The dim afternoon light, coupled with the realization that he was in the house of a dead man, made the interior feel extra gloomy. Judging by the piles of unwashed dishes in the small stainless steel sink, Wujciak apparently lived alone. Adam jumped as the refrigerator wheezed and coughed through another pointless cooling cycle. After finding the light switch, he scanned the counters and walls, but found no phone. Wandering over to an adjoining bedroom, he stood at the doorway soaking in the scene laid out before him. He reached inside and turned on a bedside lamp to get a better look at what appeared to be a curious wallpaper pattern. All four walls were covered with a collection of newspaper clippings, charts, computer printouts and photos, pasted and tacked to almost every available square inch. There were black and white, and color photos scattered about, depicting various odd looking artifacts. Pictures of gold and silver jewelry, coins, metal and stoneware, and assorted carvings of uncertain subject matter were mounted side-by-side and atop each other. Newspaper clippings and notes surrounded each with information about its point of origin, when discovered and by whom.

Many photos also had associated Post-it notes with hand-written numbers, some with question marks. In the center of one wall hung a photocopied clipping describing Mrs. Culp and her mystifying find in a lump of coal.

The same one I received in the mail yesterday.

There was a note as well, but instead of a number or a question mark, it contained a marker-inked message: SEE OLD FLORA

That name was familiar. Why was it posted near the Mrs. Culp story?

He thought there might be a phone in the doctor's office and stepped into an unlit hallway leading to the holding rooms, as he used to refer to them as a child. He shambled toward a suggestion of light at the far end, near where he supposed the office might be. Hitting the wall switch at the end of the hall fired up a sputtering fluorescent ring, animated by a distinct, but uneven hum. Adam approached the desk beneath it, outlined in a surreal and continuous cacophony of flickering light. He saw the washboard shape of the fluoroscope in a corner off to the side.

A rapping at the backdoor interrupted the almost mesmerizing, spastic humming. A shrill female voice followed. "Ben! Are you in there?"

His head began aching again. Adam heard the aluminum storm door creak open and a further knocking. He couldn't see the visitor, but called back. "Hello there. I'm a friend of Ben's. Wait a moment, I'll come to the door."

By the time Adam reached the kitchen area, the backdoor was ajar, but there was no one in sight. He stepped outside. The backyard was empty and the garage was still open. He called out, thinking that the visitor may have gone to the garage where she was about to discover Ben's body. Adam jogged over there but found no one. He was about to turn back toward the house when the hairs on the back of his neck stood at attention. He stopped. It was something he saw in the garage.

He stood in the middle of the driveway staring at the car, reviewing the scene in miniscule detail. The sun had dipped behind the trees surrounding the property, leaving the interior of the garage shadowed, making it difficult to see details. As his eyes adjusted, he caught the discrepancy and his heart shifted a few gears. The driver side door of the VW was ajar.

I know I shut that door.

He remembered being careful when he reached in through the partially open side window. He was sure that the door had been closed.

Damned sure.

Someone had been here. Adam moved in for a closer look, and nearly jumped out of his shoes. The body was gone. His head started pounding.

It took an enormous effort to control his breathing and calm down. He kept staring at the empty seat in disbelief. A sickening, nervous feeling wended from stomach to head. He glanced into the garage and back again to the empty seat to confirm that his eyes weren't playing tricks on him. Then he noticed that the car keys were gone too. He vaulted from the garage and sprinted back to the house.

I have to call the police. Someone came for a visit and took the body away. Maybe it was a killer trying to cover his tracks, and I stepped into the middle of it.

When he arrived at the kitchen, it occurred to him that getting the police involved could engender more questions than answers, especially since now that the body was gone.

How would I prove I saw it in the first place?

The police might consider him *Looney Toons,* or even worse, a suspect in the mysterious disappearance of a beloved old doctor. He wandered back into the bedroom, trying to calm himself down. That's when things went from pretty bad to clearly worse.

The walls were bare. Minutes before, hundreds of clippings covered the place. Now, there was nothing but faded wallpaper. A feeling of nausea once again flared up. After craning his head outside the bedroom door to make sure he was in the right room, Adam reached out to touch the wall, looking for some verification of what his eyes were telling him and what his mind refused to believe. His fingers felt nothing but the vague undulations of the wall and the velvet-like texture of its covering. Someone must have removed everything from the walls apparently in the time it took for him to go out to the garage and back. It seemed nearly impossible.

Was it the same person who removed Wujciak's body? Was there an accomplice? And why remove the clippings?

Adam thought about looking for the office phone and calling the police, when all at once a Technicolor image of the SEE OLD FLORA scrawl loomed up in his mind.

The doctor had written it there for a purpose.

Wuijcak was referring to his pet name for the fluoroscope—a little secret shared years ago with a young friend and his curious lump of coal. Adam ran toward the quivering fluorescence at the far end of the hallway. The office was as he had left it. Old Flora stood in the corner, unassuming and quiescent. A glance around the rest of the office confirmed that nothing obvious had changed. He also spotted a phone, an old black

Bakelite model, sitting at the corner of the desk. First, he would examine the fluoroscope, and then he would call the police.

A thick layer of dust covered everything in the office, including Old Flora. He brushed off some of it with his fingertips, especially around the name plate. According to the faded metal tag on its side, this was a Westinghouse Mobile Fluoroscope Unit manufactured in 1951. The doctor's office unit essentially evolved from the early models which were originally designed for shoe stores—a popular technological wonder designed to aid in fitting shoes before the dangers of x-ray exposure were truly recognized. This mobile unit consisted of two components, a high-voltage cathode tube to emit the x-rays and a phosphor-coated glass screen designed to light up when hit by them. The patient stood between the two as the doctor moved the screen, or washboard, to get a view. It was a museum relic.

Adam grabbed both handles to either side of the screen and pulled. The hinged screen emitted a squeal as Adam brought it up to eye level. There was nothing remarkable about it. The aged wiring was either broken or severely frayed. Old Flora had clearly been in retirement for many years.

It was probably never used again after we shorted it out.

Adam looked over the cathode ray tube housing and found nothing out of the ordinary there either. He began to return the screen to its original position when a single sheet of paper wafted to the floor. It had been hidden inside of the screen. He picked it up and found a type-written message from Dr. Wuijcak.

"Adam. Decades ago you discovered something that should not exist. Since the day you showed it to me, I began a methodical investigation into similar relics. I admit that over the years it became an obsession. Objects out of time. Findings that made no sense in the scheme of things, in the history that we have come to believe. Of the many such items discovered by others, a few fall into a remarkable category. They share a similar fate, that is, they were found, made famous, and eventually were lost. The circumstances were always the same. Usually an accident. Fire, floods, you name it. In short, I believe you have such a relic. I pray it hasn't been lost yet."

Adam found himself rubbing his medallion as he read on.

"I found out that the last coal delivery to our neighborhood was made by Samson's Coal and Oil back in 1959. In fact, they serviced your neighborhood. Checking with the company's archives, I discovered the coal came from the Knox Coal Company, located near Pittston, PA. In 1959, the River Slope Mine, run by Knox, suffered a horrific accident when miners digging too close to the Susquehanna flooded the mine. It's been closed to this day. My gut tells me that the relic and the accident may be related. The answer to the mystery of your find may well lie in the River Slope Mine. I have faith in you, Adam. God bless you and your family. Ben"

The phone rang.

Adam's heart flipped. It was the office phone. He let it ring several more times, hoping that whoever was calling would give up. However, he gave in, fumbling with the receiver and answering with as calm a voice as he could muster.

"Hello."

"Hi. Is this Dr. Woochak?"

It was a female voice, and vaguely familiar.

"No, I'm afraid he is not here."

"Who am I speaking with?"

"Just an old friend. Can I help you?"

"Is that you, Adam?"

Realization flooded over him.

"Linda! How did you know I was here?"

"I'm glad I found you. I called George and he said something about New Jersey. Then I called your mom. After she finished complaining about your habit of coming and going at all hours, she mentioned that you had received a letter from this Dr. Woochak. She came across the letter you left behind. I just figured that was the friend in New Jersey you told George about."

Quite the detective. Now, what exactly should I tell her?

"Linda. For reasons I cannot share right now, I am going to Pittston. I don't know when I'll be ..."

"Let me guess, you're headed down to the coal mines where that object of yours may have come from."

Adam froze.

Was she a mystic?

As if sensing Adam's surprise, Linda explained. "It's obvious. You and George working late at night on your gold medallion, the cryptic note about a gold chain found in a lump of coal, and now, your intention to head up to Pittston, deep in the Wilkes-Barre coal-mining region. It wasn't very hard to draw some obvious conclusions. So, you're on a mission. But why go to all this trouble now, after so many years?"

Adam replied, "I'm impressed." He took a moment to breath. "Something very odd has happened, something I am not sure I can explain."

"Adam. I think it would be a great idea if I joined you on this quest of yours."

"No way."

"There's nothing for me to do here while they're fixing up McArdle. Besides, this quest sounds like a neat adventure. An extra pair of eyes could come in handy, especially if you've got a mystery to solve."

Adam thought about the offer. Maybe it was the anxiety, maybe the need to share his experiences with someone he could trust. Whatever it was, Adam relented. "Well. Okay. I'll head back home tonight. Why don't you come over in the morning for breakfast and we'll talk."

***

The next morning, Linda arrived at Adam's house in a denim jacket, blue jeans and cross-training shoes. It was no surprise to Adam that she had also brought an overnight bag. Between slugging down freshly brewed coffee and polishing off a hearty breakfast that Adam's mom was more than pleased to provide, he related the events of the previous evening. The story unfolded over pancakes and syrup and should have been nearly impossible for anyone to believe. Linda digested it along with the food, one extraordinary episode at a time, munching and nodding, and not once questioning the incredible details. When at last Adam finished with the note left behind by Dr. Wujciak, he pulled out the medallion for Linda to see.

"So, that's it," Linda stated, rather than asked. After a brief examination of the gold enigma hanging on Adam's neck, she looked into his green eyes and said, "Let's go to Pittston."

Adam was tempted to call Wujciak's office just to see who would answer. The problem was that if the police answered, he would be dragged into an investigation that was sure to bring up the medallion and generate many more questions than answers.

And then there is the possibility of someone else answering …

Adam shuddered at the thought. He looked back at Linda. Her face was bathed by the early morning sun streaming in through the kitchen window. Her eyes sparkled and the edges of her mouth turned up slightly in a suggestion of a grin. His anxiety dissipated, and he grinned back. "Then let's get to it."

They boarded his '94 Pathfinder and took off for Pittston.

Chapter 5

A few of miles short of the exit to Pittston, Linda asked, "By the way, how is the sequence analysis coming along?"

The question took Adam by surprise, especially as they were drawing near to the former site of the Knox Coal Company, and that was all he was thinking about. "I haven't had a chance to check up on its progress. However, I have my laptop with me and as soon as we find a motel with an Internet hookup we can find out. Remember the electron microscopy that George ran?"

"On your medallion, where he found a matrix of carbon-13 in the gold?"

"Yeah. Well, he took some pictures. Can you reach the laptop case behind my seat?"

Linda retrieved the case, and pulled out a wad of photographs. She studied the pictures one by one. "These dark spots are carbon-13?"

Adam nodded.

"There are tons of these spots."

Adam flicked his turn signal.

She said, "Some of these carbon-13 blobs are bigger than others."

Adam hadn't noticed that. In fact, he had little time to examine or to think about those pictures since the lab explosion.

"Are you sure? Maybe it's just the way the pictures were taken."

"Maybe."

Adam took the Pittston/Port Griffith exit. "Which way?"

"You're asking me?"

There must have been twenty different signs at the bottom of the ramp. Blue interstate numbers, green and white local highways, hotels, restaurants and service stations taking up the rest of the rainbow, pointing in all directions. Adam had been thinking of a place to stay overnight when he noticed a beaten up little white sign which read, PORT GRIFFITH MINING MUSEUM. He glanced at Linda who was already pointing at the sign.

It took them about a half-hour to reach the older part of town near the river. At one time the neighborhood may have been a center of commerce, sporting thriving warehouses, piers loaded with goods and supplies for the mining industry, and small businesses that flourished along each side of the street, catering to the throngs of dock workers and entrepreneurs alike.

As Adam and Linda trundled toward the mining museum, they saw only deserted streets lined with refuse, windowless warehouses, rotting piers harboring a few worn out fishing and touring boats, and an occasional open liquor store or sandwich shop—pale reflections of better days.

Adam pulled up alongside the curb. The faded sign over the store-front building read, THE PORT GRIFFITH MINING MUSEUM – A HISTORY OF ANTHRACITE MINING. The main entrance was bracketed by two display windows streaked with soot and grime. They clambered out of the Pathfinder and stopped at the dusty glass. Maps outlining the locations of mines throughout the Wilkes-Barre area served as a backdrop to a variety of artifacts laid out on shelves—a miner's hat complete with battery-operated lamp, shovels, gloves, bits and pieces of coal, each with a label indicating where and when, and drill heads from the large machines. Adam focused on a scale model of a colliery—the River Slope Mine. The model was detailed, including tiny plastic mine workers entering the shafts, conveyor belts moving coal into a tall, dark breaker building, and railroad cars being loaded below it. Just beyond the colliery he made out the edge of the mighty Susquehanna. The display appeared as if it hadn't been touched in years, in fact, the dust gave the display a look of freshly fallen snow. When Adam glanced back up to the maps, fingers appeared from behind one of the hanging diagrams, pulling it aside, revealing the wrinkled face of a bespectacled, gray-haired woman. Despite being small in stature, she exuded a convincing look of self-assurance, the kind of look which he last saw on his second grade teacher. With a smile and peering over her pearl white frames, she motioned them to come in.

The door chime announced their entrance.

"Hi. I'm Adam Dove, and this is Linda Garcia. We dropped in today to find out a little about the history of coal mining in these parts."

"Pleased to meet ya. My name's Hedda Morrison. I'd be happy to give ya a little tour. Is there anything ya'd like to know in particular?"

"We are actually interested in some specifics surrounding the Knox mining disaster of 1959."

Hedda's smile disappeared, replaced by a questioning look.

"I assume yar referrin' to the flood which killed twelve miners in the River Slope Mine?"

"Yes. We'd be interested in any detailed information you may have. Perhaps how it happened?"

Adam noticed the change in Hedda's demeanor, a subtle frown. She pushed up her glasses, and replied with a slow, almost cautionary gait. "Ya know, that were a very dark time in our minin' history."

Adam saw Hedda's countenance deepen into an introspective scowl, which prompted him to explain. "Hedda, we are looking for some answers to …"

"No need. No need for explanations. I'm sorry, it's not my place. I guess we don't get that many visitors here anymore and it's just that those days were somethin' I personally don't care to recall. But, never no mind, I'll be happy to fill ya in on what happened."

The smile returned to her face and she pointed to a pair of chairs. When they were comfortably seated, Hedda told them the story of that January day in 1959 when the miner's life in the Wyoming Valley came to a sad end. It was a time for heroes and for despair. She described how one miner led thirty-two workers to safety through the maze of interconnecting tunnels, saving them from certain death in the waters of the Susquehanna river. Those that perished in the torrent were trapped by the water or were overcome by released gases. In all, twelve miners never returned to their families, their bodies never found. The surging waters penetrated deep into the mine and the surrounding network of shafts for weeks. Dirt, rocks and debris were dumped into the insatiable swirling waters but had no effect. Sixty coal cars were dropped into the raging whirlpool, which slowed the flooding enough that pumps could be used. Eventually, Knox Mine management was held responsible for digging too close to the riverbed. Indictments were handed out and arrests made. The cost of pumping out the mines made it nearly impossible to salvage the operations. Since that time, anthracite mining in the valley had slowed to a crawl, and eventually faded out.

Hedda paused for a moment as if to clear her throat, but it could have easily been a suppressed sob. The story appeared to have come to an end.

Adam asked, "It sounds as if you were there when the flood happened."

Hedda motioned for the pair to follow her to the window display where she moved aside a hanging map and pointed with her finger. "I was at home when it happened. My husband Luke was in the mine, mine shaft number 102, right here."

Hedda moved her finger from the colliery across a hill to the river.

"Your husband wasn't one of the victims of the flooding, was he?" asked Linda.

"He were in the gangway along with them buggies … those be the tram cars that carry the coal … when the river broke on through. He heard the roar of the water and ran up the gangway, but it caught up with him. After that, he didn't remember much until he woke up in a side shaft that weren't there before. He weren't sure what happened. He lost his headgear, and everything were dark, and wet, and noisy. So, he just waited until he started smellin' the black damp."

"Black damp?"

"Oh, sorry. The black damp's just old air where a lot o' the oxygen is gone and replaced with a mix o' carbon dioxide and nitrogen. Mines are full o' the stuff, and it can kill ya."

"So what happened to Luke?" prodded Linda.

"With it being dark, and he not knowin' which way to go, he started yellin'. Meantime, the river was still rushin' in, louder than him, sweeping right nearby. He decided to go up into a side tunnel away from the sound of the water. After a time, sloppin' through mud and rock, Luke came across another shaft. He yelled again and again, as there the water's noise wasn't as bad. Then he heard voices, and he thought that maybe these were others trapped like him. A few steps on, and he ran into a rescue party."

Hedda stopped for a moment to regain her composure. "It was late at night when he made it back home. I thought he were a goner, but the Good Lord brought him home to me."

Adam and Linda stared at each other in wonder. The silence in the museum was heavy, like a blanket cutting them off from the dreary reality outside. Adam spoke up first. "Hedda, it sounds like you must have gone through quite a lot back then. Do you think it would be possible to speak with Luke?"

She straightened up a bit before answering. "Luke passed away a few years back ... in a mining accident. Why would ya want to talk with 'im?"

Adam and Linda once again looked at each other, and Adam replied. "It's complicated. This is going to sound odd, but we were wondering if you had seen or heard of anything unusual being found in the mines ... maybe just before the flood?"

Hedda's eyes widened. She stood up and glanced at a glass case on the far side of the room. "Strange is right. I'm not at all sure what you mean by unusual."

Adam said, "Maybe some kind of artifact. You know, like a piece of pottery, an odd piece of metal, tools…"

Before Adam finished his hypothetical list, Hedda interrupted. "Odd piece of metal?"

Adam recognized a change in her tone of voice. It had become stronger. "Well, something you wouldn't expect to find in a coal mine."

Hedda walked over to the case and said, "You mean something like this?"

The three of them gathered around a display table with a rectangular glass case protecting a variety of artifacts within. There were lamps, gloves, nails, screws, drill bits, batteries, and a shiny gold-colored metal rod. Adam read the faded, typewritten label affixed near it. 'Metal artifact found in the River Slope Mine, January 21, 1959. Origin unknown.' Adam and Linda both bent over to take a closer look at the unassuming little metallic rod.

Adam straightened up. "This rod here. Do you know anything more about it?"

"That there piece o' metal were somethin' that Luke found the night before the flood. He brought it home with 'im, and in fact, told me that there were more like it up in the mine. He planned to get at the rest the next day."

"More?" Adam asked, letting his breath out. "Do you think we could take a closer look at it?"

Hedda reached into the back pocket of her dungarees and pulled out a set of keys. A moment later, she propped open the glass case and Adam's hands gently caressed what appeared to be a simple three inch-long solid metal cylinder. Upon closer inspection, there was the slightest hint of a groove at either end, as if the ends had diameters slightly less than the rest of the body. Hedda's mouth opened wide as Adam freed the medallion from its chain and held it up against the cylinder. He placed the end of the rod into the hole of the medallion. The two pieces slid together in a perfect union, with the end of the rod precisely flush with the surface of the medallion. The fit was snug, it was perfect, it was incredible. That this was a chance event was impossible. Adam knew that the tolerances built into the medallion were extremely precise. The rod matched the radius of the medallion's hole and its thickness. He thought about the millions, perhaps billions, of years these two parts had been separated, and now, they were united in the Port Griffith Mining Museum and held in his sweaty palm. He could be holding the wheel and axle assembly for an ancient toy car. Raising the assembly for Linda and Hedda to see, he started to spin the rod between his fingers, twirling it like a top. As the three of them were being entertained, Linda interrupted. "Adam, there's someone at the window."

The man was partially obscured by the hanging display maps. He wore a uniform, a policeman's blue uniform. The man turned away and looked into the street as if he was waiting for something. Adam had a queasy feeling in the pit of his stomach. He hunched over and moved closer to the back of the window display for a better viewing angle. When he caught a glimpse of the man's face, he turned back to Hedda with a grim, expressionless face and whispered, "Is there another way out of this place?"

Chapter 6

Adam backed away from the window.

Linda asked, "What's going on?"

"Remember the science building fire?" Linda nodded. "Well, when I went back to get my laptop, there was a policeman standing guard at the front entrance. I had a chance to speak to him. I remember his face."

"And, that policeman is out there now?"

Adam nodded. Hedda looked at the pair of them, her eyes narrowing.

"How can you be sure he's the same guy?"

"I'm sure."

Hedda interjected. "What's the story with this copper? What does he want with you?

There was no time for explanations, no time for polite conversations. There was no way that this cop was here by coincidence. Adam heard Ben Wujciak whispering in his ear, *"Get out now or you'll be next."*

"Hedda. It's too long a story to get into right now. It has to do with the medallion. I think someone is out to get it."

"I don't know what this is all about, but don't get me mixed up in it! And, give me back that rod. It belongs to me."

The rod came out with a pop, not unlike the sound of a thumb pulled from of a perfectly machined bowling ball hole. Adam dropped it into

Hedda's outstretched hand, and nodded in the direction of the cop outside. "We need to get out of here without him catching on. I think you'd better come with us, Hedda. Some strange things have happened to artifacts like these. And sometimes to the people who owned them."

He held the medallion in his hand for a moment before going on. "Just a couple of days ago, the laboratory where I had this medallion analyzed was destroyed, and elsewhere, an old friend died under mysterious circumstances, an old friend who tried to warn me."

Linda tapped Adam's shoulder. "He's turning around. I think he may be coming in."

Hedda motioned with her arm. "This way."

The trio slipped through a set of hanging drapes into a hallway. Linda, last in line, pulled the curtains together and stilled them, as the door chime sounded. They huddled behind the thick cloth, afraid to move and draw attention to themselves. The sound of leather shoes clapped across the hardwood floor. For an instant, Adam imagined Mr. Kurtinaitis looking for him again. The shuffling sounds stopped and a few moments later, they heard the visitor's voice reading aloud, "origin unknown." The man grunted and the leather slapped again. The sounds neared their curtained alcove.

Hedda was farthest along the hallway, near the back door which led outside. Adam had his arm around Linda, awaiting imminent discovery, when he heard several car doors slam in the street outside. The shoes stopped and skipped their way toward the front door. Adam rose with Linda in tow. Hedda was one jump ahead of them, opening the back door just as they heard the front door jingle again. When they regrouped in the backyard, Adam glanced along the side alley and sighted the hood of his

Pathfinder. The visitors might be entering the museum. It wouldn't take long before they realized the place was empty. The alley connected the main street with a parallel back street. Adam ran up to the front of the building, peered around the corner and saw a black four-door limo parked behind his car. The uniformed cop was standing at the museum entrance. Hedda and Linda slinked up behind Adam. The police officer was looking in through the entrance door, probably more curious about happenings within than the scant traffic.

Was this really the same guy as the one back on campus? Maybe the police were here for some other reason.

He began to think this was all just the result of an overactive imagination.

A wacky conspiracy theory.

Maybe he should simply approach the officer and find out what was going on.

What could it hurt?

Adam stood up from his crouch and was about to show himself when he heard the squawk of a walkie-talkie. "Did you see anyone?"

"Nope. Everything's quiet out here."

"They must still be inside, and it looks like they have Hedda's piece."

That clinches it.

These people, police or whoever, were here specifically for them and the artifacts. He pocketed his medallion. Hedda overheard the discussion and did the same with her piece.

The front door cracked open and orders barked out. "Go around back. Make sure no one gets out that way."

Adam's stomach tightened. The three of them stood up in the alley, faces ashen and prepared for the inevitable. They waited. And waited. Adam, closest to the corner, poked his head out again, and saw no one. He craned his neck a little farther. There was another alley on the far side of the building. The uniform must have gone the other way. Adam turned to the other two. "Let's go. Into the car. Quickly. And don't slam the doors."

As Linda ran past Adam, he grasped Hedda's sleeve. "You don't have to get mixed up in this. Those people are probably more interested in the artifact I have than anything else. You could just go back in and pretend to know nothing."

Hedda was quick to reply. "While we were sitting in this alley, Linda told me some more about what happened to you two. I know about the explosion, and about your missing friend. I don't feel like goin' missing quite yet. So, if ya don't mind, I'll be joinin' ya for now."

Hedda surged past Adam with surprising speed and jumped into the backseat of his car. Adam followed close behind, slipped into the driver's seat and turned over the engine. He moved the car out slowly, but he had only gone a few car lengths before the museum door flew open and two men came running out shouting for them to stop. He accelerated. Through the mirror he saw a third, shorter man, catch up to the now moving black sedan. The chase was on.

Adam tried to lose them with sharp turns, left and right, all with the only perceptible effect being that the pursuers were steadily closing in. In this part of town, Main Street was about all there was and side streets were only a block or two deep. Adam had to get uptown, to the middle of Pittston where there were bound to be more people, more traffic. He floored the car and proceeded to ignore a few traffic signals, but the limo kept up with him. Its tinted windshield made it impossible to see inside. There was no siren, no blinking headlights, no screeching car horn. The scene was surreal, as if taken from some action movie with the audio off. Adam approached midtown and traffic picked up. Instead of offering a chance to slip into a side street, the cars and trucks on the narrow, single lane Main Street led to congestion. Fighting a surge of panic, Adam saw an opportunity arise at the next intersection a few car lengths ahead. Spotting a yellow reflection on a traffic signal side shield, he made an abrupt turn into the empty oncoming lane, accelerated to the head of the line, and darted back into his lane across the intersection just as the light turned red. Luckily there was no cross traffic. The limo, which had been only seconds behind, now found itself faced with oncoming traffic and an assortment of screaming brakes, horns, and angry shouts.

Hedda cupped her hand over Adam's shoulder. "Take the next right."

Without hesitation, Adam made the turn while checking his rear view. Hedda positioned herself between Adam and Linda, and continued in a steady voice. "Now, take the second right."

With no limo in sight, Adam asked, "Where are you taking us?"

"One more right … the next one. Then head over the bridge, and make the first left you can. It'll be dirt road."

"That takes us across the river, but to where?"

"You'll see."

The dirt road led them south along the other side of the Susquehanna river, a route parallel to Main Street on the museum side. Adam noticed the river islands, or aits, left over from the time of the mine flood. Desperation had driven the mining community to attempt to plug up the whirlpool draining into the mines with all kinds of debris. Now all that remained were several uninhabited mounds in the river. Judging from the tall grass and the vague hint of wheel ruts, the road had seen little use in recent years.

"Slow down."

They pulled up to a rusty chain-linked gate with a weathered sign hanging askew on one surviving rivet. Adam craned his neck to the side and read out, "River Slope Mine – No Trespassing."

Linda asked, "Hedda. Why did you take us here?"

"Only a few locals like me know about this road. And there are back ways to get outta here besides."

Adam agreed. "Not a bad idea, Hedda. That bunch will likely be scouring the side streets in town, and if they are the police, they'll send out a description of our car along with the license plate number. In a small town like this, we wouldn't have a chance. At least this way we could stay here for a while, maybe until nightfall, and slip out some other way."

"In the meantime, ya might want to go on into the mine. There'll be somethin' there you'll need to see."

Both Adam and Linda threw a double take at Hedda. She got out of the car, walked over to the gate, and pulled it aside. "Go ahead. Drive on in, and I'll close it behind us."

Once Hedda was back in the car, Adam again checked for anyone following them. She directed him along a few more minutes of the bumpy road which ran alongside the river until they reached a wider expanse, a clearing made up of tall outcroppings of grass sprouting through holes in cracked tarmac. It looked as if the area was once a parking lot. A rusty chain-link fence surrounded the clearing, separating them from several dilapidated one- and two-story colliery buildings grouped together at one end. Adam noticed a tall, angular, dark and ominous structure just beyond them.

"What's that?" He recalled the model back in the museum and asked, "Is that the breaker building?"

"Sure is. Ten stories high."

It was a corrugated metal structure punctuated with a seemingly random array of square windows.

Hedda said, "It's where the raw coal was broken into smaller chunks, stones removed, and such. The stuff would move along conveyor belts to the top." She pointed to the summit of the nearly triangular building where a chute emerged. "Up there, the coal would come out and slide down into the waitin' railroad cars."

Adam followed her pointing hand to the road below, where the outline of a set of rails jutted from the ground. At Hedda's urging, they headed toward the smaller building just ahead and arrived at yet another gate. Huge patches of brown decay covered most of the dull gray metallic walls.

Hedda once again scurried out of the car and opened the gate. "Go on through to the back."

Adam noticed the 'Office' sign over the door of the nearest one-story building. As he rounded its corner, he saw a pale white VW Beetle parked alongside the office.

That looks familiar.

He stopped his car next to it just as Hedda rejoined the group. "Ya can go on inside. I'll be with ya in a couple o' minutes."

Without offering another word, Hedda walked away in the opposite direction, to what looked like several footpaths branching out toward the old mine shafts in the rear of the complex. They watched her disappear into the overgrowth.

Adam asked, "Well, what do you think?"

Linda shook her head. "I don't know what to think. Let's go inside and try to figure out what just happened."

They entered the office. Expecting broken furniture, debris strewn floors and dirt on everything, Adam found instead, an orderly arrangement of desk and chairs, working light fixtures and clean floors. There was a small refrigerator and microwave on a counter top. Adam opened the fridge and pointed out its well-stocked condition. The astonished pair sat down and waited.

"Someone's obviously been here, maybe even living here."

"No doubt." was Linda's sharp response.

The tone of her voice surprised Adam. "You know we don't have to stay here. I'm sure we can sneak out tonight and avoid those crazies that are after us, or after the artifacts … or both for that matter."

Linda nodded. "Sorry about that. It's just that I'm a bit nervous … not too happy about being chased. It's not a big town. They could easily be watching the main roads. And if they are cops, then they would have a lot more eyes looking for us."

"You're not the only one with anxiety. Here's a thought—we could simply let them catch us, and see what happens. I mean, it's not like they'll arrest us. We didn't do anything wrong."

Linda said, "Only one of them had a uniform. And what about Dr. Wujciak? What if it's the same bunch of whackjobs? Maybe they'll make the artifacts *and us* disappear."

"Yeah, but what if they're just following up on the science building explosion. These guys could be detectives who trailed us here, thinking we may know something."

Linda smirked. "Uh-huh, and what about that 'they may have Hedda's piece' remark? How do you explain that?"

Adam hunched over with his head down, staring at the floor. Linda, too nervous to sit still, got up and walked over to one of the rear windows overlooking the flat area leading out to the mines. The yard was mostly gravel and dirt, with vague outlines of narrow paths leading away toward several low-lying hills. A few weeping willows caught the late afternoon sun and threw their oblong shadows across the yard. The trees looked like they started to grow when the mines were shut down decades ago. Adam noticed Linda staring through the window and followed her gaze. In the distance, near the mines, a stand of willows moved in rhythm to a gentle breeze. The crisscrossing patterns of leaves seemed to weave a spell, drawing him into a sense of calm, a feeling that there was a logical explanation for everything that had happened these past few days.

Linda blinked. "Someone's coming."

Adam straightened up and focused. There was nothing to see but a few empty walking paths.

"Wait. There's no one there now. My eyes must be playing tricks."

She moved her head from side to side. Adam squinted but only saw scrub and high grass waving in the riverfront breeze. He rubbed her back and said, "Maybe it's just a play of light amid the trees. I don't blame you for seeing things. This whole situation seems crazy. I just want to get us out of here."

"What about Hedda?"

"She can decide what to do on her own. I don't think those people, whoever they are, mean any harm. I think they must be after this medallion and whatever they think Hedda may have. But, in the end, who knows? Maybe a black helicopter is about to land out there."

Linda turned to see Adam's playful grin, and returned one of her own. "Yeah, some secret organization … showing up in a very obvious black limo and chasing us across town. Besides, they can't be any good if we lost them."

She turned away to look out the window again.

Adam asked, "So, are we going to wait here forever? Did you see which way Hedda went?"

Linda scanned the distant shrubbery beyond the trees and saw nothing out of the ordinary. "I think she went out along the main path. That way."

Adam looked along her arm.

"Maybe we should go look for her."

Linda agreed with a nod, and they both exited the office backdoor. Adam noticed his laptop on the rear seat of the Pathfinder. "Hold on. I don't like the idea of leaving my laptop in the car."

He grabbed the case and popped into the office for a minute. Rejoining Linda by the car, the pair marched off along the main footpath. Although the trees, shrubs, tall grasses and a variety of nameless but gnarly species were claiming the trail for their own, there was a perceptible, narrow path which looked as if it had seen some occasional use, and the two gratefully stepped along its winding course.

***

The limo's engine continued its soft feline purr as a uniformed man swung open the rusty gate. Moments later, the purr changed to a growl as the limo proceeded through and into the River Slope Mine property. The driver stared ahead at the winding road while his stooped over, white-haired passenger peered at a small green screen displaying an aerial view of several buildings ahead and a yellow-green dot pulsating between them.

80

Chapter 7

Herman Borman adjusted a knob below the green screen to widen the view. His wizened hands moved deftly over the controls as the limo grumbled onwards.

"Steven, do not be too fast. Let us be careful this time."

Borman wiped his chin of a thin line of spittle. The driver silently replied with an emphatic nod and a quick sideways glance at Paul, sitting next to him. Wearing a police uniform that served its purpose at the Schill incident, Borman could tell that Paul was decidedly unhappy. His preference to wear it again plainly gave away their arrival at the museum. That did not sit well with Borman, and things that didn't sit well with him had a way of disappearing. Paul shot a nervous look over his shoulder. The old man huddled over his tracking device, face outlined in goblin green.

Borman spoke to the driver without looking up. "They are at the mine office. We do not want to spook them, so move ahead as quietly as you can. When we reach the office you and Paul will check the area. By this, I mean keep out of sight, and keep in touch with me. There may be more people involved. Once you have ascertained the situation, I will tell you what to do,"

And then, as if to himself, he continued in a whisper. "I want that medallion and I want the object Hedda has. I want both artifacts, and I do not care what it takes. *Verstehen Sie mich?* Are you understanding me?"

Steven and Paul nodded enthusiastically. Borman had a habit of reverting to German when he became excited. They had been involved in similar activities for some time now. Tracking, hunting, retrieving. He had explained to them that he was a collector of rare artifacts, with plenty of money to finance retrieval operations. For this job, he was a bit more animated than usual, breaking with tradition to join in the hunt.

They reached the outer gate.

***

Linda was the first to see it and tugged at Adam's arm. Just ahead, beyond a stand of overgrown forsythias, she made out the curved stone edges of a mine entrance at the base of a mound which blocked the view of the river beyond. The two moved off the main trail and adopted a flanking maneuver using the overgrowth as a cover. The remains of rusty iron rails protruded from the muddy trail which wound through the foliage into the bottom of a faded planking inset a few feet into the mine entrance. Centered on the wooden wall was a boarded up door announcing that the mine was closed, that there were dangers within, and that wayward trespassers should KEEP OUT. As they neared the blockaded entrance, Adam pointed at the base of the door. "Check out the footprints."

82

Between two partially buried rails shoeprints in the dirt led to the door. One such print had a feature of singular interest. Its heel was visible while its toe disappeared under the door. This anomaly drew the two closer in. Adam gave the doorknob a twist and a pull, to no effect. While Linda felt around the edges, Adam took a step back to take in a broader view. The wall consisted of unpainted planks, gray with years of oxidation. The coloring was uniform from top to bottom, except for a couple of small, nearly circular patches near the doorframe. As Adam reached forward to press down on one of the marks, the board beneath gave in just a little. Linda joined him, pushing down on the other. A faint click sounded and the door swung inward with its collage of warning placards. A plume of damp, cold air rolled over them. Instead of darkness within, a string of light bulbs glared along the roof of the tunnel and disappeared into the distance as they followed the curved shaft downward. Glistening walls and puddles caught between rails and rock debris scattered along the passageway completed the scene. They pulled the door closed behind them, careful to avoid making too much noise. Once inside, they were surrounded by the sounds of dripping water seeping into the mine from countless cracks and crevices.

Linda folded her arms."Ooo, it's cold in here."

"Take this." Adam offered up his windbreaker and wrapped it over her shoulders. He instinctively placed his arm around her waist and for a fleeting moment their eyes met, acknowledging their mutual anxiety and perhaps, something more. They proceeded onward through the ragged circles of light, careful to step over the remnants of rails embedded in the floor. The subtle tug of gravity increased with each step as the tunnel sloped downward. The rails once carried the coal cars or 'buggies' as they used to call them years ago. Rotting timbers running up either side of the wall threatened to crumble beneath their sagging crossbeams. Jagged outlines of blue-black rock reached out to them as they passed beneath the strung incandescents. The air they breathed carried a heavy dampness—a ghostly link to the miners who once worked the coal, perhaps to the miners who died here and were never recovered. There were several openings to either side of the tunnel, marking entrances to side passageways.

As they passed one such narrow excavation, something that might have once been a coal chute, they heard voices, distant and muffled. Intermittent splashes suggested vermin and other creatures of the dark scattering before them as they plodded onward, deeper into the mine. After a few minutes they could no longer make out the entrance, and instead, concentrated on what lay ahead.

Linda tugged Adam's elbow. "Do you hear that?"

They listened, trying to filter out the watery background sounds in the dank, half-lit tunnel. It was music, slow dance music—punctuated by a mellow voice, waxing and waning. The slow song, the tempo and undulating volume, mixed in with the dull echoes of trickling water and their own steps. As they neared the source, Adam heard a subtle clicking which brought to mind an image of a hand-wound record player. He recalled his father fussing with a conical megaphone contraption, probably an old Victrola, with a picture of an attentive dog pasted on its side. It was almost as if the melancholy sounds were calling out to them from another time, drawing them nearer like sirens to rocky shoals. They reached what at first looked like a dead-end, a rock fall or cave-in. The broken rails continued on under a pile of debris. The tunnel turned to the left, and as they followed the curve, they came across fresh timbers. A hundred yards or so ahead a sharp band of light from a side entrance stretched across the path. The crooning became louder.

Mona Lisa by Nat King Cole.

While staring ahead, Adam's toe grazed a discarded bottle and set off a loud and disquieting pinging as it tumbled across the floor. The noise may have been barely noticeable in the outside world, but here, in Nature's echo chamber, it was a clarion call. A moment later all the lights went out and the pair froze in their tracks. The music stopped. Seconds crawled by as they wondered what would happen next. Then Adam ventured a call out. "Hedda, is that you?"

No response. Adam tried again. "It's us, Adam and Linda. We came down here to look for you."

A spotlight flashed on at the far end of the tunnel. A moment later, a familiar voice echoed through to them. "Well, I guess ya found me. Hold on."

The overhead lights returned and Hedda emerged from the side shaft. "I thought I told ya to wait for me."

Linda said, "We started to get worried."

Hedda shook her head. "Well, I guess I'd be bringing ya here anyhow. Come along, I got something to show ya."

They followed her around the corner and into the shaft from where the music had been coming. They entered a room with whitewashed wooden walls and planked flooring. Warmth emanated from the room, cutting through the damp chill. There was a desk covered with notes and books, some chairs, cabinets, even a couple of easy chairs. In one corner Adam spotted a beaten up old desktop computer, and the grim lines of his mouth upturned into a smile, when in the opposite corner, he saw a bona fide Victrola.

"Have a seat. I think ya'll need to be sittin'." Hedda pointed to a pair of worn out and over-stuffed easy chairs. She sat down in one of the desk chairs. They stared at one another, as if waiting for something to happen. Then Hedda sighed and turned her head to the paneled wall. "Ya'll can come out now."

A panel section swung open soundlessly and a white-haired man stepped through, stooped over and head bowed. As the door reseated itself behind him, he raised his head and smiled at the visitors.

"Adam, my boy, what a pleasant surprise!"

Adam felt a shiver rise through his spine. Standing in front of him was a dead man—Dr. Ben Wujciak.

The impossibility of it left Adam breathless. The man he saw before him looked exactly like the Ben Wujciak he remembered seeing back in New Jersey, perhaps with a bit more color and certainly more lively. He looked to Linda, who returned only a blank stare, oblivious to the specter standing before them.

With both hands clutching the arms of his chair, providing much needed support, Adam managed at last to cough out a response. "But … but, how can this be? Are you really Dr. Ben Wujciak?"

The old man replied with a perplexed look. "Of course! Who else would I be?"

The VW in the parking lot.

Still dazed by the shock, Adam rose on trembling legs and walked over to Ben. He stared at his old family friend for a few seconds and then the two embraced.

"My God. Ben, I thought you were dead."

Adam's eyes were misty as the pair unclenched. When he sat down, he unconsciously flashed the splayed-finger Vulcan greeting to his old friend.

Ben smiled and asked, "And who is this remarkably beautiful girl?"

No return greeting?

Too excited to press Ben further and still confused, Adam said, "This is Linda. Dr. Linda Garcia. She's from the university. We're working on a DNA project."

Adam's mouth became dry and his tongue seemed tied in knots, unclear as to what to say next. He eased back in his chair and studied Ben. His smile faded to a thin, determined line. He needed to get past the normal niceties and drive the conversation toward enlightenment. He noticed Linda slowly shaking her head. The incongruity of the situation was sinking in.

Ben asked, "Is there a problem? It looks as if you two just saw a ghost."

Adam said, "Ghost is about right. Ben, do you remember my last office visit. Do you remember what I brought with me?"

The old man put both hands on his hips. "Well, it's been a long time."

"What was it that I showed you?"

With a shrug, as if explaining something very simple to a recalcitrant child, Ben answered, "Adam, my dear boy. I remember it quite well. It must be the reason you are here. It's the reason I am here." And after a very pregnant pause, he said, "It's the object you found in a lump of coal."

Adam slumped back into his chair. "But you're dead. You can't be here. How could you be alive?"

Ben cocked his head. "As you can see, Adam. I'm fine. Tell me why you think I'm dead."

Adam related the events of the past couple of days—the analysis of his medallion, the explosion, and the fateful and extremely odd findings in Maplewood which eventually led to Hedda and the museum. When he finished, Ben took a seat in one of the wooden desk chairs, clamped his hands across the back of his head, and appeared to be trying to absorb all the details of Adam's story, including those of his apparent death. His eyes closed and a deep silence settled amid them.

After a minute or so, Ben raised his head. "Adam, do you have the medallion with you?"

Ben's smile disappeared as at the same moment they all heard a thud in the tunnel, then another, and another. Hedda ran out of the room to investigate and returned moments later to shut off the tunnel lights. She brought her fingers to her lips and whispered, "There's someone trying to break in. They're at the front entrance."

The entry door caved in with a crash. Adam and Linda jumped. They were trapped in a dead-end mine.

Ben spoke with a calm voice. "Someone's followed you here, probably the gentlemen chasing you from the museum."

Hedda joined Ben as he rose from his chair. "No need to panic. Just follow us." Ben led the group to the hidden door and swung it open.

"A secret passageway?" Adam inquired as they entered.

Ben turned his head. "Nothing so fancy. You're in what used to be the hospital section of the mine, and this is just another way out. " He ran a hand along the wall. "I put this panel in myself, so I suppose now it's a 'secret passageway', as you call it."

Hedda secured the door behind them and flicked on a light while Ben placed a heavy metal cross-brace into position against the closed panel. Unlike the old wood used at the entrance, the panel and wall were built with oversized beams that would be able to withstand any attempt at breaching. They found themselves in a small room with rough rock walls and an exit at the opposite end.

Ben said, "If we can stay quiet, maybe we can wait here a bit and listen to what these intruders have to say. It would be nice to know who they are, or at least what they're after."

It only took a few minutes before they heard the arrival of the uninvited duo.

"Paul, shine the light over here."

Desks and chairs were moved about.

"I found the switch. There's nobody here, Steve. Borman's gonna flip."

"You sure they came this way?"

"You saw the foot prints."

"Let's give this place a good overhaul, don't leave nothin' standin'. He'll be pissed off 'cause we came back empty-handed, but I don't want him jerkin' us around 'cause we weren't thorough."

The sounds beyond the door painted a vivid picture—furniture scraped across the uneven flooring, drawers pulled and emptied, chairs fell over and cabinet doors slammed.

"Get a load of the record player."

"Leave that be."

"What about the computer?"

"Yeah, let's take it with us. They ain't here which means they're someplace else."

"There's nobody asleep in that little bird house of yours."

"What's that?"

Computer equipment cables dragged across a table top. And from the doorway, "Paul, check out that chute up ahead. They could've gone up in there. Maybe there's another way out."

"Shit, Steve, you gotta be kiddin'. Nobody's gone up that chute. Besides, I'm gonna get my uniform dirty."

"Aw, shaddup. Check it out. Borman's not too happy with you, so you better show some initiative."

When the voices faded, Hedda spoke up. "We know Borman. I know Borman. That asshole were Luke's boss. A few years ago he bought this mine. We made an arrangement to do some diggin' here. But that doesn't change anything. He's still an asshole."

Linda tilted her head and asked, "Did this guy know about the stuff Luke found?"

"Oh, he sure did. He were gonna take care of the find in the mornin'. The same mornin' the mines got flooded."

"Do you know if he got hold of the other metal pieces before the flood?" asked Adam.

"Don't rightly know, but I wouldn't be surprised if he did."

Adam turned to Ben. "Was there anything important on that computer they took? And, by the way, just what are you doing down here? If you really are Ben Wujciak, who did I see back in Maplewood?"

Adam could not let it go, and almost as an afterthought, and to no one in particular, he mumbled, "This is crazy."

Linda brought her arm around Adam's shoulders and they both looked to Ben with expectation dappled across their faces. The shadows brought on by the single light bulb directly above Ben added an eerie touch of drama, deepening Ben's eye sockets and chiseling his stubbled chin.

92

Chapter 8

Ghostly shadows danced across Ben's face, giving Adam the impression that he was staring at a phantasm more so than the warm-hearted doctor of his childhood memories. Ben took a deep breath and spoke.

"Back in 1979, when you left my office, I knew you would never let me borrow that piece of coal, even if it was for scientific purposes. It was your treasure. To me it looked like an old coin, of course, a coin stuck in a lump of coal was unusual to say the least … something that could have been around longer than recorded history."

Ben took a step back and angled himself against the stone wall.

"I couldn't get it out of my head. Was it possible that we had our history so wrong? Was it really possible that an artifact could have been made by an intelligence older than man? The next thing I knew, I was at the town library, looking up facts and theories about how coal is formed … how long it takes. I started into archeological texts, and churned through reams of microfilm and microfiche archives. I cut down on office appointments. I needed more time for research. I made weekend trips to major libraries in Newark and New York. Looking back, I was either turning into an expert in the extraordinary or turning into an obsessive fool.

"After a while, I became convinced that there must be similar artifacts buried in the rubble of human history. I made so many trips to the Museum of Natural History that the security personnel knew me by name."

Adam interjected. "It sounds to me like you went over the deep end."

Linda gave Adam the 'how could you?' look.

Ben continued. "That's quite all right. I thought so too. I followed up a lot of those old reports, seeking out the original sources, and when possible, I even checked out the locations myself to see the objects firsthand, and talk to the people who found them. I have to admit, it was an obsession. My practice suffered, but I was close to retirement, so I cut back my hours and a few years ago, cut them out altogether. I was on a mission and that mission had the potential to change everything about our history."

Linda asked, "What made you think that? There are all sorts of theories in archeology and human history. Some clearly have the potential to rock our world, but they're all in the mix, each with its own cadre of believers. None of that has made any difference in the scheme of things."

"You're right. Everything you say is true … or has been true until now."

Linda held her hands out as if asking for more evidence.

"There is something so perplexing and exciting about finding objects that just don't fit in the known scheme of things. Don't you see? They are clues. I had the feeling that I was on the brink of uncovering something of great importance."

Ben waved his arms symbolically in an arc.

"I saw myself as a searcher, a seeker of the fundamental truth, if there is one. I was, and still am, convinced the clues are hidden all around us. I think we are at the threshold of an entirely new consciousness for mankind."

Adam cleared his throat. He looked at Linda and had to fight to keep his eyebrows from rising. She lowered her head. He turned his gaze around, panning the small room, the single light bulb and finally, caught Ben's eyes. Ben had paused, no doubt catching the brief, silent exchange.

"It sounds pretty far-fetched doesn't it? An old doctor giving up his medical practice and going off into a hare-brained quest for some mystical truth."

Ben took out a handkerchief and wiped his brow before continuing.

"Hang in there, it gets better, a lot better. Every so often I came across the type of finding that would send chills through me. A story of an object out of time, an ancient pictograph or hieroglyph of a technical marvel, man-made artifacts found deep in the earth, and yes, even a story of a gold chain in a lump of coal."

Ben winked at Adam.

"Many of these tales were lost to time and indifference. I noticed a pattern, a kind of habit peculiar to human nature. People tend to disregard the abnormal even to the point of ignoring it, in particular when it contradicts their model of history. I saved the most interesting discoveries as newspaper clippings, photocopies and printouts … even hanging them on my bedroom walls.

Adam nodded. "Yeah, I saw those, or at least, I think I did."

"Over the years, the room became filled with these images. I went there to think, to meditate. My bedroom had turned into my *sanctum sanctorum*, a private refuge where I could focus. How old do you think the Sphinx is? What about finding a metal bowl in solid granite? This scavenger hunt had become a way of life for me—pasting together the bits and pieces that might make up some kind of story, or a thread of a larger story. A few weeks ago I discovered something quite by accident which changed everything."

Ben paused and said, "I'm sorry. It must sound like I'm ranting. You must understand that, with the exception of Hedda, I have not discussed this with anyone."

Adam spoke up. "Ben. I think we understand, but there're some crazies out there looking for us, probably looking for my medallion, and you haven't come to the point yet. By the way, you're not exactly coming across any more rational than they seem to be."

Linda jabbed Adam in the ribs.

Wincing, Adam clarified. "What I mean is … Ben, how come you're not dead and what's the point of telling us all about your obsession?"

Linda punched Adam in the shoulder and drew herself away saying, "Adam. Don't be so rude. I'm sure Ben has a reason."

Ben said, "Before 'I come to the point,' I am going to tell you a little story."

Adam's shoulders dropped and he slouched back into this seat.

"Over the years I came across a handful of really interesting items. I'm not talking about pottery and nails and other so-called modern odds and ends found in archeologically embarrassing locations. No, it's not the stuff that seems a bit out of place. It's the stuff that is *outrageously* out of place that really demands attention."

Ben looked down at the dirt floor, placed his hands deep within his pockets and began pacing. "I sent you the news clipping describing the Mrs. Culp find. I assume you got that?"

Ben returned Adam's nod with quick dip of his head. "What did you think of that story?"

"It shook me up. It was very similar to my own find."

"And why did it shake you up?"

"Mrs. Culp found a gold chain in coal—coal that was estimated to be at least a hundred million years old. Wouldn't that bother anyone?"

"Sure. You're shook up because of the age. It's one thing to consider archeological finds reflecting intelligence on the order of hundreds of thousands of years, and it's quite another to consider objects that might be hundreds of millions of years old. It's obvious that man wasn't around when *these* objects were left behind."

Left behind?

Adam's own findings went even further as they strongly suggested a technology which not only pre-dated mankind, but had yet to be achieved in the present day.

Adam said, "Maybe these conundrums were the result of a limited understanding of evolution on this planet, or how long it took for coal to form, or maybe they're just fraud."

"You know, I went to Morrisonville. I visited with the librarian there, who told me the story of the Culps. Mr. Martin Culp was an entrepreneur who had ventured into a variety of agricultural businesses in other parts of Illinois before settling in town to start the Morrisonville Times in 1887. His wife, Sarah, worked at home as a seamstress. The paper was a success from the start, and the two led respected and comfortable lives. In 1891, when Sarah found the gold chain, there was no need for drumming up extra sales of the paper by splashing the story on its front pages. In fact, Sarah was a very quiet person, more interested in her needlework than town gossip. When she found that chain, notoriety was the last thing she wanted, and it was upon her insistence that the news article be kept to a very modest length. It turns out that a couple of years later she gave up the chain to a cousin who lived outside of town. As the story goes, the chain was eventually lost in a fire."

Ben stopped in front of Adam, and bent over to face him squarely.

"So, is there anything about the story that bothers you, Adam?"

"It's odd that Sarah took so little interest in the chain. It's odd that she gave it away. And I guess it was odd that it was lost."

Ben's mouth began to curl up at the corners.

During the soliloquy Adam had gone from perplexed, to amused, back to perplexed and now headed straight into down-right pissed off. "Ben, what's all this got to do with anything? So they lost the chain? So what? What about you? I still don't understand how it is that you're alive, when I plainly saw you dead. Can you explain that?"

Ben's smile finally erupted as he placed both hands on Adam's shoulders. "There's only one logical explanation. You never saw me. I wasn't there."

"Come on. I know what I saw."

After a brief moment, Ben replied, "Adam, you also claim that I disappeared."

"Uh, yes, that's right. While I was in the house, someone took your body ..."

"Did anything else unusual happen?"

"There *was* one more thing. While I was outside ... I was outside for a few minutes. I had gone over to the garage to double check on you, that is, your body, when I discovered you, I mean the body, was gone. When I returned to your bedroom, the walls were bare. Only a few minutes had passed. It seems impossible that someone took all those clippings off the walls."

Still clenching Adam's shoulders, Ben shook his head from side to side. "I believe the clippings are still there, Adam. Nothing was moved. Nothing was taken."

Adam was about to begin arguing that fact, when Ben stepped back and said, "Maybe there's an explanation. Recall the Mrs. Culp story. In my travels I have chased down a few other similar findings. Whenever a particularly tantalizing find came up, the object involved was often lost or destroyed. Fraud might explain some of these events. However, a pattern began to emerge. First, a respectable person with no reason to lie finds the object. A few people see it, and the original person either keeps it or eventually donates it to a local museum. Within a short time, it becomes unnoticed, misplaced, lost, or even destroyed in an accident. Skeptics would be quick to point out that a fraudulent find is better kept away from inquiring minds, and the mystery is even better kept when it becomes the subject of a series of misfortunes. However, a very different idea occurred to me."

Ben locked his eyes on Adam and moved closer. "Adam, would you show us your medallion?"

Adam reached between the folds of his buttoned shirt front, and began patting his chest in alarm. "It's not here."

Linda said, "Adam. Don't you remember? In the alley by the museum you put it in your pocket."

"That's right!"

He checked his pockets, and his face contorted. "It's not here, either."

Linda helped him and they both went through his shirt, trousers and jacket. Nothing. No medallion.

"I can't believe this. Maybe I dropped it on the way here … outside somewhere, maybe it's just outside this door."

Adam stood up and began fumbling with the metal bar, when Ben spoke up. "Don't bother. I doubt it's here."

Adam asked, "How can you be so sure? Do you know where it is?"

Ben enunciated each word to insure its clarity. "Adam. You have hidden the medallion and only you know where it is."

The statement came across with conviction and, for a moment, Adam was speechless. His mind fought against a growing rage.

How could he know what I may have done with the medallion?

Adam was about to respond, when Linda interrupted. "Shhhhh."

Everyone turned to see her standing by the barred door with a finger to her lips. "I think I hear something. I think they may have come back."

She pressed her head against the door.

Adam asked, "What is it?"

She closed her eyes and lifted a hand, motioning for more time. Seconds passed. The back of her neck glistened in the scant light. Linda pressed her ear to the door even harder. After a few more grueling moments, Hedda angled closer to her. Linda placed her hand over Hedda's mouth and whispered, "I think someone, or something is on the other side of this door. Maybe listening, just like we are."

With an abrupt tilt of her head Linda motioned the group to get out of the room. They moved as one, as if they all had been waiting for a signal. Ben and Hedda led the way. Adam held Linda's arm as they exited through the doorway on the far side of the room. She broke away from him, preferring to take up the rear of the slow motion caravan, and gave the barred door one last look before joining the others. The group shuffled through a poorly lit winding passageway. Adam hadn't realized just how claustrophobic Linda was, or in fact, had become. He found himself trying to get past the image of a huge furry creature pressing its clawed hands against the other side of the door.

He looked back at Linda just as the tunnel began to get lighter. She nodded and grinned. She looked happy to be rid of the ghost they left behind.

Ben turned to the group. "We're coming out. You can relax now."

Adam took out his cell phone.

Linda said, "Calling a friend?"

"The police. The real police, I hope."

A minute later, Adam rejoined the group.

"Well?" asked Linda.

"I think I got through, but …"

"Your battery's dead."

Adam screwed his face at Linda. "I'm pretty sure I got through."

***

After the group emerged from the escape tunnel, the heavy metal brace which lay across the secreted door shook for a moment, then lifted on its own, and clattered to the floor. The door swung open, revealing the black maw of the room behind it and nothing else.

Chapter 9

Shades of gray streaked the river valley sky and cut long shadows across their path. A few leaves danced by—an early sign of the autumn to come. Ben and Adam paused to look back at the women. The dark triangular outline of the breaker loomed over nearby treetops. The one story mine office was a few hundred feet south of it, largely obscured by vegetation.

Adam spoke to Ben. "I don't want to depend on the police to save the day since we don't know when they will arrive, or even if they will. I was thinking that maybe we could sneak around to the breaker and go through it to reach the office building from the back? This way we could size up the situation. Get an idea of what we're up against."

Ben said, "That should be possible. What do you think, Hedda?"

Hedda voice was threaded with weariness. "Of course it's possible. We're gonna lose light awful soon, so it's best to get goin' as there's no electricity in the breaker and that's a damn dark place."

She shook her head and took Linda by the hand. Ben shrugged. "Looks like we take up the rear guard."

They carved out a path by pushing aside vines, kicking through brambles and stepping over scattered debris covered by dense tufts of grass. The remnants of several rails ran in parallel, one of which wound its way back to the Slope Mine. These were the ones used to move raw coal to the breaker. Hedda followed one of the tracks to the left. The group picked up the pace, avoiding some of the thick undergrowth, despite running into an occasional tree erupting from between the rails. The darkening gloom of early evening was already upon them. When they arrived at the rail entrance to the breaker, Adam looked up at the massive building and was at once captivated. The stark edifice was the one remaining testament to a harsh, merciless way of life that had once been the norm in the River Valley. The tattered, rust-encrusted, black and decaying corrugated metal collage soared ten stories above him, cutting an enormous black wedge into the twilight. There was little to see at the entrance. It was like the mouth of a cave.

Hedda said, "This here's where the raw coal from the mines were delivered," and with a wave of her arm sweeping upward, she added, "The coal got loaded into these bins which moved them up to the top where they got crushed and sorted."

The conveyor bins and belts were mostly gone, but some sections of the ramp and the corpse of a huge electric motor sitting astride several wheel assemblies were visible. Adam's eyes followed the ramp up to a chute perched at the very top of the breaker.

Hedda pointed to a small entryway nearly hidden by the shadowy outlines of machinery. "We can get in through this door."

The group followed her into a cavernous recess. Shards of muted light descended from a dozen small windows scattered high along the walls. The tall coal-black wooden beams could have been ebony columns majestically ascending toward an invisible domed roof of a long-forgotten cathedral. Mold and decay covered the remains of flooring. Staircases and broken gangways were arrayed at odd angles along the walls. Adam made out several mechanical sorters and crushers seemingly suspended in midair. He imagined a time when the breaker was filled with the noise and dust of coal being crushed, scoops and belts moving the pulverized rock from floor to floor.

And now, the machines stood idle, like they were waiting for something. Their dragon teeth rollers patiently waiting for their next meal.

Linda gripped Adam's elbow and whispered, "Spooky."

Hedda motioned the group to follow. They slowly padded their way along the nearest wall in single file, avoiding all manner of debris strewn over the broken concrete flooring. Minutes later they reached a side door which Hedda eased open to reveal about fifty feet of crumbling macadam, which led up to the office building. Adam's Pathfinder and Ben's VW were parked alongside, and a black limousine sat at the farthest corner near the rear entrance.

"Hey, you!"

Two figures appeared beyond the cars at the edge of the parking lot. One was in a policeman's uniform and carrying what looked like Ben's computer. The group ducked back into the breaker. They heard the two men outside scrambling toward them.

Adam motioned to the girls. "You two hide." He pointed to a jumble of twisted rubble stacked against a wall.

"Ben and I will try to get them to follow us, and if they do, you guys get to my car. We'll come around through the far entrance and meet you in the parking lot." He reached into his jeans pocket and tossed Linda the keys.

There was no time for further discussion. The girls disappeared into the shadows, and Ben and Adam ran down the center of the building making sure they stayed in view. When they reached the gnarly remains of a rusty stairway, another shout erupted from the doorway.

"Hey, stop! We just want to talk!"

Ben pointed at Adam and up the staircase, and then at himself and the opposite end of the breaker. The communication was complete. Adam started up the stairs, while Ben took off, moving fast for a man of his age. Adam leaped up the groaning staircase.

Why do people always choose to go up something when chased?

The rusty iron framework was bedecked with decaying wooden treads. He heard and felt several boards crack as he reached the second floor platform. When he paused there for a moment to look back, he saw that the men ran past Hedda and Linda, and one was now veering toward his stairs, while the other continued headlong down the center of the floor. Adam turned to continue his climb, but not before noting two figures slipping out the door.

There go Hedda and Linda.

He stared into the gloom, trying to make out where he was, and perhaps more importantly, where he was going. Each floor consisted of a narrow wooden gangway hung along the inner walls of the building, interconnected by assorted flights of stairs and wooden chutes. Caged rooms devoted to sorting screens and grinding machinery hung suspended throughout the hollow building. Many of these had sunken through the rotted flooring or completely collapsed, having come to rest on the first floor in mangled heaps. Parts of shuttles and chutes designed to move the raw coal were still visible, dangling from balcony to balcony, draped with the tattered fragments of leather conveyor belts. When Adam heard a staccato shuffle arriving at the base of the staircase, he loped up to the next level, taking care to avoid missing treads, and all the while trying to sort out an escape plan.

***

Herman straightened himself up and crossed his legs. His right hand slipped into a jacket pocket to cradle his Luger. It was his Parabellum, from the Latin, '*Si vis pacem, para bellum,*' —if you want peace, prepare for war. Holding the weapon in his pocket was a personal habit, as it connected Herman to better times. He looked up as two uniformed visitors entering the office.

"Good day. How can I help you?"

The police officers took off their caps and stared at Herman in surprise. The lead officer, a sergeant, spoke up first. "We are so sorry for the intrusion, Mr. Borman, but we received a call that there was a problem at the mine." He gave his partner a furtive sideways glance.

Herman managed a pleasant smile. "A call? Perhaps there was some confusion. There is no problem here officers. Can you tell me more about this problem?"

The sergeant held his cap in both hands, and responded in a quieter tone. "Well, it would appear that someone might be playing a prank. According to the dispatcher, a group of people were being chased here at the mine. It sounded serious, so we came to investigate."

"Hah! I've been napping here for the last hour or so. You fellows just woke me. I know of no chase. Everything in fact is very quiet."

"It's a matter of formality, Mr. Borman, but I need to ask you, why you are here?"

"I've invited a few friends to tour the mine this afternoon."

"So, that explains the cars parked outside?"

"Why, yes. They followed my limousine here. My assistants, Steve and Paul, have volunteered as tour guides."

"And who exactly are your guests?"

"You know Hedda, from the museum?"

Both officers nodded.

"And, Ben Wujciak?"

"Her boyfriend?" The two officers snickered.

"Hedda and Ben, and two out of town visitors from Schill University are at this moment in the midst of a walking tour of the colliery." Herman increased his grip on the Luger as he continued. "If you would like, we can go out and try to find them."

The officers looked at each other and shrugged. Borman was a pillar of the community. His history with the River Slope Mine had deep roots, and even they knew of him. After the flood of 1959, Herman had made Pittston his home. In the intervening years he had become a successful businessman first specializing in mining equipment and clothing, and eventually branching out into outdoor supplies for campers and hunters. His business enterprises had provided jobs for many miners displaced by the collapsing coal mining economy. After the mine declared bankruptcy several decades ago, Herman managed to purchase the land, to preserve it as a testament to local mining history. To this end, he provided funding for the maintenance of the mining museum and the research Ben and Hedda were conducting.

The sergeant spoke up again. "We are so sorry to have disturbed you. I'm sure there must have been a misunderstanding."

He turned to the door and waved to his younger partner. "We'll be on our way then. Good afternoon, Mr. Borman."

Herman stood. "It is no trouble. I understand you are doing your job, and if there is anything you need from me …" He left the statement unfinished as he walked over to the backdoor and held it open. The two uniforms emerged, turning back to tip their caps, and entered the cruiser astride the limo. Herman threw them a cheerful smile and returned their farewells with a wave of his own. He flicked on the office light as he shut the door.

***

Seeing no obvious exit, Adam continued upward, jumping two and three stairs at a time, occasionally breaking through a tread board. He paused on the fourth flight, and listened for his pursuer.

A rhythmic wheezing drifted up from the dark in syncopation with each foot step. It slowed as it neared. Someone appeared to be running out of steam.

Adam shouted, "What do you want with us?"

The reply was a rasp. "We just want to talk with you."

"About what? Why the chase?"

"Mr. Borman wants to discuss the artifact."

I'll bet.

The circumstances suggested that more than a discussion was afoot. Adam jumped when he heard a wooden plank creak halfway up the staircase. He was about to start up the next flight of stairs, but stopped short at the sight of a wide, empty space separating him from the floor above.

Parts of a wooden gangway hung from the corrugated metal wall. He sidled to the narrow walkway and edged along its entrails, careful to stay close to the wall where the metal bracing seemed strongest. It took all his concentration to focus on each step, avoiding broken slats and missing boards. He heard a voice uncomfortably nearby and almost pleading. "Hey. Come on, be reasonable."

The owner of the voice was partially visible in the darkness. He caught a flash of blue.

A police uniform.

"I don't think I can trust you. You're not a real officer are you?"

The uniform jumped to the balcony, triggering a series of metallic groans and popping sounds. Adam pictured the heads of corroded rivets decapitating, tearing loose from their moorings. He coughed as a plume coal dust enveloped him. The walkway swayed and he heard several planks land on the floor below. There was no more time for talking. A caged room with walls of chain-linked fencing was suspended at the far end of the narrow set of boards. When he moved, his world began to sway again. The planking ended several feet short of the cage. A backward glance confirmed the uniform was getting closer, almost within arm's reach now. Adam sucked in his breath and leaped across the dark void. One hand was thrown aside by an unseen metal cross bracing, while his other reached the fencing. His fingers penetrated the links while momentum swung his legs into the bottom of the cage. His loose hand groped the air, seeking purchase. He cried out when his shins crashed into the base of the cage, but at least his free hand found the wire fencing. He was four floors up, twisting above a bottomless black hole filled with the sharp-edged remnants of machinery and tangled scraps of broken wood and steel, all hidden in shadow.

... And all patiently waiting to impale my helplessly flailing body.

At precisely that moment and entirely out of context, he found himself recalling a very pleasant fishing trip that he had taken as a child with his father. Their rowboat glided over a deep, smooth portion of a lake when he happened to glance down at the vague outlines of sinewy and ghostlike shapes in the water beneath them—the vestiges of rotting tree limbs passed beneath. They called to him just like the ghostly shadows below whispered to him now. He felt his grip weakening. His shins began to burn.

Imagination was a bitch.

Chapter 10

Linda and Hedda slipped through the breaker door and flattened themselves against the outer wall. A hundred yards away, four cars sat alongside the office building. One was a police car and it was moving away. The two women ran toward the office, hoping to get their attention. Linda halted mid-stride and tugged at Hedda's arm.

"Hey, what're ya doin'?"

"The police are leaving. What does that tell you?"

"Well … That they're done here? … That maybe they finished their investigatin'?"

"Exactly. There must be someone inside the office they talked to, and that someone convinced them that everything's fine."

"Damn."

"Let's get a closer look at who exactly's inside the office and so persuasive."

The two edged their way along the perimeter of the parking lot. Linda pushed back a pine bough to get a better look. A branch snapped behind her.

It was 1978 and Linda was eleven years old. She had been waiting for her two sisters and parents on a lonely stretch of beach on the north coast of Cuba. It was a hot summer morning, and she feared that something had gone wrong. When at last she heard the purring of their outboard motor, she stepped out of a mangrove thicket and waded into the shallow waters of the lagoon. She saw a small boat approaching. That's when she heard something snap behind her. A solitary soldier stood at the shoreline staring out at the approaching boat. His grin parted a dark moustache and revealed a missing front tooth. He stood just a few feet away with a rifle in one hand. His mouth grimaced as he turned to look at her.

Hedda caught up with Linda and said, "Sorry about that. Not used to sneakin' around."

When they arrived at the back of the office building, they peered through a corner of the door window. A stooped-over elderly man dressed in a dark business suit was shuffling toward a chair in the center of the office. The tufts of white on his balding head were in the shape of a raggedy crown. As he pivoted to sit down, Hedda gasped, "It's Herman. It's Herman Borman."

The soldier motioned for everyone to come into shore. Linda saw the crestfallen faces of her family and with her shoulders slumped and head bowed in surrender, she waded back.

"Herman owns the rights to this mine. He gave Ben and me permission to run some excavations in the River Slope section …"

Before Linda knew what was happening, Hedda turned the handle and threw the door open. She marched into the office. "Herman Borman! What's the meanin' of all this?"

Herman remained seated, pushed back his chair and placed his right hand in his jacket pocket. "Good afternoon, Hedda. Are you going to introduce me to your pretty young friend?"

Before Hedda could reply, Linda said, "My name is Linda Garcia, and I'm here as Hedda's guest."

"Oh, I know you, Dr. Garcia. And where are the other two?"

Hedda said, "That's none of your business. These folks are my guests. You still haven't explained yourself."

"Explain myself, Hedda? This is my office, my colliery, my land. I do not need to explain anything to you." He wiped his mouth with his free hand. "I know Ben and Dr. Adam Dove are also on the premises." He rose to his feet and looked directly at Hedda. His face was grim, and the sneer mutated into a worm of a frown. "I also know that Dr. Dove has an artifact in his possession that is most unusual, and it is this that I've come here to see."

Hedda's face turned crimson. "So that's why you were chasing us, hunting us down like animals? You couldn't just ask? You're the same bullying dog that ran my husband into the ground so many years ago. Nothing changes."

"Now Hedda, it's not like that at all. This whole affair of the chase is just a misunderstanding. I only wish to talk to Dr. Dove and see the relic."

"Smooth talk. I ain't havin' it. We're gonna leave this place, and you ain't gonna follow us."

Hedda turned to the door with Linda in tow. They both froze at the unmistakable metallic sound of an automatic being chambered.

***

Adam felt the cage wire slicing into his fingers. His shins were screaming. In seconds the pain would begin to exceed his threshold. Dangling as he was, he knew there was no way back.

"You idiot! You're gonna kill yourself."

True enough.

Adam moved hand over hand to the left in an attempt to circumnavigate the caged room, hoping to find a way out before his fingers lost the little strength remaining. He spied the remains of a wooden platform at the entrance to the cage. He lunged and curled one hand on the base of the railing, and swung his body around the corner. As he hung there, arms embracing the metal post, the cage shook violently.

The uniform was not giving up.

Adam drew himself up and sat on the narrow platform. With a moment to regain his bearings, he rubbed his shins in an inadequate attempt to placate the throbbing, and left dark streaks on his jeans. His hands were bleeding. The cage shuddered once more. The uniform was rounding its corner.

The descending staircase was long gone. Adam stood and peered into the cage. The sheet metal floor, coated with soot and streaked with rust, sloped into the center like a rectangular funnel. The tattered remnants of a chute dangled above him.

He was looking at the guts of a crusher, a machine designed to break raw coal down to smaller pieces. Ragged metal teeth set on rollers at the base of the funnel gleamed up at him.

The uniform arrived with a grunt. In that instant, time slowed down. Everything in Adam's sight assumed an eerie, crystal clarity. He felt the beat of his heart slow, and his breathing paused. There was time enough to clinically examine the machine below and its toothed rollers. He noticed pulleys leading to the rollers, and his eyes followed them back to a set of levers nearby. He yanked one, but nothing happened. He pulled again, this time with both hands. The lever moved slightly, yielding a gravelly groan.

Did the rollers part just a little bit?

He tried again, and heard two more squeals, a mechanical one from below and a very human one from nearby. The uniform rose up on the platform and the slow-motion special effects ended.

No time left.

Adam leaped feet first into the funnel, sliding to the bottom in a cloud of black dust, down to where those dragon teeth had patiently been waiting so many years for their next meal.

***

Linda and Hedda froze, and turned their heads in unison. Herman was now standing and held a gun pointed at them. Linda didn't know which was worse—the gun or the smug look on his face.

Hedda was the first to react. "Herman Borman! You put that thing down right now. Are you insane?"

Herman's reply sent cold shivers through Linda. "Vielleicht. Maybe so. Maybe not. Sit down … both of you. No one is leaving here. Not until I get the artifact."

"If it's this you want, here, keep it." Hedda pulled out the gold rod from her jacket and threw it on the table between them.

Herman's mouth tightened into a straight line, and spoke slowly, as if to make himself clear. "And, the other one?"

Linda said, "We lost it. Just now. We don't know where it is."

Hedda was nodding as if to verify the claim.

The air that blew out of Herman's mouth sounded like something between a cough and a guffaw. He wiped his mouth again before replying. "How convenient. Do you think me the fool?" He waved the Luger. "Sit. Let's all of us sit here and wait." As they did, he continued. "My colleagues will return shortly, with Ben and Adam. And then, we shall discuss the whereabouts of the artifact."

They sat at the long folding table, the two facing the one. Herman kept the pistol raised, and stared straight ahead as if looking past them. He then turned his eyes to Linda and smiled revealing a set of repulsive yellowed teeth.

Tap. Tap, tap. The muffled sound came from above, from the corrugated metal roof—the start of an early evening shower.

Thunderclaps punctuated the downpour. The calm waters of the lagoon boiled under the cold rain. Linda started to cry, holding her hands to her eyes. When she reached the shoreline, she collapsed to her knees. The soldier seemed to ignore her. With her head bowed low, she inched her way closer until she was out of his direct view. Between sobs, she grasped a baseball-sized stone trapped in a knotted set of roots. The soldier turned toward her just as she hid the stone beneath a flap of skirt. From the corner of her eye she saw that he had resumed his watch over her family who were wading to shore.

***

"Hey! Don't be stupid!"

The voice was nearby. Adam's feet slammed into the metal teeth, kicking up a blinding cloud of dust. He reached down to the toothed rollers with one foot and traced their conical shapes, trying to gauge the size of the opening between them.

"Don't be such a jerk! Here, grab my hand!"

For a moment Adam considered the suggestion. He looked to the voice and saw the dim outline of the uniform hovering almost within arm's reach. Adam bent down and traced the shape of the corroded tips of the crusher's teeth with his fingers. With one leg through the opening, he twisted his body, trying to find a gap between the rollers.

"Give it up! You're stuck."

Every movement Adam made wedged him in even more tightly. If the rollers were to start turning, he'd come out looking like bloody Swiss cheese. Then one of the rollers shifted with a high-pitched screech. It moved only a few inches, but enough to loosen up his leg. Through the widened gap, he saw a chute descending from below the rollers.

He pushed both feet down between the teeth and let himself slip through. An incomprehensible grumble spewed from above. For a moment, thoughts of a bottomless pit overwhelmed him. He descended along a grimy slide in a spiral curve, gaining speed, slipping through mottled streaks of twilight. He passed by the third floor and as the second whipped by, he fell through empty space. The chute was gone and before he could gather enough of his wits to formally enter a panic mode, he landed on the leeward side of a shallow coal pile, tumbled down its short slope and rolled onto the cement floor in a bruised and blackened heap. A thick cloud of choking dust and stones followed him down the chute. Adam was down, in one piece. A string of curses descended from above. He stood up on bruised and shaky legs, and was brushing himself off when a figure approached from the shadows.

"Are you okay?"

It was Ben.

"I think so. What happened to you? Where's the guy that was chasing you?"

"I managed to lose him at the far end of the breaker. We need to hurry and get out of here before he figures out I doubled back."

***

Linda held her hands to her face and continued to sob. Through her fingers she saw Hedda's face turning a deep, dark red.

"Now, now, my dear," Herman purred in feigned empathy. "There is no need for emotion. I am strictly interested in the artifact. I just want to examine it, perhaps purchase it, and then you can go on your merry way."

"What will stop us from reporting all o' this to the authorities? The police don't take kindly to gunplay, even from you," Hedda countered with a contemptuous look.

"Ach, the police. Maybe you saw them leaving here? The police belong to me, Hedda."

As the message sunk in, Herman glanced at Linda whose head remained buried in her folded arms. She hunched over the tabletop, moaning. Herman, no doubt repulsed by such an outward display of emotion, turned his attention back to Hedda. "You should know this, Hedda. You have lived in this town long enough to respect my influence."

Her parents begged the soldier to spare the children. He laughed in response, and when he inhaled to catch his breath, Linda brushed back a lock of hair with one hand, and with one enormous swing landed the stone directly on his knee. A staccato yelp escaped his open mouth. He grabbed at his knee and rolled to the sand. His eyes bulged, and before he could shout out, a second roundhouse blow from the stone landed between his eyes and knocked him unconscious. He lay at the shoreline, unmoving, blood oozing from his nose and one leg in the water gently swaying to and fro.

Hedda rapped her fingers in frustration, and then slumped into her chair in defeat. Herman laid the Luger on the table momentarily as he wiped his mouth once more. Suddenly, Linda lifted the table and flipped it onto Herman. As he collapsed beneath it, she glimpsed both the shocked look and the gun flying through the air. It was a look she knew well. She leaped onto the overturned table, pinning Herman underneath it.

The rain had come to a halt. The sounds of the gentle lapping of the sea resumed, interrupted only by droplets arriving from the palm tree canopy above. A gull swooped overhead followed by its call fading into the far side of the lagoon. Her family stared at Linda in disbelief, and then, one by one, they turned to gaze at the soldier sprawled in the sand. No one spoke. No one moved. Linda tossed the stone back into the mangroves, brushed off her soaked khaki dress, and said, "I think we should get in that boat now."

"Hedda! I think you should get his gun."

Linda was no longer sobbing. Hedda waddled to the corner of the room to retrieve the Luger, all the while staring at Linda sprawled on the table and Herman's legs squirming beneath.

Herman cried out. "Get off! Get off me you stupid woman!"

The backdoor at the opposite end of the office opened a crack revealing a set of grimy fingers curled around its edge. Hedda lifted the Luger, aimed and shouted out. "Whoever you are … I have a gun and I'll use it."

The door swung open to reveal Adam's face covered in black. Ben stared over his shoulder and adjusted his spectacles.

Adam spoke up first. "It's just us … who's that under the table? Linda, what are you doing? Hedda, what happened here?"

Linda, lying spread-eagled on the table, looked up at Adam and said, "What happened to you? You look like hell."

Herman gasped, "Help me! Get this crazy woman off me!"

Adam said, "I look like hell? Who do you have under there?"

"Herman Borman. This SOB tried holding us here at gunpoint!"

Hedda lifted the Luger in her hand to show Adam.

Ben surveyed Herman's prostrate form. "Linda. I think you can let him up." He pointed to Hedda. "Since you have the gun now."

Herman, still pinned to the floor, pleaded. "Dr. Wujciak! You know me. This is all a horrible misunderstanding!"

Adam and Linda lifted the table off Herman and seated him into a chair. Ben asked, "What exactly do you want from us? Why the big chase?"

Herman looked up at Ben first, and then slowly took in the faces of the other three. He said, "I only wanted to talk to you about the artifact."

Adam brushed himself off and took a step nearer. "That's right. It's all about the artifact. How do you know about this artifact?"

"I have my ways."

Adam thought for a moment about the uniform back at Schill and then asked, "You knew about the lab work didn't you? Maybe, you had something to do with the explosion too?"

Herman stared at the floor, avoiding Adam's eyes. "I know nothing about the explosion."

"And, the morning after, it was your man going through the lab?"

Herman shrugged.

"You had no right to chase after us like this. We've called the police. You're going to have a lot of explaining to do."

Linda said, "I'm afraid that the police were here already. It looks like Herman is good friends with them."

Adam asked, "Is that right?"

Herman nodded while an incongruous smile slowly curled up his wrinkled cheeks. "Yes. Yes. The police were here. It seems someone reported a problem at the mine … clearly an error. Of course, I told them everything was fine." He took in a deep breath and sighed. "You see, this place, this mine, belongs to me. And, you are the trespassers."

Hedda interjected. "You know perfectly well you gave Ben and me permission to set up shop here. To do some diggin' in the River Slope. You know that! So what are you gettin' on about?"

Adam turned to Hedda. "You guys have been working this mine?"

"A couple of years back, Ben came to the museum. He saw the gold rod that my husband had found. It turns out he were tryin' to track down the source of some coal deliveries to New Jersey just before the mine closed down. Once we figured that the coal probably came from the River Slope, he wanted to go explore it real bad. So, we made a deal with Herman here to do some investigatin'. Herman didn't appear to mind." She paused to look back at Herman and spat out, "In fact, he was happy about it."

Herman sat up straighter. "So you see? I have a perfectly legitimate reason to be here. It is you who have attacked me. Go ahead and call the police again, and see if they believe your wild story … your fabrications."

Linda asked, "What about Herman's boys, the two who came after you in the breaker?"

Adam spoke first. "We lost them, but I suspect they'll be on us any moment now."

Ben said, "I think we should get out of here … the sooner the better. Adam, what about your artifact? Shouldn't we look for it?"

"I think I know where it might be. We can retrieve it later."

Ben walked over to the front door leading out to the parking area and looked out to see if the way was clear. "I'll take my car. You follow me in Adam's car. I know a place where we can stay tonight."

Linda and Hedda followed Ben to the door and watched him scurry out. Adam lagged behind for a moment and yelled out to the door held ajar by Linda."I'll be there in a moment."

Adam went back into the office area, walking over to the microwave perched atop a counter shelf. He opened the oven's door, reached in and pulled out his laptop. When Adam's hand emerged with a shiny gold disk, Herman gasped, "Mein Gott!" He began to sputter, seemingly incapable of coherent thought. Adam waved the medallion at him. By the time Herman could put two words together, Adam was out the door.

Linda was in the front seat of the Pathfinder with Hedda looking on from the rear. Through the rain-speckled windshield they saw the brake lights of the VW as it made ready to leave.

Ben yelled out his downturned window. "I'll wait for you at the end of the drive!"

When Ben left the parking lot, Adam turned to the two women and whispered through clenched teeth. "Give me a second."

He threw his laptop into the backseat and disappeared from view as he bent down outside the car. Moments later he reappeared on the opposite side with something in his hand.

"I found the bugger."

Adam tossed a small black box into the parking lot and eased himself into the driver's seat. Seeing that the two women were eying him curiously, he clarified. "It's a transmitter. I noticed the receiver on the floor back in the office. It's got to be how Borman tracked us here."

Hedda handed the keys to Adam and they drove out of the lot, exiting through the inner gate. In the rearview mirror Adam saw Herman staggering through the office door, pointing and shouting at the breaker. A few turns in the road later, Linda spoke up. "There's a police car sitting off to the side of the road."

A curtain of light rain caught the shimmering remains of the evening's sunset. Their headlights fell across Ben's VW parked alongside the police cruiser.

Adam said, "And there's Ben. The police are still here. He looks like he's talking to them."

As they slowed down, Ben looked up and waved them on. "Everything's fine folks! I'll catch up with you in a minute. Just wait for me by the entrance ahead."

Ben was all smiles, and as Adam slowly passed by he saw that so were the two policemen inside their patrol car. Adam's stomach tightened up.

Whatever story Ben spun appeared to be going over very well.

When they reached the city street, Adam stopped the car and turned to his passengers. "Does either of you think that any of this makes any sense? Wouldn't the police want to talk to us?"

Hedda said,"It is odd. But Ben has been visiting the mine for a couple of years now, and he knows a lot of the police around here. Maybe he just explained everything as a misunderstanding."

Adam asked, "When was the last time you saw Ben?"

Hedda wrinkled her eyebrows as she thought back. "He's been visitin' about every other week. It were about two weeks ago."

Adam continued, "And he looks the same to you? I mean the same as he looked two weeks ago?"

Hedda bent her head to the side to look at Adam more closely. The pitch of her voice increased ever so slightly. "Just what do ya mean? Sure, he looks the same."

"I don't know what I mean. Not yet."

Adam looked grim. After a glance at his mirror, he powered the Pathfinder out onto the road.

Linda said, "But shouldn't we wait for Ben? And, what about your medallion? It must be back in the mine somewhere or maybe in the museum? Aren't you going to look for it?"

Adam grinned and pulled the artifact from his pocket.

Linda was first to react. "*Dios Mio*! Where did you find it?"

Adam pocketed the gold disk and answered with a grin. "I never lost it."

Hedda stuttered, "But you said…"

"I know what I said."

Then after a moment more Adam added, "There's something not quite right with Ben, and until we know what that is, this artifact stays lost."

Adam lowered his head. The two women stared at him with their mouths open as he gunned the Pathfinder.

"What will it be? Hamburgers or pizza?"

Chapter 11

A thin ribbon of sunlight slipped through the curtains and painted a bright line along a faded blue carpet pile. It fell across a coffee stain and ascended the foot of a sofa to land on a solitary eyelid. Adam stirred to life and promptly fell off the edge of the sofa, landing on his shoulder with a thud.

It all came back to him in a flash.

The Great Adventure of the River Slope Mine.

He rubbed his shoulder, and as he regained his bearings, his hands, back and legs reminded him of the painful details of the previous day's escapade. His two roommates were snugly ensconced under the covers of a full-sized bed. A pillow shifted.

"What time is it?" grumbled Hedda.

"Time to get moving," replied Linda. She quickly sprung out of bed and in a blur launched herself into the bathroom.

***

Within the hour the trio sat at a corner table of the Starlight Motel restaurant. The sparse breakfast buffet was replete with all the trimmings of a full continental breakfast—stale coffee, yesterday's doughnuts, rock hard dinner rolls and freshly reconstituted orange juice. After a late night check-in with nothing to eat, they delighted in the repast. To the bewilderment of the motel manager, who looked on from behind his hallway counter, they indulged themselves with seconds and thirds.

"So what's your take on what happened yesterday?" asked Adam.

Linda's mouth puckered as she swallowed the orange drink. "Clearly, your artifact has captured the attention of some interesting characters."

"Intrestin' nothin'," Hedda snarled, while biting down on her marmalade smothered toast. "Herman is a ruthless bastard. For some reason he wants that medallion o' yours, and you can bet he ain't gonna stop 'til he gets it."

Adam said, "It does look that way. Maybe it has something to do with the other pieces he found in the mine."

"Found?" Hedda replied. "'Twas my husband found them relics. Herman took what was none o' his business. For Christ's sake, who knows what he did down there. The mine flooded the next morning."

Adam said, "Are you suggesting it's more than coincidence … you know, finding those relics and the flood?"

"It wouldn't surprise me." Hedda sipped at her coffee. "He's used to gettin' his way, and he'd be the kind o' asshole that'd jeopardize others' lives without givin' it a second thought."

Linda said, "These other parts … maybe they all go together in some way. Just look at the fit between your piece and Adam's disk. He could be trying to rebuild whatever this thing was."

Yeah, whatever it was, so many millions of years ago.

***

Herman sipped his morning tea and placed it back on the serving tray propped up on his lap. His maid tucked up the pillows behind his head, and straightened out the blankets at the foot of the bed before she slipped out of the heavily draped bedroom. She moved like a ghost in the wan lighting of a night table reading lamp. Herman spread a wad of butter substitute on the single scone before him, returned it to its plate intact, and stared into the gloomy interior of his bedroom.

Mumbling to himself, he proceeded to mentally outline the previous evening's events as if attempting to discover what exactly went wrong.

The two hired men turned out to be useless. One had gotten lost in the breaker, while the other idiot, still wearing a policeman's uniform, was unable to find a way down from the upper floors.

Then there was his own mistake—he underestimated the Linda woman. And Dr. Adam Dove—clearly a very resourceful man who managed to evade pursuit, hide the artifact, and make a clean getaway. The next time, and there would definitely be a next time, nothing would be left to chance.

***

Back in the motel room, Adam connected his laptop to the Internet link at the writing desk. He typed while the women finished packing. Linda zipped up her overnight bag and looked over Adam's shoulder. "Hey. What's that? It looks familiar."

Adam pointed at a corner of the screen. "See that number? It's the percentage of the DNA analyzed so far."

"That's what you're doing? Running the DNA analysis?"

"Seventy-five percent done."

Linda placed both hands on her hips. "And, what have you found out so far?"

"It's still too early to say much, since the correlation analyses really need to assimilate all the data before we can make any conclusions."

"Any trends?"

"There does seem to be one interesting trend. There are parts of this so-called nonsense DNA which might be referring to other parts of the sequence."

"And what does that mean?"

"Like I said … too early to tell."

Hedda asked, "Do you want this?"

She pulled out Herman's Luger from her jacket and held it out. "It makes me nervous."

Adam said, "I'll take it. Maybe we'll give it back to Herman, and then, maybe not." He pocketed the weapon, and his cell phone rang. He gave himself a mental pat on the back for remembering to charge it last night. He tucked the pistol into his laptop bag and flipped open the phone. "George!"

Linda and Hedda finished packing and sat at the foot of the bed as Adam spent the next few minutes in an animated conversation with his colleague, wandering from one end of the room to the other while relating the events of the past twenty-four hours.

When he ended the call, he was about to speak when Hedda stood. "Listen you two. I'm too old for this kind o' runnin' around. I'd be thankful if you could drop me off at the museum. Ben is likely lookin' for us and I expect he'll find his way there eventually. Here, ya might as well have this too."

She offered up her artifact. "It's done me no good and since Herman clearly wants it, I'd rather be rid of it than have it fall into his hands. Besides, it and your medallion seem to be made for each other. Just let an old lady get back to her life. If Herman has the gall to show up askin' for it, well then, I'll have the pleasure of lettin' him know you have it."

She finished the last remark with a smile and patted Adam on his back.

***

Linda waved at Hedda as they dropped her off at the museum, and said, "Well, where to? Are we going back to Schill?"

"We could do that. If that's what you want. But …"

"Okay. So what's up? Something you and George came up with?"

"Well, yes. That is … George has been thinking about the medallion's composition, and I guess, that goes for me too. As you know, his analysis indicated that the medallion contains tiny bits of carbon-13. He suggested

133

we get a closer look. The carbon-13 may provide further insight into the medallion's purpose."

"I suppose he also suggested where we could go to get that look?"

"Yup. But there's no reason you need to tag along. It might be best if I take you back to the university."

"Are you kidding? I'm way too curious now. There's no hurry to get back. Where exactly are you headed?"

Adam considered arguing with her, but found himself unexpectedly pleased. Linda was beginning to interest him on more than just one level.

"Okay then. We're headed out to Long Island, to the Brookhaven National Laboratory."

"Isn't that where they smash atoms with cyclotrons?"

"Among other things."

Chapter 12

The Brookhaven National Laboratories occupy about six square miles of Upton, a small rural community in the center of Long Island. The Labs were built on the site of an old Army base in 1947 in collaboration between academic researchers and the government to promote basic research in selected aspects of the atomic sciences. Adam remembered that much from a high school field trip. He especially remembered the eye-opening demonstrations—sparking Tesla coils and humongous cyclotrons, which left his teenage mind with a lasting impression—a place full of disheveled and wide-eyed mad scientists. Quivering electric arcs surrounded them while they staggered about in their cluttered laboratories, switching on all manner of convoluted, dark and noisy machinery.

And then of course, there was the sewn up body lying lifelessly on a belted gurney.

"How much farther?"

Adam blinked his eyes. "Just a few minutes more and we'll be at the front gate."

Linda shook her head. "What were you thinking about?"

"The last time I was here … as a student in high school. It was on a field trip. Did you know who made the first video game?"

"Wasn't that one of the first Atari games? Pong? Maybe around the 1970s?"

"Yeah, good guess, but Atari wasn't the first."

Linda rolled her eyes and Adam said, "Some people think it was Magnavox, with their Odyssey systems in the mid-seventies."

Linda shrugged and eased back into her seat as Adam went on. "Actually, I saw the first video game here at Brookhaven on that field trip. It was 'Tennis for Two', invented by a guy named Higginbottom, or something like that. It was an analog computer system, knobs and dials, and all of it took place on a five-inch oscilloscope screen. That was back around 1958, almost twenty years before Atari or Magnavox."

Linda interrupted his soliloquy with apparent disinterest, which in a subtle kind of way disappointed Adam. "We're here."

A large sign indicated the entrance to the Labs. As they turned into the driveway leading to a gatehouse, Linda said, "It was Higginbotham."

Adam gave her a double take. He pulled down his window to greet the gatehouse guard.

She's amazing.

* * *

A man in a white coat pulled up at the gatehouse in a golf cart and stopped in front of the two waiting there.

Adam raised his hand. "Dr. Wild … Percy Wild?"

"Quite, quite. I presume you're Dr. Dove … and the lady?"

"Yeah, that's me and the lady is Dr. Linda Garcia. We're both from Schill University as you may know. I believe George Freedman called you?"

Either his lab coat was too big or Percy was too small, or some nerdy combination of the two. His hands barely protruded from the starchy white cuffs and his face was half-hidden by the collar. It reminded Adam of the oversized winter coats his parents forced him to wear.

Don't worry dear, you'll grow into it.

Percy pushed up his glasses with his free hand, suggesting that even the eyewear was too large. Despite a diminutive frame, his voice was surprisingly deep and carried with it a tone of authority. "Yes, yes. Good to meet you. Hop in and I'll take you to my lab."

Three-across seating in a golf cart made for a distinctly perilous ride, especially as Percy seemed to enjoy making sharp turns at every intersection. Along the way he pointed out that they were headed to the RCIBI lab, short for Radiotracer Chemistry and Instrumentation for Biological Imaging. He explained that the RCIBI was where most of the innovative instrumentation was developed. They scooted past several multi-story buildings, some with metallic spheres alongside that looked like water towers. Brookhaven was a city.

Percy pointed out some of the notable landmarks. "We're passing a few of the physics facilities here. Those round towers hold liquefied gases, mostly helium and nitrogen. Many of our efforts at the moment are to complete the RHIC, that is, the Relativistic Heavy Ion Collider. It's a roughly circular track about two and a half miles long wherein heavy atoms will be accelerated to near light speed and crashed into each other."

Linda asked, "To what purpose?"

"To see what makes up matter, of course." At the next turn in the road Percy could not hide a trace of disdain in his voice. "The RHIC will be ready later this year. In fact, it's really a prototype for something much bigger being built in Switzerland."

"The LHC?" asked Linda.

Adam looked at Linda with wildly growing respect, while Percy's mouth went agape. He stuttered a reply. "Quite, quite. The Large Hadron Collider. It'll be about seventeen miles in diameter." He collected himself enough to sit up straight. "We've got teams here working on some of the magnets and detectors the LHC will use."

The golf cart came to a jolting halt alongside a whitewashed two-story cinder block structure whose square windows were sunk into a plain concrete façade. They followed Percy's diminutive five-foot frame to the building's entrance.

Adam asked, "How does your work fit in with all this collider stuff?"

Percy slid a card through a reader at the door. "Technical support and spin-offs. We come up with ways to measure things that have never been measured before. That's the support part. These efforts lead to new discoveries, spin-offs, inventions which find themselves useful for a variety of purposes."

They walked to the middle of a long central hallway and stopped in front of another set of double doors. Percy pointed to a metal box inset into the wall. "If you have any magnetic objects like watches, jewelry and so on, please put them in the container."

Adam threw him a concerned frown.

"Don't worry, they will be safe here."

They emptied their pockets of loose change, cell phones, a gold rod and an old Luger.

Percy's eyes locked in on the gun. Adam said, "It's a long story." Percy nodded and Adam added his laptop to the container.

The double doors swung open as Percy inserted a card into a slot at the side."This is my lab. The TMS lab."

Adam read the placard above the doors: TRANSCRANIAL MAGNETIC STIMULATION. The lab was filled with a variety of what looked to Adam like conventional MRI instruments—Magnetic Resonance Imaging—the kind that hospitals use to help visualize soft tissues. They gave the impression of cylindrical half-coffins to Adam, with large round heads designed to rotate around one end of a patient's body. Magnetic resonance imaging had come into vogue since it surpassed standard x-ray imaging in detailing internal organs. Based on detecting protons in different environments, and not on absorbing x-rays, MRIs were a great deal safer as well.

They seated themselves at a workbench on one side of the lab. Percy pushed up his eyeglasses. "Can I see your medallion?"

Adam reached into his shirt and detached it from its chain.

Percy held it up to the fluorescent lab lighting, pausing long enough to turn it a full 360 degrees. "Hmmm, George tells me you found it in a piece of coal, and that it contains microscopic particles of carbon-13. Is that right?"

So much for keeping secrets.

"Er … Yes. And it's the carbon-13 that has us stumped. It appears that these C-13 particles are arranged in some order and they may be of different sizes."

Adam pulled out a handful of photos from his lap top case. "George was able to obtain these photomicrographs of the object. You can see the C-13 particles there."

Percy nodded and craned his head for a closer look.

Adam said, "What do you think? Can you help us?"

"I assume you are familiar with the workings of an MRI?"

Linda and Adam nodded in unison.

"Then you know that we apply an energy field, a radio-frequency field tuned to the energies of protons, to an object or a patient. By moving this field over the object and detecting how much of the field is absorbed by protons aligning with it, we detect those protons. The instrument provides us with an image of the location of different types of protons in the sample."

He sure likes listening to himself.

Percy continued. "We can tune the field to a number of different types of atoms. Besides protons, other elements are susceptible to MRI imaging, and among these is C-13.

"So, you can get the MRI field to image C-13, but these are very small particles. Is your instrumentation really that sensitive? Especially as the particles are embedded in gold?"

"Actually, gold, or any metal for that matter, usually does present a challenge. Although it's not magnetic, the applied rf field will generate Eddy currents in gold which can result in so much background noise that an analysis becomes impossible." Percy raised his hands in nerdy triumph. "However, we have a very sophisticated set of electronics here that can dampen those Eddy currents by pulsing the sample at the right frequency.

It's just a question of whether we can generate a detection window wide enough to visualize the C-13."

"And what about the particle size? These are on a micron scale."

"That's where the TMS technology comes in."

Adam recalled the sign above the door.

Transcranial Magnetic Stimulation.

Percy arose and beckoned the pair to follow him as he walked over to a corner of the laboratory. What looked like a mini-MRI sat at the end of an elongated table. The silvery cylinder was the size and shape of a 1950s era beehive hair drier turned on its side, except this one had a chaotic array of multi-colored wires sprouting from its head. Adam looked about the lab, half-expecting to see a hunchbacked assistant limping in through the doors.

"This little guy started out as a brain-scanning application. We now refer to it as a micro-MRI. It is capable of detecting and imaging very small particles, normally limited to a millimeter-sized resolution because of the inherent movement of live biological tissue."

"Like the brain in someone's head?" Adam offered.

A living brain, that is.

"Exactly. However, in your case, the medallion is not going to move and we may be able to get the resolution down to micron levels."

Adam finished Percy's thought aloud. "Sensitive enough to get a clear picture of the C-13 patterns in the medallion."

***

Linda and Adam were purchasing coffee from a vending machine in the hallway when an undulating and ear-splitting screech cut off their conversation. A mechanical voice followed with instructions for everyone to proceed to their designated safe zones. Not knowing where their safe zones might be, they started back to the TMS lab when Percy appeared in the hallway. He waved for them to follow him to a heavy metal door emblazoned with the universal black and yellow pie-wedge radioactivity logo and big black letters spelling out SHELTER A number of other scientists and technicians were fast-walking their way in the same direction. They descended the stairway to a large and windowless basement room. The blaring above them continued interspersed by a calm robotic warning. Then silence.

Percy turned to the two visitors now that things had calmed down. "That was an automatic alarm set to engage when we detect an unusual amount of radiation." He paused to look at the digital display on the wall near the stairway entrance to the shelter. An oscillating green line illustrated the recent emission. "Based on the energy scaling factor it looks like … neutrinos. A peculiar pattern—the burst occurred a few minutes ago, and now it appears it has ceased. Nothing more. Curious."

Adam asked, "You can detect neutrinos?"

"Deep underground we have a very large system that can do just that."

Linda asked, "Are they dangerous?"

Percy explained, "Not at all. Neutrinos are very small. They hardly hit a thing at the atomic level. Actually, most pass right through the Earth with no problem."

The shelter was not designed with comfort in mind, and the proximity of so many people in such close quarters spurred Adam to look more closely at Linda. She looked pale. Adam asked, "How long do we have to stay here? The neutrinos look like they have stopped, so can we go back up?"

"Only after the all clear sounds. We need to wait a while. It's really unlikely that this type of radiation, that is, neutrinos came from our labs, although we could produce some, I suppose, by subjecting certain elements to a high-energy beam of sub-atomic particles. Most of the work here generates much heavier particles, and the usual radiation would take the form of x-rays, gamma rays and such. We are shielded from that kind of radiation. And in any case, like I mentioned to Linda, neutrinos do not pose a health threat. In fact, millions of neutrinos generated by our sun are racing through your bodies right now. The real danger may lie quite far off … something like a supernova, and if so, we should expect a killer burst of heavy radiation any moment now."

Linda moved closer to Adam.

"It's all right." Adam brought an arm around her shoulders. He was well-aware of the possibility of a local supernova wiping out all life, not only here, but for a large chunk of the galaxy, with the only warning being a surge of neutrinos preceding the ionizing barrage of deadly radiation. Neutrinos would be the first to arrive since they were subatomic particles with nearly no mass travelling at near light speed.

Leave it up to Brookhaven to come up with a way to detect them and provide a warning system to boot.

After a few minutes, the mechanical voice announced that it was safe for everyone to return to their workstations. As people began climbing up the stairway and casual conversations resumed, Adam glanced at the radiation monitor's display and took notice of the exact time the neutrinos appeared. Color had returned to Linda's face.

When they arrived at the TMS lab, they found the medallion already mounted in the beehive scanner and the MRI's output displayed on a computer screen. Adam pointed at the screen. "Is that the medallion we're looking at?"

"It certainly is Adam. Let me show you something."

Percy used his keyboard mouse to maneuver the image. With a gentle tap or two on the keyboard, it enlarged and the patterns of the C-13 particles began to emerge. As Percy continued his tapping, the tiny specks came into focus. The honeycomb pattern found throughout the medallion gradually morphed into linear strands of bright white dots on the screen.

"Take a look at this." Percy pointed with his free hand at one of the strands of particles. "Notice anything unusual?"

Linda said, "You mean you've found something even more unusual than the fact that this gold medallion contains all these C-13 bits?"

Adam fought down a grin. "It looks like these particles are not all the same size."

"Quite, quite. In fact, there appear to be four distinctly different sizes."

Another mouse movement formed a box around a string of particles.

"I've been running the data into our analysis systems. When I zoomed in, it became apparent that the particles lined up in a kind of spiral pattern—sort of like on a phonograph record or CD."

Percy pointed to another screen nearby where a continuous line of peaks streamed by like on an EKG strip, but here the peaks were of four sizes.

Adam asked, "Is there a way we could check for patterns in these peaks?"

Percy beamed. "That's just what I was thinking. In fact, that's what the analyzer system is doing right now. It would take quite a while to look at all of the data, but I can check out a substantial amount by manually isolating a number of the rows on screen."

"How much exactly?" asked Linda.

"Oh, say a couple of million peaks."

As Adam pondered over these findings, a thought occurred to him. "By the way, were you doing anything out of the ordinary at around one-fifteen this afternoon?" Adam asked.

"That was about the time when I was setting up your medallion for analysis."

"What exactly did you do to set up the analysis?"

"Well, I was positioning it in the MRI chamber."

"Anything else?"

"Not much. I just fired up the MRI."

"What does that mean, 'fired up'?"

"The machine goes through an automated alignment procedure. After a short x-ray scan, the radio frequency detectors ..."

"X-rays?" Adam interrupted. "You subjected the medallion to x-rays?"

"Quite. Quite. I used the x-ray image for the alignment. The x-rays are not harmful. Sort of like the kind you might get using a fluoroscope. Perfectly harmless." A few key strokes later, Percy added, "The log indicates that the x-ray scan ran at exactly one-fifteen."

How crazy is that?

Linda asked, "Why would x-rays cause the medallion to emit neutrinos?"

Percy pushed up his spectacles.

Adam wondered.

Why indeed?

Chapter 13

Adam had dozed off on a tattered lounge in the lunchroom just outside Percy's lab. He roused himself and his blurry vision soon zeroed in on Linda snoring on a couch directly across from him. The digital wall clock silently announced that it was approaching five-thirty. Without having windows for a clue, Adam guessed, or rather hoped, that it was the afternoon and not the next morning. They had decided on waiting for Percy's analysis, which was taking a while. As he swung his legs onto the floor, he pulled over the laptop case and found an Ethernet port on the wall nearby. Within minutes, he was looking over the DNA analysis initiated what seemed like eons ago.

Linda's snoring came to a sudden, staccato halt. "Hey. What time is it? Has Percy finished?"

"I just woke up myself. It looks like it's late afternoon and I haven't seen Percy. By the way, did you know you snore?"

"Snore? Me? I think you got that backwards."

Adam grinned. "Guess what. The DNA sequence analysis is complete."

"And did you find anything of interest?"

"You could say that." Adam waited for a reaction, but was met with no more than a noncommittal stare. "There are definite patterns, especially in the non-coding portions of the DNA They're self-referential. Other patterns seem to act as switching points, kind of like 'if this is true, then do that'."

"So, what does all that mean?"

Adam eyes glazed over as he continued. "And yet others that repeat themselves throughout the DNA as if they are commonly-used routines." His mind drifted and he went on as if mesmerized. "Commonly used routines …"

Linda waved her hand in front of his eyes. "And?"

"These features … self-referential, switching points, repeated routines. I've seen them thousands of times before."Adam put the laptop on the waiting room table and sat back with his arms folded. "They usually represent a set of instructions, lines of code, like in a computer program. The non-coding DNA looks like a program, an algorithm … a huge and complicated one, but an algorithm just the same."

Linda sat up, her eyes wide. "So the coding portions of our DNA represent the proteins, the building blocks for our structure and function, while the non-coding DNA runs the show. It makes sense, and is consistent with some of the current theory. Especially when you think about the amount of non-coding DNA *we* have compared to lower life forms."

Adam shrugged. "Does it? Does it really?"

"What else can it mean?"

"You said it yourself. Lower life forms have less of this 'algorithm'."

"Sure, because they have a less complicated system to run." She paused mid-sentence. Something wasn't quite jelling. Her hands rose to her head and massaged her temples, as if trying to force the buried inconsistency to her forebrain. Suddenly her hands dropped, and she looked up at Adam. He nodded with each word she said. "Physical complexity might not be the sole reason for a larger algorithm in higher life forms."

Adam picked up the thought. "Because the differences between these life forms are minor. They all share a basic and symmetrical structure—one head, two arms, and two legs—essentially built from a similar set of blue prints. Higher life forms share the same parts. Minor modifications lead to different species."

"And that would mean that the significantly more complicated non-coding DNA is necessary for something else, something more developed in higher organisms."

Adam opened up his arms and coaxed her on. "And that would be?"

"The brain! The more extensive development of the brain demands a larger and more complex algorithm."

"Don't stop there."

"Christ. The structures of brains are also very similar, which means the algorithm is not just responsible for the structural details … "

"… but also for its function, which means that … "

Now Linda jumped in. "That the complexity of the thinking process is somehow mapped out in the non-coding DNA, which makes sense! Just think about the concept of instinct. For generations we've accepted that given a specific stimulus, animals can and do act in a pre-programmed manner. Sure, there's some learning involved, but there's so much evidence for automatic behavior, especially in simpler species where the range of behavior is limited and easily observed. Our current view is that higher organisms learn more and rely on instinct less."

"And what about Man? Is he free of this pre-programmed instinct?"

Linda shook her head. "Not at all. We relegate that instinct to the 'lizard brain' deep within our psyche—an animal instinct for survival. We pride ourselves with self-consciousness, self-awareness distinct from other animals. And we have come to rely more on learning for survival than on instinct."

After a moment to let all that sink in, Adam said, "Yet, our DNA has the highest percentage devoted to the non-coding portion. I wonder if you can tell when it's instinct or experience that drives us? What if everything we do is preprogrammed, just like in all those lower species that rely on instinct alone? In fact, if you think about it, we may be the most programmed life form on the planet."

Percy burst into the lunchroom, and while trying to catch his breath, he wheezed, "I've found something, something incredible."

The three ran to the TMS lab. Percy led them to his main computer screen and explained. "Like I mentioned earlier this afternoon, the C-13 particles line up in a spiral, and they consist of four distinct sizes. I was able to transfer the sequence of these four sizes for a string of about a million to our data analysis systems."

Percy used an irritatingly slow delivery. Adam prodded him on. "And you found?"

He continued in an almost robotic cadence, intermittently pausing to catch his breath. "Our protocol … consists of … first storing the data in files … which in this case simply means … that I gave them the numbers one to four."

Linda caught on. "Which means you have a big file with a linear sequence of numbers limited to those four."

"Quite. Quite. And then I looked for patterns. However, after hours of analysis nothing came up. No secret messages … or anything of that sort."

Sarcasm. Nice.

Adam said, "But you did find something."

"Quite. Quite. So then I searched other databases where we store information from a wide variety of sources."

Losing their patience, both Linda and Adam blurted out, "And?"

Percy's grin widened into a full-fledged smile. "And I found a hit."

Before they could spur him on any further, he turned their attention to the screen. "You see the colored bands displayed here? The one on top is a depiction of your C-13 sequence: red, blue, yellow and green for the four particle sizes."

Linda gasped. "And the one on the bottom is a DNA sequence with the four bases displayed in the same colors."

"Quite. Quite." Percy added, "And what do you see?"

"The two bands are identical. What is that DNA sequence from?" Adam asked.

Linda looked at the coding information displayed alongside the colored band and answered, "It's the DNA code for human albumin."

Percy turned a dial on his keyboard. The two bands scrolled in tandem across the screen. "As you can see, the identity is essentially one hundred percent, all along this sequence. Other portions of the C-13 stream appear to be lining up with other protein codes. The analysis is finding more and more correspondences. It would appear that your medallion contains a transcript of DNA, *human DNA*."

The weight of this discovery seemed to overwhelm Percy. He not only pushed up his glasses, but also wiped his forehead with the sleeve of his lab coat. "Did you really find it in a lump of coal as George explained it to me?"

The two continued staring at the screen, mesmerized by the symmetry displayed before them.

Percy went on. "If that's true, this is the finding of the century … maybe the millennium … I can't wait to let my colleagues know. The implications are staggering."

Adam broke away from the monitor. "It's true. That medallion is old, very old. But, could we wait a bit before we let the world know?"

Adam could see in Percy's eyes that he was not really paying attention. He was bursting at the seams.

Percy asked, "How is it possible that this disk contains a copy of our DNA sequence?"

Linda spoke up. "A copy? Maybe not a copy …"

Adam completed her train of thought. "Yeah, what if this disk is the original?"

Percy whispered, "My God."

The conundrum left them with little more to say. The three stared up at the display in awe, surrounded by the muted hum of lab equipment. After a few moments of introspection, Adam switched the topic to something that was nagging him. "Any ideas as to how x-rays make it send out neutrinos?"

Percy seemed taken aback by the question, but managed a response, and was visibly relieved at the change in subject. "There may be some trace elements buried in the medallion, elements unstable enough to break down when subjected to x-rays." He mumbled to himself. "Although I'm not sure any such elements exist."

Percy wandered over to the MRI chamber and stared at the medallion. "Perhaps we can have some experts here at Brookhaven take a closer look?"

A knock on the lab doors stilled further conversation.

Adam asked, "Expecting anyone?"

"Not at this time of day. Most people have gone home by now. Let me see who it is."

The hallway monitor displayed a man in uniform holding a package and swaying back and forth.

"Looks like a delivery man."

"Do people normally have free access within Brookhaven? Doesn't the gate call you up like they did for us?" asked Adam.

Percy swiveled to answer Adam as he reached to open the door. "Usually, but there are some delivery services that have open access."

Adam grabbed Percy's arm before he depressed the electronic door switch. "Do you recognize the uniform? Is that one of your usual delivery services?"

"Well … no. Come to think of it, I don't recognize the uniform at all."

Adam's eyes locked on Linda's. He snatched the medallion out of the micro-MRI apparatus and said, "I think we should leave. Right now. I've got a bad feeling about this."

Percy took a step toward the door. "Just let me see who this is."

Once again, Adam tugged him back.

Linda asked, "Is there another way out of here?"

"This is most irregular. If it makes you feel more comfortable I can call security. I'm sure they'll confirm this delivery is legitimate."

"I think it would be best if we just leave now, and even better if we left quietly."

"Oh well, if you insist. There is an emergency exit at the far corner. Just press down on the bar and the door will open." In a despairing tone, Percy said, "But what about these findings? We have to let the scientific community know about this so that other experts could examine the disk, confirm our discovery. You do realize that this means we are not alone? That there is something out there that may have created us?"

"It might mean that. And I agree … go ahead and share these data. In fact, make sure the news gets out to your colleagues and the press if you like. Maybe once the discovery becomes public we could put an end to these intrigues."

Percy looked at the disk in Adam's hand. "But, the disk. We need to safeguard it."

Adam opened the emergency exit door. "That's exactly what I am doing. Go ahead and let that fellow in. If he's not who he appears to be, just tell him we left a few hours ago." A nod and a wave sealed the deal, and Percy waddled back to the lab entry doors.

They ran to the rear of the building, crouching low and moving between several parked cars. When they arrived at the side lot, they got a clear look at the front of the building where a white van idled in wait. The two emerged from the evening shadows and walked past the van.

No signage or logo on the van. That's not good.

Percy's golf cart was just a few paces ahead.

"Can you see if the keys are in the cart?" asked Adam.

"Are you serious?"

Linda quickened her pace. When she reached the cart, she whispered back to Adam, "We're in luck."

Adam took the driver's seat, and Linda slid in next to him. They purred away taking several random turns within the complex of buildings. The Brookhaven streets were nearly deserted, and dusk had arrived. After a few dead ends they found the gatehouse street and parked the cart a few hundred feet short of the entrance.

They approached the gatehouse by foot. Linda looked to her rear. "Do you really think that Borman is at it again?"

"Not really sure. I guess I've developed an aversion to surprises and a fondness for suspicion."

"I don't blame you. In any event we could ask the guard to call Percy just to make sure everything is fine."

They walked up to the gatehouse, saw the Pathfinder parked in the visitor's lot, and got out their ID badges. Taken alone, a black limo parked alongside Adam's car was not quite enough to arouse suspicion. The blue-gray security cap lodged in the foliage surrounding the gatehouse could have been a lost article of clothing. By the time Adam reached the gatehouse door, the two disjointed observations screamed out a belated warning.

The guard pointed a handgun at Adam's head and drawled, "Hold it right there."

Adam, with Linda just behind him, gasped as the buzz cut head smiled and lolled to the side to get a better view of Linda. A ring dangled from his right ear, matched by one through his nostrils. His dark knit sweater was stretched over enormous biceps. As he rose from the stool, he pulled down on the sweater with his free hand, but not before it unveiled a glimpse of solid six-pack abs.

He looks like a professional wrestler. Jeez, and weren't they all just a little crazy?

On the floor behind him lay the body of a uniformed guard. Adam gripped Linda's arm and edged her closer to him.

"Ain't that sweet?" snarled Buzz Cut.

"What do you want with us?"

Adam's mind slipped into survival mode. Stalling the behemoth seemed like a good first step, at least giving him a chance to think.

"Ain't me you should worry 'bout."

A van screeched to a halt beside them. It was the deliveryman. Momentarily out of view, Linda broke away and ran over to it.

"Get the police! This man has a gun!"

At first, the deliveryman looked shocked, and then an expression of understanding calmed his features, and he laughed. Buzz Cut arrived with Adam in tow.

Using a polite voice, the deliveryman reached out of his window. "Please give me the disk."

Adam thought about arguing with the pair, however, it was clear they knew exactly what they wanted. He reached around his head and handed over the medallion to the driver.

"Now get in," commanded Buzz Cut.

"But you have the medallion. What do you want with us?" asked Linda.

Buzz Cut shoved the pair ahead of him while the driver scurried out and opened the rear doors of the van.

"No funny business. Just get in and stay quiet."

"What the hell is going on?" asked Adam.

They were shoved into the van. Linda tugged at Adam's jacket and pointed back at the gatehouse door. "Look."

The narrow angle made the view a challenge, but Adam saw the prone guard. One leg was moving. The doors slammed shut behind them. The van was otherwise empty and a heavy wire mesh separated them from the front seats. The driver and Buzz Cut slid in. They pulled up a short distance into the visitor's lot, and lurched to a stop alongside a black limo. Its darkened rear window rolled down.

The driver said, "Got 'em, boss." He leaned out of his window and Adam saw the medallion drop into a set of very white and gnarled hands. Although the limo's passenger remained unseen, the voice was a dead giveaway. "*Sehr gut* … excellent."

"And this too, boss."

A gold rod and a Luger dropped into waiting hands.

"Ah. Very nice. You know now where we are going to."

As the limo pulled away, the van driver turned to look back at Adam and Linda. "Make yourselves comfy. It'll be a while before we stop again."

He turned to Buzz Cut and handed him a set of keys. "Here, you'll need these. See you back at the farmhouse."

Buzz Cut exited the van. The driver pulled shut a sliding panel behind his head, cutting off any possible conversation, leaving Adam and Linda completely in the dark.

***

Minutes later, the gatehouse guard staggered to his feet. He was a bit unsteady and had a difficult time focusing, as a massive headache claimed his attention. Someone handed him his cap and helped him onto the stool. As he slowly regained his equilibrium, he turned to the door to thank the stranger for his help. The door was closed and no one was in sight. The guard shook his head. He lifted a phone from its cradle and proceeded to call HQ.

Chapter 14

Adam and Linda slammed into the walls as the van turned and accelerated. They had found nothing in the dark to help them escape. Wedged into a corner, they braced up against one another for support, both physical and spiritual.

"Do you have your cell phone?" asked Linda. "Oh, oh … we left them in the bin outside Percy's lab."

"Don't forget the car keys were in there too."

Which were now with Buzz Cut, no doubt following us in my Pathfinder.

Adam felt Linda trembling, and it was not just from the van's vibrations. He recalled her anxiety in the mine, in the enclosed space behind the secret door. Despite the cold air inside the van, her blouse felt wet against his body.

"Are you okay?"

"I … I'll be all right. Just need to focus."

Her breathing came in short bursts.

"I'm guessing you're a little claustrophobic?"

"I can usually beat it down … but just now…"

Adam held her tightly. "Try to relax. We'll be okay. If these guys wanted to harm us, they would have done so already." Adam could feel her warm breath against his chest. "We'll get through this just fine … I promise."

After a few minutes the ride evened out. They appeared to have reached a highway. Linda brought her arm around his shoulders and they cocooned themselves against the chilly evening air that seeped through the van walls. The adrenalin rush had exhausted them, and it was becoming hard to stay alert, to ignore the seductive, hypnotic monotone rumbling. Morpheus soon embraced the duo in his comforting arms.

***

Adam woke up with a start. All he saw was black. Blinking his eyes, everything came back to him—they were still in the van, but it was not moving. He felt about. "Linda, where are you?"He crawled along the floor, reaching out, searching and whispering her name.

She's gone!

The doors were still locked. The sliding panel at the forward end would not budge. He slid down against a wall and sat with arms propped up by his knees. His head lolled between them and he listened. The beating of his heart was steady and loud, as if magnified. After a few minutes, his pulse slowed and he focused on the sounds outside. There were none. No traffic, no people chattering. He thought about Linda, about how stupid all this was, and in a fit of anger he swung both arms back and struck the wall panels. He beat the walls over and over hoping that the thumping might get the attention of someone outside. Time passed and no one came.

Adam leaned back against the wall, contemplating defeat. It was then that he noticed something strung about his neck and dangling over his chest. He reached into his shirt and pulled the chain over his head. He felt the disk in his hands—the weight of it, the hole in its center.

But how could this be?

As if in response, a scraping broke the stillness. Adam returned the medallion about his neck. His hackles stood on end. The scratching seemed to come from everywhere. He crawled over to the front wall and listened again. This time it came from the rear, from the doors.

"Hey! Is there someone out there? Get help, I've been kidnapped!"

No reply. The scraping ceased for a moment, as if surprised by Adam's outburst. When it resumed, it was louder. Maybe it was an animal, a bear. Maybe he was abandoned in the woods somewhere. That would explain the silence, and the scratching.

"Hey! Mr. Bear, forget about it! You can't get in here."

The scraping paused, and started up again. The van shook slightly with each unnerving scratch. He made his way to the doors. When he slid his hands along the flat metal, he found several long indentations. His hand recoiled as another scrape raised a groove.

He crawled back to the front of the van. Beads of sweat ran alongside his face, down his neck and soaked his shirtfront.

Adam stared at the back doors, or at least where the doors should be. Tiny pinpoints of light drew an outline of the door frame. The sounds changed pitch. Suddenly a crescent of light crossed his face. A gash appeared in the door. The sounds of tearing metal accompanied more slashes of light. Adam sucked in his breath and pressed his back against the front wall of the van in an effort to get as far away as possible. His eyes locked on the doors. The number of jagged gashes grew.

The slashing stopped. An elongated, ragged hole in the door revealed nothing beyond. The sounds had ceased.

Maybe the bear, or whatever, moved on.

He crawled to the hole to get a better look. It was big enough to crane his head through. Ben Wuijcak stood a few paces away with hands on hips. He stared at Adam with his bespectacled eyes wide open and his mouth in a sardonic twist.

"Ben!"

While Adam struggled to get past the shock, Ben canted his head to the side. His mouth curled up into a smile.

"Adam. My dear boy."

"Ben, help me get out of here. Watch out for the bear."

Adam was too stunned for coherent thought. His mind seemed to be trapped in a kind of psychic molasses. He should be wondering why Ben was here.

"Adam. My dear boy."

He's repeating himself.

Adam tried to reach the door handles through the opening while keeping a steady eye on Ben. He managed to grab one, but it would not move. Ben continued to smile. He seemed unconcerned about Adam's plight.

"Adam. I'll help you, but first give me the medallion."

Ben's eyes squinted. His brows lowered. His demeanor shifted from weirdly happy to bizarrely serious.

The medallion? He wants the medallion?

Ben approached the van, and with each step his body seemed to blur, shifting out of focus. At first Adam thought there was something wrong with his vision. Ben seemed to be changing as he neared. Facial features elongated, the eyes sunk into dark recesses, the cheeks became more pronounced, and the mouth grew larger. His eyeglasses fell off and long, sharp teeth erupted from the widening mouth.

Ben snarled through two very long canines. "Give me the medallion." He played out his arms and opened his hands. "Give it to me," he snorted.

The long claws protruding from his fingertips compelled Adam to roll back into the van, hoping to stay out of reach. The doors flew from their hinges with a single motion. The spectacle entering the van now looked like *Bigfoot* himself—its clothing shredded, and peeled, revealing the oversized chest and legs of this massive, hairy monstrosity.

It grunted through its yellowed teeth with spittle dangling from the hairs on its chin. "The medallion."

Adam had nowhere to run. A sudden lunge and the creature was at his throat, pinning him down to the van floor. He was powerless against its immense strength. Furry arms swiped at his chest again and again. Blood and cloth flew before his eyes. He felt detached, remote, as if he was sinking into the deep warm covers of his bed, pulling the pillow over his head. His eyelids grew heavy. His awareness dimmed out. He glimpsed the creature's hands cradling something shiny and gold, covered in dark, red spatter.

My blood.

The creature grunted. Then it turned to look down at him, cocking its head. Its arms rose for a final blow. Adam's eyes closed. Gray faded to black. His body shook.

"Adam. Adam. Get up, I think we've stopped."

It was Linda's voice. Everything was still dark. He felt her arms around him. Not quite convinced he was awake, his fingers ran over his chest. The shirt was intact, no sticky blood, and no medallion. He stiffened as he heard a scratching at the van doors.

"It's okay. Someone is opening the doors."

"Sorry, Linda. A bad dream."

The doors opened to starlight that outlined two vague shadows. It was night and the moon was not in the neighborhood. Damp air wafted into the van, carrying a pine scent. The chirping of crickets and the croaking of frogs completed the impression of a countryside venue for their evening outing. A flashlight clicked on, momentarily blinding them, followed by Buzz Cut's raspy voice. "We're here. Get out."

"Where's here? What's this all about?" asked Adam, while helping Linda out of the van.

Adam received a shove for an answer. Buzz Cut held a revolver and motioned the duo to follow the driver who held the flashlight. They single-filed their way along a narrow, winding trail surrounded by fir trees tall enough to obscure most of the night sky. As they entered the forest, the chirping and croaking faded away. The only sounds they heard were of their own footfalls crunching on uneven ground, and the lofty whispers of a meandering breeze. Minutes later, the group paused at a clearing. The hazy twilight outlined a large two-story farmhouse at its far end. As they neared, a barn and silo at its rear and a small pond to the side completed the bucolic picture. The trail led up to a wooden gate set within a six-foot stonewall which surrounded the house. Several ground floor windows sported a soft yellow flickering glow. When they reached the gate an overhead light flashed on and illuminated a backdoor astride those windows.

The van driver reached up to a post near the gate and whispered. Moments later a dull click announced the release of a spring-loaded latch and the group moved through to the farmhouse grounds. When they were several paces into the compound, the latch clicked behind them. Adam turned his head to look back.

Buzz Cut said, "Turn around and keep moving. You should be more interested in what's ahead."

The driver opened the backdoor and Buzz Cut prodded Adam. "Go on in."

They stepped into a plume of warm air and the sweet smell of burning wood. A large sofa and a pair of sitting chairs faced a crackling fire set in a huge stone hearth. Above the mantle a shotgun and two deer heads to either side spoke of a hunter's den. A framed Swastika emblem hung above the shotgun. A variety of blackened metal pots, ladles and spoons hung from beneath the mantle.

Where are the cauldron and the witch? Make that a Nazi witch.

The fireplace was large enough for a person to stand inside. Several glowing logs sputtered atop the raised grating. The fire threw off a bright buttery yellow light, which danced elongated shadows on the walls.

"Sit," said Buzz Cut.

Adam and Linda sank into an overstuffed divan replete with pillows. The driver remained standing just inside the door, while Buzz Cut assumed a position at the room's interior entryway. He looked back into the darkened recess of the house as if expecting someone. Minutes passed. Adam did not mind the wait. He was happy to absorb the heat of the fire, dispelling the chill. Gentle shuffling sounds, slippers to rug, announced the arrival of their host.

"Good evening. Or should I say good morning?"

Herman Borman entered the room wearing a silk burgundy housecoat. He eyed the couple on the settee and sat on a leather-upholstered chair next to the fireplace facing them.

"Mr. Borman, why have you brought us here? You have the medallion," Adam asked with a trace of exasperation in his voice.

Linda added, "It's outrageous. You can't kidnap people. You'll go to jail for this."

Adam placed a hand on Linda's shoulder, trying to settle her down. It was clear they were in a bad situation.

Herman tented his hands together as if praying. He placed his chin atop finger tips. "My, my. I am doing you two a favor. Consider yourselves my guests. Since you are both scientists, I thought you might like to see what your so-called medallion is really all about."

"Adam, let's leave. Now."

Linda arose and Buzz Cut moved between her and the door. She sat back down with disgust splashed across her face and snarled, "Guests? I didn't think so."

"Please try to relax my dear."

Adam asked, "How did you find out about my medallion?"

"*Your* medallion?" After a moment, Herman continued. "I have dedicated people throughout this coal mining region. After discovering the artifacts in the mine years ago it became clear they were part of a device, a device beyond our technology that was left on this planet a long time ago."

"Wait a minute. Are you saying you're the one who found the artifacts?" asked Adam.

"Why, yes. Actually two of my miners came across the find, but they were too stupid to realize its importance. So, I had some of my more trusted colleagues conduct a thorough dig."

Linda asked, "Was that by any chance the day the mine flooded?"

In the warm tones set off by the hearth Herman's face assumed a deep ruddy blush. The voice was cold when he answered. "That was an unfortunate accident. It had nothing to do with me or my men."

Adam gave Linda a quick look. Her eyes had become thin slits.

Herman turned the topic back to the find. "Once we collected the metallic pieces, it became clear that some parts were missing, and that they may have strayed away from this immediate area, possibly sent out with local deliveries. My only hope was to keep a vigilant eye. My people monitored all the nearby museums and universities as well as testing laboratories for any clues regarding golden artifacts."

"The lab explosion. I know that was you," said Adam.

For a moment Herman seemed taken aback. "The explosion was not my doing."

"But you knew about the analyses."

Herman nodded. "We were there the next morning … looking for the medallion. I assure you the explosion had nothing to do with us."

Adam recalled the near encounter with someone in the shadows of the blown out lab later that same day when he went back to retrieve his laptop.

Herman continued. "A discussion with your friend George pointed us to you."

The fake cop.

Adam followed up with a change in direction. "What about Ben Wujciak? Did you visit him too?"

Herman looked confused, but answered with a steady voice. "We never had any interest in Dr. Wujciak. He was convinced that more artifacts like Hedda's might be found. We thought him harmless enough, so we let him dig around in the mine. In any case we could easily monitor his excavation finds just in case he got lucky. He certainly seemed obsessed about the matter."

Unlike you.

Herman continued. "Back at the mine you gave us quite a chase"

Linda said, "You people had no right. To … to chase us across town and hunt us down like animals."

"Ah, yes. Linda. You certainly did not act lady-like when you threw the table upon me. Perhaps *you* are the animal?"

"And I'd do it again if I had the chance!"

She attempted to rise, but Adam held onto her.

"Tsk, tsk," Herman chortled. "You have quite the temper."

Turning to Adam, he asked, "But tell me, what did you do to my assistant?"

"The fake cop?"

"No, not that one. It took him some time but he eventually made it down. I'm referring to the other one. His name was Steven."

"Ben told me he lost the guy at the far end of the building."

"'Lost' is an interesting choice of word. Steven was indeed 'lost' in a manner of speaking. We found him along the riverbank. Rather dead."

Chapter 15

Adam felt himself go cold. "That's not possible. Ben told me himself that he lost the guy, your man Steven, in the breaker. Maybe there was an accident."

"Yes, an accident. Accidents can happen. Then there is the matter of the missing policemen. When Paul and I left the mine, we passed a police cruiser along the way. There was no one in it. We assumed the police were on foot elsewhere, but when I checked with my law enforcement connections the next morning, no one knew where they were."

Herman stood and directed his men to bring along his guests. The group followed him into an adjoining room where a small table lamp spot-lighted bookcase-lined walls. He drew aside a set of heavy drapes to expose an illuminated alcove. Linda drew herself nearer to Adam. An assembly of glimmering components sat on a pedestal—cylindrical and cubic shapes protruded from the three-foot pyramidal construct. A flag emblazoned with a Swastika draped behind the exhibit hinted at a deep and frightening purpose. The spotlight from above gave the bizarre hodgepodge a brilliant golden sheen and an unsettling feeling the alien machine could sputter to life at any moment. Adam's medallion sat squarely in the heart of the apparatus, like a centerpiece on display in a museum devoted to cutting-edge sculpture. It was at once astounding and bewildering.

"So, what do you think?" asked Herman as he clasped his hands together, rocking back on his legs.

Adam asked, "What is it?"

"It is a talisman."

Herman pointed to the center of the display. "You have investigated this disk? Yes?"

Adam nodded but his eyes were drawn to the details of the pseudo-mechanical wonder surrounding his disk.

"Then you know that the disk is not of this Earth. Yes?" Without waiting for a response, Herman continued. "We have been waiting for years for this sign, proof of the existence of a superior race on this planet. This machine is an undeniable testament to such a race. All the theories and beliefs of our forefathers are now validated. With this unearthly object we can call together our sons and daughters to prepare for a new world order, a world order that has been too long in coming."

As Adam expected, Herman relished the chance to share his story. Starting with allusions to the Aldebarans and Aryans living within the Earth, he pointed to the inevitable rise of the glorious Fourth Reich. While Herman blathered on, Adam continued his visual analysis. Since the disk contained a stream of data, it must have been read and translated into some kind of action. He spotted a rectangular component with a slit imbedded on one end. Several other suspiciously functional-looking parts seemed out of place. Logic did not seem necessary to reassemble the putative machine, rather, the endeavor appeared hasty, aimed at building an idol, a tribute to an alien god.

When Herman paused to draw a handkerchief from his robe, Linda said, "Just how do you propose this thing will act as a call to a new world order?"

Herman wiped his chin. "Scientists like yourselves will be given the chance to examine the materials and conjecture on the purpose of this machine. Its age and workmanship will provide convincing evidence that it was the work of an ancient and superior race. Their conclusion will be that this race descended from the original Atlanteans who now live beneath the surface of this planet waiting for the moment when they can re-emerge and assume their rightful place. When these findings are announced to the world, the news will call the Aryan nation into action, preparing the world for a new age."

Adam asked, "How can you be sure that these scientists will conclude so much from a few bits of metal?"

"Ach, Adam. My scientists will be free of the prejudices and biases of your stagnant society. They will be open-minded and willing to explore possibilities."

"I get it. They'll think like you do, and conclude what you want them to. Borman, what do *you* think this device was?"

"What I think is unimportant. Its original function is unimportant." Herman pocketed his handkerchief. "Once the masses are aware of its existence and origin, we will be able to shape their response. The rise of the Fourth Reich will be a certainty when we rally our Aryan brothers from all over the world. It may take some time, but we will attain our dreams of an ordered society properly ruled by pureblooded humans with superior strength and intellect. There are no limits to what such a society can achieve."

The theme was all too familiar. Adam felt like he was on the set of yet another B-movie with bad guy Nazis secretly preparing to take over the world. He looked at Herman with a kind of perverse admiration. "That's quite a plan. And what do you want with us? Isn't it enough you have the artifacts? You've got your talisman, now you can let us go."

Adam was almost sorry he brought their plight up, since the response was likely to sour Herman's disposition.

Herman extracted the handkerchief once again and wiped at his chin. "For the time being, the details of this machine will be kept a secret. Our followers will be busy for the next few weeks leaking information to the media about the finding, about what our scientists are saying, and what it all will mean. The media are easy to control. A worldwide following will require attention to detail and precise cultivation.

"Now as for you … I had a hope you might volunteer to be the first scientists to announce the artifact to the world. Fame and fortune would quickly follow. I thought it only right that your efforts in this adventure be rewarded. Of course, I can see now that will not be possible. It is a shame. Besides, we cannot have you contacting the media with contrary stories. I'm afraid you two represent an obstacle."

Linda exclaimed, "But others already know about the medallion."

Adam lifted a finger to his lips.

"We are aware of George Freedman back at your university. He had a rather limited understanding of the medallion, but even that could be a problem. A simple traffic accident will take care of the matter, isn't that right, Otto?"

So, Buzz Cut had a name.

Herman contorted his face into a look of mock empathy. "And before you ask … Hedda is an ignorant old lady of no threat to us. However, your friend Percy at the Brookhaven Laboratories was another matter." Herman paused to look at his wristwatch. "By this time an unfortunate laboratory fire has both ended his life and destroyed whatever data you were able to collect."

Adam lunged at Herman, but was slammed to the floor by Otto. Linda jumped on top wrapping one arm around Otto's thick neck while beating him about the head with the other. A moment later she flew across the study, and rolled to a stop at the foot of a bookcase.

Herman made a show of shaking his head in disapproval while closing the alcove drapes. Adam crawled over to Linda. Both Otto and the van driver had pistols drawn.

"Are you all right?"

Linda rubbed her arm. "I think so."

"Thanks for jumping in."

The moment was brief and the situation dire, but lying there on the floor, it was electric. In that instant they looked into each other's eyes and saw themselves as one. Whatever was about to happen, it would not change what they had become. Their fear was replaced with anger and a grim determination to survive.

Herman asked Otto. "You brought Dr. Dove's automobile?"

Otto nodded.

"I think it is time to bid farewell to our guests. You know what to do."

Otto and the driver ushered the two captives to the living room, and as they emerged through the backdoor exit, Herman bade them farewell with a wave of his handkerchief. "Have a safe and pleasant trip."

Don't you mean short and sweet? You son-of-a-bitch.

They trudged along the gravel pathway to the gate. Otto looked back to Herman at the farmhouse and the gate door buzzed open. When they reached the small parking area beyond the stand of fir trees, Adam nudged Linda and whispered, "Do you see what I see?"

Edging itself over the horizon, a half-moon peered through a wisp of clouds. A silvery tree line surrounded the clearing, and a black wedge jutted up in the distance against the firmament—a structure all too familiar.

"The breaker," said Linda.

Otto barked from the rear. "Hey, you two. Shut your traps and get in."

The driver opened the van doors and pushed them inside. There was no point in asking any questions. Adam noticed his car parked in front. The van started up, moved a few feet, and lurched to a stop. The driver rolled his window down and yelled, "What's wrong?"

Otto angled his head through the Pathfinder window. "Did you hear that? It sounded like a gunshot, like from far away."

They listened for a few moments. A chirrup of a Blue Jay flying overhead heralded the resumption of the normal din of forest sounds. Far off somewhere a rooster crowed.

"Damn, Otto. I don't hear nothin'. Let's get goin'."

The van pitched forward.

"How are you holding up?" asked Adam.

"I'm okay. We're in a mess aren't we?"

"As I see it, they're about to dispose of us. You could say that would be the bad news."

"And the good news?"

"We're still alive. It looks like they're arranging for us to have an accident, or else we would have been shot already. Accidents seem to be popular with these guys."

"That doesn't make me feel much better."

Adam hugged her. "We'll have to make a move when they stop. It sounds like we're following a car ... probably Otto in my Pathfinder."

Linda said, "So, I'm guessing they're going to use your car?"

"Listen, we're only going to have one shot at this. There're two of them and two of us."

Linda said, "Which one do you want?"

Adam smiled and although the interior of the van was dark, he knew she was smiling too. He brought her closer and they kissed. Their embrace became fire. Heat and passion mingled, flowed through their bodies. For a moment the terror surrounding them faded away. They rejected it. The one person they had become, alone in the void and focused on survival, refused to succumb to fear.

The van rolled to a stop.

Adam drew back. "I'll take Otto. When we get out of the van, make it look like you've given up ... get hysterical, cry if you can."

"Oh, I think I can do that."

"We need a distraction that might make them careless, even for a second. We have to attack without hesitation, without mercy. Our lives will depend on it."

"You do recall that they have guns."

"Yeah, but if they really plan to set up an accident, I don't think they'll want to use them."

***

Herman closed the backdoor. He hated the early morning chill. The dampness played havoc with his arthritic shoulders and knees. He limped over to the fireplace and stood before it soaking in the heat. His eyelids lowered as he reviewed the events of the day. His plans had worked out perfectly. The Aldebaran artifact was complete. Invited scientists would be arriving later this day. He was looking forward to their reactions. After so many years of planning and waiting, the deep feeling of satisfaction intermingled itself with the warmth of the hearth. He felt rejuvenated, young again.

He adjusted several of the smoldering logs with a poker and looked on as they flamed up while settling into the divan. With a sofa pillow in his lap he stared at the flames and listened to their sizzling and popping. He sank farther into the sofa. Then the door opened.

The man who walked in was tall, a bit over six feet. He wore a jogging suit, black with thin white stripes along the arms and legs. The cold air which followed him inside was like a splash of ice water to Herman. He focused on the face. It was oval, dark-complexioned, and sported large round eyes with a jaundiced sheen. Tiny black pupils darted left and right. The hair was close-cropped and black.

"Who are you? How did you get in here?"

As the thin-lipped mouth parted to answer, Herman reached into his housecoat and pulled out a Luger. He brought it up to aim, but the gun pulled away from Herman's grasp and flew through the air, landing in the stranger's gloved hand.

"How? How did you do that?"

The reply was slow with an exotic foreign air. "You have the … disk … the golden disk."

It was more of a statement of fact than a question. Before Herman could stop himself, his eyes betrayed him with an involuntary glance in the direction of the study. The stranger ran into the adjoining room. By the time Herman pulled himself out of the sofa, he returned with medallion in hand. Opening the door, he tossed the Luger out into the yard and turned to Herman. "You are mistaken … with your theories."

The stranger ran out into the pre-dawn darkness. Herman staggered out of the sofa and seized the shotgun from the mantle. Propping the door open with his foot he fired at the receding shadow. After a moment, the smoke cleared and Herman walked toward the gate, but found nothing. The stranger was gone. He fumbled through the pockets of the housecoat looking for his cell phone. He had to let Otto know what just happened. The phone was dead.

***

The van doors swung open to a faint glow in the eastern sky. Adam heard the rustling of leaves through nearby trees. Otto stood by the rear of the Pathfinder about thirty feet beyond the driver who was holding one of the van doors. Both had their revolvers out.

Otto spoke up first. "Let's go. Get out of the van."

Adam and Linda stepped down and the driver assumed a position to their rear, prodding them toward Otto. Adam's Pathfinder pointed away and toward a thin line of tall pine trees, black against a gray mist. The rustling sound did not come from above, but from below. As they neared Otto and the car, it changed into a dull roar, the kind of sound fast-moving water made as it squeezed through rocky channels.

We're on a cliff, and that's water below us.

Linda fell to the ground and began to sob. Both Otto and the driver stood their ground with pistols raised. Adam saw them exchanging grins. Linda looked up at the pair, and then at Adam. She screamed, jumped up and attacked Adam, slapping at him in a hysterical fit. "You freaking asshole! You got us into this mess! I hate you!"

Caught off guard by the suddenness of the assault, Adam raised his arms in defense. "Linda! Stop it!"

She came at him like a demon, beating at his arms and shoulders with roundhouse blows that Adam was barely able to deflect. He stumbled backwards and grabbed onto her, wrapping his arms around her shoulders in an effort to put a stop to the madness. Linda kicked at him as he held on, shrieking all the while. The pair grappled with each other in a kind of macabre dance, accompanied by a medley of grunts and groans.

Otto and the driver moved in, their grins became grimaces. In that moment, as they lowered their guns, Adam rushed at Otto and Linda, at the driver.

The driver was careless and his gun fell to the road as he and Linda tumbled to the ground and rolled into a ditch. Otto was not as careless. Adam's hands clenched Otto's right wrist, keeping the weapon pointed upwards. His momentum pushed Otto backwards toward the Pathfinder crashing them both into its rear. Otto's free hand grabbed at Adam's face, twisting it away, trying to gouge his eyes. The fingers found purchase on his right eye and the pain was immediate. Adam moved his right hand to deflect Otto's left away from his face. Unfortunately, this gave Otto a distinct advantage. He had the strength of two. Adam fell back as Otto pushed off the car.

The prospects of survival were fading. In a moment of inspiration brought on by sheer desperation, Adam cocked his head back, closed his eyes and smashed his forehead into Otto's nose. The sickening crunch yielded warm, wet goo splattering his face, and Otto's body and arms went limp. Adam swung his knee up between Otto's legs. The gun fell to the ground as Otto bent over and grabbed at his crotch and face. Adam wiped the ichors out of his eyes and searched for the fallen weapon. It was a few feet away, but before Adam could take a step, he rocketed forward—his arms seized by Otto's massive limbs. He toppled to the ground face first, spitting out dirt and gravel. The behemoth was on his back, pressing him to the ground. He couldn't breathe, he couldn't move. An arm cradled his head and began to pull. His spine bent backwards, nerves in his neck screamed. The pain was shutting down his mind. His vision narrowed.

So this is how it ends… damn.

Adam saw stars and dancing lights. And then the pressure disappeared. He lay on his back. Otto was gone. He shook his head and squinted. Fragments of a face floated before his eyes.

"What? Who?"

"Easy, take it easy. It's okay."

The voice was distant. It was Linda's. The jigsaw puzzle of her face gradually came together before his eyes.

"This is becoming a habit, you know. Me, waking you up."

"What happened? Where's Otto?"

"You don't have to worry about Otto."

Linda gave Adam a peck on his lips. "Feeling better?"

Adam had to admit that the kiss was a fine way to return to the world of the living. He propped himself up on his elbows and looked about. The rising sun had breached the horizon line, sending bright yellow slivers across the road. Otto lay unmoving on the pavement near the Pathfinder.

As if reading his thoughts, Linda said, "We had a little help."

She tilted to the side. Adam followed her gaze. Leaning against the van was a shadowy figure dressed in a dark jogging suit. The figure nodded and held something glittering in its hand—the medallion.

Linda said, "I'm just as confused as you."

Chapter 16

Linda helped Adam to his feet, steadying him as they walked arm in arm toward the van.

Adam asked, "What about the driver?"

She nodded in the direction of the ditch alongside the road. "Out cold."

Adam caught sight of a pair of legs splayed out near the road edge. "Great job."

"It wasn't me."

Adam took a good look at the man in black as they drew nearer. The eyes—big, round and yellow stared at him without blinking. Hints of epicanthic folds gave the stranger an oriental air. A sullen, swarthy skin tone added to the inscrutable flavor.

When they were a few paces away, Adam whispered. "Strange looking character." Linda agreed with a nod. They stopped a pace away and Adam said, "I understand we have you to thank for getting us out of this mess."

Thin lips widened into a smile. The man held out the medallion in his gloved hand and said, "I think this belongs to you."

Adam stowed it in his trousers pocket. "How did you get this?"

"From the ... farmhouse."

Impatient for more details, Adam asked, "Now, don't get me wrong, but who are you and how did you come to be here?"

"We came here because of that disk."

"That really doesn't help. We? Because of this 'disk'?" asked Adam.

The man straightened up, nudging himself off the van, and winced. A red streak stained the lower leg of his jogging suit.

"You're hurt," said Linda.

"It appears that I have been … wounded."

Adam bent down to take a closer look. He pulled up the tattered black cloth. "Looks like you ran into some BBs. I'd say from a shotgun?"

"It is a minor lesion, of no consequence."

"It might be minor, but it must hurt like hell. How about we get out of here before Herman sends more of his people out after us? I'm sure that Otto was supposed to call in or return by now."

Adam asked the stranger, "You have transportation?"

"Not here."

"Then how did you …" Adam caught himself as he noticed a dark red smear along the roof of the van.

Linda ran over to Otto and went through his pockets. "Got the keys!"

She dug farther and came up with a cell phone. Repeating the search on the driver, she tossed both cell phones into the woods and returned with two handguns. The three clambered into the Pathfinder and took off.

Dawn had arrived and the ominous outline of the Knox Coal Mine breaker followed them through breaks in the tree-lined road. They drove along a rise that followed the Susquehanna river. The colliery sat on the opposite side a few miles away.

Linda turned to the man in black seated in the rear. "So what's your name, if you don't mind us asking you? We appreciate what you did for us back there. You saved our lives."

"The name is not important, but if you prefer, you can call me Alpha."

"Alf?" asked Adam.

"Alpha. Like the first letter of your Greek alphabet."

My Greek alphabet?

"You just made that up, didn't you?" asked Adam. The stranger grunted, but it was hard to tell if it was an answer or merely a reaction to his injury. Adam thought a moment about asking about his last name, but decided that could wait. "Well, Alpha, you showed up just at the right moment. We've got a lot of questions which I'm dying to ask, but first we're going to make a stop to make sure you don't bleed to death."

Linda asked, "Where exactly are we going? To the police?"

"That would be the right thing to do, but maybe later. Right now we need a place to clean up, to talk … and to eat. I hope Hedda is an early riser. Breakfast would sure hit the spot."

***

"We won't stay here long, Hedda," Linda burbled between mouthfuls of pancakes and eggs. They sat around a wooden table in the second floor kitchen of the mining museum.

Adam sauntered in."You sure look better after washing up," said Linda.

"Herman will search for us, and it's likely he'll come by here, so we'll need to hurry," said Adam. He turned to Hedda and said, "Hedda, "Have you seen Ben since yesterday?"

185

Hedda scowled and shook her head. "Ain't seen 'im. Maybe he went back to New Jersey."

I don't think so.

"Now ya no never mind 'bout him or Herman. Eat up. How 'bout some more coffee?"

Both Adam and Linda gave her a nod. While the two dived into the pancake stacks, Alpha looked on from the end of the breakfast table, seeming to study them.

Hedda said, "Your friend there doesn't have much of an appetite."

Adam slugged down his coffee and turned to Alpha. "How's that leg feel?"

He had managed to extract several buckshots from Alpha's calf. Peroxide, gauze and an Ace bandage finished the patch up.

"Much better. Thank you."

"Maybe now would be a good time to clear up some things."

"Perhaps I should begin," said Alpha.

Hedda planted the last of the pancake stacks on the kitchen table and slipped into a chair. The sounds of munching and rattling dinnerware died down as the three watched Alpha straighten up in his seat. "I have surmised that you know something of the disk … that is, its contents?"

Adam said, "How do you?…Well … we know it contains genetic information."

"Correct. It contains all the design information necessary to build humans."

Linda paused sipping her coffee. "To build us? That's quite a claim. How would you know this?"

"Your disk is not unique. Others like it were found in many other places … in other parts of this galaxy."

Her coffee spilled. Linda hurriedly placed the cup down and wiped at the wet tablecloth with a napkin. Adam's eyes widened. Hedda shook her head from side to side.

Adam was the first to respond. "Perhaps you can begin at the beginning?"

Alpha leaned back into his chair. "Please do not be alarmed, but I must tell you that I am not from this planet."

Utter silence followed the statement, with the minor exception of Hedda's exaggerated exhale.

Adam said, "You don't look like an alien…"

"You mean that I am not 'a little green man', nor do I have the requisite bug eyes and antennae? No slim gray body with a bulbous head?"

A sarcastic alien.

Adam said, "Well, your eyes *are* a bit unusual."

Ignoring the comment, Alpha continued. "I, along with a number of others … we are on an expedition. Your discovery of the disk was reported to us a number of years ago."

Adam asked, "Exactly how was it 'reported'?"

"A neutrino emission. About twenty of your years ago, our ship detected the emission and diverted our course here. There have been several more such neutrino signals … at your university and at the Brookhaven facility. These neutrino emissions serve as a kind of signature unique to the disk."

Twenty years ago. Old Flora in Ben Wujciak's office.

"How is it you're speaking English? And why do you look so much like us?" asked Adam.

"Like I said, the same design disk was also discovered on our home world. We have all been manufactured using identical blueprints. As to English, after the neutrino detection, our ship systems enact procedures for revival and training. The trip here was a long one … about ten years of your time. As we neared your planet, we were able to calculate the geographical origin of the first emission … and we listened to your broadcasts.

Alien visitors in the movies always claim the same thing.

"Detecting neutrinos twenty years ago would mean …"

"Our ship's technology provides constant acceleration, with terminal velocities significantly approaching that of light."

Adam said, "Ten years for the neutrinos to reach you and ten years to get here. So you had the chance to observe and learn. What do you mean by revival?"

"Most of the crew is in stasis to minimize the aging effect and slow down the demands of metabolism during the long voyage. When we detect the presence of a disk from a system along our flight path, necessary course changes are automatically made and the ship's systems revive a select few of the crew to investigate and possibly undertake contact."

Adam was not sure if it was the pancakes or this conversation that was causing his indigestion. Feeling a bit disoriented, he probed further. "Let's say that you really are an alien. And, let's say that there really are these disks out there. I assume as parts of machines that are designing … no, constructing … *did* construct humans or humanoids. What's the deal? Who put these machines on all those worlds? And for what reason?"

Alpha bent forward and placed both elbows on the kitchen table. "That is the question, Adam. I can tell you this much—the coding, what you call DNA, is not limited to building blocks or structural information. The majority of the coding represents a complicated set of instructions, which directs human behavior … our behavior."

The algorithm.

Adam looked across at Linda, who said, "The non-coding DNA. That's about ninety-eight percent of our genome."

"A big set of instructions," said Adam.

Linda continued. "We had the chance to examine those sequences using statistical tools that Adam developed. Adam, didn't you find that it looked like a programming language?"

"That's true. Many sections were self-referential, almost like subroutines set up to run when certain conditions are met. Alpha, you … your people, do they have the same non-coding percentages in your DNA, in your genetic code?"

"Very similar. As is also true of all the members of our crew."

Hedda had quite enough. She stood up from the table and said, "My God. What nonsense."

Alpha looked up at Hedda and then turned to the seated two. "Have you ever wondered why humans have a need to procreate? Why they have an overwhelming urge to have children and raise them, and teach them? And why they constantly seek to discover?"

Linda said, "But that's a characteristic of most conscious organisms on the planet. It's not unique to humans, and in any case, species survival is at the heart of it all."

Hedda coughed to clear her throat. "Still sounds like nonsense to me. I'm going lie down for a bit. Let me know if ya need anything else. I'll be in my bedroom."

Adam said, "Hedda, thanks very much for the breakfast. We'll clean up and be out of here very soon."

As Hedda shuffled off, Adam continued. "So, these disk-machines created life?"

"As far as we can surmise, they have been found on planets with chemistry favorable to life. As you know, carbon-based chemistry is naturally predisposed to evolve into more complex systems. In time, self-replicating organelles form that may lead to even more complex systems given the right circumstances. A primitive form of life may have already been present when the machines arrived. They seem to have been sent out many millions of years ago, but late enough in the evolution of planetary systems to focus on solar systems containing planets with the best chance of supporting the development of humans."

Linda asked, "How can you be sure?"

"We are not sure. We can only speculate. But we do know that each planet where a disk has been found has about the same size and has similar chemistry, and is dominated by a human population."

Adam asked, "So, what is it we are programmed to do? I mean, besides procreate and making sure our species survives?"

Alpha wrinkled his brow and answered, "Humans have one other characteristic that sets them apart from other intelligent species, here and elsewhere. They have a burning desire to learn and build on technology. They, that is, we, are compelled to understand our surroundings and ..."

"...and explore," Linda thought aloud.

"Yes, explore."

Adam said, "Jeez … you're saying we were made to insure our survival over the millennia and at the same time, explore? To what end?"

Alpha smiled and raised an arm, pointing upward.

"To go into space? That's nothing new. We enjoy finding out what's what, so space is a natural. Is there something more?" asked Adam.

Alpha's thin lips straightened into a line as he responded. "Our purpose does appear to be directed at space, but not just to explore. We believe the real reason may be to report back."

Adam was taken aback by Alpha's comment and saw by Linda's expression that she was in the same boat. This conversation could go on all day. He looked at the wall clock and rose from his chair. "It's nearly nine. We need to move. Herman and his fanatics have already killed for this disk, and we are the only ones left, the only sane ones anyway, who know about him and what this disk contains."

Alpha interrupted. "That is not exactly true. You are forgetting about Dr. Wild."

Linda asked, "You know of Dr. Wild … back at the Brookhaven Labs?" As Alpha nodded Linda said, "Dr. Wild was killed in a lab fire … at least that's what we were told."

Alpha said, "Fortunately for him I was there. I arrived shortly after the neutrino burst. I saw you two leave and a man enter the laboratory of Dr. Wild. When he left, I found Dr. Wild bound and unconscious, and an electronic device attached to a cabinet, a cabinet containing flammable solvents. It was an explosive mechanism, so I destroyed its circuitry. After I released Dr. Wild, I went after you. At the outer perimeter of the complex I found the unconscious guard, and arrived at the parking area just in time to climb onto the back of your van."

Linda said, "That was rather heroic. Do you make a habit of saving people in distress?"

Alpha rolled his oversized eyes up, as if trying to recollect a similar situation, and then said, "No. But the disk is important, and I wanted to make sure that my mission was successful."

Adam asked, "And what mission is that?"

"The expedition mandates that we contact the discoverer of the disk. In addition to the genetic code the disk contains other information … what we believe may be time stamps … points of space-time origin. This knowledge will allow us to more accurately plot a course backward to their origin. It would appear that the Makers await us."

That last comment threw Adam. "Makers?"

"That is what we call them. It is the Makers that we seek."

Adam asked, "So why didn't you just take the disk and fly off?"

"That is not our way. You need to decide if I take the disk."

Linda asked, "Were you at the mine by any chance?"

"We just arrived a few days ago. A neutrino signal led me to the university, but not before the explosion. However, afterwards, I was able to follow you to the mine."

"I thought I saw someone near the mine entrance, near the willow trees," Linda said.

"Willow trees? Yes, I was there."

"And I bet you were behind the door when we made our escape through the rear?"

"Most perceptive."

Adam asked, "So, why didn't you just save us then?"

"I could not risk detection by the person you called Dr. Wujciak."

Adam legs weakened and he sat back down.

"This Dr. Wujciak is from our ship. He is of a human species very capable of mimicking, of appearing like someone else." After a beat, Alpha said, "He belongs to a group of subversives that have infiltrated our expedition. Their number on our ship is uncertain but we think it is no more than a few. This is the first instance of one leaving our ship."

"That seems like a crazy thing to do. He's opened himself to discovery."

"Fanaticism. These individuals believe that the purpose of the expedition is flawed, that it is against Nature … against God's will. And that our expedition represents an unholy blasphemy."

Adam nodded. "I visited Dr. Wujciak's office before coming back up here. I found him dead. But then his body disappeared, along with clippings and notes describing a variety of strange discoveries through the years. When he showed up at the mine I was shocked, but he seemed like the real deal. More recently I found out that he may have killed one of the pursuers at the mine … and maybe others. If you know about him and the other subversives, why don't you just remove them from the ship, or at least lock them up?"

"We have many individuals on board. Of these, a small number are either of his species or one similarly capable of disguise, so in this case we have a list of suspects. However, our centralized instrumentation shows that everyone is presently accounted for. We have only two crewmembers awake right now, and I am one of them, thus making the search for the missing crewmember problematic. I have no doubt our monitoring devices were altered. However, he will need to return, at which point we should be able to identify and secure him."

"Assuming he does return," Adam said.

"True. That he went to see Dr. Wujciak would be logical since the original signal could be traced to that location. To these fanatics, how do you put it, the end justifies the means, and this false Dr. Wujciak will do anything he can to destroy the disk, including killing you or me."

"Or himself, no doubt."

***

Hedda chose not to lie down. She sat at her bedroom window and stared out at the street below. Adam and Linda were in deep trouble. Now they've tangled themselves up with this stranger, Alpha.

Alpha the alien.

Whatever he is, he's in danger too. The police were likely to be in Herman's pockets, so that meant just about anything was about to happen. As she mulled over the situation, a black limo pulled up outside the museum. She undid the safety of the 45-automatic in her lap.

Chapter 17

Hedda looked in through the kitchen doorway. "Quick. Ya need to get out o' here now. Herman's limo just pulled up outside." The three followed Hedda to a window at the head of the stairway."Ya can get out that way. The fire escape'll take ya down to the back where your car is parked."

Adam asked, "But what about you?"

"Don't worry 'bout me. I got a score to settle with that bastard, and it might as well be now."

Glass shattered on the wooden floor below, and the door chime jingled.

"Get goin'. I got some customers downstairs that need tendin' to."

Adam hustled the other two out the window and onto the railing of the fire escape. He handed Linda the keys. "Wait for me in the car."

Hedda slipped her revolver into the folds of her dressing gown and descended the unlit staircase. When her line of sight cleared the ceiling of the first floor, she saw the outline of a man standing in an overcoat silhouetted by the light from the front doorway. He leaned forward at the creak of a riser. She continued down the stairs, slowing, trying to avoid setting off any further alerts.

"Hedda, is that you?"

She knew Herman's voice. Fighting down an urge to answer, she steadily made her way to the base of the stairs.

"Now I see you. It is you, is it not? I have come here for the disk. Dr. Dove's car is in the rear, so I know he is here. My people are surrounding the place as I speak."

Hedda took a few steps forward. Something in his hand glinted. It was the blue-black barrel of his Luger.

"What're ya thinkin'? You're trespassing, breakin' and enterin'."

"Hedda, I have no argument with you. I just want that artifact returned to me."

"No argument with me? You bastard!" Tears welled up in Hedda's eyes as she recalled the day Luke died. "It wasn't enough that you took that damn treasure for yerself, sendin' twelve miners to their watery graves while ya did it. Luke knew what you did. You made sure he got the worse shifts … the most dangerous jobs. You had to keep 'im outta the way, keep 'im quiet … and then another damn accident, and he were gone."

Herman's shadowy figure began to drift. "You are a crazy old woman. Get out of my way."

"Yeah, you were cleared by the company, but you and I know different."

While Hedda reached up with her free hand to grasp her eyeglasses and wipe at her eyes, Herman snarled, "So what does it matter? Your husband was a loser … and so are you."

In that instant Herman moved forward and raised his gun, an action which precipitated several nearly simultaneous events. Three shots rang out. Hedda stared at the figure before her, staggering and then crumpling to the floor with a sigh. She dropped her gun, fell to her knees and clutched her thigh. A loud moan brought Adam racing to her from the base of the stairway. A red stain oozed through her gown.

"Hedda. Are you all right? Were you hit?"

She slumped to the floor and curled up in a fetal position, rocking back and forth. Her hands grasped a leg and were covered in blood.

Sirens approached. Adam heard a car, the limo, start up and screech away. He began to shake as the rush of adrenaline raced through his body. He had never fired a gun at anyone before. He ran over to inspect Herman's prostrate form, rolling it over. The overcoat opened to reveal a white cotton shirt with a large dark stain in the center. Herman had died instantly. He pocketed his gun and turned back to Hedda. The smooth wooden floor was broken by a patch of upraised splinters surrounding a small round hole in the floor.

Was that Hedda's shot ... or mine?

***

Officer Bloustein sipped at his Styrofoam cup yet again, apparently using the action to gather his thoughts. He replaced it next to his keyboard, looked hard at the screen, and then at Adam seated across the desk. "It looks like I have everything I need. I still don't get why Mr. Borman pulled his gun."

"He seemed out of control ... yelling something about an artifact and that Hedda better hand it over or else."

"Yeah. You already told us that. Shooting at Hedda just doesn't make sense."

"He seemed very angry. Is she going to be okay?"

"The EMT boys said it was a flesh wound. No major blood vessels, no bones broken."

"Thank God. She was just trying to defend herself."

"Yeah. You told us that too. We'll get her official statement at the hospital."

"What about the guys in the limo?"

"We have an APB out on that limo. We know it well. It's just a matter of time."

And just a matter of time before you visit Herman's little farmhouse and make some more interesting discoveries.

Adam had been careful not to mention the kidnapping and the attempted murder the night before. Right now he just needed some time. Bloustein had also asked about the missing policemen. Their last call came from the mine, and their abandoned patrol car was found near its entrance. Everyone knew the mine belonged to Borman, however, as there was no obvious connection between Adam and the mine, the questions appeared to be routine.

"Then we're done here?" Adam asked.

"For now. But I want you to stay someplace local. I don't want you leaving town until we get the coroner's report and forensics finish up. It may take a few days to get everything straight. Here's my number."

Adam took the card. The police report would say that Hedda defended herself, that two shots were fired, the fatal one striking Herman Borman in the heart. The coroner's report would corroborate Adam's story.

But the forensics report could be another matter. Ballistics might point to a third shooter, and we don't want to forget the hole in the floor.

Linda and Alpha were long gone. After the shooting and before the police arrived he gave his gun to Linda. They agreed to regroup at the Starlight. The challenge of explaining Alpha to the police was happily avoided. It was late afternoon when Adam was finally released.

***

The early evening news hissed through wavering shades of green and orange, slightly out of synch with the anchorman's undulating mouth. Adam stepped out of an incredibly refreshing shower, but was still worn out. Donning the clothes he wore for the past several days did nothing to revitalize, rather it had the effect of reminding him of the twisted situation in which he and Linda were ensnared. Each step seemed to take all his concentration. He passed Alpha seated on the edge of a bed and angled himself into the single desk chair in their room.

The police had escorted him to the Starlight Motel. Linda and Alpha arrived by foot shortly afterward. They all knew that the half-truths Adam told the police would eventually unravel. Their time at the motel was going to be short.

Linda held out a box of cold pizza. "Here. Have a slice. It'll do you wonders."

Adam gratefully accepted it. "What a crappy TV. I guess the digital world hasn't quite arrived at the Starlight."

"Excuse me," said Alpha. "My fault." Alpha's left hand moved over his glove and the image cleared up.

"What does the glove do?" asked Adam.

"It is an electromagnetic device which allows the user to attract or repel anything made of iron or any other ferrous-like metal."

Such technological eccentricities from their guest were becoming the norm. Adam found himself accepting that the man was not from the neighborhood and in so doing, found Alpha's story surrounding the disk more believable with each passing minute.

"What are we going to do now?" asked Linda.

The question verged on the rhetorical. Before anyone could take a shot at an answer, a familiar scene unfolded on the twenty-inch screen. A reporter announced that she was at the Brookhaven Laboratories, and that a statement was forthcoming from one of their leading scientists. She started to say that it dealt with the discovery of a prehistoric artifact when a mob of reporters spilled out of a building behind her. Adam recognized the building. The broadcast cut to a different view, a close-up of the reporters gathered around a scientist. Only the top of this head was visible. It was Percy Wild. In his hands he held printouts and a photo.

The camera zoomed in and swayed with the movements of the throng. "Ladies and gentlemen, by now you know that we have analyzed an artifact millions of years old. Further investigation has revealed that this relic, a disk made of gold, contains data. The ramifications of the findings are staggering and will change the way we view ourselves as a species forever."

A reporter in the crowd yelled. "What kind of data?"

Another asked, "Where did you get it?"

Percy took his time answering, which had a two-fold effect—giving the mob a chance to simmer down, and hyping the drama, something that Adam guessed was the principle objective of the interview.

"Quite, quite. We can announce today that we have found an artifact estimated to be millions of years old that contains a coding which appears to be a copy of human DNA."

The crowd noise ebbed for a moment, as if letting the news sink in, and then, as if a bomb was set off, the mob exploded with questions. They converged on Percy, jostling his body and jabbing at his face with microphones and cameras. In spite of being swallowed by a riot of reporters, he managed to go on, screaming into the nearest camera. "These are pictures of the artifact and printouts of the analyses. We are currently studying the data with the help of scientists from around the world. These findings will revolutionize our thinking about the origins of humans on this planet, and perhaps the origins of life itself..."

Percy was abruptly swept away by the force of the crowd. The camera shot cut back to the network anchor who closed with a promise of more information as it became available.

Linda continued staring at the screen even as a commercial came on. "I guess the cat's out of the bag."

Adam said, "The reporters will dig out the source of the artifact, and then we'll be in the news and the whole sordid story will catch up with us."

Alpha said, "It is time I make my position clear. As I pointed out earlier, it will be your decision to give me the disk or not."

Adam asked, "Remind me again. Why don't you just take it?"

"Our collective mandate is one of discovery and respect. We will only take the disk if you are willing to give it to us."

Adam reached into his pocket and brought out the medallion. "This may be of great value to us, here on Earth, but it seems it might serve an even greater purpose in your quest."

Alpha said, "There is one more decision you will need to make … and that is whether you would like to join us on this expedition. I offer you both the opportunity to become part of our quest, to search for the origins of our human race, to seek out the reason for our being. In short, to confront our Makers and obtain the answer to the fundamental question of all time … why we were created."

That was the Krakatoa of proposals. It left both Adam and Linda speechless and nearly breathless. A tidal wave of questions inundated Adam's mind. "You have room for us? How long do you think it will take?"

There were many more questions—the problem was that they all tried surfacing at the same time.

Alpha said, "We can spend hours going through the details. There is room on the ship. After a short training period you will be placed in stasis. You will be integrated into our automated duty schedule and be awakened periodically. The schedule will allow you to meet others and to study the data collected during the journey. When we reach our destination everyone will be revived."

Linda asked, "And the trip … how long would we be gone?"

"Our current estimates place the home of the Makers approximately two hundred light-years distant."

Adam and Linda looked at each other.

"Afterwards, we plan to return everyone to their respective planets … to report on our findings. In your case the round trip is likely to take about five hundred years."

That would pretty much make it a one way trip.

Alpha continued. "It is a decision I expect will need some time to consider. However, as you know, we have very little time. Might I suggest that you talk it over with your family and friends. If you choose to join us, you must do so with full realization of the commitment. It will be a long voyage, but rest assured that you will have comfortable quarters and your ageing process will be slowed considerably by both relativistic effects and biological stasis. We should journey back to your home town this afternoon before the police are aware you are gone. We can meet again tonight. I will need your decision by then."

"What if only one of us wishes to go?" Linda asked.

"Then you must both remain. It is our policy to add crew in pairs, compatible pairs. From what I have observed, you are such a pair."

Adam looked at Linda.

Was she smiling or was that a smirk?

They agreed to return to their Scranton suburbs. They further agreed on a meeting place if indeed both decided to accept the invitation—a secluded portion of the Schill campus, behind the practice football fields at 11:00 p.m.

The trip back was uneventful and silent. Adam's suspicious nature insured they would not be followed. After taking a circuitous route with many unnecessary turns, he dropped off Linda at her home about a mile from his own and promised to call her later in the evening for her decision.

She handed him his gun. "I won't be needing this."

Minutes later he bade Alpha a goodnight from the brick stoop of his own home. As Alpha disappeared into the evening, Adam found himself wondering if what happened this week was not some daydream fantasy—that he would suddenly wake up and find himself lecturing organic chemistry. He was staring at the front door when it opened. His mother scolded him for staying away so long without a word. She questioned him about the dark stains around his jacket collar, and whether he had been hurt. He hugged her and held her with his eyes shut tight, taking in the sweet smell of her, and for a moment, welcoming a flood of long-forgotten childhood memories. He was so happy that he hardly noticed that she kept up the chastisement as they entered the house.

The door clacked shut and she said, "I can heat up some soup, or maybe you'd like a sandwich too? There's meatloaf in the fridge."

It was suppertime.

Chapter 18

In 1980 Adam and his father had just returned home from a film festival honoring the flying saucer movies of a quarter century before. Adam was standing in the driveway staring up at the night sky. Billowy clouds were illuminated from beneath by city lights. He stared at a black patch between the gray, cotton-like masses, and then he saw them—three lights moving between the clouds maintaining a steady formation. His heart leaped into his throat so much so, that for a moment, he was frozen in place and could do nothing but stare. His father waited for him at the front porch.

"Dad! Come over here! Look up there! Flying saucers!"

Adam focused all his attention on the black patch and now saw a fourth, and then a fifth speck of light join the formation. They flew behind the clouds.

He heard his father approach along the driveway and as he turned his head, the corner of his house came into view. When the clouds drifted behind the roof line, his heart sank. He was looking at stars, and the moving clouds had fooled him into thinking something entirely different.

"What is it son?"

"Aw, nothing dad. Just thought I saw something."

***

Adam sat on the front porch of his house gazing at those same stars drifting between puffy gray streaks. His eyes were moist. He had told his mother about the adventures of the past week, the analyses of his medallion, the chases, the kidnapping, the shooting and finally, Alpha and his offer … an offer for the Ages. Anyone else listening to these stories would assume they were made up, and in fact, that maybe Adam was delusional. His mother took it all in stride, listening to every word with no more alarm than she would if Adam had just returned from high school and was catching her up on the latest teen gossip and intrigue.

He wiped his eyes with a handkerchief and blew his nose. His mother followed him out to the porch swaddled in a woolen wrap and carrying a tray of cookies and coffee."I brought you some dessert, honey."

She sat down in an Adirondack next to his, placing the tray on a small table between them. The night was cool with a mild breeze. Adam pulled up the collar of his wind breaker. "Thanks, mom."

She sat back in the chair and held a cup to her mouth, gently blowing over it and absorbing its aroma and warmth. For a while, she stared straight ahead, looking to be deep in thought. When she turned to Adam, her face appeared placid, relaxed."You look troubled, honey. Is there something you haven't told me?"

"Oh … I think I told you everything. It's just that I don't want to leave you." Adam's voice cracked and he sighed to cover the near sob. "I don't know if I can do this. I'm going to miss you."

"And I, you."

She placed the cup down on the arm rest and put her hand on his shoulder. "Now look. If what you told me is real, which I still have a problem getting my head around, then you have an opportunity that no other human being in history ever had, or perhaps ever will have." She looked up at the stars and pointed to them. "We've been staring at those buggers ever since Man crawled out of his cave."

She leaned back into her chair. "When I was a child in Lithuania, I remember sitting out in a pasture one night, a warm summer's night. Our family had a farm in the countryside, miles from the nearest village. There were no clouds, no moon and the stars were so bright it was like everything glowed. You could see the grass and road and trees sparkling all around. The Milky Way looked like a river up there, a beautiful silver river made of thousands … no, millions of stars. Of course, I didn't know it was called that but I could see so many, so many."

She took a sip and smiled at Adam. "They taught us in school that each one was a sun, kind of like ours. So looking at all those little specks, I wondered which ones had planets, which ones had people. What kind of worlds were out there that we could never know. Were there people out there staring up at the same sky with our sun one of their stars? Were we going to be kept away from each other forever, never to know each other even existed?"

Adam was taken aback. That his mother was so philosophical wasn't something he expected.

A dreamer, a dreamer like myself.

Adam said, "That's the question we all have at one point or another. *Now* I know … we know, there are people out there, just like us."

"And you have an invitation to meet them, speak with them … to see other worlds."

"But at a cost, mom. I'll never see you again. I'll never see my friends again. If I do return, it'll be hundreds of years from now. Nothing will be the same. Everything I know and everyone I love would be gone."

His mother smiled and nodded. It was a vision he knew would be etched in his mind forever. "You're worried about me. No need for that. I've had a wonderful life. Your dad and I were very proud of you … our little scientist. I'll be fine. Besides, there's always my sister in New Jersey." She laughed. "I'm sure if your dad was standing here, he would give you the thumbs up. It's the price of knowledge, Adam." Her face turned solemn. "You know, I would not hesitate to take the trip if it was me."

"Even if it meant leaving dad?"

She paused a moment and said, "It would be a terribly difficult decision, but I think I'd still go."

Adam wiped at his eyes with his index finger, and shook his head.

It must be where I get it from.

***

"Are you stupid?"

Linda was tempted to throw her kitchen phone against the wall. Instead she held her temper and the phone a little longer. Her sister, Terry, raised her voice. "Do you hear me? I asked if you were stupid?"

"I'm going to slam the phone down."

"Don't you dare! You listen up, girl. You got yourself mixed up with something that's got nothing to do with you. First of all, you have a career, a real job. You're a friggin' biochemist with a real future. What are you thinking about? Leaving with some jackass who claims he's from outer space? Do you know what that sounds like?"

"I told you. He has proof. One look at him and you'd know. He knew about the medallion and he knows what it contains. How do you explain that?"

"Sister, he's got you bamboozled. Any two-bit con man could talk you into anything. He's probably after the damned thing. You said it's made of gold. That's it. He's working you."

"It's not like that. He had it and gave it back to us. I told you what happened. If mom and dad were still alive I'd be talking to them and not you. They'd listen and understand."

"*Dios mio*. They're probably listening now, and anyway, what do you mean you wouldn't talk to me? I'm your older sister, you better talk to me."

"I need you to listen and not shout at me. I'm old enough to know what's real and what's bullshit. I trust your judgment but you're not listening to me."

There was a pause in the debate, long enough for Linda to wonder if Terry was still on the line.

"Hello? You still there?"

After a moment more Terry replied in a muted, calmer voice. "Yeah, I'm still here. If I wasn't a thousand miles away I'd be there, knocking some sense into you. Did you tell Celia. Did you tell your little sister you're about to go flying into outer space with a man you hardly know and a mysterious, tall, dark and alien stranger, and I stress the alien part?"

"No, I haven't. I just thought I'd talk to you first. After all, you're the oldest of us three. You're the one that I always relied on for advice." Linda paused to suck in a sob. "Besides, I may be in love with Adam."

"That's just great. Love and outer space. Are you listening to this?"

Linda held her tongue.

"Linda, you've unloaded a story and a half. It's just that it's so screwed up. I'm not sure what to believe."

"Believe me. Better yet, believe *in* me."

"I do, Linda. You've always been the smart one, the tough one. All I can offer is my experience."

They were both silent for several long minutes. Once again Linda worried that Terry had hung up.

Then Terry said, "You know what? I can't really help you here. This one's in your court. If you're sure that this alien, Alpha, is telling you the truth, take him up on it. And if you love Adam, or at least think you do, then stick with him. I have to say I don't believe half of it, but I do believe in you, Linda. I really do."

Linda could hear muted breathing, as if a hand covered the receiver on the other end. She began to cry.

"Now stop that," Terry said between her own sobs. "I know you said you'd be gone a long time, but girl, I'll wait for you anyway. I don't give a shit if it takes a couple of hundred years. You know damned well I'll be here waiting for you."

"I know."

***

Adam's coffee went untouched. An earlier call from Linda confirmed that she had decided on the expedition. The voyage of a lifetime was about to happen. Fate shrugged and extended its fickle hand to embrace a little known organic chemistry professor and a promising young biochemist, offering them a spectacular chance to represent Earth in the quest of all time—to discover other worlds and the origin of mankind, not only on this planet but on countless others. In return it asked only that they give up their careers, family, friends and all that was dear and familiar to them. In short, give up everything.

Adam had moved the chairs together and had his arm wrapped around his mother's shoulders. This was to be their last evening together and he intended make every precious moment count. With his eyes tightly closed, he could see his dad standing alongside them. Dad looked happy and that was a good feeling.

Undulating colors, red and blue, seeped through his eyelids. Adam flicked them open and caught sight of a distant patrol car approaching. No siren. The cruiser came to a stop at the corner traffic light.

"Mom. I think the police may be coming for a visit."

She stirred and said, "How can you be sure that they're headed here?"

He stood to get a better look. "I did promise to stay at the motel in Pittston, so they're probably a bit ticked off. I'll know in a moment."

When the light turned green, the cruiser shut down its flashers and continued on a steady pace as if searching for a house number.

"They are definitely looking for something nearby."

He took a look through the porch window at the clock mounted over the mantle. "It's almost ten. I think it's time I go."

They embraced a final time. Adam wanted the moment to last, but his mother gave him a shove. "You need to go, so go now. Don't disappoint me or dad, do a good job out there. Be brave my honey. I love you very much."

"I love you too, mom. If there's any way I can get back sooner, I will. I promise."

He entered the house through the front door, and ran to the kitchen. He did not look back because he could not bear to, and besides, he did not want his mother to see him blubbering. He grabbed the kitchen phone and called Linda. A few short moments later he was in the back yard. A glance up the side alley confirmed that the cruiser had stopped in front of the house, alongside his Pathfinder. Linda would be coming around with her car to the back of his block in a few minutes. Adam slipped through the neighbor's shrubbery and waited in the shadows.

Chapter 19

"Looking for something, Dr. Dove?"

Adam almost broke into a run. He straightened up and a uniform stepped out of the shrubbery and into the faint light of a distant street lamp.

"Over here, sir."

"Sorry, you surprised me."

The officer brought hand to mouth. "I found him. Come on around to the other side of the block."

"I'm sorry, officer. How can I help you?"

It would be mere seconds before the patrol car showed. The officer hadn't yet drawn a gun.

"It looks like headquarters has some questions … about the death of Mr. Herman Borman."

"But I've already given my statement."

"We're going to need you to come with us."

The officer brought one hand down to his holster. A pair of headlights turned into the street. The corner lamp reflected a blue hood—Linda's Corolla. When the officer looked around, expecting to see his partner, Adam pounced and brought him to the ground.

"I'm really sorry about this."

In the struggle, he struck the officer across the chin as hard as he could and winced at the pain in his knuckles. The officer groaned, spewing garbled invectives. The Corolla pulled up and the passenger side door swung open.

"Get in. We need to move fast. There's a police car coming up the street."

Linda's hoarse whisper sprung Adam into action. He jumped in, slamming the door shut. They took off with a mewling screech just as a patrol car entered the street, flashers on and siren blaring.

Linda turned to him as she floored the accelerator. "You have the medallion?"

She was wearing a sweatshirt with the hood pulled over. Her voice was low and raspy, strained with tension.

"Yes…of course."

He looked in the side mirror and saw the cruiser pause. Then its headlights burned bright as it picked up speed.

Linda said, "Hold on."

The car veered. Tires screamed as they shot through a narrow line of streets. Linda found a side alley and shut off the headlights. While they coasted along the unlit passage, Adam searched the rear view for any signs of blue and red. "Take care not to step on the brakes."

Linda threw him a curt nod of her hood. "Let me see the medallion."

For some reason Adam felt his flesh crawl. The hairs on his neck stood erect and his heart began pounding. "Why do you need to see it?" He glimpsed at the dashboard clock. "Shouldn't we be more worried about getting out of here? It's early, but I wouldn't mind waiting at the football field … assuming we can get to it without being stopped by the police. I'm sure they've called in for backup by now."

Linda shut down the engine. Her cowled head craned forward to face him. "Give me the medallion."

Her voice was a snarl. An image of a howling beast flashed before Adam's eyes. The cowl hid most of her face. She wheezed.

"Are you okay?"

Linda's right hand flew off the steering wheel and snatched Adam by his jacket collar, pulling him toward her. Her left grabbed his head, forcing him to look into her face, a face that appeared to be squirming. Her nostrils flared, the cheeks puffing in and out. The eyes were pulsating. Sweat was pouring down along her temples. One moment she was Linda, in the next, she was Ben Wujciak.

"You're … you're not …," he sputtered, while struggling to get free. "You must be the other one, the one Alpha warned us about."

"In this you are correct."

The alien heaved Adam into the dashboard. He was in a world of pain and confusion, dazed by the knock on his head. Not waiting for the interior of the car to stop swirling, he pushed open his door and tumbled out, hoping to put some distance between him and the monster in the car. Instead, he ran into a pair of arms that held him with a steel grip, and then tossed him onto the narrow alley sidewalk.

He crawled for cover where there was none and was hauled up and thrown again, this time landing against a chain-linked fence. His legs felt rubbery. With his back against the fence, he slid down to the pavement and watched as a blurry figure approached.

"The medallion, please."

Adam merged several images into a single fearsome one. The scant light in the alleyway made it difficult to make out details, but he had the impression the face continued changing.

"Did you kill Ben Wujciak?"

The alien paused before answering. "That was a regrettable error. I came to him for information, and he became extremely agitated. After a lengthy interview, his heart failed him."

"So, you took on his looks, you became him. And you went to the mine …"

"Seeking out further clues as to the location of the disk. And then you showed up."

"Why didn't you just take it from me then?"

The hood moved side to side. "You had hidden the disk. I would have interviewed you, but there were too many witnesses that would need to be removed. For the last time Dr. Dove, the medallion."

The alien took a step forward into a faint sliver of light descending from a nearby window. He was holding his hand out. Adam noticed that the other hand, still poised on the alien's hip, was gloved in a metallic mesh. He reached into both of his jacket pockets. With his left hand he withdrew the medallion and tossed it into the air toward the gloved hand, and said, "Here, take it."

When the alien reached for the golden disk, Adam pulled out a revolver with his other hand. Quick to catch on, the alien moved the gloved hand toward Adam's gun. The trigger caught on Adam's finger and the weapon fired as it was whisked away. The alien grunted, dropped the gun and fell to the sidewalk. Its face had stopped writhing. It had a neutral, pale featureless quality. It coughed with every inhale. Dark splotches mottled its thin lips.

"You do not know what you have done. That medallion cannot ever be made known. Destroy the cursed object. Destroy the evil for the sake of your planet."

"Hold on. I can get you back to your ship. We're going to meet with Alpha in a few minutes. Just hold on."

A deep gurgling issued from the open mouth. The alien spat and coughed some more. "The expedition must be stopped … in the name of all that is holy … God cannot be known by Man. It is a blasphemy … a sacrilege."

"Linda. What did you do with Linda?"

Dark red bubbles emerged from the alien's mouth and it seemed to pass out. A second floor window slid open. Shadows moved behind curtains. Adam pocketed the medallion along with the gun. Precious seconds ticked by as he dragged the alien's body into the rear seat. Once in the driver's seat and after confirming no car had entered the alley, he moved off in the dark. At a cross street, he flicked on the headlights and blended into the traffic. The dashboard clock read 10:46 p.m.

Nearly ten minutes later he pulled up to Linda's house. No lights had been left on. The front door was unlocked. He ran inside, afraid of what he might find inside.

"Linda. Linda, can you hear me!"

He sprinted from room to room, turning on lights and calling out her name. He stumbled over a half-filled backpack at the head of the stairs, a sobering discovery. The house was dead quiet, but as he moved along the upstairs hallway, he heard a distant humming, a kind of mechanical purr.

It appeared to be coming from the other side of the house. He hurried to the window at the end of the hallway. The one-car garage had its paneled door pulled down

It hit Adam hard. He had no time to lose. He sprung open the window, hung suspended from the sill for a moment and dropped into a juniper stand below. When he rolled up the garage door, a cloud of white exhaust fumes billowed out and revealed a rusty white VW with its engine running.

Linda was slumped over the steering wheel. He almost tore the car door off its hinges, scooped her up, and dragged her out of the garage. There was a raised bruise on her forehead and her lips were red.

Please let that be lipstick.

He laid her on the asphalt drive and shook her shoulders. She stirred, choking, gasping for air. Her eyes opened and fixed on Adam, and then she retched.

"Damn, I'm sorry about that."

He lifted her to a seating position. She coughed a few more times and then steadied herself with both hands on the driveway. "I don't know what happened. I remember throwing some things in a backpack. Then everything went black."

"It was Wujciak, or rather, the alien Alpha warned us about. He pretended to be you and tried to get the medallion."

"Pretended? Where is he now?"

"Nearby."

Linda tried to get up and Adam caught her as she teetered.

"Whoah. I'm dizzy … and boy, what a headache."

"You'll be okay in a little while. You really need oxygen, but I'm afraid we have a deadline to meet."

"I think I'll be okay."

Adam steadied her with his arms beneath her shoulders. They toddled to the front of the house, and leaned against the Corolla.

"We've got a couple of minutes to meet up with Alpha. Are you sure you want to do this?"

Linda opened the driver's side door. The overhead car light illuminated her face and Adam saw some color returning. She rocked back and forth for a moment and said, "I'm certain."

She ducked her head as if to enter the car, but instead, turned back. "I think you better drive." She vomited again, this time making an effort to avoid hitting Adam, which was only partially successful. "I think I feel better now."

On the way to the campus Adam related the alien encounter and its unfortunate conclusion. They both glanced at the body in the back seat several times during the recap. Although it remained still throughout the drive, it was hard to shake off a feeling of dread, of an imminent threat.

It was 11:00 p.m. when they eased through the main gate. Except for the dorm, most of the university buildings were dark. They circled around McArdle Hall. Even after a week of repair work, streamers of yellow tape, orange traffic cones, and scaffolding surrounded it. Light, noise and music spilled out from nearby student quarters. It was just another school night. They motored farther on, headed to the dark outline of the Schill University Stadium.

Adam said, "The practice fields will be just past the stadium."

A minute later, they arrived at a gravel road that led to the fields. Adam caught sight of a flashing light in his rearview mirror.

Police?

He pulled over to the side, hoping the patrol car might pass them.

No such luck.

He rolled down his window as a campus security guard greeted them. "Good evening folks."

Adam conjured up what he hoped was a pleasant smile. "Hi, officer. What's up?"

The guard bent down to look inside the Corolla, panning the occupants with his flashlight. "Whew. Something stinks." He looked closer at Adam. "What happened to you? Did you throw up?"

"Oh … that. My wife here had a little too much to drink at the party … you know, back at the dorms. I was just driving her back home."

The guard pushed back his cap and asked, "Who's that in the rear seat?"

Linda said, "That's … that's just a friend of ours. He's wasted. We're going to let him sleep it off at our place."

"Can I see your driver's license and registration, sir?"

Adam handed over his license and Linda fumbled through the glove compartment for her registration. Adam said, "We're both faculty members, teaching here."

"Are you really?"

The guard shone the flashlight on the license. Adam thought the reflected light gave the guard's face a demonic glow. Time was running out.

The guard was about to return the license, but paused. "You're Dr. Adam Dove."

Adam nodded and offered up Linda's registration card.

"Please step out of the car," said the guard. He backed away and unholstered his gun.

"What's the problem, officer?"

"Sir, just relax and step out. Keep your hands where I can see them."

The guard motioned Adam to come out, while pulling out an oversized walkie-talkie. Adam swung open his door. While the guard whispered into his two-way, a variety of escape scenarios flew through Adam's mind. He was still deciding on an option when the guard grunted and slumped to the ground. Like the finale to some amateur magic act, in his place, stood Alpha with yellow eyes visible even in the darkness.

"You are late."

"We had a tough time getting here. Linda is in the car, and your friend's in the backseat."

Alpha looked into the car. His eyes appeared to be able to see quite well in the dark. He reached into the rear seat with his ungloved hand.

"Did you shoot him?"

"I'm not sure. I was holding the gun when he used his glove, and…"

Alpha pointed to the dorms in the distance and said, "We must go now." Several blue and red flashers came into view. The real police had arrived. "Follow me in the car."

Alpha took off on foot toward the practice fields. Adam leaped back into the car and roared after him. A quick glance to his rear confirmed that, indeed, the police were closing in.

About a hundred yards later he skidded to a stop along the gravel. Alpha bounded over a low barrier on his way to the fields. Adam and Linda scrambled out of the car. The soft glow of the night sky outlined a cylindrical shape where Alpha was headed. It stood on one end and was about twenty feet high. A slit of light appeared at ground level, and while it grew into the shape of a door, Alpha ran back toward them, motioning with his arm. "Get in the shuttle."

There was no time for questions. Long purple shadows intersected ahead of them. Linda was the first to enter. Adam paused for a moment to look back at what could be his last view of Earth. Alpha jogged toward them carrying a hooded body over his shoulder. He laid it down in the tight quarters of the entryway just as the police reached the Corolla and began blaring commands through cruiser-mounted speakers. The door slid shut cutting off all the noise outside. They had finally reached safety. The silence underscored an abrupt disconnection with the outside world. For Adam it held a much deeper meaning.

This was the end and the beginning.

He felt a mild vibration and embraced Linda. "Wow … just like in the movies."

Linda returned the hug. She closed her eyes. "In the movies, the hero always kisses the damsel in distress."

Adam's eyebrows arched and they both laughed.

Chapter 20

The Schill University student center building was virtually empty. Although the cafeteria on the basement level offered a wide range of early morning entrees, the two security guards seated at the counter stuck to their usual coffee and doughnuts. Their customary daybreak grunts and shrugs were replaced this morning with wide-eyed animation.

"Did you see that damn thing take off last night?"

"Damnedest thing I ever saw."

"Shit. That was a damned spaceship, man."

"Maybe."

"What do you mean, 'maybe'? That sucker was a rocket ship. It flew right up and disappeared … and you saw the other one, right?"

"Yeah. That one must've been about a mile out. Seein' two of them fly up was a sight I'll never forget. You know, for a second I thought they might be missiles."

"What do you think it was all about?"

"Roger was on patrol last night and he said that he chased two faculty down to the fields. They cold-conked him, but he got himself back up and chased 'em over to the practice fields. By then a couple of the townie cops showed up. Roger said these folks stopped at the fields and ran into a goddamned spaceship. Then a third guy carrying something, maybe a body, arrives and they just took off."

"Where is Roger anyway?"

"He had a meeting this morning … in town. Seems now, that some folks from the government want to speak to him."

"I came in through the back entrance. The state police were running roadblocks around those practice fields. Must've been ten, maybe twelve cars, and behind them, and I think I saw a Humvee or two, you know, the kind the military uses."

"Shit. Sounds like a big deal."

They gulped and swallowed, and then gaped at the TV above their heads as a news story came on.

"According to Scranton police, the two rockets seen by hundreds of witnesses last night were nothing more than small model rockets fired off by hobbyists. Officials declined to identify those responsible but did indicate that a full investigation into the matter would be forthcoming."

"Bullshit."

"Yeah, bullshit. Those were big suckers. I believe Roger. He was close to the one takin' off from here and he ain't one to exaggerate."

"You're damn right. Just look at the fuss out there this morning. Those weren't no model rockets."

The two slugged down the remains of their coffees, stood up and left for their rounds.

***

In a matter of weeks the discoveries made at Brookhaven became a worldwide sensation. Broadcast and cable TV networks carried the story and video clips of interviews with Dr. Percy Wild flooded the internet.

"…It appears that two scientists from Schill University presented Dr. Wild with a gold medallion claiming that it was millions of years old. In a stunning revelation, Dr. Wild stated that using his advanced MRI imaging system, the medallion was found to contain humankind's genetic code…"

"… The implications of the find, if indeed it is not a hoax, are enormous. Religious groups claim the find is a fraud while scientists remain skeptical. Curiously, the medallion itself may have been lost…"

"… Dr. Wild claimed that some fanatic attacked him. The Schill University professors, Dr. Adam Dove and Dr. Linda Garcia, who found the medallion have disappeared without a trace…"

"…Wild stated that the medallion was found in a coal mine. Although it is now missing, all the data collected at Brookhaven is secure, along with a three-dimensional image of the medallion itself…"

Percy Wild had achieved fame. The media hyped the discovery of the medallion, the revelation of its contents, and the mystery surrounding the missing university scientists with daily updates for weeks after the incident at Brookhaven. Dr. George Freedman of the Schill University analytical labs had come forward to confirm the existence of the artifact, providing even more details of its composition and underscoring its likely extraterrestrial origins. Sightings of UFOs peaked that September and continued on for several months thereafter. Meanwhile, the implications of the discovery began to percolate up through the dogmatic layers of organized religions throughout the world.

In light of the DNA sequences found in the artifact, fierce arguments ensued between fundamentalist and moderate leaders of major religions, questioning the origins of the human race in a way that was never addressed in ancient scripture, in a way that pointed to a possible alien origin. These arguments were only the beginning of a religious upheaval the likes of which the world had never known.

***

"Where, where am I?"Adam's voice was hoarse, his mouth felt numb. Lying on his back, he squinted at a single light fixture embedded in an otherwise featureless metal ceiling. He sat up and fought down a spasm of nausea. A portion of a wall mirror reflected back an image of a nude man whose feet dangled a few inches off the floor. Transparent, flexible tubing containing a clear liquid hung from a device at his side. Its pointed nozzle left a trail of droplets on the table.

A red streak ran down and across his forearm. The room seemed to move, forcing him to grab hold of the table he sat upon with both hands. Everything was the color of dull, sterile gray—cabinets, or what looked like cabinets, counter tops, floor and ceiling. The place reminded Adam of a doctor's examination room.

And, where is the doctor?

Adam extended his feet to the floor and stood, swayed a little more, and lunged forward to a counter to catch himself on the rim of an embedded sink. A single handle provided water that he splashed into his face. He shook his head and looked about.

No towel ... that figures.

He wiped his hands on his chest, and staggered over to a small rectangular glass pane set in the wall. His legs felt heavy, sluggish. He gazed through the glass and saw only darkness outside. The glass looked like part of a door with its edges barely visible.

There's no handle, of course.

He stood for a minute, trembling with the effort to remain in one place. He thought back to the shuttle—the chase, Alpha carrying a body, and the door sliding shut. Then things got foggy. He recalled embracing Linda, and kissing her.

A great kiss.

He brought his nose closer to the glass and looked again. His pupils were growing accustomed to the low light and now he saw muted floor lighting in what was taking the shape of a hallway. It dead-ended to his left, and to the right it disappeared from view.

His hand brushed against the door and two panels slid open.

***

Hedda was released from the hospital and no charges were filed, pending further investigation. Preliminary findings pointed to self-defense. The Pittston police liked Hedda and the crime lab somehow failed to provide a complete ballistics report. Fortunately, Herman's bullet had passed through her thigh and no major arteries were severed. A few stitches and a few days rest, and Hedda was back at her museum hobbling about on crutches, doing what she could to straighten out her collections and sort out her memories. The events of the past week would long remain with her. A knock from the front door interrupted her broom mid-sweep.

"Ma'am, you be Hedda, Hedda Morrison?"

The visitor wore khaki overalls, held a large brown metal box and sported a low-slung and fully stocked leather tool belt. He was a big man with a dark clay complexion with long black hair tied back into a ponytail.

"And, you must be the carpenter, right?"

"Yup. That's me. Name's Windstorm, Jay Windstorm, ma'am. I guess this here's the door you want fixin'?"

Hedda's eye was drawn to a fragment of yellow police tape still caught on the edge of the frame. A breeze kicked up and fluttered the tape, carrying with it a scent of fallen leaves. "Windstorm. Unusual name."

"Yup, it's native American or what I guess the English translation would be. My father's side … his family was part of the Sasquehannock tribe, descended from the Algonquins." He gave the door a closer look. "You're gonna need a whole new door. I can probably save some of the hardware and rebuild the outer frame. Was this here a break in?"

A shudder ran through her as she nodded.

Windstorm gave the museum a quick glance while he made a show of fishing in his belt for a screwdriver. "You must be a lover of history. The stuff you've got in here … It's like the story of mining in this valley."

"It only goes back about a hundred years."

Windstorm nodded. "This valley, this whole area has a rich history … and yeah, more than just mining. It goes back thousands of years."

"You mean native American history?"

"Yup. The real history of this country."

Hedda paused in reflection. "Mr. Windstorm, I were wondering, and I hope you don't mind me askin'… askin' you about Indian, eh … Native American religions. What I mean is what do the Susquehannock believe about creation, ya know, how we came to be?"

Windstorm tilted his head to one side. "Hey … there's a question I don't hear too often in this job." He looked down at his boots. "I don't mind tryin' to answer it. Our beliefs aren't much different from most other native Americans."

He found the screwdriver and squatted to work the bottom door hinge. "I guess you'd call it a creation myth these days. Honestly, I don't recall all the details, and there are a lot of versions among the Nations, but here's how I remember it. There was a great Earth mother who had two sons, one good and one evil. After their mother died, the good one—his name was Glooskap—made plants, animals and humans, while the evil one, Malsum … well, his job was makin' snakes and poisonous plants. It turns out neither one was immortal, so in a fight with Malsum, who used some trickery, Glooskap was killed. But he managed to resurrect himself and eventually kill the evil one. He kept making good things, while Malsum went underground and became a kind of wolf spirit, hasslin' humans ever since."

"And do you believe in this story?"

Windstorm tossed a loosened hinge to the floor and started on the next. "It's as good a story as any I suppose."

Hedda grinned and resumed sweeping the floor.

***

Adam lurched into the curved hallway. He took an extra step to catch himself from falling. The panels hissed shut behind him. When he touched the door, the panels parted once again.

He staggered along the hallway, fighting off a compulsion to retch. The brightness of the floor lighting increased and the illumination kept up with him, brightening ahead and dimming behind. He saw several more glowing glass doors ahead to his right.

The next-door panel revealed a room much like the one he left, but empty. There were four more to go before the hallway disappeared to the left. Adam was about to conclude each room was vacant when he reached the last in the line. It was occupied.

"Linda."

She was stretched out on a table, much as he had been, naked and with an arm attached to a line hanging from the ceiling. He parted the door panels with a light touch. Linda seemed unconscious, but breathed steadily. He shook her, but there was no response. He brushed back a displaced lock of hair and bent down, kissed her on the cheek and whispered, "Linda … it's me, Adam. I'm going to find out what this is all about. I'll be back real soon."

He left the room and continued his walkabout. His gait and equilibrium were improving, and he began to feel steadier.

About a dozen paces later, he came upon an expansive unlit area, a kind of alcove into which the hallway emptied. When he stepped forward into the awaiting gloom, a set of lights arranged on the facing wall powered on. As their intensity grew, details of the semicircular room were revealed. Mounted below each light was an instrument panel of some kind, and below that, something that reminded Adam of a casket.

There were six rose-tinted metallic containers positioned in an arc, radiating out like spokes on some bizarre half wheel. As Adam edged closer he saw that each container sported a little window where a head might be if there was a body within. A dim glow from inside the portal of an end unit outlined the face of a woman, seemingly at rest. A scan of the panel above her head told Adam nothing more than some parts of the display, possibly monitoring gauges, were undulating in a slow but steady rhythm. He studied her face—the eyes were closed, bluish lips slightly parted, and dark hair pulled back. No signs of life. A small placard atop the viewing pane displayed several undecipherable symbols. He was about to move on to the next casket when his eye caught a movement beneath the glass. He leaned over to take a closer look and saw a tiny bubble caught in the frame. A moment later, it was gone.

Asleep in a fluid.

Three other caskets were occupied—two men and a woman. The next was empty. Its window held a card with his name, ADAM. He leaned across to the last casket, also empty and as he expected, it displayed the name, LINDA.

These must be the stasis devices Alpha talked about. Maybe we're on the mothership.

Adam headed back to his room. If Alpha was going to show up, it would be there. He trotted off down the hallway while a mesmerizing lighting display followed him. He checked on Linda's compartment and found her undisturbed. He fought off an urge to go in again, but instead, he blew her a kiss. Moments later he was seated on the table in his room.

Not knowing how long the wait might be, Adam lay down. After a while, his eyelids grew heavy. He dreamed of spaceships, new worlds, stars and galaxies. A deep voice reached him from among the stars.

"Adam. Relax. No need to get up."

"Alpha! I knew you'd come."

Adam's eyes flickered open. The ceiling light kept the figure floating above him in a blurred shadow. He felt a pinch on his forearm and the glowing workings of the universe folded about him like a warm blanket. He was at peace, cozy and safe, all the while streaking through the dark void, passing planets whirling about their suns.

The voice returned. "Adam. I've re-attached your medications, getting you prepared for the trip."

Despite his spectacular flight through and between galaxies, a tiny portion of Adam's thinking brain was aware that it was about to succumb to an even deeper slumber. It took what he had left of his concentration to force out one slurred question. "Alpha … the guy … the bad alien … what happened to … him?"

Adam plummeted toward the enormous black hole at the center of the galaxy and began to feel his body being delightfully torn apart. The voice echoed between the vestiges of torn spacetime in a most melodious manner. "Fortunately, we were able to save him. No need to concern yourself. Just enjoy the ride. Good night, Adam."

Alpha checked the tubing, insuring that it was properly inserted, and scanned Adam with a small hand-held device. He nodded in satisfaction and turned to leave when the door panels slid apart. Atall man stepped in.

His features were pale and expressionless. He wore a hooded sweatshirt, open at the front, revealing a heavily bandaged chest.

Alpha smiled and said, "I thought that went rather well, don't you?"

Part II

The Makers

Chapter 21

The Visitor followed his Greeter through a maze of tunnels to a room illuminated by a glowing ceiling. An aroma of freshly made caramel cloyed at his nostrils. Before he could ask the Greeter even one of a myriad of questions whirling through his mind, she smiled, nodded, and left without a word. Recessed doorway panels slid shut behind her, leaving him alone amidst an array of instruments and machinery. Tethered to the wall by pipes and cables, a large sarcophagus-like construction stood upright in the center of the room with its single door swung open. Its silvery exterior threw back his thin, elongated image, while its dark maw glistened with tiny pinpoints of reflected light.

He felt as if someone held him by his shoulders and legs. An unseen, viscous fluid wrapped itself around his body, coaxing him toward the awaiting opening. His attempts to cry out yielded no more than anemic whimpers. His toes skated along the floor as he was maneuvered into position inside the device. A thinning halo of light surrounded the shadow cast by his head, reflecting off each long needle fixed in place only inches from his face. The movement halted and the pressure ebbed away He thought that he might flee, escape the nightmare. Some control returned to his limbs as the door behind swung shut. He dared not move for fear of the surrounding needles. A humming met his ears. His screams were faint and short-lived.

***

Adam did not feel as if three centuries had gone by. He sat up. The room was much as he remembered it—mousy gray walls and cabinets, and a cold table. His eyes had a little trouble focusing, but when at last they did, the wavering shadows coalesced into a tall, black-haired, sallow-skinned man wearing a dark blue, skin-tight suit. He stood before Adam with hands on hips. "So, how did you enjoy the nap?"

"Alpha. It's you isn't it?" Adam coughed up some phlegm.

"Here's a tissue. Your eyes will need a few moments to adjust to the light."

Adam squinted. A loose IV line swung from his side. Alpha stared back at him with unblinking yellow orbs.

"Did you say three hundred years?"

Alpha nodded. "Of course, those are your years—years that have passed back on Earth."

Adam brought his hand to chin and rubbed.

"Don't worry … the combination of relativistic effects and stasis have slowed your aging to a mere week or so."

Adam recalled his mother and their final moments together before he left.

Before I left for the stars.

He rubbed his eyes and searched for a wastebasket. "Are there clothes or do we strut around here exposed? And, hey, what about Linda? Are you going to awake her too?"

A voice from behind startled Adam. "I'm already up, Dr. Dove. You're the sleepy head."

He turned to see Linda dressed in a red, full-body leotard. Her long, silky black hair swung side-to-side as she parted her lips. Reflected light from the ceiling danced across her dark brown eyes. Her dimpled cheeks widened.

"Linda! It's great to see you … what's so funny?"

Adam turned to look at a wall mirror—no gray streaks in his dark brown hair, no new wrinkles under his green eyes, no horn sprouting from his forehead. Dangling from his neck, a gold medallion caught the ceiling light. He caressed it.

"Hey, I look pretty good."

Linda patted Adam on his back. "Yeah, not bad for three hundred something."

"So, that would make you a three hundred twenty-something, or is that thirty-something?"

She punched him in the shoulder. Memories of that day crept into view.

Alpha's shuttle. We were both giddy with the adventure before us. Tracking down the origin of the medallion and the ones who created us … and the others on this ship … from other worlds.

"Some nap. Are we there yet? The home of the … what did you call them?"

"Makers," replied Alpha.

"Yeah, the guys who sent out and planted all those medallions. Three hundred years? I thought we would be taking turns running the ship."

Alpha's shoulders arched upward. "That was an approximation. Recent data suggest the location to be somewhat more distant."

"An approximation?"

Alpha bowed his head and stared at the floor as he replied. "We now know the location to be in what you call the galactic halo."

"And where exactly is that?"

"It is roughly eight thousand light-years above the galactic plane, in a zone known to contain the oldest stars in the universe."

Adam's stomach tightened as he thought about the distance.

"Six trillion miles per light-year makes it ... forty-eight quadrillion miles," said Linda.

Adam's eyes widened. "You did that in your head?"

Alpha said, "We were able to detect radio signals from a red giant system in the halo a short time ago."

"And these signals … what makes you think they're from the Makers?" asked Adam.

"They consist of a simple pattern—a sequence of numbers using only the digits one through four."

"You're kidding."

Alpha shook his head. "The transmitted sequence represents our genetic code."

An eight thousand year old signal.

"The time has come for you and Linda to learn much more about our ship and your duties."

"That sounds so exciting," Linda said. "We are looking forward to it, right Adam? And, here, you can put this on."

Adam accepted a single piece of clothing, dark blue and silky. As he slid off the table, he waved the crumpled tissue at Alpha.

"Just toss it into the sink."

He lobbed it across the room and it disappeared with a tiny whoosh.

***

She gazed up at the night sky while sitting alone in the middle of a field of grass. The distant banter of Greeters and Visitors carried on the gentle evening breeze, reaching her in broken whispers. It was midnight, and the horizon encircling her view was a deep crimson line beneath a cloudless sky. The majestic sweep of stars cast a radiance upon the land, as if a master silversmith had cast the field and village beyond with details etched in starlight. She stood up, her naked body at once silhouetted and shimmering. Someone approached.

"Fay. What are you doing out here?"

"Supervisor Mar … nothing really."

"You know you should be in the Welcome Center greeting the Visitors."

Mar scrolled his finger across a small pad, and looked back at Fay. "Do this again, and I will report you. That means you go back to the Learning Center, and if that does not help …"

"Do you not wonder at the lights in the sky?"

Mar hesitated a beat, and then said, "They are the tapestry of the Source. You know this."

"But the Visitors … do they not come from there? Can it be that the lights are like our Source, and they come from places like our own?

"There is but one Source."

Mar skewed his head as if to get a better look at Fay. "Are you questioning the Truth?"

She caught the threat. "No, no. Just random thoughts. I will clear my mind and return to the village."

Mar shook his head.

She was a Greeter, and knew her job well, but unlike the others, who carried on without question, she found herself thinking, perhaps thinking too much. Why these duties needed to be carried out. Why the Source imposed so many rules. In her heart there was a longing. She often wondered about the Visitors and where they came from. She wondered what happened to them after the Greeting. She had been instructed that everything came from the Source, and her work was a sacred trust, handed down by the Source. Generations upon generations before her had carried out these tasks, these most holy obligations to the Source. But that did nothing to quell her curiosity.

"I must be defective," she whispered to herself.

Maybe it just took some time. She would eventually be like the others. A shudder ran though her frame as she recalled what happened to defectives. Then she noticed Mar. "Do you wish something more?" she asked.

"I will escort you back to the Welcome Center."

***

"What's that?" asked Adam.

Alpha placed a pea-sized pink sphere into the chamber of a large syringe. "This is a translation node. I will place it beneath your frontal lobe."

"Whoa, whoa. Remind me why I need this?"

"I had mine put in yesterday," said Linda, her face adopting a cheerful expression.

Alpha raised the loaded syringe. "It will allow you to communicate with all your fellow passengers. Once the device attaches itself to your language centers, it will automatically interpret incoming audio signals and process them into understandable patterns."

"It will attach itself? Is it alive?"

"It is no more than a miniature computer with wiring designed to automatically interface with your brain's language and audio centers."

Adam sighed. "Well, I guess if the lady here can take it, then I can too."

Linda smirked, "It'll just hurt for a second."

"What?"

Alpha inserted the syringe into Adam's nostril, and at first, everything went black. Then a lightning flashed and a bolt of pain shot through his sinuses, down to his toes and back again. When the room lights came back on, he saw two hazy figures. Alpha and Linda took their time returning from the edges of a dark universe.

"Remind me never to listen to you again. It was like having ten root canals."

"Don't be such a baby."

"It will take a day or two to become fully functional," said Alpha.

Are you talking about the node, or about me?

"In the meantime, I will introduce you and Linda to the ship."

Adam got up off the table, and with Linda's help, wobbled out of the room to follow Alpha along a darkened hallway. Adam recalled the magical floor lighting coming on as they moved forward.

"So, how many are on board? Did we stop to pick up some more?" asked Linda.

"We made several stops. We are now at capacity with one hundred twenty individuals, in pairs representing sixty star systems."

"Wow, so that's sixty medallions?" asked Adam, while tracing the contours of his own disk beneath the thin material of his tunic.

"Exactly. It is likely there are many more scattered among the systems we passed."

Linda asked, "And each one of those medallions had the same DNA coding?"

"Yes. Essentially, all our genomes began as identical sequences. However, the evolutionary processes on each planet resulted in subtle changes dictated by environment and selection. It would appear that the time required for sentient species to arise was from several to a few hundred million years."

They followed Alpha along the curved hallway, passing several rooms similar to the one they just left. Alpha pointed to one. "These rooms are for preparation and recovery. Ahead you will see the chambers we use for storage."

"Stasis chambers?" asked Linda.

"Yes. They produce a kind of stasis, slowing metabolism to nearly zero with the help of drugs."

"I couldn't help but notice there's gravity on this ship. How is that possible?" asked Adam.

"The ship is under constant acceleration providing the equivalent of approximately eighty percent of your Earth's gravity."

"Wow, that means you have engines which can produce thrust for hundreds of years?"

"Much longer, if necessary. You will learn more about our propulsion systems shortly."

Adam asked, "At speeds like that, what about the chance of running into something?"

Like a rock.

Linda joined in. "And what about the radiation? These speeds can turn simple radiation to deadly … a blue shift, I think?"

Alpha gave her an approving nod. "All in good time. Interstellar space is nearly a pure vacuum, and the ship is equipped with the means to avoid damage by particles or radiation."

They entered a darkened foyer, which immediately brightened, revealing a semi-circular arrangement of casket-like compartments. The doors to two were open.

"Those chambers were, and are, yours. You will return here after your scheduled duties are completed."

"For another three hundred years? You said our destination is about eight thousand light- years away. Exactly how long a trip will this be?" asked Adam.

"We will not stop for any more passengers. We are about to head out toward the halo, and assuming we have correctly identified the home of the Makers, the remaining trip should take no more than a thousand years. Of course, I am referring to the time passing aboard the ship. And, your shifts will occur quite often … about every fifty years, for waking intervals of several weeks at a time."

Adam said, "That leaves of lot of dead time between shifts. Doesn't someone have to steer the ship?"

Linda shook her head.

Alpha seemed unmoved. "Automated systems handle the navigation. If an unforeseen circumstance arises, I will be alerted. There will always be two crewmen on duty. There is nothing to worry about."

They walked past the stasis room and into a small alcove. A set of double doors parted revealing a small compartment.

"Please get in. This elevator will take us to the control room … or the bridge … I think you would call it that."

The doors shut and the small cubicle purred, hinting at the barest sensation of movement.

Adam asked, "Who built this ship?"

"A consortium representing several planets. Once the medallions were discovered and found to contain mankind's genetic makeup, their contents were compared. Scientists from these worlds determined that the disks contained clues to our origins. That discovery led to an interplanetary agreement to seek out the Makers."

"How long ago was that?"

"A few thousand years."

"Why so long?" asked Adam.

"At the onset, we detected a number of medallions in our galactic neighborhood. After correcting for the movement of the galaxy over the estimated age of the medallions, their locations appeared to occur in an arc running through one of the spiral arms. Our scientists speculated that they were distributed by an intelligence, and that intelligence had an origin …"

"At the start of the arc," said Adam. "After detecting our medallion, why exactly did you stop to pick us up? You certainly didn't need our expertise to help run this ship."

Before Alpha could reply, the humming came to a stop and the doors parted. Adam had been expecting Hollywood's version of an interstellar spaceship's bridge—a panoramic screen depicting a vast star field, instrument stations with blinking lights scattered in an arc manned by a colorful variety of hunched-over humanoids, and in the middle, the captain's chair—one perfectly molded to the contours of his body. Instead, the room they entered was small, dark and quiet. A single monitor at its center displayed a blob of blue-white dots. Below that, two people, looking quite human, sat at a shared console.

Well, at least there're some blinking lights.

Alpha said, "When we, that is, the consortium decided on the expedition, the decision was made to offer the opportunity to join our quest to any willing to take the risk. Such offers were extended only to those who had discovered the medallions, and had a demonstrated minimal level of technology."

"But why the choice?" asked Adam.

Linda said, "Yeah, we could have easily opted to stay on Earth."

Alpha placed his hands on the shoulders of both. "I mentioned that it was an ethical issue. We do not believe in forcing anyone, and in addition, it is much better if you are willing and motivated to join. The quest to understand our origins and purpose is likely fraught with danger, since we do not know what lies ahead. It has been millions of years since the disks were sent out. Perhaps the Makers no longer exist, or they may find us to be a pleasant surprise, or …"

"Are more than happy to vaporize us," Adam offered.

"Or they'll delight in the arrival of new specimens for their collection," suggested Linda.

They chuckled as they approached the pair seated at the console.

Adam said, "Whatever the case, they must be very different from us. Just think of the patience—seeding the galaxy with an experiment that takes at least a million years. What kind of people could do that?"

Alpha said, "That is our purpose. We will find the Makers and we will then know why we were created."

"Alpha, there's something I've been meaning to ask you about. Back on Earth, you said that one of your passengers was a religious fanatic intent on disrupting the mission. That guy tried to stop us … he tried to kill us. I shot him. Did you say that he survived, or was that just my imagination?"

Alpha showed no surprise at the question. "Yes, he survived."

"And where is he now?"

"He is in stasis and will not be revived until we reach our destination."

248

Chapter 22

"Ouch."

"Now, who's the baby?" asked Adam.

Linda stretched her leg backward, poking Adam in the stomach. He teetered backwards and landed on this butt. Splotches of black grease covered his hands.

Linda pulled her head out of the metal cowling. "I didn't expect this either. Alpha said that maintenance is critical on long voyages." Seeing Adam on the floor, she said, "Oh Adam, I'm so sorry. My leg was cramping up."

"Yeah, yeah."

He hauled himself up and sidled up to her. When she reinserted her head, he wedged his in with hers. "So did you find it yet?

"It isn't going to be any easier with your blockhead taking up breathing space in here."

"Don't you find this situation kind of odd?"

"You mean the two of us with our heads in this duct?"

"Yeah, there's that, but I'm talking about Alpha. He's the one who contacted us on Earth. It was his shuttle. He prepared us for space travel, and now he's the one waking us up and getting us oriented."

"So?"

"So, there's a hundred twenty people aboard the ship. That's an even number."

"Let me guess. You're wondering where Alpha's mate is." Linda screwed up her face and reached farther into the cowling. "Found it." She turned a valve, and draped a meter around a tube. "Can you see the readout?"

"It's white."

"Then we're good."

Adam extracted his head. "Well, that's two. How many more?"

"Like you don't know."

Most systems in the ship were automatic, but some needed manual oversight. One of these was aptly referred to as Waste Management. Alpha had provided them a detailed map of all valve locations, as well as twenty-four hours of intense training for this and other ancillary systems.

Adam was still getting used to one of the peculiar side-effects of chemically-induced stasis—it made sleep unnecessary for several weeks. According to Alpha, that increased the efficiency of the shift protocol. Adam and Linda were the official maintenance engineers, at least for the next few days.

Linda flipped back her pony tail, and Adam pointed at her face. "There's some stuff on your nose."

She wiped at her nose with a free hand, which had the effect of lengthening a dark smear already there. "Did I get it?"

"Yeah, it looks perfect."

***

"My name is Markas, and this is Jule."

"It's a real pleasure to finally get to talk with you, if only for a few minutes," said Linda.

"Yeah, Alpha will be back any moment now," said Adam.

"To escort us back to our stasis chambers," said Markas.

The two seated at the control room console looked every bit like humans. With pale and freckled faces, and rust-colored hair, they could easily have just stepped out of an Irish pub, and with quaffs in hand, settled themselves on a shaded park bench. Instead, they hailed from a planet called Moors, located some five hundred light-years back along the Milky Way's Orion-Cygnus arm, and held drinking containers equipped with straws, filled with a dark, frothy liquid protein tasting more like dishwater than stout.

"Is navigating the ship very difficult?" asked Linda.

Jule said, "You'll find it much easier than the maintenance duties."

Everyone laughed at that.

A sense of humor that spans hundreds of light-years.

Markas said, "Most of the controls are automatic and configured to respond to almost any situation. The engines provide a constant thrust. The acceleration gives us the equivalent of gravitation. By the way, how does it feel to you?"

Linda said, "About right. Maybe a bit light."

Jule said, "To us it is nearly perfect."

Adam asked, "If the whole trip is going to take more than a thousand years to complete, and that's one way, doesn't that mean the fuel has to last for the same amount of time? That's a huge amount of fuel."

Markas chuckled before responding. "Actually, the fuel has to last for at least 10,000 years, and yes, it would be, if we carried normal fuel. You will soon learn that we have three types of engines aboard. The main systems are antimatter-based, and these provide most of our thrust. We have ram jet systems which compress interstellar particles, mostly hydrogen, which take over once we achieve sufficiently high speed. And, finally, we have chemical engines used to make simple changes in the ship's orientation."

Adam was about to ask another technical question, but realized he had little time before Alpha would return. "Just out of curiosity, do you remember who contacted you on Moors? Was it another member of the crew?"

"It was Alpha," said Markas.

"And was Alpha alone at the time, or did he have a partner?"

"He was alone."

Jule interjected. "Markas, don't you remember? There was someone else. When we boarded the shuttle, there was someone already at the controls."

Before Markas could offer more details, the control room doors parted and Alpha stepped through. "Well, are we ready to return to stasis?"

Markas and Jule rose with their drinks and followed Alpha to the elevator. Just before they entered, Jule looked back and said, "Good luck. We'll see you later."

They exchanged smiles and nods.

Alpha stepped in behind them. "I will return shortly to orient you for navigation." As the doors closed, he said, "Please do not touch anything until then."

"Adam, this is so exciting."

"I'll say. Can you imagine trusting a couple of chemists to run an interstellar starship?"

Adam reached up to touch the instrument panel. Linda swatted his arm aside and skooched over on the interconnected pair of seats. Her arm curved around his shoulders, and he returned the favor. Their eyes closed, and the ship, its alien cargo, and the enigmatic Alpha all faded away, replaced by a certainty of an everlasting future together that no force in the universe could place asunder.

***

"Well, that wasn't too bad," suggested Linda.

Adam sipped at his protein drink and turned his gaze past her. They sat opposite each other at a small table, one of four in the room. Inset into the far wall was a counter, over which three spigots stood out. Each offered up a tasteless repast brimming with vitamins, minerals, carbohydrates and proteins. Variety came in the form of the three choices: liquid, solid and mush.

"Are you kidding? This stuff is the pits."

"That's not what I meant. I'm talking about the control room training."

"Yeah, beats toilet training."

"Now, now. The plumbing is for our benefit. Besides, you seem to have a natural talent for that type of work."

Adam chose to ignore Linda's dig. "I'm not complaining about the work. It's necessary and important. It's just not the first thing that came to my mind when Alpha described this mission. Here we are, on a noble quest, something that mankind has imagined since the day we crawled out of our caves, headed out to one of the oldest stars in the universe to find our creators. And when we do, we can ask them just what exactly were they thinking? In the meantime, we need to make sure our crappers don't get stopped up."

Adam finished slurping up his meal and tossed the container into the disposal sink in the counter. "It's a little hard to get used to running around all day without sleeping. I keep expecting to fall on my face any moment."

Linda said, "I like it. It's like being on a caffeine high, 24/7."

"And what about the crash afterwards?"

"Alpha ran through the biochemistry with me. It sounds like it should be gentle on our systems. Once the stasis drugs get metabolized and our circadian rhythms return, we simply slide back into normal."

"I don't think that we'll ever be normal again."

Adam looked at the wrist timepiece Alpha had provided. "Hey, how about a little adventure?"

Linda threw him a perplexed look. "I thought we were already on an adventure."

"We've got a little time left, you know, before getting back to the control room."

"And what exactly did you have in mind?"

"I was thinking of doing a little exploring."

"And what exactly will we be exploring?"

"Ah … If I knew that, there'd be no reason to explore."

"I guess it wouldn't hurt to look around a bit."

Minutes later, the two were back in the elevator which connected the control room with the stasis sections. Adam pointed at the top of an array of illuminated panels. "So, we know this one goes to the control room. The next one down is where we eat, wash up, and …"

"I got it." Linda pointed to the lowest. "And this one's for the engine room," adding with a snicker, "and other critical plumbing services."

"So, in between the snack shack and shuttle terminal we have ten levels, or whatever you'd call floors on a ship."

Adam recognized the symbols on one of the labels. "That's where our caskets are."

Linda said, "Ten floors, six chambers apiece…"

"Makes sixty," finished Adam.

"That would account for all of our passengers," said Linda.

"Presumably the extra stasis chambers for Alpha and his shy buddy should be on one of these floors."

"You're so sexy when you're logical," purred Linda.

She lunged at Adam, apparently with the intention to whack him in the shoulder. Adam was quick to step to the side, allowing her to slam into the side of the elevator.

"Your three hundred plus years are beginning to show."

Linda snorted as Adam closed in on her. His arms held her against the wall, and his head tilted to the side. She closed her eyes.

"Whoa … what's this?"

Her eyes snapped open. Adam stared at something over her shoulder. "Are you going to let me go?"

"There's a little door here. It looks like your klutzy move jarred it open."

Adam released her and swung open a hidden wall panel exposing a single button. "What do you say? Give it a push?"

Linda was shaking her head 'no' when Adam leaned forward and depressed the curious little button.

Chapter 23

It was early morning. A ruby red horizon cast long, purple shadows among the naked Greeters gathered for the ceremony. The night before had been devoted to welcoming the Visitors and processing them. It had taken all night to insure that each Visitor was incorporated in the manner demanded by the Source.

An enormous space vehicle came into view as it neared the Great Circle. Greeters positioned themselves along the rim, standing on the lowest rungs of raised platforms. The Visitors' ship glided several meters above the ground, as if suspended by invisible strings.

"I love this part. It's so beautiful," said Naia.

Fay nodded in feigned agreement. "It's my favorite part of the ritual also."

She glanced up at the highest row behind them where the Supervisors sat. In dark uniforms and heads cloaked by hoods, they began a rhythmic, low chant, repeating a guttural mantra in a mounting cadence. The Greeters swayed in time to the undulating refrain, raising their arms in synchrony, clapping hands to the beat, and stomping with their bare feet. The chanting and dancing increased in volume and pace as the spaceship glided into the arena. It stopped over the center of the Great Circle. The chanting and dancing ceased. All paused, allowing complete silence to descend upon the spectacle. Both Supervisors and Greeters bent forward and held their heads low. No one moved.

***

The sensation of movement in the elevator was so subtle that Adam and Linda were not sure if they were going up or down. Seconds later, the doors parted.

"The hallway's dark," Linda muttered.

"These corridors are always dark."

They stepped out, and the usual floor lighting came on. They were in a short, straight section that ended at a main passageway, which like most other passageways in the ship, curved in either direction.

"Let's go left," Adam suggested.

"I like the right," Linda countered.

They went right. Unlike the stasis sections, they saw no preparation rooms. The hallway was entirely unremarkable. They followed its arc to a point roughly opposite the elevator access and came to a single, windowless door set into the inner wall.

Adam reached out with his hand and touched the door. Unlike all other doors in the ship, this one remained shut.

"Adam, I don't like this place. It's downright spooky. Let's get back to the elevator and back to the control room before Alpha finds us. There's probably a real good reason this level is kept a secret. Maybe it's dangerous."

"How about we go a little farther? Maybe there's something just around the bend."

They took a few baby-steps, when Linda grabbed Adam's shoulder. "Hold it," she whispered.

They froze in place, trying not to breathe. Footfalls. Someone approached. Adam looked in one direction, and Linda, in the other. The floor lights were pressure-sensitive and could give their presence away.

"There."

Adam followed Linda's extended forefinger. "I see it."

The curved hallway was brightening. The two scampered on tip-toes in the opposite direction until they reached the elevator doors. Adam felt like he was back in grammar school, trying to avoid getting caught in the school's attic where he had been searching out bottles containing dead babies. He never did find any, but remained convinced they had to be there somewhere.

"Damn. That was close," Adam said, out of breath more from tension than action.

"Who do you think that was?" asked Linda.

"Who else? It had to be Alpha."

They scooted inside the elevator. After selecting the control room level and insuring that the button was hidden once again, Adam said, "I don't know why we're acting so scared. We're all on the same mission, on the same team, aren't we?"

Before Linda could answer, they felt a subtle loss in momentum as the elevator glided to a stop at one of the stasis levels. Several levels short of the control room. The doors parted.

"Greetings," said Alpha, as he stepped inside. "I just prepared Markas and Jule for storage. On your way to the control room?"

They both nodded, and then gave each other a stare.

***

"I thought you said the galactic halo was sparsely populated. This screen display shows that we're approaching a dense cluster of very bright blue stars." said Adam.

"As you know we are constantly accelerating, and after some time, we begin to achieve a speed approaching that of light. Some unusual visual effects begin to be noticeable as we approach that speed. The cluster you see is actually a view of all the stars around us, even to our rear."

"I don't see anything around that cluster. It looks like empty space."

"That is an aberration. The faster we travel, the more the visible radiation from the universe becomes confined to a tighter cone of observation in the direction of travel. What you see on the screen as a cluster, actually represents the stars around us."

"Exactly how fast are we moving?" asked Linda.

Alpha pointed to one of the displays. "Like most readouts on the ship, this one is graphical in nature. The black bar represents the ship's velocity as a percent of light speed."

Adam asked, "And the hash marks below it? No, wait a minute, let me guess … one, two, three. So that's either seven percent the speed of light, or … "

"Adam, I think you need to count the larger marks before these," suggested Linda.

"Ah … that means we're going at ninety-seven percent the speed of light?"

Alpha nodded.

Ok, I'm impressed. Too bad you couldn't use the same technology to make the food taste better.

Adam looked back to the screen. "I guess I had expectations based on movies and TV. I was hoping to see stars glide by as we zipped along."

Linda laughed. "Me too. I guess space travel is not as romantic as Hollywood would lead us to believe."

Alpha pointed to several of the bright blue stars on the screen. "The aberration includes what you call a Doppler shift. Since we are approaching them, these stars blue shift. That is not their normal color. However, it remains true that the brighter stars are closest to us."

"With everything bunched up like that, how do you know where you're going? I mean we *are* going incredibly fast. Wouldn't the slightest error put us off by a zillion miles?"

Seeing the perplexed look on Alpha's face, Linda added, "A zillion miles is a very large distance."

Alpha touched several knobs below the screen. "These controls provide a virtual image of our travel by taking the distortion into account, producing an image that may be more intelligible to you."

Alpha turned a knob that had the effect of spreading out the dots. The resulting view showed separated points of light shifting to warmer tones and moving slowly off screen.

The next hour was filled with lessons and drills, including the meanings of key functional readouts and procedures, and the general layout and use of the ship's engines. Alpha handed out a small plastic sheet with English symbols. "You should have this for reference at all times during your shift. It summarizes most of what we went over today, and will help you remember the most important aspects of your duties in the control room. Do you have any questions?"

Adam asked, "Just to make sure … are we all done with waste management?"

"Your entire waking shift should run about three weeks. Each week you will need to go through the waste management protocol."

Adam slumped in his chair, pouted and looked at Linda. "She's actually much better than I am at that chore."

Linda punched Adam in the shoulder, which was becoming sore.

Alpha clarified. "If you will check the sheets, you will see that the protocol requires that you both carry out that duty."

Adam asked, "But it's just the two … or three of us. Where's all this waste coming from? I mean, Linda does like to eat, but really?"

Adam ducked away, avoiding a roundhouse blow.

Alpha said, "The waste flow includes material generated from all of the stasis chambers and the food production machinery, besides your personal contributions."

Linda chuckled at Adam's pallid demeanor.

"Your training is complete. You have your schedules. If there are no further questions, I will leave you now."

Linda asked, "Alpha, will you be checking up on us from time to time?"

"From time to time. If there is an emergency requiring my assistance, use one of the call buttons."

Alpha pointed to one such button, a six-inch wide round disk emblazoned with black and white stripes. They had seen these mounted throughout the ship, on all levels and in all rooms.

Adam asked, "So, are you going into stasis yourself?"

"My duties are to act as trainer and guide, and as a result, I occupy a special chamber which provides many of the benefits of stasis, but from which I can be roused in seconds."

"So you're not on any of the storage levels, since there're only six chambers per level and ten levels make up our total of sixty couples."

"There is an additional level which, for reasons of security and privacy, is off limits to the crew."

"And, you're alone on this trip … no partner?" asked Linda.

There was a hesitation in Alpha's response as he took a hard look at the seated pair. "That is correct. I have no partner."

"It must be tough to travel alone, to be responsible for the crew and ship on such a long voyage," said Linda.

"I was one of the original scientists who helped design the ship. It was my choice." Alpha turned to leave the control room.

Adam said, "Let's hope our shift is unremarkable. See you in a few weeks, right?"

Alpha smiled through the closing elevator doors and said, "Stay out of trouble."

Fat chance.

***

Fay heard a popping sound, followed by another. That was the signal. She straightened, as did everyone else, including the Supervisors. The small explosions mixed in with metallic tearing and screeching, and became more frequent and louder. The Supervisors grunted in baritone synchrony, again and again. The Greeters joined in, adding their alto voices to the chant. The throng echoed across the Great Circle. The groans, squeaks and cracks from the suspended ship provided a kind of rhythmic accompaniment. Fay felt her heart throb—a primal pounding within her chest.

Of a sudden, the floating ship fell silent, and in the same moment the chanting ended. The sun cleared the horizon, bathing all with its warm red rays. A bloody aura surrounded the ship, glowing and pulsating. Fay could feel its reflected heat suffusing her body.

Although her training compelled her to focus on the ritual, she managed a surreptitious glance to the side. Naia's eyes were wide and fixed, and her face, expressionless. With her arms to her sides, her trim body seemed statuesque, as if carved from the precious pearl rock lining the river Manx.

Fay dared another glance, backward this time. The Supervisors had pulled back their hoods, revealing hairless pates. They, too, stared straight ahead with large, round eyes set in alabaster faces. Before Fay could turn her head back to look upon the glowing silver ship, her eyes were drawn to a slight movement. It was Mar. She looked away, but felt certain that it was too late, that he had seen her break protocol.

The hovering ship began to dissect. Two long, graceful fins mounted to either side floated away from its sleek body. Panel sections, having been part of its smooth skin, peeled away. Engines and their mounts descended. The interior came into view, and components of that were extracted, and those too, drifted away. Walls, desks, chairs, equipment and wires, were all separated, taken apart with invisible tweezers, care being taken to avoid damaging even the smallest specimen. The glittering mix of shapes coalesced into a huge sphere rotating above the Great Circle, casting long shadows that danced across the entranced witnesses.

A small round hole appeared in the floor of the Great Circle directly below the sphere of debris. Like a camera iris, it grew larger, accompanied by a faint whisper, betraying the presence of hidden machinery of mysterious design. The expanding rim of the hole halted a few paces before the curved line of Greeters. Fay saw nothing but darkness within the gaping orifice. The rotating mass that was once a starship lowered, whereupon everyone resumed the hypnotic chant. Their voices echoed off the metallic debris, and they waved. In synchrony, their lolling arms surrounded the mass of spaceship particles, until it disappeared into the ground. It was the final tribute to a technology having arrived from the stars, now incorporated into the Source. The perimeter of the hole shrank noiselessly as the Greeters dropped their arms. When it disappeared from view and the floor was once again whole, both Supervisors and Greeters screamed shouts of joy. The ceremony was over, and all began their trek to resting stations scattered throughout the neighboring village.

Fay walked alongside Naia and said, "Once again, a successful ceremony. The Source will be pleased."

Naia agreed. "Oh, yes." She looked to the stars, difficult to see in the waxing light, and asked, "Do you think this day will bring more Visitors?"

"As nearly each day appears to bring," answered Fay, frowning at the realization. She had to be careful lest she be accused of calling into question a ritual older than time. She waved at Naia as they entered the village.

Naia nodded and slipped into a nearby cabin, one of a number of simple one-room buildings constructed of cut stone and wood.

Fay walked toward her lodging, only steps away. She once again wondered if there was something wrong with her. None of the other Greeters appeared to be concerned about the Visitors, about what was happening to them, and to their ships. Why was she so unsettled by it?

She paused at the door to her hut. A Supervisor stood across the way. It was Mar. She waved at him and threw him a quick smile. In response, he frowned, sending a shiver through her. His finger moved across a hand-held pad.

Chapter 24

"Is this number forty or forty-one?"

Linda turned from the monitor and cast a stern look. "Are you really keeping count of our shifts?"

"Why not? Besides babysitting the ship, sneaking around looking for Alpha's secret buddy, and cleaning up after ourselves, what else is there to do?" Adam slurped up a mouthful of malted protein. "You know, I think I'm getting used to this gruel."

Linda slapped at her shoulder.

"What's that about?" Adam asked.

"I don't know. I think something stung me."

"An insect in here? And through that leotard? No way. Let me see."

For the present shift Linda had opted for a white leotard over her usual red. She moved her hand and uncovered a small red stain.

"Whatever it was, it looks like you shmushed it."

"The bite feels funny. It feels deep, like a needle."

"Here, let me take a closer look."

Adam lifted her arm. "Oh, oh."

"What do you see?"

He scratched his head. "You've got another bite right on the other side of your arm."

"Adam. Your forehead … it's bleeding."

Adam looked at his hand, but before he could comment, he was overcome with a sense of nausea. He stammered, "Hey. You're floating."

Linda held onto the back of her seat. Her legs lifted from the floor. "You too."

The lights in the room became brighter, the doors slid open, and an irritating screech of an alarm began wailing in the corridor. They held on to each other, while rising and rotating above their seats. Adam glanced at the main instrument panel. The ship's acceleration was at zero. The engines had cut out.

He tried reaching out for the emergency button when his eyes caught the movement of the elevator doors in the corridor. Alpha flew past him and alighted at the monitor station.

Adam asked, "What happened? The engines seem to be off."

Alpha remained silent. He wedged his legs between seats and panel while his hands methodically moved from one display to another.

"What's going on?" asked Linda.

Alpha twisted his torso to gaze up at the two floating crew and shook his head. "We have run into an unexpected circumstance. We have struck a small dust cloud. The result is that some of the particles have penetrated our hull and reached our engines. Such penetration threatens a breach in antimatter containment, thus the engines automatically shut off."

"Breach? That sounds awfully dangerous," said Adam.

"Indeed. However, the antimatter containment module is a very small target and the probability of its breach is nearly negligible."

Linda asked, "What if it was, as you say, 'breached'?"

"Total annihilation would ensue. But you should not worry, since it would happen instantly, so there would be no time to …"

"Feel the explosion?" asked Adam. He pointed at Linda's stained arm. "The dust. Is that what these bites are about? Are these pinholes from the dust particles?"

Alpha looked them over. "Very likely. Even very small particles impacting our ship at near light speed can be dangerous. Space is a nearly perfect vacuum and the region of the galaxy's halo is expected to be clean enough for our passage to be uneventful."

"So we're getting peppered by unexpected particles. And these are passing right through the ship?" asked Linda.

Adam asked, "Is there anything we can do before the ship and we become Swiss cheese?"

Alpha paused a moment and shook his head. "This collision is a rare event. I believe we have already passed through the cloud, so I do not think you need to concern yourselves any further."

Alpha turned down the alarm and rechecked the monitor panel. "There is no significant damage. The ship's hull will self-repair as long as the particles are small. Sensors confirm that the majority of the dust has passed. I will need to go down to the engine compartment to reset the system. It should only take a few minutes."

As Alpha pushed himself off the console toward the open door, Adam extended his bloodied hand, and pointed at Linda's shoulder. "What about our personal damage?"

"As long as there are just a few instances and the particle sizes are small, there should be no threat to your lives."

Adam slapped at his arm as another tiny red spot appeared.

I guess we're not completely past that cloud.

Alpha disappeared through the doorway, and moments later the pair heard the swish of the elevator doors beyond. They floated above the console in a kind of macabre orbit around each other. Linda kept moving her arms and hands about her body, looking for new bloody little dust bites. Adam began doing the same, and then reached out to Linda, catching her with both hands.

"Hey. Did you notice something unusual?" he asked.

"Which is it? Us getting skewered by dust particles or us floating upside down over the control console?"

"Neither. Take a look at the doors."

"Yeah. I see the doors."

"And?"

"They're open."

Linda turned back to Adam. "So, they're open … and?"

"It must be the alarm. No artificial gravity and the doors open."

Realization ran across Linda's face as her brow flexed. "I can't believe what you're thinking. If all the doors are affected, then …"

"We've got a few minutes. Are you with me?"

"I don't know Adam. A few minutes isn't very long. I'm not used to flying through the ship. Neither are you."

"It's not that hard." Adam executed a somersault, grazing the ceiling and seat back. "See? I'll make it quick. Anyhow, that mystery door will probably be closed, so I'll be back before you know it."

He pushed forward, bouncing off the rim of the open control room doorway, using his fingers to guide himself to the elevator doors. A quick wave to Linda was all he could manage as the doors slid shut. Seconds later he was floating in the hallway leading to Alpha's secret lair.

The flooring of the curved hallway was brightly lit throughout. The pressure-activated systems appeared to have defaulted to an on position. Adam bounced his way from inner wall to outer until arriving at the door. As hoped, it was wide-open, inviting Adam to enter. His fingers curled around its edges.

Diffuse ceiling lighting illuminated the expansive room, nearly as big as a stasis level, and curved away in either direction. He glided in. The hairs on his neck and arms prickled. He was floating in a huge donut-shaped space. Obscure instrumentation decorated the walls and countertops. A small bottle floated by as he pushed himself along the walls and ceiling.

He was almost halfway around when he passed over a cushioned bed. Set into the counter running along the outer wall, the molded cushion had the shape of a prostrate human. An alcove inset farther into the wall revealed another instrument panel within.

A faint high-pitched beeping enticed him to nudge his way farther along the donut. The sound became a more distinct, clipped mechanical blip. He spotted another recess and caught his breath as a bare foot came into view, followed by second. He had no way to stop his flight and could only hope that the body attached to those feet was unconscious. His outstretched hands caught the second alcove's ceiling He was hovering above a naked body held in place by the curved outlines of molded cushions. The eyes were closed and the chest bore evidence of scarring. The upper torso appeared to belong to a male, however, this male was hairless from head to toe, and the genitals appeared to be missing. That last observation brought an involuntary pang to Adam's groin.

The face was nearly featureless, as if the head belonged to a manikin—pale and bloodless, sculpted from wax, but as yet unfinished. Part of the back wall, embedded with lights, flickered in synchrony with a chirping sound. Several cables erupted from a panel below and wound their way into the chest cavity of the body. A thick one entered the back of the head.

This has to be the guy who tried to kill me and Linda back on Earth, the one who Alpha claimed was a fanatic, the one I shot in the chest.

A bead of sweat floated in front of Adam's eye. Something nagged at the back of his mind. Something he just saw—letters on the panel, labels perhaps. He ducked his head into the recess. Unlike the control room, where everything was essentially unmarked, these labels sported some odd symbols. Adam expected alien symbols on an alien ship, but some of these were familiar. These were the enigmatic symbols he had seen many times before—on the edges of the medallion—an object created by the Makers.

Adam fished out the medallion from around his neck, and stared at its edge, hoping that he was mistaken. He was not.

He pushed off toward the entrance. As he did so, the lights in the room dimmed, and in that instant, he fell and struck his head on something hard. Gravity had returned. He tried rising, but was too weak and his vision was overcome by a whirlpool of color through which emerged a pair of feet. Feet that were bare. He lay back down. Everything dissolved to black.

***

It was a familiar voice. His eyes fluttered.

"Adam, it's me, Linda. Can you hear me?"

Linda's face splashed into view.

"Are you okay?"

He couldn't remember where he was. "Linda. What happened?"

A fuzzy outline moved behind her.

"Alpha brought you back. He found you in the elevator, passed out. He thinks you bumped your noggin when the engines kicked in."

Adam rubbed his head. "I must have fallen on my head."

"You were unconscious. Can you remember what happened?" asked Alpha, who peered over Linda's shoulder.

"I left the control room to check on something …"

Linda flashed a look at Alpha and interrupted. "You remember, Adam. You said you wanted to get a snack from the dining level."

Adam's eyes locked in on Linda's. She nodded an exaggerated nod.

"Yeah, that's right. I was feeling a bit hungry."

Alpha said, "When I restarted the engines, you must have been floating in the elevator. You are fortunate to have only a minor injury. I administered some medication that should relieve your headache."

Adam sat up and found he was on the control room floor. Linda and Alpha helped him to the console seat.

"There now. Are you feeling better?" asked Linda.

The two figures and the room remained stationary. His headache persisted.

"Yeah, I guess I'll be all right."

Alpha handed Linda some pills. "If the pain returns, these should help." He turned to Adam. "Please try and rest through the remainder of your shift. I will return in several hours to check on you."

When the control room doors shut, Linda grasped both his shoulders, and looked him straight in the eyes. "That was a damn fool move. You're lucky you only knocked yourself out in the elevator."

Adam kept blinking.

"So what did you find? Were the doors open? Did you get in?"

"Linda, I don't know what you're talking about. You heard Alpha. I was in the elevator when the gravity came back. Just bumped my head, that's all."

"Adam. Look at me."

Linda pushed her face to within inches of Adam's. "You do remember why you left the control room, don't you?"

Adam broke out with a grin. The tension lines in Linda's face began to fade as she shook her head from side to side. She made as if she was about to punch him when he said, "Sure, sure. Like you said … it was to get something to eat."

***

"You were gone for about five minutes."

"Maybe I was on the way back from the snack shack."

"I don't get it. You appear to have lost all your short-term memory … even counting the time before you set out. You do remember that Alpha brought you back here? And our conversation a few minutes ago … after Alpha left?"

"Mostly. This is really weird. I hardly remember leaving the control room. Now, even waking up here is a bit spotty."

Linda leaned over. "Hold still."

She ran her fingers through his hair while turning his head from side to side. Then she ducked down below his chin. "Don't look down, look up. I want to see into your nostrils."

Adam felt her fingers stretch open his left nostril. A couple of seconds later, she said, "Looks like a little blood. Did you have a nose bleed?"

"Not that I recall. Of course, with my current level of dementia, there's no telling what I was up to."

"Maybe you got it when you fell. Maybe it's from one of those dust particles, and then maybe…"

"Someone erased my memory?"

"Yeah. Something like that. Short-term memory is converted to long-term through protein synthesis in the brain. If that doesn't happen, you end up forgetting recent events."

"Isn't that a bit of a stretch?"

"It's theoretically possible to interfere with the conversion. Our understanding of the subject is incomplete, however, something like a direct injection of RNase into the brain could do the trick."

Adam rubbed his head. "RNase would block the synthesis of new proteins, proteins needed to store the memory."

"I'm impressed … Biochemistry 101. That's assuming RNase was used. Alpha comes from a civilization far more technically advanced than ours. Maybe he used something more specific, especially since it affected your memory from about the time you left the control room."

"Maybe I found out something juicy."

"You must have gotten into that room, and discovered something we're not supposed to know."

"Wouldn't hitting my head in the elevator do much the same?"

"Not likely."

"Any chance that some of my memory could return?"

"Maybe. Short-term memory only lasts about a minute. If it was particularly strong, that is, if it was a big surprise or really important, your mind would consciously start to go over it, reinforcing it. That process begins the chemical conversion. There might still be a trace."

Linda paused for a moment and embraced Adam. "This must be so hard for you."

"Something really important may still be in here somewhere?" Adam asked, pointing to his head with his index finger. He closed his eyes and imagined floating into the mystery room. He tried relaxing, letting his mind wander. After several minutes slipped by, he sighed. "It's useless. I'm getting nothing."

"Not even a kind of feeling, an intuition perhaps?"

Adam remained motionless for a few more minutes and then opened his eyes. "Nothing. Well, almost nothing."

"Almost?"

"Ah, just some old stuff. Don't see what it has to do with Alpha's secret."

"And, this old stuff is?"

"Symbols. The symbols on my medallion. For some reason I'm getting a feeling they're important."

Chapter 25

Fay followed Mar into the windowless Learning Center at the outskirts of the village. They slipped in through the wide, doorless entryway, which brought back memories of her training not long ago. Unlike the joyful expectation she felt when she had achieved novice status, a foreboding clung to her like a dark mist. No explanation for the visit was given. Mar marched into the dim hallway with his head erect, apparently expecting Fay to follow closely behind. This she did, adopting a quick stride to keep up.

"Mar, slow down, please."

Her voice echoed off the sleek walls, mingling with the staccato of Mar's boots on the polished stone. The cold floor numbed the soles of her feet. He gave her a quick sideways glance and resumed his pace. Fay began jogging.

She could not understand what had driven Mar to this action. She did not recall making any errors in greeting protocol, at least, none that were significant in her mind. She was sure she had followed all the rituals faithfully. She had even avoided questioning dogma, in particular, in public. However meticulous she had been, there must have been something that caught Mar's attention. He was an unpleasant Supervisor, often impudent, always demanding. She focused on his broad-shouldered back and the dark robe swaying to and fro, certain that she would soon come to learn about her failings, and their consequences.

The Learning Center was one of a number of similar modules scattered in the forests surrounding the village, each with a singular purpose as deemed by the Source. This Center was devoted to studies of history and ritual, and to the training of novices. They passed a recessed entry to the Library, which was used primarily by Supervisors and Clerics. Fay's stomach clenched as a cowled figure glided over the floor within the Library nave. She had never seen a Cleric before, but was aware of their manner of dress. She understood that they communed directly with the Source, and spoke only to Supervisors, commanding unquestioning loyalty, respect, and fear.

Mar raised his arm. "We have arrived."

Fay stopped short, catching her breath. They were deep into the Center in an unfamiliar section. Mar depressed a wall panel and an opening formed as if the wall had been an illusion that now dissipated like a mist. A recessed chamber came into view, and within it, darkness.

Mar directed her with his hand pointing the way. "Enter."

Fay had no choice but to obey Mar's direct command. If there were danger, he would have warned her.

She fought back a sudden urge to bolt, to step away and run, and instead drew a deep breath and stepped forward into the gloom. Mar's footfalls followed closely behind. They stood together in the small space, waiting in silence.

The floor disappeared and Fay felt herself falling. Her hands shot up to her mouth, stifling an urge to scream. She was in free-fall, a feeling foreign to her experience. Her wide eyes found Mar behind her, his solemn demeanor unchanged and his robes flowing up from his shoulders. A growing twilight replaced the dark as the two continued to plummet. Lighting streaked by, glinting off silvery walls. After a time, the sensation of weight return to her legs. They were slowing down.

Mar spoke in a calm voice. "We are about to land. Prepare yourself."

Fay had no idea how to do that, but she focused on keeping her legs in the downward direction and braced herself. The landing was as abrupt as the start of the fall, and was so smooth that she found herself standing on firm ground before she could even react.

They were in an identical alcove to the one in the Learning Center, except this one had to be very deep within the Source. They stepped into a corridor and Mar directed her straight ahead. "I will wait for you here. Go on."

Her heart was pounding so loudly she could hardly hear him. At least, she thought, she was expected to return.

She steadied herself and looked out into what was more of a tunnel than a corridor. Subdued lighting mounted on its walls seemed to go on forever. A quick glance confirmed Mar remained behind, draped in the shadows of the alcove. She had the impression that he was smiling, a disturbing thought which caused her to swallow. She felt his eyes on her and the skin on her back crawled. A wave of cool air brushed her bare back. When she looked, Mar was gone. She stared at the empty recess, wondering what was next, what was to become of her.

"Come with me, child."

The words were at once startling and comforting. The voice was deep, resonant, and had the lilt common to a female. She turned to see who it was. A Cleric stood before her. The face was hidden by an overly long hood, part of the pure white robe that covered the rest of the body.

"Easy now," said the Cleric as Fay staggered backward.

The Cleric pulled back the cowl. "You see, I am like you. Nothing to fear."

Fay saw what could be a female, but like no female she had seen before. Her hair was long and white. The face had soft features, creased around the eyes and mouth. The cheeks were sunken as were the hollows of the eyes. Even the hands that steadied her had a desiccated look, their skin folded and thin.

"Take this, dear Fay, and put it on."

The Cleric handed her a robe, much like her own, but without the hood.

"We will be travelling farther into the Source, and the temperature is not always as you are accustomed to."

Fay donned the robe, finally getting past the shock of not only meeting a Cleric, but also having one talk directly to her. She began to think that perhaps all this was a dream. Maybe she passed out during the fall. She was moving, but could feel nothing. She was listening, but could not bring herself to speak.

"Are you ready?" asked the Cleric.

Fay challenged the dream. She trembled, but summoned up her concentration. "Where are you taking me? Why?"

Her own words surprised her. Were they too defiant?

The Cleric flashed a smile. "You may address me as Deirdre. I already mentioned we will be travelling farther within the Source. As for why, well, you have been nominated for the Study."

"The Study?"

"Why, child, you will be trained to become a Cleric, of course."

***

"It's not here."

Linda took a close look at the area that Adam just finished poking with his fingers. The wall of the elevator seemed the same, but the hidden panel was gone, or perhaps, hidden elsewhere.

"You're right. I guess Alpha figured out we knew," said Linda.

Adam continued his sweep, depressing the walls at random locations. Linda did much the same on the opposite side of the elevator. He slumped up against a panel. "This is getting us nowhere."

The elevator doors opened to a cacophony of voices from farther along the hallway. A number of the crew were lazing in the corridor, chatting each other up, sipping drinks. The scene reminded Adam of his early days in academia. The gathering ahead could easily have been a group of faculty awaiting the start of a seminar. Some members of the group even resembled graduate students he had known.

"I must say, it's quite a change from the early days," said Linda as they emerged.

"You got that right. I'm beginning to miss the peace and quiet."

"You don't mean that. Come on, let's see if we can find some old friends."

For the past several weeks an increasing number of the crew was awakened from stasis. According to the radio signals they had been following and Alpha's calculations, the ship was now only a few hundred million miles away from the planet of the Makers. They had been under deceleration for the past several thousand light-years, and soon that would come to an end as the ship assumed a flight path designed to enter orbit, which according to Alpha, was going to happen within a week's time.

They headed for the snack shack.

Alpha squeezed between several crew and waved. His smile faded as quickly as it came. "All is well in the control room?"

"Uh, yeah. We've got a full view of the red giant, though we can't see the planet as yet. We just came down here for a little break and some food. There sure are a lot of people hanging around these days," said Adam.

"There are adjustments to the monitor that will allow you to see the planet, and I have awakened nearly all the crew."

"Any problems with that? I mean, is everyone okay?" asked Linda.

Alpha lowered his eyes. "We lost two. A malfunction caused by the micrometeoritic bombardment we received some time ago."

"Damn," said Adam, unconsciously rubbing his forehead. "Where are all these people going to hang out? I mean, there's only a couple of tables in the cafeteria."

"We are only a few days away."

Linda asked, "Are you sure we're in the right place?"

"I am sure. The radio signal now carries a different message."

Adam looked at Linda, and they both shrugged in that 'and you're only telling us now?' body language.

"Well, what's the new message?" asked Adam.

"I will announce it and our plans to land as soon as I have all the crew revived. We will meet in the shuttle level where there is sufficient room."

Alpha angled past Adam and Linda. "I will be busy for the next few hours."

Alpha made his way down the corridor and into the elevator.

"You look a little peeved."

He shook his head. "Way more than a little. That guy runs the whole show here, doesn't he? And you'd think at least he'd have the courtesy of letting us know about the new message."

"It's just the way he is," said Linda, bringing her arm around Adam's shoulders. "No need to get uptight. After all, if you think about it, we've been on this ship for nearly nine thousand years. Let Alpha have his moment."

Adam rubbed his forehead again. "I wish I could remember."

Linda skewed her head. "Oh, yes. How's that going? Have you had any flashes, anything at all?"

"Just the same ole, same ole … Symbols. I can't shake the feeling that there's something about those ancient symbols that could change everything. It's so damn frustrating."

"Just what is so frustrating?"

It was Markas. He held a drink in one hand and had his other feathered around Jule. The two redheads made a striking pair.

"Hey, we do keep running into each other don't we?" asked Linda.

"Fate. You must be excited by the prospect of our arriving at the planet of the Makers," said Jule.

"Is something bothering you, Adam?" asked Markas.

"Tell me, is there anything about this whole expedition that bothers you. You know, anything that doesn't seem quite right?" asked Adam.

Markas stopped mid-sip, and looked at Jule as he answered. "Perhaps." He checked the hallway, as if expecting someone to suddenly appear, and while still looking past Adam's shoulders, asked, "Is there anything specific that you are referring to?"

"I guess it's the 'why' of it all."

"Go on."

"If you believe what Alpha says, he was part of a very advanced civilization. Based only on the medallion and its DNA code, he and his folks decide to build a ship capable of interstellar travel. They build a huge ship that uses antimatter for propulsion, one that has a hull which repairs itself, stasis chambers, and there's other technology like the neutrino detection system."

"It is quite impressive," said Markas.

"And don't forget about the translation implants," said Linda.

"And why did these builders then set out to pick up others along the way?" asked Adam.

Jule chimed in. "Alpha told us that each medallion had some kind of information that pointed to its origin."

"So he needed sixty of them?" asked Adam.

Markas shrugged. Jule grabbed his drink and said, "Markas, tell them what you told me this very day."

"We were discussing the trip, and that we had to leave the arm of our galaxy to head out to the galactic halo."

"Yeah, that's right. Alpha said it was a surprising finding … that we had to redirect the ship," said Linda.

"I get it. If the medallions had the information, why the surprise?" asked Adam.

***

The Study took place in a labyrinthine network of tunnels. Fay was now a member of a group of Acolytes, each of whom had been nominated by their Supervisor. They came from different regions of the planet, representing the various specializations demanded by the Source. Each had traits considered important in carrying out the duties expected of a Cleric.

They gathered in a domed room, numbering a dozen. The ceiling held a single, subdued source of light, much like others scattered throughout the tunnel system. They formed a circle around a raised platform. Deirdre stood atop the dais and addressed them in her low, velvety voice. "One of you has been determined to require resorption."

The words seemed to hang in the air for a moment. Fay's heart pounded. She was sure that Mar nominated her for resorption. It had to be her—the free thinker.

The group remained in formation, with nary a whimper or gasp. Whether the silence was the result of resignation, respect, or fear, it did not matter. Someone's fate was sealed. Each Acolyte avoided direct eye contact with the Cleric, in hopes that this simple avoidance would somehow protect her.

Deirdre took a step toward Fay, raised an arm, and placed it on the shoulder of the Acolyte next to her. It was all Fay could do to remain standing. The chosen one collapsed to the floor and sobbed.

"Now, now dear. It is the way of the Source. There is nothing to fear," said Deirdre.

In spite of the placation, the crying continued, the grief made all the worse by the fixed and indifferent stare of the remaining Acolytes. Deirdre stepped off the platform, took hold of the stricken Acolyte's arm and helped her stand. At once, she floated up, swaddled in her robe, arms dangling to her sides. The ceiling lighting gleamed off her wet cheeks. Her sobbing halted and her eyes grew wide. She continued rising as Deirdre stepped back. She hovered directly over the center dais.

Deirdre nodded to the group. "The Source knows all. It is the wish of the Source that the Acolyte before you is resorbed. So will it be."

All eyes looked down as a dark round opening formed directly below the suspended Acolyte, and in that instant, she dropped. Fay heard no sound, no scream. A moment later, the platform was restored.

Deirdre spoke once again. "Your comrade was the weakest of this group. During the course of the Study, the Source will conduct additional assessments." She led the Acolytes out of the chamber. "We will now begin your formal training. Are there any questions?"

No one spoke. Fay was sure none would dare. They followed the Cleric in single file. After some time, Fay managed to shake off her inhibition and snaked through to the front of the line. She whispered to the Cleric. "Deirdre. Is it permitted to ask how many of us are expected to complete the training and become a Cleric … like yourself?"

Deirdre craned her head as if surprised at the audacity of the question. She closed her eyes and replied, "My child, it is expected that none of you complete the training."

Chapter 26

The announcement seemed to come from the walls. "Please assemble on the shuttle level. Once there, you will be updated regarding the plans for orbit and departure to the planet of the Makers."

"Alpha sounds so formal," said Linda.

"He's way too stuffy for one of the scientists who built this boat," said Adam. "You'd think he'd be just a little excited."

"Like the rest of us," commented Markas, pointing to the throng piling up by the elevator doors.

They joined the party and were in the last group to reach the shuttle level. People milled about the two shuttlecraft. For the first time, Adam had a chance to actually see most of the crew. Animated and talking, each in a different language, but speaking intelligibly thanks to the chip in his head. Aside from minor differences in color and height, they seemed to be cast from the same mold. The few exceptions that jumped out were the scaly-skinned couple that could pass for giant frogs back on Earth, and two pasty-faced, rotund humanoids that appeared to enjoy licking each other's hands. For many this was the first time they had a chance to meet others. A number moved to the center of the bay and stared up at Alpha who walked out atop a gangway. He called out. "Please listen closely."

The crowd below hushed and a recording played. The acoustics of the bay focused the voice—soft and melodious. "Welcome visitors. Welcome to our home. We are so pleased you have arrived. This world is not only our home, but yours as well. You will find our atmosphere and temperature acceptable. We look forward to meeting you."

"The message repeats," said Alpha. "As you can see, we are expected."

A murmur ran through the bay. Adam turned to Linda. "Expected? After travelling for nearly ten thousand years, following a path based on gold disks set out millions of years ago?"

Adam pointed to his forehead. "Funny how these translator chips were able to figure out the language of the Makers so efficiently. Usually, there're a few words lost, especially at the start of a conversation."

Alpha spoke up. "The message included instructions and coordinates for landing. The Makers await our arrival. Within an hour we will enter orbit. Please take note of the handrails, as we will lose gravity. I have prepared a schedule with lists of passengers. As a precaution, we will use one shuttle. It is capable of carrying ten passengers at a time. Please check for your names and times of departure posted at the entryway. Each flight will be announced a few minutes before departure."

Adam and Linda, who happened to be near the entry, read the list. Each pair of names was written in a different script. Their own names stood out, since those were the only ones in English. There were six groups, and they were in the last one.

"We are on the same flight," announced Markas, draping his arm around Jule.

Adam shook his head and smirked. "Obviously, they've left the best for last."

And that is when he saw it. A pair of bare feet wended through the crowd lining up on the floor of the bay. Everyone on board normally wore the equivalent of slippers or moccasins. Adam's hands were already sweaty when he cupped them over his ears, fighting back a wave of nausea. An image leaped up in his mind—an image of a pasty-faced manikin.

***

Fay placed a ball the size of a walnut on a ramp. She released it and followed its travel down a short, curved chute. When it reached the end, it fell into a cup with a clank. She walked to the cup, retrieved the ball and began the process again. It seemed to her that she had been doing this for hours, as were the other Acolytes in her Study group. The clatter of balls dropping into cups strewn about the room provided an uninterrupted and an eerily comforting cacophony—a kind of audio mesmerism, disguising a surreal lesson plan.

"Stop. Come to me," commanded Deirdre.

They all obeyed at once, forming a circle about the Cleric.

"Now, when I point to you, you will tell me how many times you have rolled your ball."

Fay had guessed at the nature of the hidden task within a task. She could see by the strained faces of her colleagues that not all had shared her vision. Deirdre nodded in recognition as each individual submitted her number. When Fay announced her tally, the Cleric's eyes widened for a moment. A trace of a smile flitted across her lips before she summoned the next Acolyte.

$$***$$

Time was hard to measure during the Study, but Fay guessed that several weeks had gone by—each day demarked by Deirdre's visit, arousing the group from slumber. They always slept at a different location within the underground domain of the Source. There were now only four Acolytes remaining. Unlike the first ritual resorption, members of her group had disappeared without ceremony. One day they were there, the next, gone.

Tasks became more convoluted, bordering on the bizarre. As far as Fay could tell, each was designed to test an Acolyte's perseverance, as well as analytical and tactical ability. Deirdre's commands were to be followed precisely and without hesitation. On one day, the most difficult challenge began in the form of an innocent request.

"I will ask each of you, in turn, to follow me into the adjoining room," announced Deirdre.

All stood silently. Fay wondered what kind of morbid deception awaited them. The Study had proven to embody the contrasting effects of heightening anxiety against a growing empathic rapport with the Cleric. Fay had the feeling that Deirdre wanted them to succeed, but knew well that she would not hesitate to eliminate any one of them.

Fay was last in line, and watched as each was escorted to the next room. After an Acolyte entered, she heard only whispers followed by silence. And so it was, until she was called upon.

Deirdre led her by hand into a darkened chamber with a beam of light descending from the center of a domed ceiling. The light illuminated a slim, round table, upon which rested a small dagger. They walked together to the table.

"You see the knife?" asked Deirdre.

Fay nodded. "I do."

Its curved blade glinted up at her. The hilt sported an ornate carving, suggestive of a deep and inscrutable history.

"When I command you to do so, I want you to take the knife and plunge it into my chest."

Fay thought a moment. This must be yet another test. She looked about the room. There was no other exit. Where had the others gone?

"Are you ready?" asked Deirdre.

"Yes."

One more look around, and she confirmed that they were alone.

"Now."

Without hesitation, Fay wrapped her fingers about the smooth hilt, brought it up, and thrust it into Deirdre's chest. It slid in with almost no resistance. The Cleric's mouth opened, and a puff of air escaped through her parted lips. Her eyes bulged as she doubled over. Fay released the knife, and the Cleric fell backwards, her hands clutching the protruding hilt, blood seeping out onto her white robe. She rolled on the floor, gasping for air, legs writhing. In a few moments, she was still.

Had Fay passed the test? Was she supposed to follow orders without question? Or had she made a mistake? Maybe she should have refused the command? Doubts weighed heavily on her mind as she staggered out of the chamber.

"Well done, my child."

Fay looked. Deirdre smiled at her, her white robe unsoiled.

"I don't understand," she croaked.

"You have met the final challenge."

"But I stabbed you. You fell to the floor and died."

"All an illusion."

Fay calmed herself. "And, what of the others?"

"Either they would not follow my command, or they took too long to decide. Disobedience or indecision is not acceptable in a Cleric." Deirdre looked into Fay's eyes. "They have been delivered unto the Source. They have been resorbed."

"Then…"

"You are the sole survivor of the Study. Your real training will now begin."

Deirdre waved Fay to follow, which she did without further discussion.

***

Adam tugged at Linda's elbow. "We've got to talk. Let's go back up to the control room."

"Where are you off to?" asked Markas.

Linda gave Adam a questioning look.

He said, "Fine. They can come. We need to move now, before Alpha catches on to what we're doing."

Linda motioned for the Moorsians to follow. She ran after Adam and the two piled into the elevator.

Adam asked, "Are they coming?"

"I don't know. They were…"

Before the doors closed completely, the two redheads angled through the narrowing opening.

"What's going on? Don't you want to stay and see the shuttle launch?" asked Markas.

Adam depressed the control room button. "What if I told you that the Makers built this ship?"

All three remained speechless as the elevator arrived at the control room level.

"So, you finally remembered," whispered Linda.

"How can you be sure?" asked Markas.

"A while ago, I was able to get into Alpha's quarters." Seeing the confusion on the Moorsian's faces, Adam explained. "We found where he stays between shifts. I came across his invisible buddy." Adam paused to look at Jule. "You know, the guy that was your shuttle pilot." Then he turned to Linda. "The same one I shot back on Earth … the crazy one Alpha told us had survived."

"Alpha may have a good reason to keep him away from us," said Jule. "Just because you saw this person, doesn't mean that there's a secret plot of some kind."

"Maybe so. I have to tell you, the guy looked more artificial than human."

"That might be it," said Markas. "It may be some kind of android or something, and Alpha may feel uncomfortable with it being on its own.

"All that may be true, but I saw something else. Did your medallion have some writing, some symbols on its side?" asked Adam. He pulled out the gold disk and showed Markas.

"Yes. It did. Four symbols, as I recall they were the same as yours," answered Markas.

"Then, what would you say if those symbols showed up on this ship?"

Before Markas could answer, his arms splayed out in an attempt to steady himself. Adam felt light-headed. Linda's hair rose from her shoulders. Jule began floating toward the ceiling. An announcement bellowed from the wall.

"We are entering orbit. Prepare for weightlessness."

Thanks for the warning.

They careened through the hallway and into the control room. Adam grabbed the console seat to steady himself. "Assuming the monitor displays color in much the same way we see it, the planet's sun is a red giant. The curved surface must be the planet. Is there any way to control the view? Can we get a better look at the whole planet?" asked Adam.

Jule pushed herself off the ceiling and landed between Adam and the console. "These sliders should give us a better look."

The other three grappled their way toward Jule, coming to rest behind her. Her fingers danced beneath the monitor, and the planet came fully into view, revealing a pink sphere with no remarkable surface details.

"Looks a little like Mars, but with fewer canals," remarked Linda.

"That's funny. There do seem to be some regular features. Can we zoom in a little?" asked Adam.

While Jule made a few adjustments, Markas said, "Adam, what exactly did you see?"

"Well, it's still a bit fuzzy … but I know I saw the medallion's symbols. They were up on a panel along with many others. That's about when I blacked out."

"Maybe the symbols you saw were being analyzed along with others. That's something Alpha could have been working on," said Markas.

"Those symbols were part of the panel, permanent tags, right over where the android thing was stretched out."

"Here we go," said Jule.

What had at first looked smooth became a regular series of light and dark square patches. It was as if a checkered tablecloth was stretched over the entire planet. Although there was no ocean, there were some hints of small rivers appearing as dark, sinuous cracks. No cloud formations or any other signs of weather were evident.

"What are those patches?" asked Linda.

Jule expanded the view. "Could be vegetation in the dark areas … maybe forests."

"How high up are we?" asked Adam.

"Units of measurement are arbitrary, but I can say that our orbital distance is about equal to the radius of this planet," answered Jule.

"Do you have Earth's size in the directory?" asked Linda.

Jule twirled a knob below the monitor and brought up an image of Earth—a depiction in three-dimensions, complete with an orbiting moon.

Another touch on the panel split the screen, allowing a comparison of the two planets.

"It's smaller than our moon," said Adam. "Way smaller."

Symbols scrolled across the screen representing comparisons of gravity and rotation.

Jule said, "It does appear quite small for a planet. However, its gravity is about the same as on the ship, and its rotation is equivalent to a twenty-hour Earth day."

"Small place, big mystery," said Markas.

"In the meantime, we have our own 'big mystery' right here," said Adam. "If the ancients built this ship, and Alpha is one of them, why didn't he simply tell us that? What's the big secret?"

Chapter 27

Time passed, and Fay had put aside her dream-like musings—the warm embrace of the sun and the cool breezes wafting through treetops above her home. She was a model student, focused on becoming a Cleric, on assuming the unique mantle of responsibility that would permit a view of the world and the Source unlike any she had ever imagined.

She had been introduced to the hidden realm of the Source. She knew that Greeters and Supervisors originated from growing chambers managed by machinery, complex and mysterious. These were overseen by Growers, who themselves were included in the production, as were all beings on the planet. Only last week, she was introduced to the Sustainers, those that grow and process food. Of all those in service to the Source, Caretakers held the greatest fascination. As a Greeter, she had not even known of their existence.

"Today, you will be introduced to the Source," said Deirdre in her now very familiar baritone.

Fay had just awakened from a deep sleep and was quick to don her white robe, outfitted with a black hood, which identified her as a Cleric-in-Training. Deirdre was standing at the doorway of her quarters.

"I am ready, Deirdre."

"Will you not partake of the morning meal?" asked Deirdre, pointing to the untouched dish and glass at Fay's bedside.

"I am not hungry."

"Very well. Follow me."

Nonetheless, a sudden dry mouth compelled her to take a quick sip from the glass. The pair walked along corridors long familiar to Fay. They took one of the central elevators to the lowest level, the only one as yet unvisited.

The doors opened upon a bright, white wall, very different from the dimly lit tunnels above.

"Follow," said Deirdre. The Cleric's command echoed its way along the corridor, as if enticing them onward.

Fay noticed odd symbols embedded in a nearby wall panel, embossed over narrow rectangular grooves. "What are these markings?"

Deirdre paused and said, "Sacred symbols of the Source. Their meaning is unknown to us."

She turned to go, but Fay asked, "Is there a door here?"

"Such markings often designate entryways. This one is not functional."

Fay followed the Cleric a few more paces to another wall panel. Deirdre touched it and they stepped through.

"Good day, Cleric Deirdre."

The man bowed. His long blond hair fell over his shoulders revealing a circular bald patch. He was clad in a gray body suit. A mesh-like extension of the suit covered his hands and feet.

"Good day, Caretaker Ebbe. This is Fay. She is here for the introduction."

Ebbe straightened and swiped his hair back. "Welcome to the Source, Fay."

***

"Here comes the shuttle," said Jule.

The monitor screen automatically locked in on any moving objects near the ship. The shuttle was about a half-hour away.

"Looks like we should be getting ready for our trip," said Markas.

Jule pushed herself off the control console and joined Markas at the door.

"We'll see you on the shuttle. If you run into Alpha's buddy, give him, or it, our best regards," said Adam.

Jule's voice adopted a measured, almost reproachful tone. "Alpha's companion is a mystery to us as well, but we never had an issue with him … or it."

"I agree with Jule," said Markas. "It is perplexing to me that you are so engrossed with Alpha's companion, whatever he may be. You are losing sight of the enormity of our present circumstance. After a flight that took thousands of years to complete, we have at last arrived at the planet that may have originated our species. Don't you feel at least a little excitement at the prospect of meeting our creators?"

"Point well taken, Markas, and we are just as excited as you, but you're ignoring the possibility that the Makers may have built our ship. I just don't like the secrecy," said Adam.

"Conspiracy theories can weigh a mind down," noted Jule.

Markas nodded. "The use of symbols similar to the ones on the medallions could be a coincidence, or perhaps they were copied from the medallions ..."

Adam shook his head. "I know what I saw."

He looked to Linda for support. "I'm sorry, but I'm with Adam. Besides the lies Alpha has told ... that alien sidekick tried to kill me too. We know that Alpha's keeping him from the crew, and that's not a theory."

"I guess we'll find out the truth very soon," said Markas. They pushed off into the hallway and waved.

Adam and Linda perched themselves on the console, gazing at the monitor in silence. Adam heard the sound of labored breathing, and turned to see Linda holding her hand to her nose while a single, translucent drop hovered above her face. She was crying.

"Hey, what's going on? Are you okay?"

Linda brushed the back of her hand across her face, dislodging a few more tears. "It's nothing. It just ... It just sunk in how much time has really gone by. All that we knew back on Earth, everything's gone. And not just gone, but after nine thousand years, who's going to remember us?"

Adam wrapped his arms around her. They held themselves this way, letting time come to a standstill in their control room sanctuary.

"Let's get down to the shuttle bay."

Linda pulled back her hair, which had the annoying habit of assuming a Medusa look without the help of gravity. "And what do you expect to find there?"

"Don't know. We're supposed to wait there anyway. We'll just be a little early. Are you all packed?"

Linda threw Adam a smile. "Thanks."

They pushed off. Adam led the way using railings mounted along the corridors. They soon found themselves in the elevator, along with several other passengers.

"Isn't it exciting? We're finally here, at the home of the Makers. I can't wait to meet them."

The person addressing them was tall, dark, and skinny, saddled with a markedly long face made even more horse-like by a prominent and full-lipped frown.

"My name is Adam, and this is Linda. We are from Earth. I guess our paths haven't crossed before. Where are you from?"

"It's none of your business."

Horse-face looked up at the ceiling of the elevator. An awkward silence followed.

I guess politeness is not necessarily a universal.

By the time they reached the shuttle bay level, they were alone in the elevator. The doors opened to a wide, dark blue metal floor with the second shuttle, a yellow streak, crouching in the shadows. Its far end was secured to an airlock, while the open door on the near end invited entry. The subdued lighting of the bay gave the place a cavernous feel. Adam and Linda floated into the center, stopping just short of the shuttle with the help of floor railings.

Adam scanned the curved walls.

"What are you looking for?" asked Linda.

Beads of perspiration launched off his forehead as he turned. Before he could answer, they both heard a low, guttural, and familiar voice. "Perhaps what you seek is here."

A figure floated up from behind the shuttle, and drifted into a cone of overhead lighting.

***

Fay did not see Deirdre again for what seemed like weeks. During that time, Ebbe had demonstrated and described all the different maintenance duties Caretakers undertook. These included everything from mundane cleaning to complex repairs. Although the Source was never revealed, all the machinery and systems required for its existence made her head spin. The thrill of learning about the underground workings of the Source made the time pass quickly. Ebbe had introduced her to a number of different Caretakers, each with specific tasks and responsibilities, and each of whom reported to him.

Ebbe greeted Fay as she arrived at his quarters. "Good day."

Fay nodded. Ebbe pulled on a pair of meshed gloves. "I trust you slept well."

The greeting was always the same, and Fay, as usual and as expected, produced yet another nod. When Ebbe finished with his gloves, he yawned and bent backwards to stretch.

"Today, I will be your instructor," he said, with particular emphasis on the 'I'.

He motioned Fay to follow. Within minutes they were at the main elevators. When Fay took a step toward the doors, Ebbe grasped her arm. "No, no. We are here."

Surprised by the physical contact, she considered launching a reprimand. Although she was not yet a Cleric, she expected a significant degree of respect.

Ebbe took a step back. "Fay, please excuse me. We have arrived."

She looked about. This was where she and Deirdre had first entered the domain of the Caretakers.

"And where exactly have we arrived?"

Ebbe pointed at the embossed symbols. Below them were a series of faintly perceptible seams. Fay recognized the location.

"I was told that the meaning of these particular markings is unknown, that the doorway, if there is one, has never been opened."

Ebbe grinned. He raised both gloved hands and depressed the symbols, touching some simultaneously, others one at a time. The seams widened and a doorway appeared before them.

Chapter 28

Linda and Adam looked up in horror at the alien who had disguised himself as a family doctor, was behind the disappearance of several people, including police officers, and later tried to kill them both. Linda gasped as his face began to blur. "Adam, he's changing."

Alpha's little secret floated upward, nearing a gangway atop the bay. His face fluttering and settled into a familiar look—the jaundiced skin, the dark hair, and the large yellow eyes with pin-points for pupils.

Adam said, "You're not Alpha."

The alien held on to the support struts below the gangway. "Are you sure?"

"You're the maniac we ran into on Earth."

"Your imagination limits you."

Adam said, "You're some kind of chameleon, and besides, you're insane."

The alien lifted his dark blue tunic and exposed a hairless chest. "What do you see?"

The chest was smooth. No scars.

"So, you had your scars removed. Big deal," said Adam, stressing his words in a vain attempt to conceal his growing lack of conviction.

"What are you, anyway?" asked Linda.

"Who or what I am is not important. Soon you will join your colleagues on the surface. The Makers are expecting you."

"Are you one of them?" Adam asked. "You must be artificial. Did Alpha build you?"

The alien said, "Then you remember what you saw in our quarters?" He bowed his head. "They made me … just like they made you."

Adam looked to Linda and pointed to the opening in the shuttle with his eyes. She answered with a wink.

"Now," whispered Adam.

They flung themselves through the air, aiming for the shuttle entryway. Halfway there Adam felt something land on his back. He tumbled to the floor, bounced off, and floated up a meter. The alien grabbed a railing and flung himself toward Linda who was at the shuttle door. He gripped her hair and tugged backwards. She turned into the pull and pummeled the alien with a right hook. He loosened his hold long enough for her to twist away and head back to the shuttle.

Adam wedged his foot on a floor railing and launched himself, wrapping both arms around the alien's neck. Linda drifted into the shuttle, and then the bay rotated in a dazzling display of light and dark. The alien had thrown him off, and he spun, heading toward the ceiling. His arm caught a gangway railing with a jolt. He rubbed at his elbow, struggling to regain his orientation and a direct line on the alien.

Adam glanced at the bay entry, hoping for some early arrivals. The few remaining crewmembers were still on upper levels and likely would not arrive for several minutes more. By then, Linda and he would have met with an unfortunate accident.

Adam swung over the gangway in time to avoid the alien's grasp from below. "Linda! Fire up the shuttle!"

The alien's lips curled up as he hissed. "Nice try. You have not been trained to pilot the shuttle. I will take care of your sweetheart right after I deal with you."

"That's where you're wrong, champ. You, or Alpha, didn't have it in our training schedule, but we spent long hours going over the shuttle and its operation."

The running lights on the shuttle's exterior came on.

That's my Linda.

When the alien glanced down, Adam kicked out with his right foot, catching it on the side of the head. The motion flung Adam in the opposite direction and he hung on to the gangway frame to avoid flying off. The alien twirled downward like a pinwheel and landed with a bounce. Its body assumed a fetal position as it curled around a protruding handrail.

Linda's head emerged from the shuttle entryway. "Looks like you won't be needing my help."

"Very funny. We have to get out of here before he or it wakes up."

Adam propelled himself down to her, arms extended. They embraced and he asked, "Think you know how to pilot this shuttle?"

"Yeah, right."

***

Six crew, including Markas and Jule, joined Adam and Linda in the shuttle bay. The talk was filled with expectation and wonder. Adam and Linda decided to keep their adventure to themselves, electing instead to observe and learn. A warning clang sounded as Alpha's shuttle reached the outer airlock. The hull hissed open and the shuttle clacked into place. A few minutes later, the inner airlock doors parted and Alpha stepped through. He scanned the bay with the pretense of checking on the crew, but Adam and Linda knew better, especially as Alpha gave the other shuttle a long look. He turned to the small group. "Is everyone ready?"

Markas asked, "Can you tell us about the Makers? Are they as friendly as they sounded? Do they know who we are?"

The group surrounded Alpha, as if they were news reporters eager for a story.

"All your questions will be answered. I promise you will not be disappointed. Now please get in the shuttle so that you can join your fellow crewmates in the meeting taking place below." Alpha motioned for all to enter.

When Adam and Linda passed by to take their seats, Adam diverted his eyes, but not before he caught Alpha staring at him.

He knows.

Before securing the door, Alpha paused at the entryway, giving the bay one last look. He took in a deep breath, exhaled, and glided over to the pilot console."Please strap yourselves in. It will not be long now."

Adam secured his seatbelt. The other shuttle remained visible through a side portal. The airlock doors unclamped and as their shuttle inched out of the bay, a hand jutting up at one of the other shuttle's portals. Fingertips scraped at the glass, and then moved across the pane, as if bidding the last of the crew a fond farewell.

***

"Cleric Fay, five sets of arrivals have been processed."

She acknowledged the Supervisor's report with a slight nod. The sixth and final shipment of ten was currently on its way.

"Thank you, Serv. Please inform me when the remaining Visitors have been incorporated."

Serv nodded and left Fay alone in her compartment. She should be feeling a sense of deep satisfaction in the processing of new arrivals , but instead was struggling with a troubling sense of doubt. Despite the intense training she had undergone, and survived, she was prisoner to a gnawing belief that somehow nothing was as it seemed. Her early days as a Greeter brought back images of Visitors with happy, friendly faces, of people not unlike herself. Were they really just conduits of information for the Source to absorb? Did they not have lives of their own? Did they not dream?

"How are you, today?" Deirdre stepping through the doorway.

"Of sound mind and body, Cleric Deirdre."

"No need for formalities, Fay, especially as there is only the two of us here."

Fay bowed before she could catch herself.

"I just spoke with Serv. He tells me all is well … that the processing is on schedule."

Fay gave no outward reaction, instead she asked, "Deirdre, what brings you to see me this day?"

Deirdre's lips tightened as she spoke. "My time is short. As you know, I will soon join the Source." Her deep voice cracked, causing her to pause a moment before going on. "I just wanted to say goodbye."

Fay was taken aback. Although she knew of the eventuality, her mind had relegated the thought to some indistinct future time. Deirdre had become a fixture in her life, and this news was unwelcome. She breathed in deeply. "I wish you a pleasant joining. I am sure the Source is satisfied with your work over the years."

The words threatened to ring falsely. Fay cringed at the image of joining the Source, but managed to keep her facial features steady and her tone pleasant.

Deirdre took a step closer and embraced her. Fay returned the gesture and fought down an urge to sob. Deirdre had become something more than a mere teacher, something Fay was not sure she could describe. The lines on Deirdre's face deepened as she closed her eyes.

When they separated, Deirdre said, "You wonder about my looks, the lines, the sagging features of my body."

Fay nodded.

"Someday, the Source be willing, you will have similar features. What you see before you is the work of time. Our bodies were created to function for limited periods. Greeters and Supervisors are resorbed more frequently. Caretakers and Clerics are more difficult to train and are designed to function for a much longer time."

Fay recalled that many of her previous Greeter colleagues were taken by the Source. It was the way of things. Of the fate of Caretakers and Clerics, she knew much less.

"Why must it be so?"

Deirdre chortled. "Even now, you have the curiosity—an excellent trait … to a point. The reasons for decay and absorption are beyond our understanding. They are a mystery onto the Source."

"When will you … go?"

"When I leave this room, it will be the last time you see me."

The statement impaled Fay's heart. Deirdre gazed at her with that analytical look she knew well, as if this was yet another test, perhaps a final exam. "Then, farewell and thank you, Deirdre. It has been an honor to learn from you. I shall miss you."

Deirdre's eyes became rheumy, and with a trembling voice she replied, "I will miss you as well, Fay. Someday you will be called upon to conduct a Study and identify a replacement for yourself. Be strong and faithful to the Source."

Fay watched Deirdre as she was swallowed by the gloom beyond the doorway. Her mind raced. Perhaps it was not a test. Perhaps Deirdre was sincere in her feelings.

She shuffled away from the door and slumped into a chair. With elbows on knees, she held her head with both hands and closed her eyes. How was she ever going to get off this world?

Chapter 29

"I am Mar. You will follow me."

Adam and Linda joined the column of twos. Mar, draped by an over-sized cloak, exposed only his bald head. Even through the pinkish hue thrown up by the setting sun, Adam could make out his distinct yellow eyes. They hiked across a concrete-like surface that covered a wide, flat expanse. The shuttle behind them gleamed in the fading red light and was the only craft visible in any direction. They appeared to be heading toward a distant copse of trees. Linda held Adam's hand with a vise-like grip. Alpha was last in line.

Adam spoke loud enough for Alpha to hear. "Are you nervous?"

"Just a bit."

"A bit? My fingers are numb."

"And you're not the least bit worried?"

Adam threw a brief, tentative smile. "It's all I can do to keep my knees from shaking."

He looked back at Alpha and asked, "Your brother's not joining us?"

Alpha paused mid-stride, and then skipped a step to catch up with the pair. His voice seemed very controlled, very calm. "He is not my brother. And, no, he will not be joining us."

"Any reason why he tried to kill us?"

"He is sometimes a trifle impetuous."

"Impetuous? That madman wanted us dead back on Earth."

"Of course, you know by now that we are representatives of this planet. Our mission was to convince as many as possible to join our expedition … our gathering."

"And the purpose of this … gathering?"

Alpha remained silent. Adam pushed ahead. "I guess there's not much time for a discussion, but tell me this … was he supposed to scare us into joining?"

"Adam, we're slowing down. It looks like a building of some sort ahead," said Linda.

Several hundred meters ahead stood a grove of palm-like trees, and beneath, a one-story building with a group of people gathered in front.

"Are those women … naked?"

Linda sighed and shook her head. "I'd be more worried about what they plan for us, than how they're dressed."

Adam stopped to block Alpha's forward motion. Linda swung around as the rest of their group continued unaware. Adam's speech became a distinct staccato. "Are you going to tell us, or don't you want to spoil the surprise?"

Alpha's face screwed up, and he raised his hands. "It is the will of the Source. The people here serve the Source, and they will guide. All your questions will be answered then." Alpha kept his hands raised, a motion which now prodding the two forward. It was clear no further explanation was forthcoming so they rejoined the procession.

When they were steps away from the awaiting reception, Adam asked, "Where are the others … where did all the crew go?"

Alpha lowered his head. "They are one with the Source, or soon will be."

Several figures paused at the arched entryway of the building. They waved and turned away, escorted by a number of naked females.

Alpha moved to the front to join Mar.

Adam nudged Linda. "I don't like any of this. It all seems a bit too ritualistic."

"Like the natives are about to load us into a giant pot and have us for dinner?"

"My gut tells me to get the hell out of here."

"But, to where?"

"Anywhere, but into that building. Seriously, what's the worst that could happen to us?"

Linda was about to reply when Mar addressed the group. "Welcome to our world, the world of the Source. The Greeters you see before you will escort you to an area for refreshment, and later you will convene with the Source at which time all your questions will be addressed."

"Okay, so the first part doesn't sound too bad," said Adam.

Adam saw Markas look back. He wanted to point out the obvious connection between Alpha and the Makers, but Jule gave Adam a look of reproach and turned him away.

Mar said, "Please come forward and meet your Greeter."

As the group advanced a few steps, each Greeter introduced herself to a pair of the crew, and the three split off onto a trail through the trees nearby. They headed out to a small glen in which stood a structure covered by a thatched roof somehow illuminated from beneath.

"Did you notice anything funny about this place. I mean here, by the trees?"

Linda squinted, and then wrinkled her nose at the air. "Outside of a very pleasant, sweet odor? Can you be more precise?"

"No insects … in fact, I don't see any signs of birds or any other wildlife."

"I'm impressed that you can pay attention to details like that. I'm half out of my mind."

Adam pulled her closer. "I guess it's my way of dealing with that same apprehension. I have to say, that for a culture millions of years ahead of us, the thatched roof and naked women don't impress me. Well, maybe the women … "

Linda jabbed him. "They do seem to be primitive." She pointed back to the landing site. "But, don't forget. They built the ship that got us here."

"How? Have you seen any technology?"

A cream-skinned, blonde girl approached and bowed. "My name is Naia. Welcome. Please follow me. I will take you to refreshments."

"Lead on, fair lady," replied Adam, trying hard not to stare at her.

Linda said, "Her facial features are remarkably similar to those of Scandinavians back on Earth."

"Facial features?"

Linda jabbed him again. Adam rubbed his side, making sure to exaggerate the injury. He noticed that Alpha lagged behind. He had just finished talking to Mar.

Adam said, "You did notice her navel, right?"

"No, is there something unusual about her belly button?"

"Yeah, I'd say so. She doesn't have one."

The roof was weaved using the wide leaves of the trees surrounding the glen. The open hut was large enough to accommodate a gathering of twenty or more.

"My God, the smells," said Linda.

The vague sweetness of the air at the landing site had now become a strong, heavy aroma, at once familiar and unknown, laden with meaty flavors and exotic spices.

"You'll have to speak up. My stomach is making too much noise."

The place had the appeal of a Hawaiian luau—long tables laid out to the sides, each covered with dishes and trays, loaded and steaming. The rest of the landing party spread themselves out among the delicacies and drinks. Adam picked up his pace. In his mind's eye he saw a cartoon character lifted by wavy lines shimmering in the air. The lines tugged at his nose, pulling him onward, toward the wondrous repasts on display.

When they reached the canopy, Adam said, "I'm sorry, Linda, but thousands of years of that tasteless, gray spaceship slop and I'm ready to eat anything that smells good."

Naia directed them to the center of the structure. "Your journey was long and hard. Please take a moment to relax and sample our food and refreshment. As you can see, we are human like you, and I assure you that everything here is compatible with your digestion. In a little while we will visit the Source."

Adam shuffled past Naia to the nearest table. Linda quick-stepped up to him and grabbed his elbow. "Adam, before you start pigging out, stop and think."

"I know what you're about to say. It's just that this stuff looks so damn good."

"Where are all the others from our ship? Wouldn't you think some would stay and enjoy the food … the drink? "

She steered him away from the tables to make the point. Adam reached over her shoulders to grab a scrumptious looking pastry-like dish on the table nearby. Linda pinched his arm.

"Yeesh. You don't have to do that. By the way, we're being watched." With a roll of his eyes, he pointed out Mar, who stood just outside the canopy. Alpha was nowhere to be found.

Adam pivoted around Linda's hold on him and gave her a quick peck on the cheek. "I get it. Make like you're sampling this stuff … just don't swallow anything, no matter how delicious it looks or smells."

After a few minutes of feigned munching and drinking, they rejoined in a corner and watched the rest of the party.

"Everyone's getting pretty happy," said Adam, while making chewing motions.

"Maybe too happy. What's our plan?"

Adam looked out across the landing area. "Well, the shuttle's still there."

"We can't fly it."

"Alpha's the guy we need, and I didn't see him go back to the shuttle."

Linda wrinkled her brow. "I've been keeping my eye on that building, and he definitely didn't go there."

"I don't see anyone there now."

Mar's deep voice sported a resonance that instantly broke up the chatter. "The time has come for you to meet with the Source. Please follow your Greeter. We will proceed along the walkway."

He pointed to a narrow trail that wound through the trees to the building beyond. Their Greeter once again met each pair of visitors, and the trio joined the processional. Many talked loudly, overjoyed at the prospect of meeting with their Makers. No one seemed interested in staying behind to sample some more food or just talk it up with the Greeters.

Adam felt a lump in his throat. This could be the most important meeting in humanity's history. After millions of years of evolution, humankind-representing planets strewn across the galaxy was to finally have a chance to discuss its purpose with the creators themselves.

Naia took Adam by the hand. "Come, let us go now." She threw the pair a wide smile. Although pleasant, it struck Adam as rather artificial, something that she had done dozens of times before.

He returned the greeting with an artificial smile of his own, and spoke loudly. "I can't wait. This is so exciting."

Linda tossed up a set of nods. "Adam, I don't know what to say."

The trio fell in step with the rest of the group at the rear. Mar followed closely behind.

When they reached the beginning of the trail, Adam grabbed Naia by her shoulders. "Sorry about this." In one motion, he threw her into Mar. The two flailed as they tangled and fell to the ground.

Adam pointed to a second trail, which led into the woods in an opposite direction.

"Adam, do you know where you're going?" Linda shouted.

They sprinted headlong into a darkening forest. The sun, already low on the horizon, was nearly invisible under the broad-leafed canopy. A few minutes later, years of inactivity caught up with them, and both lay flat on the ground, gasping for air. A red-black gloom erased the trail ahead. They listened for a pursuit, but heard only the raspy sounds of their own breathing.

***

"I'm feeling a little sleepy." Adam sat up. He rubbed his eyes and squinted. No matter what he did, he saw nothing. The forest was black. Beyond the pleasant sweetness wafting through his nostrils, there were no sounds, no light. He aimed his voice at where Linda should be. "The stasis effect is wearing off. I think we might pass out any moment."

"Comforting thought."

The evening had transformed the forest into a virtual prison. The darkness pressed against them like invisible iron bars.

"No wonder no one's chasing us," said Linda.

Adam could hear her voice crack. Her claustrophobia was rearing its ugly little head.

"Keep talking, so I know where you are."

"I'm right here. Oh!"

Adam found her and wrapped his arms about her. After a moment, he said, "You'd think the natives would have flashlights."

"Maybe they do. Maybe there's some other reason they don't come in here."

Chapter 30

Fay straightened her robe and pulled back her hood. Mar had just finished recounting the events surrounding the loss of two Visitors. As he was once her supervisor, Fay felt somewhat awkward speaking to him thus, but duty to the Source required discipline.

"Why do you suppose these two ran off?"

"I cannot say, Cleric Fay."

"Did they not partake of the welcoming feast? Should they not have become cooperative?"

Mar continued to stare at the floor of Fay's inner chambers. She watched his eyes follow the stonework patterns to her feet, and then drift upward.

"Cleric Fay, I can only surmise that they were suspicious of the feast. The Gatherer, Alpha, had mentioned to me that those two may have discovered that the ship was ours."

"And what precautions did you take to insure that these Visitors would be processed according to ritual?"

Mar gaped at Fay, as if searching for words or explanation. When he did speak, his voice lacked vigor. "I assumed the feast would entice the pair. I was sure they had eaten and drank. They should have been becalmed." His voice cracked and he lowered his head. "I took no precautions, Cleric Fay."

"You were told they knew of the subterfuge. You *surmised* that they were suspicious. And yet, you did nothing to insure a smooth delivery to the Source."

Fay saw Mar tremble. Was she being too severe? Was she being spiteful? Her introspection seemed to make things worse, as Mar's trembling increased to visible shaking.

"Have all the other Visitors undergone Incorporation?"

Mar raised his eyes. She saw his distress lift with the change in topic.

"Nearly all, Cleric Fay. Several await outside the Incorporation chambers within the Greeting Center."

"And Alpha … where is he?"

"I am not sure. I thought he had gone back to the shuttle."

"You *thought*?"

His trembling returned.

"You are a Supervisor. Your function is to obey instructions, not to *think*."

She turned away from him. When she spoke again, the words tumbled out in an emotionless, mechanical cadence. "Return to your duties and oversee the remaining Visitor Incorporation. Contact the Supervisors in the neighboring sectors to begin searching for the two missing Visitors. I fully expect they will be secured, sedated by force if necessary, and processed before my morning meal. Further blunders will not be tolerated. Do you understand me?"

"Yes, Cleric Fay."

She walked away, making it a point not to look at Mar. She heard him exhale as if he had been holding his breath all the while. After insuring that he was gone, Fay looked to the dark recess of an adjacent room. "You may join me."

"As you wish, Cleric Fay."

A figure wearing a dark, skin-tight leotard broke the hard edge of light falling from the inner doorway. He tossed his head back, flinging a comma of black hair from his yellow eyes.

***

"Listen."

Linda stirred. "I think I was sleeping. With this darkness, I'm not sure what I'm doing."

"You're not the only one," replied Adam. "Shhh. There it is again."

Adam could feel the muscles across her back tense. Their bodies pressed to one another, the rhythm of their respiration, synched and syncopated. As if on cue, both held their breaths. The soft pulsing of their hearts threatened to mask the subtle sounds of the forest.

Footfalls. Several in a row. Then nothing. Then again.

"Someone, or something, is getting closer," Linda whispered.

"Maybe that something doesn't know about us. Maybe it's just following the trail."

Adam got up on all fours, jostling Linda to do the same. He grasped her hand and tugged her along, while extending his other hand to avoid

323

knocking into a tree. After shuffling a few meters in a direction he hoped was off the trail, they reached the base of another tree.

"Let's stay here. Get close, tuck in, and pray whatever it is doesn't trip over us."

Linda threw her arm around Adam's neck, and the two pushed up against the trunk. The irregular shuffling sounds continued, becoming louder. Adam peeked in their direction. At first there was nothing to see, but soon a dim, blue glow danced through the woods, steadily growing and brightening. The approaching light sketched in the layout of their surroundings.

"I've got an idea. Stay here."

Linda glanced around the trunk. Softly illuminated fronds and branches stood motionless while the distant, shifting blue light skittered shadows to and fro.

A few moments later, Linda studied the sinuous cracks of the tree bark behind her. Her toe was caught by a shard of light and she squeezed even closer to her tree. The source of the blue light stopped moving.

"Please step out and show yourself."

The voice was soft, likely female, with an air of assurance, a kind of commanding quality. Linda remained hidden. Maybe it was a bluff. Maybe the searcher stopped every few meters and called out as a way to flush her quarry. She would wait and see.

Of a sudden, she heard a single grunt, followed by the sounds of a scuffle. The encounter was brief. The subsequent silence was broken by a familiar voice. "You can come out now, Linda."

It was Adam. Linda stumbled out toward the glow, at once shielding her eyes and willing them into focus. Adam lay on his back with a sandaled-foot resting on his chest. The foot was attached to a bare leg that disappeared under the edge of a robe. It was a hooded robe that kept the owner's face in the shadow cast by a torch, a torch without a flame that danced overhead.

"Adam, are you alright?"

"Yeah, yeah."

The leg lifted.

"I think my pride might be damaged … and maybe my collar bone."

Adam rubbed his shoulder and the hooded figure stepped back, allowing the two to rejoin. Linda helped him to his feet. Adam directed his gaze at the stranger. "So, who are you? Are you the Source?"

The figure stood unmoving but for the torch, a floating orb of light which shifted to a point midway between the three.

"My name is of no consequence. More importantly, you are Visitors that do not belong here in this forest. You were directed to meet with the Source. Why have you refused the kindness of our people?"

Still holding his shoulder with one hand, Adam replied, "Our mentor, by the name of Alpha, lied to us. He claimed to have been a scientist who helped build our ship. His expedition was to gather up volunteers from any planet that discovered the nature of the medallions … that is, the disks containing our genomes. According to Alpha, the mission was to meet our creators on this planet and find out what was behind our making." Adam paused for a moment before going on. "Does any of this make sense to you?"

"He did not lie."

Linda said, "But your people built our ship. Alpha was from here. His story was untrue."

"He and others did build the ship. As a Gatherer his mission was to collect individuals from different planets and to bring them here. You will discover your purpose when you meet with the Source."

Adam shook his head and Linda jumped in. "Alpha built the ship about twenty thousand years ago. Even in our Earth years, that is a very long time. How is it you remember him?"

The stranger kept silent.

"But why the deceit? Couldn't Alpha just tell us the whole truth?" asked Adam.

"Truth is a relative concept. If you knew of your real purpose, you may not have volunteered to join the expedition, as you call it."

"Oh? So, why don't you tell us what this is really all about? And who are you, exactly?" asked Linda, taking a step closer. Adam could see that she was beginning to lose it.

The orb wavered slightly as the stranger stepped away. "Know this. Supervisors are at this moment surrounding the forest. There is no way for you to escape. In the morning, follow the trail to the reception area."

The light went out. There was no sound of footfalls, no scraping of the dirt or brushing up against dangling fronds. Adam took several steps forward into the blackness. With his arms stretched out, he felt for the stranger and almost immediately ran into a tree.

"She, or it, is gone," said Adam.

"Damn spooky. She could have left that light with us."

"I'm not sure what we should do."

"How about doing what she suggested?"

"Give ourselves up, like the ghost lady of the Maker planet commanded?"

"It's either that or get lost in the woods and hope for the best."

"I'm sure there was a plot in a Star Trek episode that involved something a lot like the Source, and I don't think it ended well for the crew."

"Are you wearing red."

Adam chuckled. "I sure would like to know what we've gotten ourselves into … what this place is all about."

"Maybe we should follow the lady's advice. Maybe she's on our side."

Adam sensed a faint tremolo in Linda's voice. "Anyway, it's too dark to move through this forest. We'll settle in for the night. I feel like we haven't slept for the last eight thousand years."

"Very funny. At least the temperature here is pleasant, even at night."

"Let's hope it stays that way."

The two stretched out on the ground. After several minutes, Adam edged closer to Linda.

"Hey, don't get any ideas."

"Just a precaution, you know, just in case it does get cold."

They snuggled a bit closer.

"At daybreak, we'll decide what to do."

Chapter 31

"What is this all about, Mar?" asked Hai.

A look of contempt passed over Mar's face."Two Visitors have wandered into these woods."

The group of Supervisors gathered into a circle around Mar. A single blue orb of light hovered above them, casting their shadows outward like the elongated spokes of a wheel. They were standing at the entrance to a trail leading into the forest. Sunrise was expected within the hour.

"Most unusual. Does Cleric Fay know of this?" asked Hai.

"Cleric Fay has ordered that these two are found as soon as possible."

Hai was second in command of Greeters in the sector. There was a resentful quality to his voice, reflected in his countenance. Years ago, he and Mar were close. When Mar was selected as the Principle Supervisor, Hai had congratulated him, but it was clear that a deep line remained between them. After the selection, their relationship went cold, and in the intervening years had become ice.

"As you know, there is no precedence for this circumstance. Cleric Fay indicated to me that the Source has no use for Visitors of this kind. We are to capture them, and if necessary, destroy them."

"Destroy them? Those words do not sound like they came from Cleric Fay," said Hai.

Mar felt the heat rise through the skin of his face. His eyes narrowed. "You and the others will obey my exact instructions without question."

Hai dropped his head in obeisance.

Mar said, "Bring them to me. I will take them to the Cleric for final disposition."

Although it was unlikely that anyone would seek to verify a Cleric's order, Mar needed to insure that the operation was conducted in a manner which would not alert her. "I want three Supervisors stationed at each of the four trail entrances. I will stay here, at the entrance closest to the Incorporation Center."

A thin orange line appeared at the horizon. "Go now before the sun arrives."

Hai took charge of one group, but as he led them off he threw Mar a long look. Three groups moved off, each followed by a floating orb of light. Mar turned to the two Supervisors remaining with him. "Station yourselves by the shuttle."

"But that would leave you alone at this trail entrance."

Mar glared at the Supervisor who dared speak. He was the least experienced of the lot, not yet fearful. Mar pointed at the landing area, and with a failed effort to keep the irritation out of his voice said, "Do as you have been commanded."

He watched them move out and when their orb was but a distant fleck, he activated a hand-held beacon and entered the forest. His other hand held a rod, whose end glowed a deep crimson.

The tallest fronds were first to catch the rising sun, glinting as they swayed in the slight morning breeze. Vague outlines of the trees and the path before him took shape. Mar held out the beacon and picked up his pace, careful to avoid making any noise to alert the two wandering Visitors.

Fortune smiled upon him. Two prostate bodies lay directly ahead. He turned off the beacon and secreted it within his robes. Stepping lightly, he moved from tree to tree. When a few meters away, he saw that the Visitors were still asleep. Cleric Fay would have them brought before her this morning. However, there was nothing mentioned about what condition they might be in. The Source would be unhappy with two dead Visitors. How would Fay explain her failure?

The glowing end of the rod throbbed, throwing a pulsating red cone of light toward the unconscious pair. Mar considered which he would impale first.

He brought the rod down, but before it could sear its way through unwary flesh, someone grasped his shoulders and threw him to the ground. Rolling onto his back, he held the rod high, trying to focus its light on the intruder.

"Hai, how dare you?"

"You do not have the authority to kill these two." Hai stood at Mar's feet and grinned. "I expect Cleric Fay will be very interested in your actions, Mar. I am sure you two will have a lively discussion." He waved his hand at Mar. In it he carried a glowing white rod.

Adam and Linda stirred.

"Give me your weapon," Hai commanded.

An empty feeling ran through Mar. He was caught in a forbidden act. He turned over the rod in his hand and said, "Help me up."

Mar took hold of Hai's hand as he got to his feet and moved back a step.

"The rod?"

Mar lowered his shoulders and bowed his head. "How could I have been so stupid?"

"Now, now, Mar. Perhaps Cleric Fay will be merciful. Perhaps she will recommend re-education instead of resorption."

"Yes. It was stupid of me. Here."

Mar extended the rod's handle toward Hai. The motion had the effect of illuminating Mar's face from below, sculpting his features in sharp shadows. Hai's eyes wandered from the rod to the scarlet visage but for a moment—a moment long enough for Mar to flip the weapon, and slash it up in an arc.

Hai screamed. His severed hand tumbled to the ground.

Adam swiveled up to his knees. He shook Linda, but she was already awake and rising.

Hai fell to the ground, grabbing at his severed wrist, trying to staunch the half-cauterized stump. Mar took a step closer and raised his rod.

"What are you doing?" The words leaped out of Adam's mouth and he stepped toward the pair. In that instant, the rod glowed even brighter, turning into a fiery arc as Mar swung it. Adam heard an abbreviated grunt, and had to blink to clear his vision. The rod's afterglow bathed Hai's head in a crimson wash. Hai's eyes were open wide, staring at Adam. They rolled upward, and his head tilted back, revealing a dark, smoldering slash beneath his chin. His body snapped forward to the ground, landing in a lifeless heap.

Mar pivoted. "Stop!"

Linda reached Adam and pulled him back. They stared at Mar, unsure of what had just taken place, unsure of what to do next.

Mar lowered his rod, and with his other hand focused the beacon. He swept the area, blinding Adam for a moment.

Adam said, "I know you … Mar … isn't that your name? You met us when we arrived."

Mar nodded. It wasn't a nod which made Adam feel any better, rather, it spoke to impending doom.

"What happened here? Were you attacked?" Adam asked, giving Mar a chance to defuse the situation, to provide an explanation, even if it was a lie.

Mar straightened up and spoke to the beheaded body. "There was an attack. Poor Hai—taken by surprise."

Linda moved behind Adam and whispered, "It seems that this fellow, Hai, was on his knees when Mar slashed his throat. Some surprise."

Mar looked to Linda as if he heard her plainly. "Oh, there was a surprise. Hai never expected you two to attack him, least of all, to kill him in such a horrible manner."

"What are you saying?" asked Linda.

Adam took a step forward. "What kind of game are you playing at?"

"A game? Yes, I think this *is* a game," said Mar. He lifted the rod and moved his thumb over its end. A bright white light replaced the dull red glow. He pointed it at the pair.

Adam turned away to hold on to Linda. A surge of pain leaped through his back, and everything winked out.

Chapter 32

"I heard shouting. Hai was calling for help."

The subterranean hall echoed Mar's words. Fay sat upright and alone at the dais. Her eyes wandered over the Supervisors lining the walls of the circular room. Hai had an excellent record in this sector, and was considered for eventual promotion. That such a dismal fate should befall someone with promise was a misfortune. The circumstances leading to his death, a death without Incorporation demanded a full reckoning. Her eyes narrowed. "Tell us what happened next."

"I ran along the path toward the sounds. On the way I could hear Hai pleading for his life, begging for mercy. When I came upon him, the two fugitive Visitors were standing over him. They had forced him to his knees."

Mar paused a moment, perhaps to gather his thoughts, but more likely to heighten the drama. He drew in a deep breath and went on. "I shouted at them to stop, but they did not seem to hear me. Then I saw that Hai was holding his wrist. A blood trail led to what was left of his hand."Mar cleared his throat. "Somehow they must have taken his rod. The male Visitor held it high over his head. The female prodded him on, saying 'finish him', 'kill him'. Before I could draw my own weapon, the male slashed at Hai. He died instantly. When he turned his attention to me, I fired. The wide dispersal rendered both Visitors unconscious." Mar hung his head low and shook it slowly back and forth. "If only I had arrived sooner."

Light tapping of Fay's fingers on the polished stone surface of her table broke the silence in the chamber. The rhythm beckoned Mar to raise his head.

"And when did the others arrive?" she asked.

"Only minutes later, Cleric Fay. I ran to Hai to see if I could do anything for him. He was beyond help."

"That would explain the blood on your robes?"

Mar nodded. "When the other Supervisors arrived, I had already retrieved Hai's rod from the two Visitors. We secured his body and the Visitors, and brought them back here."

Fay once again directed her gaze to the attendants. "We have heard the testimony of Mar and several Supervisors who were first on the scene. Does anyone else wish to speak?"

No one offered a word and all eyes fixed on Mar. After a moment more, Mar said, "Cleric Fay, I realize that such events are without precedence, however since the Visitors are clearly guilty, may I suggest that we dispose of them in a public forum as a kind of lesson to both Greeters and Supervisors?"

Fay looked upon Mar with something approaching admiration. It had been mere hours earlier that she had admonished him for his lack of oversight, and now he painted himself as a hero—his actions being swift, perhaps even saving the lives of other unwary Supervisors searching for the two Visitors. It all made for a compelling story, except for one or two points. What motive could the Visitors possible have had to drive them to such a killing … after all, they were trying to evade detection. And besides, she did not trust Mar.

"I agree that the evidence provided thus far is consistent with their guilt. I shall inform you and the Supervisors of my decision regarding the fate of the Visitors after interviewing them myself."

The proclamation prompted a collective gasp. Mar lowered his head and seemed as if he was about to speak, when Fay stood. All bowed as she exited the hall. Once inside her chamber and sure she was beyond direct view, she collapsed onto a nearby chair.

"Is there anything you would like for me to get for you?"

It was Serv. He had been standing in the shadows, and had taken a step forward into Fay's private chambers. She shook her head for a brief moment, clearing it of the tangled events of the present hour. "A glass of water. Thank you, Serv."

The fates of the accused Visitors rested upon her decision. The killing of a human was an abomination, especially in such a gruesome manner. The death of Hai would displease the Source, and the loss of two Visitors made it worse. Everything that she knew of the incident relied upon Mar's statements. Ordinarily that should have been sufficient, but it was not sufficient—instead, it was worrisome.

"Here is your water." Alpha stood before her with glass extended. "With your permission, I dismissed your servant.

Fay took a long swallow. "You heard the testimony?"

"Mar provided many details."

"And, what do you think?"

"Cleric Fay, I am but a Gatherer. I am not in a position to counsel."

"Nonsense. My research in the archives has told me much about you. Gatherer, though you may be in name, is barely an adequate description of reality."

Alpha paused a moment, giving Fay a sidelong glance before gazing beyond her at the opening to the hall. "Details are where the truth of a matter hides."

Fay looked up from her glass. "And what is the truth?"

"Mar claimed he heard Hai shouting for help. Two points bear mentioning—that Mar could hear anything at all from his position on the trail, and that he could recognize Hai's voice."

"Troubling points, I agree. However, he could have been far enough along the trail to hear the shouting quite clearly."

The thin line of Alpha's lips broke as he stifled a laugh. "You posit a point which you yourself disbelieve."

Fay shrugged and placed the glass on the table. "I think that I will need your help."

***

"I don't feel anything."

Adam opened his eyes.

"I think I'm blind."

Every muscle of his body ached. He flexed his arms and legs, or at least thought he did, but felt nothing but pain.

"Adam. Adam is that you?"

"Hey, Linda. Can you see?"

"Blind as a bat. Everything's black. I'm not even sure my eyes are open ... and I'm awfully sore ... all over."

"Same here. Numb and in pain, a great combo."

"What do you remember?"

Adam grasped at the shredded tendrils of recent memory. "Snippets. Back in the forest, some guy ... I think it was Mar. He killed someone. Then he turned that gizmo, the lighted stick in our direction."

"I remember a flash, and bam. That's about it," finished Linda.

"Yeah, bam."

An eternity later the lights came back on.

***

Fay sat back in her chair. She felt exhausted. Perhaps she had shared too much with this Gatherer. There was no choice, really. No one else would have understood her. For the first time in many years, she faced uncertainty.

"They are ready for you," said Serv.

Fay swiveled in her chair, careful to hide her surprise. She was lost in thoughts forbidden to those loyal to the Source. Perhaps she really was defective, just like Mar had suggested so long ago.

"Thank you, Serv."

She walked along the labyrinthine passageways to an elevator leading to the Incorporation Center. As the doors slid shut, she shook her head—

an ineffective attempt to cast off doubt. Her life as a Cleric had been a lonely one. Service to the Source required her to be objective and distant, always impersonal. Ever since the Study and the training that followed, she was steadfastly true to its rigid customs. That is, up until now. She considered a new direction, an irreversible step, and one that promised either enlightenment or certain death.

***

Gray. Everything was gray. Adam turned his head away from the subdued lighting overhead and squinted.

Not dead yet.

A pair of fuzzy feet wandered into his view—next to them, another pair. He looked up and focused on a row of three figures sitting on a bench. Something touched the side of his head.

"Adam. That's you isn't it?"

Adam swiped away Linda's hand. "You found me."

The three seated blurs remained unmoving. They seemed to be staring at the wall opposite. Adam raised himself on one elbow.

"Can you get up?"

"My arms are good, but my legs are asleep."

"Same here. Must be the after-effects of that flash."

Linda propped herself up. "Probably some sort of electrical shock to our nervous systems. I'm starting to feel my toes. Hey, is that Markas and Jule?"

Adam looked again. The seated figures were now only slightly out of focus. Two had red hair.

"Could be. Hey, Markas. Jule."

"They don't seem to hear you," said Linda.

Adam scanned the room. "Lots of empty benches. Looks kind of like a doctor's waiting room."

Linda sat up. "Whoa, don't get up too fast. The room's spinning."

Adam kept his head down and dragged himself toward Markas and Jule. He lifted his arm and waved it. "Markas. Wake up."

His vision was cleared up enough to see that all three were staring out into empty space.

"They looked drugged."

He felt a whoosh of air pass over him. Without a word, a naked female stepped around him, leaned over to the figure seated next to Markas and whispered something into his ear. The man arose and followed her out of the room. The door slid shut behind them. Markas and Jule remained as they were—grim and lifeless statues.

"I don't like where all this is going," said Linda.

"How are your legs now?"

"They're starting to tingle."

"Mine too. We've got to get out of here."

Adam forced himself to sit up. Everything in his view wobbled.

"Man, I hate this feeling."

"It'll pass, just give it a minute."

He rubbed his legs. Linda did the same. The air moved again. A white-hooded figure approached.

"Haven't we met before?" asked Adam.

The figure stopped a few feet from the two. The hood fell back, revealing an oval face framed by long, brown hair with a streak of white. Even the subtle lighting of the room could not dull the brilliant blue of her eyes, which seemed to provide their own internal illumination.

"My name is Fay, Cleric Fay"

Adam used a bench as leverage to swivel up and sit. Linda reached out and she joined him. Adam pointed at Markas and Jule. "What happened to those two?"

"They are awaiting Incorporation."

"What does that mean?"

"They will become one with the Source."

"And, after that?"

"There is no after. Their bodies will be absorbed."

"Is that where we're headed?"

"You must tell me why you killed Supervisor Hai."

Adam felt the room move again. Linda steadied him and said, "You can't be serious. We tried to stop the killing. That other Supervisor, what's his name … Mar. He's the one that did the killing."

Adam said, "Two men awakened us, arguing. One of them was on his knees, holding his hand. Before I could figure out what was going on, the guy standing … Mar … swung that glow stick of his through the other's throat."

Adam rubbed his temples.

"And what occurred next?"

"He turned to us. The stick changed color to white and … that's all I remember."

Cleric Fay dropped her head as if contemplating.

Linda asked, "I bet that Mar told you a different story."

"Did he say *we* did the killing?" asked Adam.

Fay nodded, and Adam asked, "It's our word against his, isn't it?"

Fay said, "Perhaps this may be the custom where you come from, but not here. We are all in service to the Source. There is only truth in our words."

"You're telling me nobody here lies?" asked Linda.

Adam could not contain himself. "I guess not telling us the true nature of our trip here was not a lie? What about Alpha's buddy trying to kill us? And, what the hell are you doing to our crew? Drugging them and that incorporation business … you're killing them, aren't you?"

Fay raised her hands. "Enough. I understand your perspective, and the situation here must frighten you. We have been receiving Visitors like you for many, many years. It is the will of the Source to gather its probes from the far corners of our galaxy. They serve the Source. They provide the Source with data, information about civilization and history."

Adam had a suspicion that such might be the case, but when laid out in such a direct way, he felt the air leave his lungs. He grasped his head with both hands, elbows on knees. "A civilization and history that the Source put into motion?"

"Our archives do not provide the exact time it all began, and in any case, my understanding of the matter is inadequate."

Linda said, "We believe that life on our home world, Earth, began as simple one-celled organisms nearly four billion years ago. That's in our years of course."

"Rotations about your sun?"

Linda nodded and Fay said, "A minor difference between our worlds."

Adam asked, "Has the Source been in existence that long?"

"I cannot say. The archives suggest a beginning before time."

Adam looked back at the redheaded pair. "So this Source of yours has been around a long time, planting 'seeds' as you call them. And now, you're busy harvesting the crop, enticing members of all the humanoid species that managed to survive millions of years of evolution to take a trip to visit with the Source … only they find out that it's a one-way trip. All they're really needed for is to have their data downloaded for the Source's pleasure."

"A crude description."

Linda asked, "Why are you here? I mean, right now. Why are we having this conversation? Shouldn't we be executed, or whatever it is that you do with murderers?"

Linda trembled as she held Adam's arm. The corners of her eyes were moist. He began to feel the weight of their hasty decision to join this expedition.

"I am here to ask for your help." The two stared at Fay in silence. "You will not be, as you say, executed."

Adam said, "No? So, instead it's incorporation for us? I guess that's something anyway."

Fay raised her voice. "You don't understand. Escape. I need your help to escape this planet." Both were too shocked to answer. Fay stood. "Come, we must act swiftly." She approached the wall and the doors slid open. "You must trust me."

Linda pointed to Markas and Jule, "We can't leave them behind."

Adam said, "They are our friends. If we are to escape, then we all go together."

Fay shook her head. "Those two are under the influence of a powerful drug. They will slow us down. Do you not want to survive this situation? Do you not want to return to your world?"

Adam felt Linda's hands grip his arm. She spoke first. "There's no point in returning. Our families are gone. The world will have changed, leaving nothing for us, no one waiting for us."

"Yes. Families—a concept foreign to our existence. However, I can imagine such a close relationship with other humans. But you must want to survive. Every creature wishes to continue its existence. That reason alone should compel you to follow me."

Adam said, "Maybe we've lost our families, but we have friends here now. We don't go without those two."

Fay shrugged. "Very well. Whisper in their ears to follow us. They are becalmed, and will follow any direct order. Do it now, we have little time."

Adam stood, teetered a moment, and in short order joined Fay and Linda at the doorway with the two Moorsians in tow. The group shuffled along the hallway to another set of sliding doors. Fay depressed a few symbols embedded in the frame, and the doors parted.

"Well, well. What do we have here?"

Fay froze. Beyond her shoulders Adam saw Mar's smiling face, and several more like him. An old woman next to Mar was garbed in a white robe much like Fay wore. She spoke with a gravelly timbre. "My dear Fay. I see you have elected a rather unorthodox approach to justice."

Fay stammered. "Cleric Deirdre … I thought you were …"

"Incorporated? All in good time, Fay. It appears that some more work remains for me."

A red gleam emerged from Mar's upheld hand.

"And with the able assistance of Supervisor Mar and his charges, we will see to it that it is completed properly … in the name of the Source."

Chapter 33

"How do you think they're doing this?

Linda shook her head. "I don't believe you."

Adam turned enough to see Linda. They were hanging in the air about a meter above the floor. "Your ponytail looks good … subtle, yet provocative."

"Seriously?"

A smile creased Adam's cheeks. "What I'm saying is, it's not antigravity. We're held up by some invisible force field or something. These guys are really a lot more advanced than they look."

"Duh."

They were in a domed chamber with one arched exit and a single source of light illuminating a raised platform with a dark hole in its center.

Adam said, "Which means it's got to have a source."

"How about *The* Source? Isn't that the thing that runs the show here?"

"Can't be much of a Source if it let us get loose."

"Does this look like loose to you?"

Adam pointed with his nose. "What do you think that hole is for?"

"Garbage disposal."

***

After what seemed like hours, a hooded figure swathed in a white robe walked in. At first Adam thought it might be Cleric Fay come to rescue them. The hood fell back and revealed the white-haired crone that intercepted them earlier. She paused a moment to look at the two. Then Fay appeared at the doorway.

"What did you do to her?"

Fay's hood was missing. Judging from the ragged edges of her robe, it was torn off. Both her nostrils were caked with dried blood. Dark circles surrounded her eyes. One was swollen and nearly closed, and below it, a cruel red streak ran down her cheek.

Mar appeared from the shadowy recess behind her. Grinning up at Adam, he made a show of caressing Fay's cheek with the back of his hand. She winced as his hand glided over the wound.

Linda almost choked. "You people are sick. I can't believe your Source would condone such barbaric behavior."

When Cleric Deirdre spoke, the hollow voice they had heard earlier was gone, replaced with one of strength and command. "Silence. Your words are meaningless to us. We are here to witness the resorption of this unfaithful ward of the Source."

Adam and Linda struggled with their invisible bonds, which brought a wider smile to Mar, who looked on with obvious delight.

Linda raised her voice. "She was just trying to help. We did not kill anyone. He was the one … Mar."

"Blasphemy. His record is without blemish. He is a loyal servant of the Source." Deirdre sneered as she moved closer to the suspended pair. "You have caused a great deal of harm. You have deceived us, and tried to escape to avoid the Gatherer's efforts. It was not enough that you killed a Supervisor. Somehow you managed to convince this poor girl to help you … to turn her back on all that is holy … to betray the Source itself."

Before Adam could fan the flames even further, Fay rose into the air. Hoisted by an invisible force, she remained as if standing, her arms at her side. She drifted upward and then over the raised platform.

Deirdre spoke again. "Witness her resorption … the final moments of her life. What has come to be now returns."

Linda said, "You can't do that."

"Fear not for her, fear for yourselves."

Adam and Linda glided across the room. In seconds they were but an arm's length away from Fay.

"May the Source be swift and just."

There was no sound, no air movement, no last words. One moment Fay was before them, the next, she fell away into the darkness.

Adam fought down the image of a rabbit with a watch. This was no Wonderland. "Stop. You must listen to us. We just wanted …."

Linda disappeared into the hole. No scream, no sound.

"Linda!" Adam strained against the unseen bonds as he floated above the sinister blackness. Sweat ran along his temples. He stared down at Deirdre, and at Mar, anger contorting his features. He refused to believe that this was how it would all end.

A journey of a lifetime.

He opened his mouth to have at them one more time when everything went black.

***

Adam was sure he was screaming, but however much he shouted, he heard nothing. The air offered up no friction. There was nothing to see. His middle ear cranked out a growing sense of nausea. He had become weightless.

Minutes went by. Was he falling? He had read about sensory deprivation, and how it led to hallucinations. The silence was getting to him. He tried singing, speaking, humming and shouting yet again, with no effect. There simply was no sound.

His mind wandered. He thought about the landing. If he was falling all this time, he probably wouldn't even feel the landing.

Splat. Just like that ... I'm Spam. Bon appétit Mr. Source.

Adam had lost his sense of time. In its place, images sprouted up in the dark before him. Vibrant colors, reds and greens, they grew like stop-motion flowers, intersecting, and fading in and out. Rainbow spirals wormed across his vision, bursting through the flowers, breaking them into flashing Mandelbrot geometries.

I'm going insane.

He began hitting himself. This was a sensation he could feel. He pinched his cheeks, tugged at his ears, and scratched his stomach. The colors grew fainter, fading into a lighter, dreary gray. Thinking it was the

350

pain that pushed back the dark, he turned up the effort, gouging his thighs, punching his ribs.

Sensation returned. He felt air, or water, or both streaming across his face. He was falling though something thick, like a dense cloud of droplets. But these were not rain drops. They had an acrid odor, a sour taste, and stung his eyes. The featureless mist brightened. The liquid surged up at him in sheets, like a monsoon disgorging itself. The stinging of his eyes became excruciating. His skin started to burn.

Liquid forced its way into his mouth, choking him. He coughed, trying to clear his throat. He flailed his arms and legs, and shut his mouth and eyes, holding his breath. Soon, an inevitable, irresistible urge to breathe would fill his lungs with the excoriating fluid. The end would follow—swiftly, he hoped.

Something pulled at his arm, dragging him through the bubbling fluid. He groaned with the burning, contorting his body. Liquid flames licked at his skin. He twisted his torso, hoping to buy his lungs a few more seconds before succumbing.

Air. Cool air swept across his face. Adam blew the acrid goo out his nostrils and opened his mouth wide, sucking in the sweetness. He shook his head and along with it, the stinging, fiery liquid. There was light, and in that light, Adam saw a hand reaching for him.

The world was a streaked blur. Searing pain ran along every sinew. Something pulled him from the seething morass. He panted and coughed, spat some more, and breathed in air. Glorious air.

"Don't touch your eyes. Keep them closed."

He lay down. At once, a cold fluid drenched him, different from the burning—first his face, then his body. The liquid felt cool, refreshing, pushing away the pain, washing it off. He lay still for a few minutes, catching his breath and allowing his senses to calm, to return.

"You can open your eyes now."

Adam winced. His eyelids flickered, afraid to open.

"You're going to be in some pain for a while, but I think not very long. Wash your eyes out with this."

Unable to focus, he reached out. He felt a bowl, cupped his hands around it, and splashed the liquid on his face and eyes. "Oh, God. I thought I was going to die."

"You would have. However, you have a friend that has other plans."

Adam squeezed his eyes clear, enough to see more than shadows. The stooped person talking to him was balding, had long blondish hair and a smile he would not forget for the rest of his life.

"My name is Ebbe. I am Caretaker." He turned to point at two other figures lying on the floor. "Your friends are recovering same as you."

***

"Tell Cleric Deirdre what you told me."

Mar pushed Serv closer to Deirdre.

"I overheard Cleric Fay speaking to someone in her compartment."

"Do not refer to Fay as a Cleric. She is no longer functioning in that capacity … or any capacity for that matter." Deirdre frowned and pressed a finger to her temple. "Who exactly was she talking to?"

Serv said, "She spoke with the Gatherer, Alpha."

"And ...?"

Serv lowered his head. "I could not hear what they said."

Deirdre looked to Mar. "Is this all you have for me?"

Mar shoved Serv. "Tell Cleric Deirdre what else you know."

"Cleric ... Fay, before she met with the Visitors ... the ones who killed Supervisor Hai ... she and I descended to the Caretaker level. She dismissed me, saying that she would be along shortly, that I should wait at the Learning Center."

"And that is when you informed us of Fay's activity," said Mar.

Serv nodded.

Deirdre said, "Leave us," and turned to Mar. "Ebbe ... she must have gone to see Ebbe ... but why?"

"Perhaps we should ask him."

***

"Linda!" Adam stood up, but promptly slipped back down.

"Adam, you're alive!"

"Please take care, sir. As you can see, the flooring is wet," said Ebbe.

Adam's skin felt like he had just rolled through a bed of stinging nettles. Red welts ran along both hands, and he could only imagine what his face looked like. It felt like hell.

Adam said, "Ebbe ... My throat is killing me."

"Please take a drink of this."

Ebbe offered the running water from his hose. After gulping down the cool, soothing liquid, he thanked Ebbe and got up on his feet. Linda was already standing, helped up by Fay. Their clothing was shredded in places, as was his. Both had rashes running over their faces and hands. They looked like half-boiled lobsters.

"Cleric Fay, aren't we supposed to be …what did that woman say? Resorbed?"

Fay said, "Yes, resorbed. We were meant to be broken down into basics. Thanks to Ebbe, we are yet intact.

Ebbe said, "I was more than happy to be of service, Cleric Fay." He bowed and stepped back, while hosing down the platform.

Adam caught the acknowledgment. "You knew this was going to happen?"

Fay said, "In a way."

Adam was about to explode, when Linda interrupted. "What is that stuff? Some kind of acid?"

Fay said, "Enzymes, though not the type you are familiar with. These are engineered to digest flesh and bone."

Linda said, "Like proteases, and lipases, and such."

"Much more efficient than those. The purpose of this system is to recycle amino acids, carbohydrates, fats … even the minerals in your bones."

Still reeling from the revelation that Fay had willingly risked their lives, Adam asked, "Recycle to where?"

Ebbe shut down the sprayer. "To the Growing Chambers, and to the Sustainers." He offered the trio a set of towels.

Adam wiped his face. An image of prancing Greeters filled his mind. *Greeters without navels.* "So all these resorbed people become new people? You grow human beings down here?"

Linda asked, "What about children? We haven't seen any."

Ebbe nodded. "Humans are grown to full term, each programmed to carry out specific duties. Further training is provided in the Learning Center. There is no need for immature versions."

With the exception of you and Deirdre, it seems there's no need for old ones either.

Linda asked, "What are Sustainers?"

Fay stepped between the two. "They produce the food we eat."

Chapter 34

"What do we do now?" Adam asked the question of no one in particular. The wind had left his sails. He was exhausted, hurt, and hungry. He had trouble standing, and a glance at Linda confirmed she was in about the same sad shape.

Fay said, "We will proceed to the surface, and with your help commandeer the shuttle and return to your ship."

Adam said, "That's quite a plan."

I only see about a thousand different ways it could go wrong.

"Who is going fly the shuttle? And the ship? Surely, you must know we can't do any of that."

"Steps have been taken."

Ebbe said, "Watch your heads."

The platform began to move. It glided over the roiling sea of digestive juices, bobbed by foam gurgling up from beneath. Several low-hanging pipes came into view through a swirling mist.

Adam ducked and said to Linda, "You weren't far off."

"Far off?"

"Yeah … the natives and their cook pot."

An edge appeared. Then more lines as they approached a wall. Seconds later, the raft docked to a small outcropping of flooring, a pier of stone, which led to an arched doorway.

Ebbe was the first to step off. "Follow me."

Adam caught hold of Ebbe. "Wait a minute. What about Markas and Jule?"

Fay said, "They are beyond our help now. They have been incorporated."

Linda asked, "What exactly does that mean?"

"Their bodies and minds have been linked to the Source. Their personal data is now part of a great collection of information about our galaxy."

Adam said, "You're not really suggesting that the whole reason to come here was to provide data? I got the part about your Source responsible for the creation of humans, or humanoids. And that was a few million years ago. So, now you're telling us it's harvesting its creations, simply to get data?"

"Crudely put, but accurate," said Fay.

"And you see nothing wrong with this? It's fine with you that humans are used in this way?"

Linda said, "We're more than some interstellar probes ..." Her voice faded and Adam draped his arm around her.

Adam looked beyond her shoulder into the dim reaches of the hall. "Maybe we're missing something. It can't be that simple ... that cruel."

Fay said, "As a Cleric, I have the privilege of learning, of seeing how the inner functions of this planet work." She looked to Ebbe, who had his head bowed low. "With Ebbe's help, I became familiar with all the systems supporting the Source. And I know that we have all been programmed, and that includes you. Humans are driven to seek us out, and we, to incorporate your knowledge. This is the way of things."

"But you're not like the others. You told us you wanted out, to escape," said Adam.

Ebbe's face froze. He croaked, "To escape?"

Fay placed a hand on his back. "My desire to leave this world, to seek out the *real* Truth, is my own. From my beginnings as a Greeter, I questioned this reality, our rituals and our purpose. However, Ebbe, I have always been loyal to the Source, and would never do anything to harm it."

She stepped away. "I thank you for your help in saving our lives. You can now return to your duties. We will find our own way."

Ebbe sagged and shook his head from side to side. Adam saw the deep relationship the two had developed, almost like father and daughter—a disappointed father and a rebellious daughter.

"I wish you well, Cleric Fay."

He remained on the platform as the three disembarked.

As they entered the hall, Linda asked, "Are Markas and Jule dead? Is that what happens to people who get incorporated?"

Once farther along the hallway, and away from the burbling noises of the immense digestive vat, Fay said, "I believe they are still alive."

"For how long?" asked Adam.

"They are kept … linked forever.

Adam said, "At least take us to them. Can you do that?"

"It is likely that Deirdre and her Supervisors will initiate a pursuit. Like me, she is very perceptive, and after a time may find reason to suspect that we have survived." Fay stepped out ahead of the two. "I will take you to the Incorporation Chambers. It is along the way, but we must hurry."

Fay's pace was swift, forcing Adam and Linda to jog every once in a while to keep up. They traversed countless corridors, side passages, and hidden doorways, pushing ahead at an unrelenting tempo. Not once did they encounter anyone else in the Makers' underworld. Adam was about to call for a break, when Fay spoke. "We are here. The Incorporation Chambers are beyond this doorway."

The door dissolved, and he and Linda followed Fay onto a balcony which overlooked a shadowy open expanse. Adam leaned over the railing, but did not see any walls other than the one they stood within, which disappeared to either side, swallowed by the gloom. As his eyes grew accustomed to the muted light, small rectangular objects took form in the void, each with a subtle blue glow illuminating its bottom surface. At first he saw dozens, then hundreds of casket-like containers suspended in the air, arranged in a three-dimensional pattern of rows and columns as far as he could see in any direction. The suffuse lighting came from a small round portal set into the top panel of each container.

"What is this? asked Linda.

"Each chamber contains a Visitor."

Adam asked, "How many are there?"

"Of this, I am uncertain. During my tenure as Cleric, I oversaw the processing of several thousand Visitors." She hesitated a moment, as if thinking back. "That was over a period of about ten years. However, our archives suggest the processing began at least ten thousand years ago."

"My God," said Linda.

Millions by now.

Adam took a beat to let the statistics sink in. He was almost afraid to ask. "Is there any chance you could find our friends?"

"I brought you to the most recent end. Look closely." Fay pointed to a specific row of chambers.

Adam followed her finger and said, "There are no containers beyond that one."

"It was the last to be processed."

Linda said, "So that one, or those two at the end, could be the ones containing Markas and Jule."

"How do we get there?" asked Adam.

"The process is irreversible … you will not be able to revive or retrieve them."

"You know this for certain?" Adam pressed.

Fay opened her mouth, but waited a moment before going on. "No Visitor has ever returned from Incorporation." She shook her head at the pair. "I can bring us closer."

The balcony lunged forward, nearly sending Adam over the rails. Linda grasped him by the arm.

"I should have warned you. Hold on tight."

Fay played her fingertips across a part of the railing. In moments, their platform hovered over the last container.

A myriad of deep blue lights surrounded them, like beacons alerting the world to occupants within. Cables emerged from the ends and sides of each rounded box, creating a kind of mesh that connected each to its neighbor. Wires snaked from the portal ends and joined thicker cabling. The columns of containers reached downward beyond Adam's vision.

"As you can see, there is nothing you can do."

Adam turned to Linda, who widened her eyes and gripped his arm tighter. She said, "No you don't."

"Be right back."

Adam leaped over the railing and landed atop the nearest chamber.

***

Ebbe spat out a tooth. He watched it arc, bounce once and skitter along the floor.

"Enough." Mar lowered his arm and looked to Deirdre. She stepped closer to Ebbe and said, "For the last time, tell me what you discussed with her."

Ebbe continued to look down at his tooth. His mouth was numb, and felt as if it was sagging. The tooth was blurry, melding with the floor. His right eye was shut and his left filled with tears. He knew the dark spatter on the floor was his, but it held no terror or fear, for his mind had already retreated to a warm, safe place.

Mar raised his hand. A fierce red glow sparkled before the one good eye. Ebbe looked up and saw two smudges, distorted images of people he once knew, people he once considered colleagues. When he spoke, the words oozed out in a slur. "I have nothing to say. Cleric Fay is my friend, my good friend."

The Deirdre smudge nodded, and Ebbe's crimson sun set.

***

The suspended Incorporation container remained in position as if the whole matrix was made of stone. Adam crouched beneath the one above. A downward glance soured his stomach and threatened a spat of vertigo. Before skipping across to the last two in the row, where he hoped to find Markas and Jule, he focused on the small, six-inch circular portal at his feet. He knelt and lowered his head into the soft blue light. The transparent pane held a face frozen in the throes of terror—eyes wide, nostrils flared and mouth agape. It was vaguely familiar, maybe one of the last shuttle passengers. The features were so distorted that he wasn't sure if it was male or female. A closer look revealed needles. They transfixed the face, locking it in place. A picture of the infamous medieval Iron Maiden flashed through Adam's mind—a permanent imprint on an impressionable young mind wandering the darker recesses of museum alcoves. In this incarnation, each needle-like projection likely served a special purpose, perhaps gathering biological samples and data from the specimen trapped within.

Linda leaned over the balustrade. "What can you see?"

Adam rose, steadying himself by gripping the chamber above. "It's not good. These people have been skewered by some kind of network of wires or needles." He looked at Fay, and asked, "Are they completely impaled in there? I can't see much past the face."

Fay nodded. "The process of Incorporation is irreversible. They are in direct communication with the Source."

Adam stepped over to the next container in line, which was only about two feet away, then the next, until he reached the last one—the most recent addition. Markas stared up at him—his open-eyed visage painted with deep shades of blue. Adam shook his head in disgust. He was about to check on what was probably Jule's chamber, when he caught a movement from within the portal. The eyes—the eyes were following him.

Adam dropped to his knees and tapped the translucent pane. "Markas, can you hear me?"

The face looked as if molded in wax, but the eyes blinked.

Adam turned to Fay, now some distance away. "Markas is alive. He can hear me."

Her silence suggested she was as surprised as he.

"Is there a way to open these coffins?"

Fay leaned over the railing and said, "The panel you are standing on is a door. However, I have never seen one opened once closed."

Linda angled over the railing and jumped to the nearest chamber. "Adam, I'm coming."

Moments later, she stood on the container nearest Adam. "It's Jule, and her eyes are moving too!"

Fay said, "The process of Incorporation may take some time to complete. Perhaps that would explain the eyes."

Adam worked his fingertips around the edges. "There's a lip here. I can get my fingers beneath it, but it isn't going anywhere as long as I'm standing on it."

Linda said, "How about we try and free Jule first. You stay there and I'll get on the one behind me."

"Then we'll pull on the door from opposite sides," finished Adam.

It took almost no effort at all. The door swung up with a whisper. A network of needles automatically recessed into the doorframe, leaving only bloody tips protruding. Additional sets withdrew from Jule's body to the sides of the chamber. She remained motionless. A regularly spaced series of dark patches appeared along the sides of her face and all over her body suit—nasty little pinpricks.

Linda was closest to her head, and reached down, rocking it gently to and fro. "Jule, it's all right. It's Adam and me … Jule." She used a hand to wipe the blood from the sides of Jule's face.

"Is she breathing?" asked Adam.

Jule spasmed. Her body shuddered and then lurched. An arm shot up, catching Linda on her shoulder, causing her to lose balance and slip off the container.

Chapter 35

Adam's eyes locked onto a dark streak where Linda was perched only a moment earlier, and his gut jerked when he heard a thud from below. His mind filled with an image of Linda cart-wheeling between containers, careening off hard corners, her bloody and torn body disappearing into the bottomless abyss. He edged back enough to peer through the gap between.

"Linda. Are you okay?"

She was on her back, propped up by her elbows on one end, while the heels of her feet rested on the rim of an adjacent casket door. Her sagging butt filled in the span between. She looked up, and even in the gloomy lighting Adam could see the pained expression on her face. He wasn't sure if it was from an injury or she was just plain embarrassed.

"Do I look okay?"

"You look great."

Jule's head bobbed up. It was streaked with blood and staring right at Adam. Her voice warbled. "What a curious thing to say."

Adam said, "Jule! How do you feel?"

"I'm not sure. My arms and legs are numb." She looked at her hands. "And is all this my blood?"

Jule angled her elbows onto the door's rim, trying to lift herself out of the chamber.

"Whoa, hold on. We'll have you out in a minute. Just relax right now." Adam looked at the door panel. "No more needles."

"Thanks for nothing," Linda said. She was straddling the tops of two chambers, and lifted her arms toward Adam.

Adam said, "For a moment I thought you were a goner. Hey, help me out with Markas' chamber door." Working together they managed to flip it open.

In minutes Markas and Jule were sitting up, rubbing their arms and laughing. Fay, who had been a silent witness to the dual resurrection, called from the railing. "You must hurry. The Source will be aware of your activities."

Adam and Jule helped Markas to stand. Both Jule and he were swaying, trying to find firmer footing, when a clacking, grinding sound stopped them cold.

Adam looked to Fay. "What's that?"

Fay said, "Get back up here now. It may be an automaton."

Maybe it was the way she said it—'an automaton.' Hackles ran up Adam's back. The dim lighting made it worse, leaving too much to his imagination.

I can see it now ... a huge electromechanical spider, using its specially designed twelve legs to drop from chamber to chamber, preceded by a mandible equipped with giant pincers jutting from its three-eyed head.

"No time to lose," Adam said. He helped Markas up, and the two followed Linda and Jule across several containers.

Markas said, "I want to thank you for coming back for us."

"That's okay, Markas. I'm sure you would have done the same."

"Indeed."

The clacking turned into whirring. Something was definitely making its way closer, something metallic. Adam saw only dull blue chambers receding into the distance.

Linda was the first one over the railing. She reached down and helped Jule up. Adam positioned Markas for the next haul up. The whirring stopped. All three women stared at something behind Adam. All three had eyes the size of saucers.

The spider has arrived.

Adam let go of Markas, and did a slow one-eighty. At first, the silhouette of the thing standing a few paces away atop the adjacent chamber appeared to be a man—human size, two spindly arms, and two spindly legs. When it bent at the waist, the similarity came to an abrupt end. It had no head, but it did have an extra set of arms.

When its forearms touched the chamber, it used the middle set to lever its way across the gap between. It clacked away from Adam, reached the edge, whirred and extended its torso. The movement allowed it to drop onto the next chamber. It moved like a cross between a caterpillar and a Slinky toy. Clacking and whirring, it headed to Markas and Jule's recently vacated accommodations.

Adam turned back to Markas. "Let's get the hell out of here."

He gave Markas a boost up. Once over the railing, Markas reached down toward Adam's extended hand. The clacking-whirring sound returned, drawing closer. Slinky landed on the far end of his container. Three-fingered paws snapped open, and its torso whirred.

Adam stepped to the side and jumped to the next container. Slinky regained its compact shape and turned to follow Adam.

"I don't think it knows about you. Stay quiet and don't move. I'll try and circle around."

Adam leaped from chamber to chamber in an arc designed to return him to the balcony. Slinky clacked and whirred after him, following his exact trail like a bloodhound. It was fast, easily keeping up, forepaws narrowly missing him more than once.

As Adam passed the railing, he jumped and grasped the connecting cable between two chambers above him. Slinky landed on the chamber below just as he swung his legs up and over the cable. He waited. The thing was like a robotic bloodhound. It hesitated, perhaps sniffing the air, trying to pick up Adam's scent. It clanked and whirred onto the next chamber, appearing to have decided to continue its search along the circular path they just completed.

Adam lowered himself to the container below before getting hoisted up and over the railing.

"What was that?" asked Adam.

"Part of the automated repair systems. It was investigating."

Fay led the quartet back into the tunnels. Quick exchanges along the way caught up Markas and Jule on the situation—Fay wanted escape, Adam and Linda wanted the same, but not before meeting the Source. Markas and Jule were happy to be alive. They did not remember much beyond the luau.

"What about after you were placed in those chambers?" asked Linda.

Jule grimaced and her eyes rolled. "I do remember that. I felt completely helpless. And when the door closed, I was sure it was the end."

"Did you sense anything? Was there something communicating with you?" asked Adam.

Markas said, "Fear. I only recall being scared out of my mind. After the door closed, I felt the needles." He stopped a moment, swallowing hard, and lowered his voice. "I remember screaming when the door shut and the needles … and then, nothing."

Fay turned and said, "Keep moving. The Source knows about us."

Markas and Jule limped, but their balance and strength seemed to be improving with each step. The group seemed to be wandering aimlessly through a maze of interconnecting hallways. Several robed figures, dressed much like Ebbe, passed by without incident.

Fay raised her arm, halting the procession. "It is time to make a decision. These elevators can take us to the surface, and the way back to your shuttle. This passage leads deeper into the Source's domain."

Adam asked, "Have you been that way? I mean, have you seen or spoken to the Source?"

"There has never been a reason to meet with the Source. It provides for everything we have here."

Linda said, "It sounds like you don't really know anything about the Source, do you?"

Fay rubbed the side of her face and scowled. Adam wasn't sure if that was a look of disgust or a reaction to pain. She replied in a voice so distant as to be a whisper. "To my knowledge, no one has ever directly visited with the Source."

Adam said, "Then for all you know, you could be serving and worshiping something made up … made up by your ancestors. Your people could be following a ritual that has no real purpose anymore."

Fay scowled even more.

Linda said, "Is there actually a place down here … where the Source resides?"

Her head moved side-to-side, as if discounting the present discussion. "There is a location, a forbidden place."

"Okay then," said Adam. "That's where we're headed."

Jule looked back at Markas, and said, "I'm not so sure we should take the time to go looking. Markas, we already got a taste of what the Source has in store for us. I would rather we get away from here … even if it means never discovering what the Source is. I don't want to die here."

Markas dropped his shoulders and looked to Adam and Linda. "I guess I'm with Jule. We're lucky to be alive. Why test that luck? I think we should get out of here while we can."

Adam turned to Fay. "Why don't you just show us which way to go, and take Markas and Jule up to the surface?"

Fay depressed several embossed symbols on the wall. As the panels glided open, she spoke to Markas. "This elevator will take you to the surface. You will arrive in a Sustainer Unit, a structure designed to provide food. It will be well away from your original landing site. Someone will meet you there and take you to the shuttle. Inform him that we will follow shortly."

"But who will fly the shuttle? We have some knowledge of the controls, but neither of us is capable of flying it," said Markas.

"That will not be a problem," said Fay.

As the elevator doors began to close, Adam said, "We'll be right up. Don't leave without us."

Fay said, "I can take you to the Source, or at least to its location, but cannot promise a meeting. Also know well, that it is aware of us and there are forces here sworn to protect it that are also aware of us."

Chapter 36

Weariness turned their meandering into a brutal slog. Adam's throat burned with thirst, made all the more acute by the earlier acid wash. Linda's grip on his arm loosened as they trudged farther into the maze of passageways.

"We are approaching the Birthing Pavilion. It is where we are manufactured."

The Greeters without navels.

Linda asked, "Is that something we could take a look at?"

"We will need to pass through the facility. Just be sure to avoid eye contact with the attendant. No one will question a Cleric or her party."

The way ahead widened into a brighter expanse. They entered a circular, domed room, about a hundred meters across. A bright silvery tube, perhaps six feet thick, dropped from the center of the dome, sprouted narrower, flexible arms from beneath which extended outward in every direction. These reached the curved outer walls of the room, where massive instrumentation received them. Translucent panels set within the walls of each radiated a pulsating emerald green.

"What are we looking at?" whispered Adam.

Fay said, "These are the growth modules. The attendants are Growers, responsible for the production."

There were Growers standing at each module. Adam counted at least twenty.

Linda asked, "Can we take a closer look at one of these modules?"

Fay appeared to shake her head, and continued on a steady course aimed at the mouth of an exit at the far side of the room. Before they reached the egress, she changed direction and stopped alongside one of the growth chambers.

"Stay close to me. Do not touch anything."

Several child-like bodies bobbed within a green window.

"Are you growing these individuals to adults in there?" asked Linda.

A male Grower, clad in a green tunic and leggings, turned to Linda and was about to speak, when Fay explained, "These two are Visitors for whom I am providing a tour. I will answer their questions. You may resume your duties."

The Grower pivoted and examined a gauge-like device mounted on the chamber. He sidled away to make some adjustments on an adjacent panel.

"Each chamber is designed to grow up to ten individuals. They are kept in here until early adulthood."

Adam asked, "I noticed that you seem to have specialists … like Supervisors, and Greeters. Are these individuals trained or is there something more involved?"

"We use prescribed genetic codes to create individuals with the proper traits." Fay pointed to the window. "These will be Greeters. After they complete their growth cycle, they are given a short period of training, focusing on duties and customs."

Linda said, "Genetic codes. You're talking about designed genomes?"

"We have all been designed—on this world, as well as on yours."

Adam said, "But what about family? You're creating people incapable of having children."

Fay dropped her head. "It is the way of the Source."

"What about you? You're not like the rest," said Linda.

"No, not like the rest. I am defective. That is why I must leave."

Linda cupped her hand about Fay's shoulder and said, "There's nothing defective about wanting to find out more. It's in our nature as humans."

"The Source has instructed us—here, we carry out our duties without question … while you seek and discover, and eventually return to the Source."

Adam said, "To provide the Source with information. That's our duty? And it's written into our genome? I don't think I like this Source of yours."

Linda watched the Grower making adjustments. When he finished, he walked off to join another. She took a few steps toward the viewing panel and gazed inside. "It's an impressive technology—growing humans without umbilical cords. How long does it take?"

"A few months."

"Fast. And all that time, they just sleep in here?"

"There is some learning provided by the Source." Fay pointed to a set of thin wires protruding from the nostril of one of the children. The wires led to a bundle, which disappeared into the upper reaches of the tank. "They have no awareness of the outside world until they are ready to emerge."

Linda gasped as one of the floating children opened her eyes. "I think this one might be ready."

"An autonomic reaction … similar to dreaming. It is an involuntary response to the information she is absorbing."

Adam moved closer to the control panel. "This stuff here—for monitoring the kids?"

Fay acknowledged with a quick nod.

"And what's this?" He bent down to look at a rectangular faceplate sporting a thin horizontal slot.

Fay said, "We really must be on our way."

Adam was about to argue with her when he noticed that the Growers had congregated into a group on the far side of the room. He tugged Linda's arm as he caught up with Fay.

"Hey, what's the rush?" asked Linda.

"Check it out," said Adam, and pointed to the huddle.

"I get it."

The three fast-walked through the exit. The lighting improved and a set of embossed lines on the wall caught Adam's interest. "Let me guess. This is another elevator."

Fay looked weary. It was a wonder that she had kept up such a frightful pace. Her injuries were severe. She said, "The entrance to the domain of the Source."

Linda said, "Is it farther down?"

"No, my dear. We will not be taking the elevator."

Fay nodded at the wall. Adam followed her gaze and his jaw dropped. Linda croaked, "Oh my God."

Fay asked, "What is it that surprises you so?"

Adam said, "The symbols."

Fay spoke in a low, reverent tone. "The symbols are ancient, written in a form long lost to us. Even Caretaker Ebbe did not know their meaning, however he taught me the proper touch sequence to open this door."

Adam gave Linda a glance, and then said, "Would you mind if I tried?"

Fay stepped back, her eyes wide and mouth open.

He reached up to the wall panel and glided his fingers over the extruded symbols, tracing them, feeling their shapes. He brought up his other hand, and tapped several symbols in sequence. "Well?"

As nothing happened, Fay said, "The entrance remains sealed."

"Really?" Adam touched one more symbol. The panel slid up and out of sight.

Fay stammered, "How could you know?"

Adam said, "These symbols, the ones you call ancient, are well known to to us. They spell out the instructions for opening the door. Right here … OPEN BY DEPRESSING NUMBERS ZERO THROUGH NINE … It's written in English."

Chapter 37

"How is it possible?" asked Linda.

"That's the million dollar question," said Adam.

The three stepped through into a wide hallway, but only about twenty feet long. The door behind them whooshed shut. The walls themselves glowed.

Fay said, "English. That is your native tongue?"

"Yeah. Why would our native tongue show up on a doorway here, eight thousand light-years from our home?" asked Adam.

Linda said, "You mentioned it was an *ancient* language?"

Fay barely nodded, and replied as if to herself. "Our beliefs hold that it is the language of the Source—the ones who created this world."

"Well, I guess it must be some hell of a coincidence that we use the same language. You said there was a way to meet with the Source … a forbidden access."

"The means is concealed among these texts." Fay swept her arm through the air.

The walls were pure white, with raised symbols covering most of their surfaces.

"You've never been through here?"

Fay remained silent.

She's been inside.

Linda moved to the opposite wall. "There are hundreds of letters and numbers. Most seem to be the alphanumeric characters we know, but they may not necessarily be part of the English language. A few are quite different."

"Those are the ones on the medallion, and the ones I saw on the ship."

Linda faced Fay and asked, "Aren't there any scientists in your community?"

Adam thought about the complete absence of technology on the surface.

Yet these people are comfortable with space ships, robots and killer glow sticks.

Fay said, "You met Ebbe, the Caretaker, and you saw the Growers. There are specialists of all kinds here."

Adam could see she wasn't getting it. "Your specialists are what we would call technicians. We're talking about people who develop *new* technology, inventions that make life easier."

Fay said, "We have everything we need. There is no necessity for improvement." After a moment she added, "We live to serve the Source."

"Who built the machines? I'm talking about the growth chambers, that resorption stew that we swam in, the incorporation systems, and even that six-legged Slinky that chased me?"

"The Source provides everything."

Linda said, "I don't see any instructions. None of the lettering makes up any words, and the formulas look to be nonsense."

The two moved along the wall, looking and feeling their way through the pictographic murals.

"Whoa … did you see that?" asked Adam. He pointed to the featureless wall at the end of the corridor. As the two took several steps closer, a door took form—an ordinary office door with four recessed panels and a brass doorknob.

"Jeez … is it real?" asked Linda.

Adam said, "Only one way to find out."

He turned the knob. The door swung in and disappeared into a black void.

Fay moved up behind them. "You are looking into the face of the Source."

Adam and Linda stepped up to the threshold. At first they could see nothing but pitch black with a blurry white blob suspended in the middle, possibly a consequence of the strong contrast with the corridor's bright lighting. Gradually though, details emerged—staggering details. An arc of clouds coalesced into thousands of pinpoints of light. Another, and then another came into view. Together, they formed a set of curved arms—a spiral, the center of which now glowed even brighter.

Adam said, "We seem to be looking at stars. Is this our galaxy? I swear it's what the Milky Way might look like from above its plane … from the halo … from where we are right now."

When Fay spoke up, her voice assumed a deep resonance. "It is the tapestry. It is the Source."

Adam moved side to side. "Damn if this doorway isn't some kind of window." He looked Fay in the eyes. "You've been here before."

"Few have had the honor."

Linda asked, "Is this it? What about the Makers, our creators?"

"This can't be real." Adam reached out with his hand, extending it beyond the doorway.

"Don't." said Fay.

"So, you didn't actually meet the Source."

Fay said, "To gaze at the wonder is enough."

"And I bet you didn't try this." Adam stepped through the doorway and disappeared.

"Adam!"

Fay wrapped her arms around Linda. She threw off Fay's embrace. "What happened to him?"

Fay looked confused. Suddenly her eyes widened. Linda turned to look at the dark opening. First a finger emerged from one of the galaxy's arms, and then four more joined it, forming a hand.

Fay choked. "It is the Source. It comes for us."

As the hand moved closer, it brought with it an arm covered in tattered cloth. Linda stepped away from Fay, who was bowing her head for fear of gazing into the face of the Source. She drew nearer to the extended arm. With its palm up, the fingers curled, as if beckoning.

She reached out and grasped the proffered digits and was pulled in.

"Surprised?"

Linda blinked several times and shook her head. "Adam! You're all right."

"Quite the special effect, isn't it?"

"What is this place?"

"That's what we're about to find out."

The room was a box about ten feet on a side. The open doorway cast their shadows on empty walls. Through it, they saw Fay, now resting on her knees.

"Cleric Fay!"

Fay seemed oblivious.

"Apparently, the visual effect is not the only thing that's one-way," said Adam.

"This looks like a dead end," said Linda.

"So far, nothing about this place looks like what it really is. Why don't you look for a light switch?"

"Ha. It would be nice to have a light switch."

Linda walked over to the open entrance. "Holy shit."

Adam whirled about and saw Linda staring at the doorjamb.

"What's up?"

Linda depressed something on the wall, and the room became illuminated. "A light switch."

Adam looked to the ceiling, but found no specific source for the lighting. The walls and ceiling seemed to glow from within. "Great work."

"Adam, do you recall seeing this switch when you came in?"

"Not really ... I guess I was too pleased with myself for figuring out the galaxy scene was an illusion."

"I don't recall it either. In fact, I'm sure it wasn't there."

Linda joined Adam in the center. "Look at each wall. Do you see anything?"

"Nada. The walls are bare. There's no exit, except for the doorway behind us."

"Now, what do we want? I mean, is there something specific we want right now?"

Adam scratched his head. "Besides getting back on the ship, and heading for home?"

Linda glared at him.

"I suppose we want to find out who these Makers are. So we want a way to get out of this room, a way which will lead us to them."

"Great. Let's both visualize what that might look like."

"Yeah, right."

The second glare mollified him.

"Well, okay. I guess we want another door … this time one that leads to the Makers."

Linda enunciated slowly. "Let there be a doorway which leads to the Makers."

"You *do* know how silly that sounds."

There was nothing to announce its manufacture, no gaudy lighting effects, not even a whisper. They both stared at the new doorway for a full minute.

"Should we fetch Cleric Fay?" asked Linda.

"It's bad enough we've questioned her religion, her belief in the Source. There's a good chance that we're about to destroy that religion."

"Or confirm her suspicions," said Linda.

"Either way. The last thing faith needs is an inconvenient truth. Sometimes faith is all we have."

"My, my … an adventurer *and* a philosopher."

"Wonders never cease."

Linda gave Adam a peck on the cheek.

Adam said, "Now … let's see who's behind the curtain."

The two held hands and stepped through the doorway.

***

"We have found them."

Cleric Deirdre unaccustomed to intrusion, especially within the confines of her compartment, struggled to keep from reprimanding Mar. Though she suspected his integrity, she knew she could rely on his ruthlessness. The incident involving Cleric Fay and the two Visitors unsettled her, made her deeply concerned. She had been the one to select Fay, and now, the traitorous devil had undone her work. In addition, she sensed the displeasure this had brought to the Source. The sooner the matter came to an end, the better.

"Exactly who have you found?" she asked.

Her steely tone should have unnerved Mar, but a single breath later, he showed no signs of it. "Fay and the two Visitors have passed through the Birthing Pavilion. They appear to be headed toward the central elevators."

"And of the other two… the red-headed Visitors, the ones released from Incorporation? Were they with Fay as well?"

"No Cleric Deirdre. They must have separated."

"That much is obvious."

While Fay and her two Visitor companions represented no more than a housekeeping issue, the escape from Incorporation was a most serious event. It was without precedent, and it happened while Deirdre was in charge.

"Fay … have you retrieved her and the other two?"

"My men have arrived at the Birthing Pavilion, but have not secured them as yet. All other elevator exits are blocked. It is just a matter of time."

"I wonder."

She dismissed Mar with a wave of her hand. And then considered what Fay would do to avoid capture. Where would she go?

Chapter 38

Adam walked through an ordinary-looking door, and now as he looked down, the same doorway was at his feet. Linda fell into him, knocking them both to the ground. They rolled a turn and sat up on their haunches.

A musty odor rode upon a mild breeze. Adam looked up to see a yellow mid-day sun, not quite bright enough to engender a squint, but sufficient to cast an eerie soft-shadowed twilight, as if the orb was running on low batteries.

"What happened to the red giant?" asked Linda.

"I don't think we're on the surface. This is someplace else."

Adam moved his hand in an arc. "Take a look around. We're sitting in the middle of a town square, a New England town square if I'm not mistaken."

A small white steeple protruded from the trees that ringed the square. Brick buildings, walkways set in stone, shrubs and grass, a wooden bench and a statue completed the picture.

Adam stood, helping Linda up. A bright, copper-colored sculpture of a man dressed in an unfamiliar uniform stood in the center of the green. He was hairless and postured at attention with a scroll tucked under one arm. His free hand pointed upward, in the general direction of the white steeple.

The rectangular metallic plaque at the base read 'CAPTAIN JAMES A. MAKER, FOUNDER.'

"Well, that's either a whopping coincidence, or we're in a *Twilight Zone* episode," said Adam.

Linda said, "Not to mention that it's written in English. You know, if I'm not mistaken, only one person ever referred to this place as the planet of the Makers."

"You're right."

Alpha.

Adam's eyes wandered farther along the plaque. "These look like dates."

Linda read aloud, "Twenty-five ninety to twenty-seven thirty-one, ET. If these are dates, this guy lived a full life … a hundred forty-one years."

"ET?"

"Earth time?" said Linda. "But that's impossible. That would mean …"

"That they arrived here about six-hundred years after we left."

"And more than nine thousand years before we arrived," said Linda.

"Breaking the laws of physics," added Adam. "Besides we know that the gold disks originated from here some millions of years ago. I don't get it." He shook his head. "Anyhow, we're definitely not outside."

"How can you be sure? Maybe we've been transported to another dimension, another place … there's no telling what the Makers, the Source, or whatever, are capable of."

"Take a look down that street."

Four narrow streets met at the square and extended into the distance like crosshairs. The square was actually more of an oval island of grass, or what passed for grass, and ringed by what looked like low-lying shrubbery and flowers. The landscaping had the disturbing quality of a recent manicure, as if the gardener might be working the earth just out of view.

"Oh, my."

"You see it, right?" asked Adam. He pointed at one road and raised his arm. "See how the street rises and disappears like into a mist."

"They all do that," said Linda. "And I don't see any cars. No traffic lights, no people, no birds … this place is either deserted or everyone's hiding."

"It's like we're inside a bowl," said Adam.

"A hollow sphere."

"Damn, this can't be a planet. It's more like a ship."

Linda said, "Some ship. It's enormous."

Adam said, "We need to find these Makers, and get the hell out of here." Adam looked back at the church with its white crossless steeple and two broad columns to either side of a set of bronze doors. "We could check out the church."

"I've got a better idea." Linda pointed to a two-story red brick building next door.

"City Hall. Yeah, maybe the Mayor's in."

On the way, Adam gave the green behind them a quick glance, half-expecting a munchkin to leap out from behind a shrub, perhaps laughing wildly at the great joke he had pulled off. They stepped across the asphalt street and a minute later stood in front of a set of oversized ebony doors.

"Well?" asked Adam.

"Did you notice how clean everything is? There's no litter in the street."

The gardener and street cleaner are both invisible.

"Not to mention how quiet it is here."

Linda reached up and turned the brass handle. It rotated easily, as if it was recently oiled. She pushed the door in and the two entered.

"Nice," Adam whispered, and wondered why he felt compelled to whisper.

They stood in a small foyer with a maple-stained hardwood floor covered by a broad oval rug that looked Persian. Two mahogany side-tables framed a center hallway while an unlit glass chandelier dangled inches over their heads. Framed portraits hung on the walls. The furniture and décor were typical for the twentieth century.

He closed the door. Dim and colored lighting suffused through two narrow stained-glass sidelights built into the frame. "Let's see if we can find the guy in charge."

Linda cupped her hands about her mouth. "Hello!"

"Anybody home?" asked Adam.

They padded along the carpeted corridor to a receptionist desk. A bronze nameplate read 'Angelina Bounty.' Angelina was not in. A spotless green blotter rimmed by pens and pencils stacked in leather-bound cups lay centered on the desk. A black typewriter perched atop a dictation slide and a candlestick phone completed the incongruity.

"Check out the relics," said Adam. "Nineteen-twenties Americana." He walked around to the other side of the desk and lifted the receiver. "Nada."

Linda examined the typewriter. "It's a *Royal* typewriter. The keys look worn out. I guess it got a lot of use."

"Yeah, like a million years of use. For an advanced civilization, what we're looking at just doesn't make any sense. Unless we've stepped into a time warp … you know, a parallel universe, an alternate reality, maybe a dimensional rift in space-time." Adam moved his hands in waves.

Linda looked beyond him and said, "Well, if anyone has the answers it ought to be the guy in that office."

Going by the name embossed on the door, the office belonged to the Mayor, Harold Avery.

"Probably out to lunch along with everyone else," said Adam. He knocked on the door out of politeness, and after waiting a beat, the two stepped in.

Venetian blinds spilled thin bars of light between partly drawn heavy drapes. The wide maple desk with only a phone standing on its corner seemed too neat. Adam's expectations had already moved past the absence of people, in fact, he was starting to get used to the silence, and would have been bowled over if the Mayor happened walk in.

He rubbed a finger over the smooth wood. "Another thing … there's no dust. Just like the outer office, everything here appears as if it just got cleaned and polished."

Adam sat in the leather-bound chair and said, "So let's think this through. The few written words we've seen are in English. The architecture, furniture, everything … looks to be from early twentieth century. And the whole place is deserted."

Linda said, "The Founder, that James Maker, he died in twenty-seven thirty-one."

"Yeah, assuming we didn't slide into some cosmic warp hole, what's been going here since then?"

"Your summary is giving me something," said Linda.

Adam looked at her with expectations curling up the corners of his mouth.

She said, "A headache."

The two spent the next hour going through desk drawers, cabinets, and storage rooms to no avail. They found not a scrap of paper or book, no records of any kind. Upstairs offices offered no clues. Everything was clean and in its proper place.

"There's water, and the toilets flush," said Adam as he ambled out of the ground floor restroom.

"Wait for me here," said Linda, who entered the ladies room next door.

Even with no one here, she prefers the Ladies Room.

Adam leaned back and stared at the receptionist's desk at the end of the hall. His eyes fixated on the typewriter, and a scene from a movie played out in his head. The body of a woman lay dead at the foot of her desk. A detective stood nearby, scanning the room for clues—a note, a button, anything. Then he drifted to the typewriter. Although there was no paper inserted, he smiled nonetheless. His hand reached for the …

Ribbon.

Adam ran to the desk. Sure enough, there was a ribbon still in place. He lifted the cover and yanked out the reels.

"Hey, what are you up to now?" said Linda. "Had to figure you wouldn't wait for me."

Adam lifted the ribbon to a nearby window. Nothing. It was fresh, with no markings whatsoever.

"Just wasting my time," said Adam as he tossed the reels on the desk.

Linda was walking toward him when they both heard a scream.

Chapter 39

Adam and Linda flung the entry door open. At first, everything seemed as it was before—uncomfortably silent. Then a head bobbed up over the shrubbery surrounding the statue of James A. Maker.

Linda was quick to recognize who it was. "Cleric Fay!" The two ran to her.

Her face was pale. Her eyes wandered upward as if she was about to faint. "I must return. I cannot stay." Lines creased her forehead and cut across the corners of her eyes. The fading light added years to her countenance.

"There's nothing to be afraid of. There's no one here but us," said Adam.

At least no one that we can see ... right now.

"Why did you come? We were going to return for you," said Linda.

"Cleric Deirdre was about to enter the chamber."

"How do you know that?" asked Adam.

"I could hear her outside commanding others to stay away. The entry code is a sacred trust, kept by Clerics and Caretaker Ebbe."

Fay looked behind her at the rectangular hole in the ground. "You must seal this door."

"You've never been here before, have you?" said Adam.

Linda said, "You don't speak English … the language of the ancients, the ones who created the Source."

Fay nodded.

Linda looked at Adam. "English is the spoken language recognized by the Source. I bet no one here knows what it sounds like."

"Which explains why no one has visited this place." Adam stepped over to the doorway. At the same moment, a head draped in a white hood began to rise through the opening.

Linda pointed. "It's her!"

Adam shouted out, "Let this door be sealed." It was too late. Deirdre squirted out and rolled onto the ground. The door disappeared behind her, leaving no trace of it in the stone.

Deirdre moaned, sat up and drew her knees to her chest. Her cowl fell back, and she looked up at the trio, focusing on one at a time, as if making sure her eyes were not deceiving her. "Are you … are you the Source embodying my failures? Or are you the three blasphemers, kept alive by the Source to torment me, to remind me of my failings?"

"Some choice," said Adam, "How about just apologizing for trying to kill us?"

Deirdre dismissed Adam with a scowl. She lowered her head, grasped it with both hands, and groaned. "This is my punishment. May the Source forgive me."

Fay said, "Stop it. You sound like an Acolyte."

The insulting appellation caught her attention. "How dare you?"

Fay continued. "I can understand why you condemned me, but to resorb these two was a mistake. They were innocent witnesses to a murder, a murder committed by your lackey—a sadistic brute overcome by ambition. That despicable coward cares only for himself. How you came to trust him is beyond me."

Deirdre said, "The Source will decide who is guilty. Now help me up."

Fay gave her a hand and the two settled on a nearby bench. Deirdre looked about while avoiding eye contact with her new companions. When she spoke, she stared at the ground where there was a doorway only a minute ago. "How did you open the portal to the Source?"

"It was not I. These two, Adam and Linda They speak the language of the Ancients. They commanded that a portal appear, and it became so."

Deirdre's eyes widened. "The language of the Source? Spoken by Visitors?"

Adam pointed to the statue and said, "The mystery is even deeper than that. It seems that this guy here is the Founder, maybe your first 'Ancient.' Trouble is, he's likely from our planet, Earth, and the dates on the plaque suggest he left *after* we did. That would be fine—we would expect space flight technology to catch up after a time. But this guy, and presumably his crew, may have arrived here a few million years ago, assuming his people were responsible for the disks."

Deirdre remained stone-faced.

Linda said, "This town, this place you believe is the home of the Source, was built using architecture common to our past. As far as we know, there's no one here now"

A short blare, like a distant foghorn, made everyone jump. Another, and another followed.

"So much for being deserted," said Adam.

The booming ended as abruptly as it began. The four stood, each peering down a length of street. Deirdre had shaken off her anxiety enough to speak. "The Source knows we are here. It comes for us."

Adam said, "I'm not so sure about the Source, but something's coming."

Far off, a reflected wedge of the fading light emerged from the mists. In seconds, other glittering bits joined in, spreading themselves across the road. Adam looked about and saw that the same phenomenon was occurring along each street.

Linda said, "Do you hear it?"

Adam thought of a crab skittering on a stone surface. "Sounds like tiny little feet. I think it might be a good idea to get off the green, off these streets."

"How about up there? In the steeple."

"Let's hope the church is open."

The trio ran to the church, leaving Deirdre behind, standing on the green, transfixed by the coming chaos.

Adam tugged at the oversized handles and the doors swung out. "You girls get inside. I'll be right back." He leaped over the shrubbery to face Deirdre.

She said, "We will all answer to the Source."

"You're probably right about that."

He looked beyond her. The sparkles of light had morphed into silvery lines connected at odd angles. The scuffing, scraping cacophony grew with each passing second.

The army of the Source.

With one smooth move, he scooped up Deirdre in his arms. Her protests were lost to the oncoming, clattering hoard. He ran to the church and through the doors held open by Linda and Fay.

Deirdre squirmed out of his arms, straightened her robe and threw him a baleful look. When the doors swung closed, red and blue glass windows at either end of the narthex cloaked the group in a jigsaw puzzle of plum shades. Adam pressed his hands against the wooden doors leading to the nave, hesitating for a moment, thinking that perhaps the town seemed deserted because everyone was attending church. Even now, they could be properly seated in their designated pews, looking up at the pastor, their spiritual leader, anticipating a soul-inspiring monologue, little knowing that their peaceful respite was about to be shattered by a stranger from another world. Adam pushed open the doors.

No parishioners.

About twenty empty pews bracketed a wide center aisle. The altar and pulpit stood as silent testaments to the missing congregation. There were no crucifixes or religious statuettes to identify the denomination.

"Empty," breathed Adam. He looked back at the three, and glimpsed a side door. Motioning to Linda, he asked, "Where's that go?"

The noise outside was making it difficult to hear. Linda raised her voice. "Stairs."

"Lead on."

Adam coaxed the two Clerics to follow her. The stairway zigzagged into a kind of left-handed spiral ascending through the steeple tower. About a half-dozen turns later, the group entered a small room, much of which was taken up by a large bell suspended in its center. To Adam's relief, there was no pull rope evident. Faint slivers of light shone through the down-facing louvers on all four sides. Adam stepped up to the one opening onto the green.

"At least it's less noisy up here," said Linda.

"The sun seems to have gone down, but the lights have come on."

The other three positioned themselves behind the remaining louvers.

Linda said, "Street lamps. I didn't see any before."

"The Source is wonderment. The Source will find you and punish you," said Deirdre.

The lamps could have been taken directly from the foggy streets of a nineteen-century Sherlock Holmes' London, except that instead of a romantic gas flame flickering in the mist, these burned with a steady blue, the same blue color Adam last encountered in the forest.

"What are those?" asked Linda.

Adam knew she wasn't asking about the lamps. Odd things scurried along the walkways and streets, reflecting flashes of silver-blue as they moved. They were mechanical, like the accordion Adam danced with atop the Incorporation Chambers, and they moved with a purpose, spreading out into side streets and houses. The few units remaining behind trundled around the green.

One went into the shrubs and flowerbeds, and began digging. Another moved along the curved road, sweeping it. Others entered the buildings.

"They're the cleaning crew. That would explain why this place is so …"

Something noisy entered the narthex.

Linda whispered, "Let's hope they don't come up here."

"Yeah, they might consider us litter," said Adam.

The four were frozen in place. Adam continued to peer through the louvers, trying to see if anything was leaving. Whatever came into the church produced no sound, as if it had paused to consider next steps, or perhaps it was sniffing the air, determining the source of an exotic odor. Adam wiped his brow and turned to check on Linda, who had shifted her position. He bumped her shoulder, and as she reached out to steady herself, the bell moved.

They stared at the super-sized chime, mesmerized by its swing. It clanged—a brief strike of the clapper, which in the confines of the belfry sounded like the deafening blast of Archangel Gabriel's horn heralding the end of days.

Adam peaked through the louvers. "It doesn't seem like the little mechanical wonders down there even noticed it."

Then they heard the clanking from below. This time it was louder. Something entered the stairway. A shuffling, grinding sound vibrated the planks beneath their feet, thumping its way upward. There was no door to close, no barricade to erect. The four stared into the dim recess of the spiral stairway.

Deirdre stepped forward and spoke into the stairwell. "I am Cleric Deirdre. I tried to stop these non-believers. I am not one of them."

Whatever was ascending did not pause. The groaning mixed in with the metallic choir outside.

Fay tugged at Deirdre and said, "Stand back. That which ascends is no more the Source than a servant is a master."

Shadows along the stairway lengthened, encouraging the group to move back, to use the bell as a shield. They crouched and shifted their heads to catch a glimpse of what was arriving. When the clattering ceased, something stood at the threshold of the belfry. Although the play of deep shadows and the louvered blue light distorted its features, it was plain to all that it was a robot. A parade of mechanical men marched through Adam's addled mind, but none compared to the marvel standing before them.

Its shape was the first to take form—a smooth, silvery body similar in size to a man. Its head swiveled to and fro, revealing a single slit of an eye, no nose, and no mouth. Two arms and two legs were joined at the torso in a fashion normal for humans, except that the shimmering appendages seemed to wander from their expected shoulder and hip locations. The slithery impression was not unlike that of a snake dancing to the exotic strains of a charmer's pungi.

They couldn't cower forever. Adam winked at Linda and stepped out from behind the bell.

She gasped. "Adam, no."

Deirdre moaned and whispered in a deep voice. "It is the Source. May the Source bless us with its mercy."

Fay said nothing and remained huddled next to Deirdre.

The metal creature's head stopped mid-turn. Its eye slit glowed fiercely and in that moment Adam ran a hand across his chest checking for burn holes.

And then it said, "Welcome home."

Chapter 40

The robot's name was Angel. It had been awaiting the return of the Makers, and was, for a while, convinced that they had come. After some discussion, the group decided to take Angel's advice and return to the green, that is, all except Deirdre, who was convinced Angel was an unholy abomination.

"Is Deirdre still up in the belfry?" asked Adam as the group assembled on the green.

Angel said, "Yes, she preferred to stay."

The short staccato of a statement was delivered without emotion. Angel had no body language to betray an inner thought, no tick of an eyebrow or wandering looks to trigger unease.

Really?

Adam turned to Linda. "Maybe we should go back up there and take Deirdre with us. We may have been too hasty to leave her behind, and I know how much she means to you."

She's looking at me like I just turned into a talking banana.

Angel stepped between them and said, "Cleric Deirdre will not receive guests. I provided her with the route back to the surface, which she will take once daylight returns."

Adam swore that its speech was a half tone higher in pitch, as if it was anxious. He closed his eyes for a few seconds, thinking that testing Angel any further could be dangerous. When he opened his eyes, Linda stared at him.

Fay asked, "Is there a reason we cannot go back to the surface right now?"

Angel said, "As you can see, the maintenance units are busy at work. They are scattered throughout the town, performing all manner of upkeep and cleaning. They are not capable of rational thought, and could easily harm you by accident. It would be best to wait for daylight, when they return to storage."

Linda asked, "But why are they still needed? According to you, the humans from Earth are no longer here."

"Maintenance of the town is as critical as the work that is conducted on the surface. Our collective mission is to insure that all is kept as it was when the crew was alive."

Adam asked, "How long ago did you arrive here?"

"A difficult question to answer. Our journey was interrupted by a wormhole. The space-time distortion was severe enough to damage our engines. Our ship has been in orbit for a very long time."

Adam asked, "Are there any Maker descendents still alive?"

"All that remains are their records. Their bodies were long ago resorbed."

"I'd be interested in seeing those records. Any chance of that?"

"There is much that will be explained in due time. Right now, I suggest we leave the square. There is a safe place reserved for you." Angel walked past the Maker statue and waved the group to follow.

Reserved for us?

Adam drew himself close to Linda and pointed down. "What about using the portal to get out of here? I bet we just have to ask it to show up."

"We came all this way to find out something."

"Yeah, but there's a better than even chance *that something* could be fatal."

"No risk, no gain."

Adam took a closer look at Linda. Blue sparkles glinted off her dark pupils. He was staring at the most beautiful woman in the universe. Even in his mind, the cliché failed to irk him. She pecked him on the cheek, and said, "Let's move. Angel doesn't seem to be the patient type."

"Did you see the blood on its arm?"

"Yeah, and I think it knows we saw it."

And doesn't care.

Linda tugged at Fay's robe and the three followed Angel. They walked along the center of one of the four streets. There were no parked vehicles, no bicycles chained to lampposts, no sign of any transportation.

Adam said, "I assume that at one time there were quite a few people living here. Did everyone walk, or was there a faster way to get around?"

Angel turned his head slightly. "No need for vehicles." It pointed to a faint rectangular outline in the gray stone walkway at an intersection. "There are portal drops at every intersection."

A pole at the corner displayed a street sign with the names 'Bank Street' and 'Main Street' emblazoned in bronze on black.

"Was English the language spoken here?" asked Linda.

"It was an English very similar to your early form. It is the language recognized by the portals."

They passed by several blocks of two-story houses, all seemingly cut from the same mold—pastel-toned wood framed units with clapboard siding. Each had a two-step brick stoop leading to a windowless entry door. To either side, casement windows in rabbeted frames decorated with diagonal metallic strips exuded a European aura. The roofs were gabled and looked like they were covered with ceramic tiles—a design feature which struck Adam as odd, since precipitation wasn't likely, especially in view of the lack of sewer gratings in the street.

"If I didn't know any better, I'd say we were strolling down a village street somewhere in England," said Linda.

"Looks like the folks who set this up wanted something to remind them of home," said Adam. "Cleric Fay, what do you think of all this?"

Fay seemed to be in a trance. After a moment, she said, "We have always considered this domain forbidden—the sacred home of the Source. I'm beginning to think we were wrong in that belief. Everything here would appear to have been made by the hand of man, lived in by man."

Adam could hear her voice slip. Faith was a difficult state to achieve, and horrible to lose.

He said, "I wouldn't assume that the Source doesn't exist, here or anywhere else. As a matter of fact, back on Earth, we have a similar set of beliefs among our people that have lasted for thousands of years."

He took Fay's hand. Her face was still flushed from the resorption bath— one swollen eye and a scabbed gash along her cheek. Her hair hung in chaotic tendrils, imparting a doleful Basset hound look.

"We'll get through it. We'll find out what this place is all about, and we'll get out of here alive. You'll get the chance to discover what's out there among the stars."

A smile flitted across her weary face.

"We have arrived." The metallic timbre of Angel's voice carried with it an air of disquieting normality, as if this procession was routine, which they were playing out a part in a pre-scripted vignette. The front of the house looked very much like all the others along Main Street. Angel clambered up the brick stoop and depressed the doorbell. A moment later the door swung inward and Adam's nostrils were assailed by sweet, meaty odors.

His stomach rumbled. "My God, that smells like food, real food."

The three followed Angel inside. The foyer opened onto a dining room with a crystal chandelier suspended from a vaulted ceiling. Its faux candles illuminated a wide center table and cushioned chairs. These were pulled out slightly, as if inviting someone to be seated. A plain linen cloth was stretched out beneath steaming serving dishes, casseroles and soup bowls. Adam's eyes began to tear up.

Angel said, "I believe you must be hungry and thirsty after your ordeals. Please sit and help yourself. Afterward, I will address your questions."

As if noticing the incredulous looks passed between them, Angel added, "Fear not. This is not a Visitor reception. There are no drugs in these foods."

Adam and Linda angled into the proffered chairs, while Angel stepped back. Adam's eyes flitted from one dish to another. He was stunned. Here he was, on the planet of the Makers, eight thousand light-years from Earth, and he was staring at oven-baked turkey, sliced ham, and what was most certainly a large roast beef still simmering in its juices. Several carafes of wine, white and red, were centered on the table along with salads, bread rolls and a host of other sides, including baked potatoes, vegetables, and even a bowl of cranberry sauce.

"How is this possible?" asked Linda.

Adam shook his head slowly, mirroring Linda's confusion. He reached over to the wine and was about to ask her what she preferred, when he realized they were alone.

"Where's Angel?" he asked.

Linda turned around and said, "And where's Cleric Fay?"

Chapter 41

Adam called out, but there was no response. With a turkey leg still in his hand, he bolted out of the dining room. "They didn't go back outside, did they?"

Linda caught up with him in the foyer. "We would have heard the door."

Adam pointed to the back of the staircase. "Lights."

The narrow hallway opened onto a kitchen. Angel was standing at the sink, holding Fay's shoulders. She was hunched over, making gurgling noises.

"What's going on?" asked Adam, all the while thinking about Deirdre and the blood on Angel's arm.

Angel braced Fay as she launched into a retching fit. It turned to face Adam. "Cleric Fay is dying."

Linda said, "What do you mean? She was fine a moment ago."

Angel said, "She has no immunity. The disease will kill her. I will put a stop to her suffering."

Angel brought its hands over her neck and head.

"Hold it!" screamed Adam. "Don't do that."

Angel held his hands in place, and said, "The illness will cause her much suffering and a very painful death. Is this your wish?"

"What disease does she have?" asked Linda.

"A fatal bacterial infection. It begins as a stomach upset, progresses to breathing difficulty, and ends in convulsions. It has no name."

Adam said, "Where did this infection come from? I didn't see any evidence of sick people on the surface."

Fay grasped the edges of the counter and raised herself. She shook as she spoke. "There is no such illness … on the surface. This is a punishment … the Source is displeased."

Angel said, "Cleric Fay is correct. This disease does not exist on the surface."

Linda said, "Did these bacteria kill off the original humans … the crew, their descendents?"

"Not exactly. The bacteria are all that is left of the crew—a mutated remnant of gut flora, I believe."

Adam felt his jaw drop.

Linda said, "Radiation."

Angel tilted its head at her. "Gamma. The red giant we orbit produces gamma radiation at levels unhealthy for humans. The ship's gravitic systems are incapable of shielding the occupants from it."

Adam asked, "How long did the crew survive after arriving here?"

"Several thousand years. During that time their population gradually declined because of reproductive issues. Eventually, all that was left were several strains of bacteria hardy enough to resist the radiation."

"And the people on the surface?" asked Linda.

"They have been manufactured asexually to avoid mutational effects. All are recycled periodically before undergoing significant damage."

Angel glanced at Fay, who was now dry-heaving over the sink. "Even Clerics are recycled, but at a lower frequency."

"Is that what happened to Cleric Deirdre?" asked Adam.

"I chose to provide her with a quick and painless termination. I apologize for the deception, but I felt there was no reason to alarm you."

"What about us? Won't we catch this infection?"

"It is possible, but since you have not exhibited any symptoms as yet, it is unlikely. In any event, it is probable that evolutionary pressures on your planet have provided immune systems that ward off such infections. This is not true of the surface units here."

"We will not allow you to terminate Cleric Fay. She's with us," said Adam, who realized he was waving the turkey drumstick at Angel. He bit off a morsel and chewed.

Angel said, "I cannot allow Cleric Fay to return to the surface. The infection could easily spread and cause a massive disruption."

Disruption ... apparently more important than the loss of life.

Linda asked, "Don't you have drugs here—something that would kill the bacteria, antibiotics?"

"Such medicines were available long ago. A great deal of time has passed and there is nothing left of them."

"You've been incorporating Visitors for thousands of years. You mean to tell me that of all the information you've assembled, there's nothing on antibiotics?"

"The machinery of the ship runs autonomically. We, meaning I, cannot access that information. Neither can the humanoids on the surface." Angel lowered his head. "The system was set in place by the Founders, and could only be accessed by them."

Linda retained her incredulous look, and as Adam snagged yet another bite from the drumstick, she said, "So for thousands of years you've been collecting Visitors and processing them into some kind of electronic network which serves no purpose?"

"The information has been stored by the Source and will be accessible to true humans. Regardless, it is not something I can change or affect."

Adam asked, "How long does she have?"

"Several hours. The disease moves swiftly."

"Then we need some way to quarantine her while we make our way back to the surface," said Linda.

Angel appeared to consider the suggestion, and was about to speak when the doorbell chimed. The door opened automatically, admitting three figures into the foyer.

Adam craned his head around the edge of the staircase. "Alpha! Markas, Jule!"

The Moorsians ran to Adam, while Alpha kept a pace behind. Linda joined the group at the kitchen doorway. After pleasantries were exchanged, Alpha entered the kitchen.

"Good day, Alpha. Welcome back," said Angel.

"Good day to you, Angel. What are you up to?"

The four humans fell silent.

"I brought these humans here to replenish their strength. This surface unit," Angel pointed to Fay, "is dying of the illness. We were discussing possible options."

Alpha said, "We will need to take her with us to the shuttle. There is medication on our ship that may help. That is the only option you need to consider."

"As you wish, sir."

The appellation surprised Adam. "You two know each other?"

Alpha said, "For many years."

Linda asked, "How did you gain entry to this town?" She looked at Angel. "I thought the portal only responded to spoken English."

"English is the language I have been speaking all along."

Adam said, "Then you knew. You knew Earth was the home planet of this ship."

Alpha nodded.

"But how…?" asked Linda.

Alpha said, "How is it possible?"

"I told them the ship had passed through a wormhole, sir," said Angel.

"My God," said Adam.

"What's going on?" asked Linda.

Adam shook his head and looked at both Alpha and Angel. "Exactly how long did you say that you've known each other?"

"I didn't say. But you might as well know. I was the last creation of the surviving members of this expedition."

Linda said, "That would make you …"

"Over seventeen million years old."

"The wormhole," said Linda. "It didn't just send you here."

Adam said, "It sent them back in time … about seventeen million years back."

Chapter 42

"I feel guilty eating this food," said Linda.

Markas and Jule both had mouths too full to speak. Adam glanced at the floor, where Fay lay unconscious. She was wrapped in blankets Angel had appropriated from an upstairs bedroom. Angel and Alpha were seated at opposite ends of the table. Neither ate.

"Forget about it. There's nothing we can do for Cleric Fay right now. Just hurry up. We have to get back up to the ship. I have a feeling we'll need our strength."

Markas had just finished relating how Alpha had stepped in to save him and Jule on the surface. Mar was killed in the tangle, and though tragic, the news lifted Adam's mood.

"So you were here when the medallions were sent out?" asked Adam.

Both Angel and Alpha tried answering at the same time. Angel deferred to Alpha, who confined his answer to a curt nod.

"But why? Why send out machines which were designed to create human life?" asked Linda.

Alpha said, "When the crew and its descendents realized that their time here was limited, they became desperate to let others know that human life existed elsewhere in the galaxy. That they were not alone."

Fay stirred beneath the blankets, and let out a groan. Her eyes flickered for a moment before she passed out again."

Angel said, "Excuse me sir, but we are losing time."

"Of course." Alpha rose from his seat.

"Wait a minute," said Adam. "I can understand sending out messages in a bottle … you know, letting others know about you and where you are. But I don't get why your machines were designed to create humans."

Alpha stepped away from the table and said, "The probes had a second purpose—to create human life wherever possible. You already know that DNA is an algorithm. It was designed by the ship to infuse humans with a specific behavior. The code compels human beings to seek out their origins. In other words, to find this ship."

Adam raised his eyebrows at Linda.

Markas pushed back his seat and said, "But when we arrived here, you treated us as if we were no more than robotic probes, returning with information to be absorbed by your machines." His voice rose in pitch as he went on. "Where is your humanity? How could you be so callous?"

Before Alpha could answer, Adam cleared his throat. "If what you said is true, then this is the paradox of all paradoxes. Your crew, this ship, created human life on Earth, which over millions of years evolved into a civilization capable of space flight. I wonder, would they have even existed if they chose not to send out the probes?"

"A paradox, indeed," said Alpha. And without a moment's hesitation to ponder the immensity of the revelation, he said, "Angel, you will carry Cleric Fay. Make sure she is wrapped in that blanket to minimize the threat of infection."

They all rose at once. Adam staggered for a moment, catching himself on a seatback.

"Are you okay?" Linda supported him by his elbow.

"I must have gotten up too fast. All this food, and I'm still trying to get my head around the human race creating itself … I guess it got me a little dizzy."

They followed Alpha through the front door. It was still dark outside. Most of the maintenance units were gone, likely having returned to concealed storage locations to await their next call to duty. Alpha led the troupe back to the central green, and shouted out. "Open the portal to the surface." To Adam, the words sounded the same as usual—a dull monotone translation unreeling within his mind. The chip in his head must be dealing with English the same as any other language.

A rectangular hole appeared at the base of the Maker monument. Adam half-expected an army of Supervisors to come piling out. Nothing stirred. Alpha stepped into the hole while motioning to the others to follow.

Regardless of his mental preparation, Adam still flailed like a rag doll when he popped through to the other side. He was on the floor of the room fighting back nausea and looking through the mystical one-way screen. Several Supervisors sat on the floor with their backs against the vestibule walls. "Those guys must have come with Deirdre."

Without a word, Alpha walked through the screen. In seconds all three were lying flat on the floor. Adam had seen no more than a blur. Alpha waved back at the screen, beckoning the group forward.

"That was fast work," said Linda. "With you along, I don't think we'll have any trouble getting to the shuttle."

Alpha stooped over the unconscious trio and said, "What we will encounter is beyond imagining, and it will use all its resources to stop us from leaving."

Adam said, "What exactly is *it*?"

Alpha retrieved hand weapons from the unconscious men and handed them out. He stooped over the bodies again and began undressing them.

"Adam and Markas put on these uniforms."

Adam passed a tunic to Markas, and turned back to Alpha. "So, if you're not going to tell us about this thing that's 'beyond imagining,' I was wondering … you're part of the system here. Don't they call you a Gatherer? Why are you helping us?"

Alpha pulled off a leotard bottom and said, "The time has arrived." Seemingly as an afterthought, he said, "I speak of the ship. A mechanism is in place to insure that all continues here as originally intended."

Great.

A muffled cough and a short series of raspy groans stilled the conversation.

"Place her down. I want to see how Cleric Fay is doing," said Linda.

With the exception of Alpha, who positioned himself at the doorway exit, the group gathered around Angel. It folded back the blankets, uncovering Fay's face. Her eyes were shut, the lids forced together by purple swellings above and below, and her face was covered with fierce red hives. Short wet gasps passed for breathing.

Linda touched her brow. "She's burning up."

Alpha said, "We have no time to lose. Cover her. We need to go now."

Adam stumbled once again.

Linda asked, "Are you sure you're okay?"

He felt his forehead become moist and a chill ran up his spine.

"It's just a little headache. I probably ate too fast back there." His eyes were watery, and he was sure his head was about to explode. "I'll manage."

Alpha depressed a series of raised numbers by the exit and the doors slid apart. He gave the corridor a quick glance to either side, and disappeared into the gloom.

The four humans and Angel, with Cleric Fay draped over its shoulder, followed close behind. They stepped up their pace to stay with Alpha. Adam reveled in the cool air.

Linda asked, "Why don't we take this elevator? Doesn't this one go all the way to the surface?"

Alpha said, "They all do that. This one is most likely monitored, as it was the one used by Cleric Deirdre. There are others we can use."

Linda turned to Adam. "Give me your medallion."

"Why?"

"I'll explain it later. It was something I remembered from before."

Adam pulled the stringed disk over his head.

Jule said, "Don't do anything foolish. You may risk our capture. We must stay close to Alpha and do what he says."

Markas, who had been quiet all this time, agreed with Jule. "Alpha is our only chance."

Minutes later, the procession reached a familiar area. The corridor widened and several figures in green stood by a series of large chambers. They had reached the Birthing Pavilion.

Alpha said, "Follow me and do not lag behind. The Growers will think we are part of the Supervisor team sent down here to capture the fugitives. He looked at Linda and Jule, and said, "You are the fugitives."

They moved into the Pavilion, careful to walk at a steady pace and appear as casual as possible. From the corner of his eye, Adam noticed that the Growers had paused to watch the procession, in particular, they seemed most interested in the mechanical man taking up the rear with its mysterious bundle.

The minute it took to walk across to the opposite entryway felt like hours. They turned the corner and were well past the Pavilion, when Adam's heart skipped.

"Linda. She's gone."

Chapter 43

"No, I'm not."

Linda shifted her head from behind Angel, and skipped to catch up to Adam.

"Where did you go?"

"Silly, I just got behind for a moment. What's the big deal?"

Adam gave her a long sideways glance. "If you don't tell me, I'm going to ask Angel."

Linda shrugged. "You can't trust that robot."

"Silence."

Alpha's single word stopped the procession at an intersection. He peeked around the corner and said, "We are here. Wait for me," and disappeared.

Adam sidled over to the wall's edge just enough to get an eyeful. Two Supervisors stood about twenty paces distant, talking to each other. Silky lines of reflected, undulating light ran along their black uniforms. One laughed so hard he had to brace himself against a wall.

When Alpha approached, the two stiffened and drew weapons. The nearest one said, "Identify yourself."

Even from his limited view, Adam saw the muscles along Alpha's back tighten. As he drew nearer, the Supervisors recognized him, calling him by his name. Their weapons lowered. In that instant a high-pitched banshee wailing shattered the stillness. Adam snapped his head around and saw Fay's arm protruding from between the folds of the blanket. Angel lowered her to the floor. She squirmed and cried out as it rearranged the covering. A light came on in the hall, catching Adam's attention. He looked back to see two glowing weapons. Their colors went from red to white, and then the beams arced up. Alpha broke into a run aimed directly at the two. Several paces short of the pair, an intense white burst blinded Adam. He rubbed his eyes to clear his vision of purple silhouettes just in time to see Alpha stagger up from the floor. A second blast followed and Alpha careened into the opposite wall. Adam kept his eyes closed and turned back to Linda.

She asked, "What just happened?"

"I think we're in deep…"

Shuffling sounds rounded the corner. Everyone, including Angel looked up.

"The way is clear. Here take these."

It was Alpha. He handed two-rod weapons to Adam and rested his body sideways against a wall.

"How did you survive that?" asked Linda.

Adam said, "Yeah, we got a dose of that electrical blast from Mar, and I'm still numb."

Alpha took a deep breath, and said, "My makeup is quite different from yours. I may look similar to a human, but I am far from such a simple biological entity."

Not to mention you're millions of years old.

"How do you feel? You *do* look a little shaken," said Linda.

"I will recover. We must move quickly. The Source is aware of us," said Alpha.

"I thought there was no such thing as the Source," said Adam.

"I speak of the survival systems on this ship. The Makers designed a combination of machine and human components to maintain the ship perpetually. These same systems created me."

Adam said, "I still don't get it. You're a Gatherer."

Linda said, "And you're helping us to escape."

"The time has come. The circle is complete."

As obtuse as usual.

"I take it there are more Gatherers?" asked Adam.

"Only one more. You met him on Earth, and on our ship."

"The one who tried to kill us ... twice?" said Adam.

"He was my prototype. Not as intelligent, and I'm afraid he may be defective."

Markas approached the trio, looked back at Jule, and said, "We must hurry. Angel says that Cleric Fay is nearly dead ... and my wife ... she is showing signs of the infection."

Jule was sitting on the floor with her head down.

Alpha said, "We have only to ascend to the surface using these elevators, then cover a short distance to the shuttle."

Adam lagged behind to help Markas with Jule. They squeezed into the elevator and seconds later stepped out into an arched hallway. There was no welcoming committee awaiting them. In fact, there was no one about at all.

Alpha whispered, "We are in the Learning Center. There are usually a number of novices and teachers about. Their absence is troubling. The Source knows where we are."

They followed Alpha as he slinked along the wall toward the faded pink of daylight seeping in from the exit archway. When he reached the opening, he crouched and pointed. "There is the shuttle. I see only two guarding it ... most likely Supervisors."

There was a strained tone to Alpha's voice. He held an arm out and signaled the group. All the while, his head darted back and forth, as if he expected someone or something to show up.

As they waited in the shadowed entrance, Adam considered the group—a robot servant who kills and lies about it, a Cleric who wanted to explore other worlds and was now dying of an infection, the only two friends they had—two carrot-tops from another world brought back from terminal Incorporation, he and Linda, naively seeking out the answers to humanity's most pressing questions, and Alpha, a walking enigma.

What an odd bunch. And right now, they're all my best friends.

Alpha stood up. "Now." He set off in a slow jog toward the shuttle, which stood a few hundred meters across a flat expanse of barren stone.

Adam sneezed, wiped his nose with the back of his arm. "Go. I'll take up the rear."

Linda paused a step to help Markas with Jule, and the three loped out of the building. Angel made no perceptible sound or head movement. It slung Fay up unto its shoulder and fast-walked, swiveling its hips to maintain a steady, level gait to avoid jostling the Cleric. Adam glanced down the hallway, scanned the woods nearby, and shuffled into the crimson clearing after Angel.

They were stretched out in a line about thirty paces long when Adam heard a low rumbling sound. More than a sound, it felt like the ground beneath his feet was vibrating. The guards stationed at the shuttle ran off into the woods at the far end of the expanse. The whole planet-ship seemed to shake and a dark slit appeared in the ground ahead of them. Alpha lurched to a stop and motioned for everyone to do the same.

The slit turned into a round hole, and it was expanding. The tremors beneath Adam's feet brought him to his knees. Seams appeared in the ground and widened. Flat stones slid beneath each other. In seconds, the opening spanned the distance between them and the shuttle, stopping short a few meters from swallowing both. The guttural grinding ceased and a faint dust cloud hovered over the dark abyss—an unfathomable black opaqueness, which spoke to a harrowing and deadly depth.

"Is that it?" asked Adam. "Is that all the ship can come up with? We can go around that."

Alpha looked to either side of the newly formed canyon. "There will be more."

A howling gust of wind bore down on the group. Directly in front of them, poised at the very edge of the hole, a dust devil took shape. Like a small tornado, it spun, forming a vortex of silver white. The red giant sun behind them painted the growing funnel a brilliant shade of crimson. The whirlpool coalesced, solidifying, draining the cyclonic cone until a solitary figure appeared in its center.

It was robed, and its face obscured by a hood. The folds of its cloak hid both hands and feet. When it spoke, the melodic lilt of its voice sent a shiver of recognition through Adam. Its singsong timbre belied a deadly intention. "You cannot leave. Return to the Learning Center and submit to Incorporation and Resorption."

"Adam, isn't that..." said Linda.

"The same ghost lady we met in the forest," said Adam.

Alpha turned to the two. "This entity is neither man, woman, nor ghost. You are being addressed by the Source."

Adam spoke to the cloaked figure that stood mere steps away. Perhaps a direct approach could work. "We do not wish to stay. We thank you for your hospitality, but feel we must return to our own worlds."

The figure said nothing. After a moment, it turned away from the group and raised its arms. Adam caught sight of silvery fingers protruding from the ends of its robe. Then it spoke again. "You cannot leave."

The thing that Alpha called the Source pointed its arms in the direction of the shuttle. Adam sucked in his breath as the small ship rose, rotating from shadow up into the rays of the sun. Several electric arcs sprung from its lower panels to the ground.

"Stop it!" screamed Linda.

Adam took a step forward. Alpha lunged at the figure, crashing into its back. There was no perceptible reaction to the attack. It continued moving its arms as if it was conducting an orchestra through a particularly delicate movement, but in this symphony the shuttle was the only musician and the final crescendo was drawing near. Alpha knelt by the figure, shaking his head.

Adam tried turning on his rod weapon, but it did not respond.

The shuttle was now poised above the center of the gaping pit. Adam spoke up once again. "Hear me Source, you *must* obey our commands. We are the Makers, and we command you to restore the shuttle and to help us leave this ship."

The shuttle stopped revolving but remained suspended. The figure turned to look at Adam. It threw back its hood, exposing a brilliant, silvered head with no perceptible facial features. The reflected image of the sun appeared as an oval in the center of its face. When it spoke, a thin line cut through that oval.

"You are not the Makers. They are no more."

Adam took a moment to get past the distinctly inhuman veneer of the creature and said, "Do we not speak the language of the Ancients ... the language of the Makers? Do we not look like them? Is not our genetic makeup identical to them?"

A pause.

"Points well taken. But you are not a Maker."

A thread of hope. The creature, the Source, was now engaged in a conversation.

"But they came from Earth, just as we did."

Before the Source could reply, Adam caught hold of an inspiration and said, "What if I told you we are the ancestors of the Makers ... that it was *we* who created *them*?"

A paradox. Computer programs and paradoxes are like water and oil.

"You speak nonsense."

"I'm guessing you were built sometime after the Makers arrived here. Is that right?"The lack of an answer prompted Adam to go on. "Can you access the history of the arrival ... I mean exactly what occurred to maroon the ship here around this sun?"

"The Makers were always here. They were our creators."

Linda jumped in. "Can you scan our DNA?"

"You are attempting to delay the inevitable."

"Can you?" persisted Linda.

"Of course."

"Then, do so."

The creature reached out to Linda with its silvery digit and rubbed it along her bloodied cheek. She winced as it scraped off portions of a long scab. The blood on its finger disappeared, seemingly absorbed, and a few seconds later it said, "Your DNA is essentially the same as programmed on the probes."

"Now, compare it to the Makers. Can you do that?"

The creature stood still. Adam could imagine its brain, possibly a part of a huge electromechanical wonder located throughout the ship beneath their feet, retrieving the data and running it through billions, maybe trillions, of comparisons.

After a few seconds passed, it replied, "It differs in some respects, but as I stated, essentially identical."

"Not *completely* identical, right?"

No answer. The Source turned to face the suspended shuttle.

Linda asked, "Could you determine which DNA came first? Think it through, the process of evolution on Earth was the same for us and as it was for the Makers. Look at the minor discrepancies in our genetic codes. The evidence is there."

The Source seemed to ignore Linda's request, and concerned itself with the shuttle's disposal. It waved it's arms and the shuttle began moving.

Linda said, "You must see it. Even over the course of a few thousand years, you must be able to see that some of those differences are due to normal mutational changes. Just look. Please."

"Damn it," yelled Adam, "You're about to destroy our only way back home."

Adam looked to Alpha, who drew himself up, as if ready to pounce on the Source again. Markas shook his head and held tightly onto Jule's limp form. And then there was Angel, who had no special expression, but continued to hold Fay over his shoulder. She was still alive, judging by the slight movement beneath the blanket.

The shuttle glided through the air, hovering a scant few meters above the void. Adam began to abandon his vague theories of escape, and accept what fate was about to dish out. He held Linda in what he imagined would be their last embrace. She buried her head against his chest and sobbed.

Then the impossible happened.

Instead of dropping into the ebony abyss, the shuttle continued to glide, drawing closer. Alpha backed away from the Source and joined the group as they stared at the approaching craft. It settled on the ground not twenty meters away.

The Source turned back to the group. "You may go. The circle is complete."

Adam was about to say something when Linda put a finger to his mouth. Alpha was standing by the shuttle's open entryway by the time Adam finished kissing her. Markas and Jule were the first to reach Alpha, with Angel close behind. The Source stood silently by, apparently watching, though it had no obvious eyes.

As Adam passed near it, he said, "What will happen to you and this ship?"

"With your arrival, we have completed our mission."

Linda asked, "What of the people on the surface?"

"All will continue as before. We have been programmed to carry out the instructions of the Makers."

Adam said, "What about coming with us?"

The question must have stunned Linda, since her mouth remained open, waiting for the response.

"I am the ship. I cannot leave."

"So, the humans will be allowed to live on?" asked Linda.

Its head bowed slightly.

Linda said, "And that means all support systems will continue, including the Birthing Center?"

"Until there is nothing."

As they walked to the shuttle, they turned to wave at the Source. It was a perfectly instinctual, human thing to do, and they fully expected the farewell greeting to go unrecognized. Inside the shuttle, as the door slid shut, Adam caught a glimpse of the Source standing at the edge of the precipice.

Perhaps the most powerful and loneliest entity in the galaxy.

The door hissed as it mated with the wall. Adam slipped into a seat next to Linda. He was happy to have made it back to the shuttle, but couldn't shake the image of the planet's guardian—an entity beyond understanding, filled with the knowledge gathered from countless civilizations. He played out the scene over and over, and each time, he became more certain that the Source did wave back.

Chapter 44

The shuttle docked without incident. When its airlock systems cleared, Alpha opened the door to a darkened bay.

Adam said, "Whoa, it's cold. Looks like your buddy's not here."

Alpha bounded to a handrail a few steps out. Adam stayed behind with Linda hovering at his shoulder, both armed with rod weapons in hand. Alpha had explained how to use them, just in case the need arose.

"Well?" asked Adam.

Alpha drifted behind the spare shuttle. The silence was beginning to creep out Adam.

"Perhaps I should assist?"

He jumped at the mechanical voice. Angel had come up from behind, exhibiting a surprising talent at weightless stealth. Linda smirked as Adam composed himself and said, "What about Cleric Fay? How is she doing?"

"Not well, I'm afraid. She is unconscious."

Fay was wrapped in a blanket and strapped down across several seats. Jule and Markas chose to remain behind. Jule's breathing was short and raspy. Markas said, "If you need me, I'll come, but I would rather stay here right now."

"Understood."

Adam felt feverish himself. Whatever the Ancients left for them to catch was a dilly. He held back a cough, cleared his throat, and said, "I think we can handle this."

Alpha returned from the second shuttle. "The sick should stay here."

"What about..." Adam began. "Does he or it have a name?"

"No name. He is not in the bay. Judging from the emergency lighting, he has shut down the ship's power."

Linda asked, "How do we get it back on?"

"Systems controls are located at the Engine level."

"Let me guess ... without power, the elevators are out," said Adam.

"In order to obtain the medicines we need, power must be restored first. Adam and Angel, come with me. Linda, stay here with the rest. You have heat and light. Keep the door closed until we return." Alpha pointed at the weapon in Linda's hand. "And do not hesitate to use that if the prototype shows up."

Adam glided through the door and gave Linda a quick nod.

The three entered the connecting hallway in a single line with Adam last. They passed below the occasional suffused emergency light from a recessed fixture. Long shadows followed them along the flooring and walls. The weightlessness, silence and cold made it feel like they gliding through a deep sea wreckage of a sunken ship, with air bubbles replaced by puffs of condensed water vapor. As for fish, Adam strained his eyes for one particular breed—a nameless predator lurked in the shadows, waiting for the moment to strike. His hand tightened about his weapon.

By the time they reached the central elevator, Adam shook uncontrollably and his nose cast off beads of sweat. Alpha grasped the edges of one of the doors and directed Angel to do the same with the other. The panels moved aside, opening onto a sinister shaft.

"Follow me."

Alpha floated in, and pulled himself down. Adam and Angel followed closely behind. There were no handholds or cables. Adam copied the movement of the other two as they gripped gear-like projections along a strip that ran the length of the shaft. After descending two levels, they encountered the elevator cab. It appeared to have stopped at the Engine level.

Alpha called up. "Adam, turn on your weapon."

Thumb pressure on the handgrip produced a weak white light—a stand-by mode. The light was more than enough to illuminate the top of the cab, and a rectangular arrangement of bolts set in its center.

Without a word, Angel gave one of the bolts a tentative turn with its spindly metal fingers. A few seconds later the twisted panel floated past Adam, and the trio dove into the elevator.

Adam held his weapon high while Alpha forced the sliding doors. Angel launched itself into the gloom, and flew directly toward a concentric series of rings embedded in the opposite wall. Alpha eased out with Adam close behind. Two amber ceiling lights provided ample illumination.

Adam asked, "Is that where the antimatter is held?"

Alpha threw a quick nod and drifted closer to Angel.

"What about the containment ... doesn't that need power to work?"

While Angel began turning and pushing a variety of dials and buttons on a panel below the rings, Alpha drifted up and over the control panels, seemingly more concerned with what may be lurking behind them. The room was in the shape of a circle with the antimatter containment and engine infrastructure part of the solid donut hole in its center.

A sharp thud shattered the stillness. They both looked in the direction of the sound, toward the curved edge of the rounded containment section. Alpha floated out—his body slowly rotated with arms and legs stretched out like a child's doll. Dark red spatter covered his forehead.

Angel moved its hand over a section of the panel and the lights came on. "We have power," it said. "Turn up your weapon."

Adam did as he was instructed. Angel lifted off and glided to the opposite side of the paneling. It looked back at Adam for a moment and placed a single, silver digit over its mouth. Adam held the glowing red rod pointed directly ahead of him and slowly drifted up to check on Alpha, all the while certain that a monster was about to leap out at him.

He latched onto the body and swung it around to get a better look. A few drops of blood lifted off Alpha's face. He appeared lifeless, however, Adam felt a pulsation at the neck. He steered Alpha away from the containment system toward the elevator doors, and squat-thrusted upwards to get a better view. When Adam reached the ceiling, he clung on to a cross beam and watched Angel disappear around the opposite corner below.

Beads of sweat hugged Adam's forehead, and he felt a slippery dampness seep between his fingers and the weapon.

Something broke—a complex sound, like a burst of small cracks happening so fast that they gave the impression of a single event. A silvered object the size of a football twirled up from behind the containment rings. Angel, or rather, his head, drifted up, slowly rotating, a darkened slit eyeing Adam with each revolution. Oily droplets oozed out of the jagged remains of a neck and scattered in every direction as it drifted by like a newly launched satellite.

Adam tore his eyes away from the cranial specter and focused on the hulking figure emerging from behind the containment rings. Shirtless, and with a long bloody gash running along its neck and shoulder, it held something that looked like a pipe. It gave Alpha's body a poke, sending it adrift to the opposite wall. Its head swiveled, taking in the rest of the room. That it didn't look up was an astonishing bit of fortune.

As Adam brought up his hand to stifle an urge to sneeze, he heard a grunt from below. He had forgotten his hand weapon was lit, and its moving beam caught the ogre's attention. The face that stared up at him was a gnarled mish-mash of undulating flesh, in one instant looking like a plastic store manikin and in another, a furry beast replete with an extended snout and protruding canines. It seemed it couldn't decide what to resemble, perhaps drawing upon memory for the most fearsome facade in its facial portfolio.

Nice choice of looks. Either way, you're one ugly son-of-a-bitch.

He squeezed the rod and let loose a brilliant white beam. The thing cringed, and then squatted as if preparing to spring up at him. He sent out a second shock wave, which rocked it back a step. It shook its head and leaped. Adam blasted it yet again mid-flight and at the same time launched himself down toward the open elevator doors.

When he reached the cab, he heard a loud groan that sounded as if the beast was at his neck. He slipped through the open ceiling panel just as an arm reached out, searching. The hulk's body was jammed, a bit too wide to fit through. Adam depressed the rod and swung it's crimson tip in an arc, severing the arm at the elbow. A quivering jet spray from the stump released a thick cloud of red droplets. The thing pulled back its stump and let loose a shriek. Its forearm thumped into the shaft wall, fingers still twitching, seeking out Adam's neck.

The cab hummed to life and began moving. Adam grappled with the gearing strip trying to use it pull himself through the shaft, but his fingers slipped on the blood-coated teeth. The rising cab slammed into his backside, driving him upward. The dead-end top of the shaft was seconds away. A square of light two levels up marked the open doors leading to the shuttle level. Adam timed his leap, caught a leg at the doorframe, and bounced through and into the corridor ceiling with a satisfying thwack. The beast would waste no time backing up. He careened from wall to wall in the connecting corridor, pushing off toward the shuttle bay.

Adam spotted Linda at one of the shuttle portals. "Hey. Open up, fast. That damned prototype is after me."

She pointed to her ears. Adam pointed back, making 'open the door' motions and looking behind him at the same time. A shadow filled the corridor and the floor lights sputtered on. It was coming.

The shuttle doors slid open. Linda hovered at entry. "What's going on? Where are the others?"

"Shut the door, quick!"

Adam bounded up, grabbed a handhold on the shuttle's skin and swung himself onto its topside. He lay flat as he could. The image of a long ago basement encounter loomed up in his mind. He wondered if his butt was floating up for the psychotic android to see. Unlike getting caught by a curmudgeonly old fart, consequences this time would be deadly.

"There is no place you can hide."

Its voice was slurred and came from directly below. Adam pressed his fingers against the shuttle and shifted a few inches forward. The creature stared into the door portal, while holding on to its stub of an arm with the pipe floating at its side. The bleeding had slowed to a trickle, and its breathing came in long, heavy drafts. Adam brought his weapon forward.

"This blasphemy ends now," it growled.

The creature smashed the pipe against the portal glass. It paused a moment and slammed it again. The second move caused it to rebound a few meters from the shuttle door. Adam pressed his head against the cold metal, hoping that it would not look up.

"There you are."

The words were like ice water running along his back. Adam stiffened and depressed the rod and released another nerve-deadening flash. He pulled himself into a squat and shot up. The scene seemed to play out like his last encounter. He grasped the metal framework of the gangway, and pivoted to its upper side, fully expecting to see the android rising toward him. He saw nothing. The creature could be anywhere. He depressed the rod until its tip turned a bright red.

The door to the shuttle flew open. Linda and Markas emerged, their weapons glowing.

Adam yelled down to them. "I can't see it. It's out here somewhere. Be ready."

Rumbling laughter erupted from above. When Adam looked up, the creature's face was inches from his. He brought his weapon up, but it was swatted away. The android grabbed him by his neck and squeezed. Adam grappled with the massive arm, trying to pry the fingers back. The creature's face warped, like melting wax, transforming.

It rasped, "There is no need to struggle."

A thin mist of blood swirled about them. Adam's lungs strained to suck in air as its grip tightened. Its face writhed. Its yellow eyes widened. It held Adam out for the audience below to see. "Throw your weapons aside, or I will kill him."

Linda said, "Why are you doing this? We intend you no harm. We just want to get back home."

"The weapons."

Two rods, their tips fading red, drifted up from below. Adam felt the hand at his neck ease off. The android pushed off the gangway and landed with him in tow on the decking a few meters from Linda and Markas. A fine drizzle of pink droplets followed. It released Adam and shoved him toward the two.

The thing angled into the shuttle's entryway, taking a survey within before speaking. "I cannot allow you to return to your home worlds. The location of the Makers' ship, the world of the Source ... These things cannot be revealed."

Adam wiped at his eyes to remove some of the salty ichor. "You can't believe that killing us is justified. You must have some morality, some sense of right and wrong."

The creature sighed. A grimace belied the pain of his arm. "It was a mistake to gather humans. And it would be a bigger mistake to let them return." Its speech slowed as if each phrase demanded more effort. "I have corrected the mistake."

Linda asked, "What do you mean?"

It looked at Linda for a moment, and then lifted the pipe.

Adam tried to reach the weapon. Linda and Markas joined in, extending their arms around the two, desperately trying to get to the pipe. They were dancing a weightless tango when the android grunted. Its black pupils dilated. The pipe wandered away from its open hand while its fingers spasmed

Jule's head bobbed up from behind the hulk. She pulled something from its back, and looked at Markas before drifting away like a rag doll, head over heels, back into the shuttle. Her rod weapon rotated in the air, casting a spiral of black smoke and the sharp odor of burning flesh.

Markas pushed off the android's body and glided into the shuttle after Jule. Adam was about to speak, when everything fell. He found himself lying on the floor alongside Linda and the dead hulk.

Linda gasped, "The ship. The ship is moving."

She may have said more, but a bone-rattling siren stole her words.

Chapter 45

Adam clambered into the shuttle. Markas was on the floor, kneeling next to Jule.

"How is she?"

"I think she just passed out."

Adam looked back at Linda who stood at the shuttle entry and said, "We need Alpha. We need him now."

The two took the now funcional elevator back to the engine level. Alpha was gone and Angel's body lay behind the containment module with its head near the elevator door. Adam had half-expected Angel to repair itself. He noted a black and white disk mounted on the wall by the doors and realized what the wailing siren meant. "Alpha must be in the control room."

"But why is he using the emergency siren?"

Seconds later they arrived at the control room level. Alpha hovered over the console and when he saw them, he slapped the alarm disk, cutting off the pealing signal.

Adam's breath caught at the sight of the instrument panels.

Is this what that psycho meant by "I have corrected the mistake?"

He imagined a pipe bashing switches and dials, splintering monitors, and crushing the sensitive electronics within.

Adam asked, "Alpha, are you all right?"

Alpha turned his head slightly, enough to reveal several lines of clotted blood running from his forehead. "I am now. I presume you have dispatched my prototype?"

Confidence, or just stating the obvious?

"It's been dispatched, thanks to Jule. I'm not sure it can be fixed."

Linda looked over the damage. "Can *this* be fixed?"

Alpha said, "The chemical engines are running. We are accelerating. However, the heading is unknown. This can be repaired, but we need to stop the ship first."

"Is there a backup system somewhere?" asked Adam.

"Follow me."

"But what if that nutcase got to that as well?" asked Linda.

"Not likely."

They entered the elevator. Alpha depressed several buttons simultaneously.

"Aha," whispered Adam and nudged Linda.

They followed Alpha along a familiar hallway to the entrance of his private quarters. He touched the door and it slid open.

"It's programmed to open only for you, right?" asked Adam.

"I will need your help."

They shuffled around the curved inside wall. Adam said, "This is it. I was here. This is where I saw those symbols ... the ones on my medallion. By the way, where is my medallion?"

Linda pouted.

When Alpha reached a berth along the outer wall, she asked, "Where are the controls? And what's this for?" She pointed at the body mold.

Alpha canted over the counter edge and slipped into the rubbery mold which seemed to caress his body. With a free arm, he reached over into the wall niche and pulled out a black cable with a plug-like end. "Once I connect, I will access the ship's systems. You will need to remove the cable when and if I correct our course."

He placed the plug end to the back of this head and after a muffled click, his eyes rolled up under his eyelids. His body shuddered for a moment, and then he spoke in a low, almost mechanical cadence. "We are headed toward the red giant. A collision course."

"What just happened? Are you part of the ship now?" asked Linda.

"Can you stop the ship? What about changing course?" said Adam.

Alpha remained silent.

"Can you hear us?" said Adam.

The room spun. Adam and Linda floated toward the ceiling. Adam said, "The engines just stopped again."

Linda grabbed hold of a cabinet top. "Careful, remember what happened last time."

Adam got the hint, though he had little recollection of the details. Using Alpha's leg as an anchor, he pulled himself down to the floor, towing Linda with his other hand. He didn't have to wait long before a second attack of vertigo hit. A beat later, his stomach settled into place as gravity returned the missing weight to his legs and arms.

He took in a deep breath and exhaled in relief. "Looks like Alpha managed to turn the ship."

"Time to decide."

It was Alpha who spoke.

Decide what?

Alpha's body shuddered. His arms jerked upwards and fell back.

"Adam, I think we should disconnect him."

Linda reached behind his head and gave the cable a light tug to no effect. "Oh, what the hell." Using both hands, she yanked it out. Alpha's torso jerked up, casting Linda back. His eyes reappeared from below the lids like the winning line in a slot machine—black dots on yellow.

He said, "Time to decide your fate."

***

"Are you ready?"

Adam frowned and avoided Linda's stare. "I've been thinking about this whole idea of going back," he said. "By the time we get to Earth, about twenty-thousand years will have gone by."

"That *is* a long time."

"There's no way we'll recognize anything. Jeez, whole civilizations have come and gone in less time." He looked at Linda, eye-to-eye. "There'll be no one there to remember us."

Linda leaned back in her chair. "But I thought that's what you wanted ... to go back ... back home."

"Yeah, but home is where the people we knew live, where they work, the neighborhoods we grew up in. It's where family is."

Linda's voice cracked. "You have family here, Adam."

Her eyes were moist, and he wasn't far behind.

"Of course I do." He pushed back his chair, and stepped around the table. She reached up, wrapped her arms around his neck, and their lips met.

"You are next."

Adam held the kiss a bit longer, and then the two turned to the voice. Markas stood at the entryway with Jule behind him and said, "We are headed up to the prep rooms now. Just thought we would say good bye, and thanks for everything."

Jule said, "Especially for saving our lives."

"It was a team effort," said Adam. He and Linda embraced the pair, and waved until they disappeared into the elevator.

Adam looked back into the snack shack and said, "You've been very quiet. How are you feeling? You must be very excited."

Fay sat at a corner table alongside Angel. It was Angel who responded first. "I am feeling well, thank you. I am also quite excited."

It was the first time Adam had heard Fay laugh. Her recovery had been difficult. Unlike him and Linda, or even the Moorsians, her immune system was immature and unprepared for the simplest of bacterial insults. That was two weeks ago, and she was still weak. They had opted to stay in orbit around the red giant until everyone was healthy, including Angel.

Fay said, "I have learned a great deal about our world ... the ship of the Makers. All my life, I wondered about our purpose ... about the Source ... about us."

"It must be very hard for you," said Linda.

"Now ... I'm not sure of anything."

Adam said, "Welcome to the club."

"Perhaps the trip to your world will help her," said Angel.

Statements like that coming from a robot made Adam's head spin. He said, "I was thinking about that myself." He turned around to Linda and said, "I think I know where we should go ... where our real home is."

***

Ten year old Brady should have known better than to challenge Sean. Older by two years, he stood a full hand taller than his sister. Brady stepped up to him, forehead to chin, and set her mouth in a tight line.

"Give it to me."

Sean glared down at her. "Make me."

Brady took a step back and before Sean could react, she launched herself at her brother, sending him sprawling to the ground. The ball that he had held flew into the air.

"Got it." Angel held the ball up high. "Are you two fighting again?"

Sean brushed off his knees and straightened up, perhaps too embarrassed to answer.

Brady ran over to Angel. "It's mine. It's mine."

"Is there a problem?" Adam called out from the picnic table.

"Oh, no, sir. I am just playing a little keep away."

Adam looked at his two children. "Is that right? You weren't fighting?"

Brady and Sean stared down at their bare feet and both shook their heads slowly from side to side. Adam turned back to Angel, who looked back with its inscrutable slit of an eye and canted its head.

"Time for a break," said Linda, who held a pitcher. "Come on children, have some lemonade."

In seconds, the two were seated and gulping, and the argument, a faded memory.

She said, "Jule and the kids will be here in a few minutes. You two better be on your best behavior."

"Where does this go?" Alpha stood at the gated entrance to the backyard, cradling a large cake outfitted with a huge array of candles. Adam couldn't help grinning at the incongruity—Alpha, who was at least a million year old android, powerful and unafraid, logical and ruthless, had agreed to bring along a birthday cake to a surprise party. Apparently, baking was yet another talent to be added to the list. It was Fay's birthday. The date was selected by Alpha, and no doubt made up, but the sentiment was very real.

Adam snatched up a glass of lemonade and walked around to the front porch. There was no traffic in Maker town, but the streets were bustling with pedestrians. For the past thirteen years, with the help of the Source, several thousand of the Incorporated were successfully revived. Hundreds of the surface dwellers were given a chance to learn how real humans worked together, played together and procreated. Thanks to Linda's efforts and Adam's medallion, many were now capable of having their own children. People from all over the galaxy opted to make a new life in this subsurface spaceship town. In a few years' time, Adam expected their combined efforts and a little help from the Source would succeed in reconfiguring the gravitic drives. The technological innovations born of these diverse civilizations would serve well to repair the Maker planet-ship and prepare it for the long voyage along the Orion arm—an epic journey that would take more than ten thousand years. He thought about the eons that would pass and his descendents, children of children, who would know nothing of their home worlds except what was passed on from their ancestors. They would be returning to new worlds.

He flopped into one of two Adirondack chairs on the front porch and placed his glass on its broad armrest. Several guests waved at him as they walked by the side of the house to the garden. Adam leaned back and closed his eyes. He let his mind drift, thinking of the future and of the past.

"It's everything you imagined, isn't it, son?"

It was no more than a whisper. He fought the urge to open his eyes—afraid to spoil the impossible. A minute went by, and the voice changed.

"Adam, the guests are waiting."

When he opened his eyes, Linda sat on the arm of the empty chair. She smiled at him and said, "Penny for your thoughts?"

Adam sighed and looked into her eyes. She leaned over and cradled his head in her hands. The kiss lasted only a second, but in that brief moment, the stars and planets stopped in their tracks, and the immense void surrounding them collapsed into a singularity.

They rose as one, holding each others' hands, and descended the porch steps.

Acknowledgments

I would like to thank my number one supporter and first reader, my wife Lidia, without whom I would not have had the courage to undertake this project. Special thanks go to my colleagues at Bristol-Myers Squibb who graciously volunteered their time and effort to provide critical feedback as well as great suggestions: Stephen Johnson, Dora Schnur, Brian Claus, and Jano Jusuf. I also want to thank the Melbourne, Florida writers group and the Florida Writers Association for their support and insightful critiques along the way.

Background research was instrumental to the successful telling of a tale involving mid-twentieth century coal mining in Wilkes-Barre Pennsylvania. For this, I would like to thank the Pennsylvania Anthracite Heritage Museum in Scranton and its curator, Richard Stanislaus, for providing detailed information and references about the industry and the tragic Knox Coal Mine disaster of 1959 which took the lives of twelve miners.

The inspiration for the story came from a variety of real accounts describing the discoveries of objects out of time. Among these was the singular finding of a gold chain in a lump of coal, a stunning report which appeared in the Morrisonville Times, Ohio, June 11, 1891. Thanks to the efforts of Linda Sheedy of the Kitchell Memorial Library in Morrisonville, and subsequent follow up by the staff of the Abraham Lincoln Presidential Library in Springfield, I was able to obtain a facsimile of the original 1891 publication.

There were many technical details cited in this work, all of which accurately depict actual analytical instrumentation available through 1999, as well as our understanding of the human genome at that time, which has remained consistent through to the present. The description of a MRI device capable of microscopic analysis was based on an extrapolation of similar devices and was brought to life with the help of timely insight and advice from another BMS colleague, Keith Constantine.

Lastly, and foremost, I would like to thank my agents, Frances Black and Jennifer Mishler of Literary Counsel, who provided expert help and guidance in getting through the daunting task of producing a quality manuscript.

www.ingramcontent.com/pod-product-compliance
Lightning Source LLC
Chambersburg PA
CBHW030645120726
47905CB00001B/71